Nettleflower

TERRI BECKETT
CHRIS POWER

Cerridwen Press

What the critics are saying...

❧

5 Hearts "This tale evokes so many emotions. Many times it's a headshaking feeling of gratitude that we don't live in those violent times. Sometimes it's awe that these people can do so much with so little and still feel joy. Quite often it's just respect for this writing duo who has penned such a great tale. There's plenty of action and great dialogue to keep the story moving. [...] It was a hard book to put down, keeping my interest from first page to last."~ *The Romance Studio*

"***Nettleflower*** is a wonderful addition to the historical romance genre. Terri Beckett and Chris Power take great care in making not only the names but the actions of those in the story represent what was happening at the time. I found myself drawn into the story and rooting for Leofric and Regan as well as for the bard Daffyd. I thoroughly enjoyed ***Nettleflower*** and think you will too if you like tales from around the turn of the 1st century." ~ *Joyfully Reviewed*

A Cerridwen Press Publication

www.cerridwenpress.com

Nettleflower

ISBN 9781419959530
ALL RIGHTS RESERVED.
Nettleflower Copyright © 2007 Terri Beckett & Chris Power
Edited by Helen Woodall.
Cover art by Philip Fuller.

This book printed in the U.S.A. by Jasmine-Jade Enterprises, LLC.

Electronic book publication March 2007
Trade paperback publication September 2009

With the exception of quotes used in reviews, this book may not be reproduced or used in whole or in part by any means existing without written permission from the publisher, Ellora's Cave Publishing Inc., 1056 Home Avenue, Akron, OH 44310-3502.

Warning: The unauthorized reproduction or distribution of this copyrighted work is illegal. Criminal copyright infringement, including infringement without monetary gain, is investigated by the FBI and is punishable by up to 5 years in federal prison and a fine of $250,000.
(http://www.fbi.gov/ipr/)

This book is a work of fiction and any resemblance to persons, living or dead, or places, events or locales is purely coincidental. The characters are productions of the author's imagination and used fictitiously.

Cerridwen Press is an imprint of Ellora's Cave Publishing, Inc.®

Nettleflower

Dedication

Dedicated to everyone who believed in us and encouraged us.

Chapter One

※

"I said *no*, Ranulf!" Regan shoved hard against his wide chest. "And I meant it. Let me go or I swear you'll regret—"

"Don't be foolish, sweeting." Supremely sure of himself, Ranulf fitzRobert smiled, tightening his hold around her. "The Abbey's no answer for a wench like you. You can't mourn forever. Besides, we both know that Gifford—God rest his soul!—would have made you a poor sort of husband. See sense, girl! I can give you what you need—"

"Swine!" Goaded beyond control, Regan dealt him an open-handed blow that staggered the Norman, big as he was, and left a burning imprint on his smoothly handsome face. "Out!" She wrenched free of his loosening embrace. "Out of my garth or I'll have my carls throw you through the gates!" Her headrail had been torn from her hair by her struggle, a square of white linen tangled among the rushes strewn on the floor. The embroidered fillet that had held it in place was under his heel and anger shook her again. She hadn't spent hours of eye-strain stitching the wretched thing for this oaf to ruin it with impunity. "Out!" she shouted again, reaching for a weapon of some kind—anything. Her hand found the smooth shaft of a broom and she swung it up before her body, holding it two-handed, like a quarterstaff. "Out!"

Ranulf was no longer inclined to laugh. With her loosened copper hair wisping in bright tendrils about her face and the single hip-long braid seeming to twitch like the tail of an angry lioness, her features had a fierce beauty that was heightened by the dark-lashed eyes flashing with emerald fire. Though she was slender-made, she was tall for a woman and the blow she'd given him had plenty of strength behind it. She was balancing the broom-shaft now as if she knew exactly what she could do with it. Last but not least, Northman-born as he was, he'd stood in a battle-line against marauding Danes and heard that ancient Saxon war-shout barked at the enemy. He did not relish it thrown at him now, even by a woman.

"She-cat!" he growled, half-angry, half-admiring. By the Rood, he'd be a year taming this woman and he'd enjoy every moment of it. He backed a step and tried another tack. "Have you no thought to guest-right or kin-right?"

"Neither gives you the right to force yourself on me! I say this one more time—out, fitzRobert! I want you gone from here by noon!"

"But it's snowing," he objected. He had not planned to leave so soon. His tone softened, became cajoling. "Regan, I meant no harm. You should take it as a compliment."

"Well, I do not and maybe the cold will cool your ardor. Get you gone from here, man! I won't tell you again."

Balanced and ready to crack his pate for him, Regan watched as with a muttered curse he retreated to the door and let himself out, dark face scowling, brown eyes coal-hot in the shadow of his brows. The door swung closed and she drew a deep breath, letting it out in a ragged sigh. Then scrubbed the back of her hand across her lips to rid herself of the taste of him and his ale-laden breath. That two men born of the same sire should be so different! Gifford's kisses had been gentle and caring, a promise of shared warmth to come when their marriage was made. Whereas Ranulf—if she'd faltered just once, one minute more and he'd have had her down on the rushes with her skirts up and no benefit of clergy.

But her anger was as fast to fade as it was swift to rise. Regan was shamed to see that her hand was shaking as she put the broom back in its place by the door post.

"In truth a warrior queen," said a mild voice, light and rich and musical as a skald's dream of heaven. "Hippolyta, I salute you. But that, for certain, was no Theseus." Regan turned to find Dafydd ap Gryfydd by the dais table, hands behind his back. His lean body was relaxed but the top of a short hunting bow stood up above his shoulder, while the bulk of the ever-present harp-bag was safely out of the way across the table. She found a smile for him, grateful that he had not rushed to her aid nor smothered her now with concern. "Going hunting, were you?" she asked, scooping up headrail and fillet. One could be shaken free of rush-shreds, but the other was muddied and scuffed and would need more care.

"I thought there might be a rutting boar not far from here, my lady," he said, laying down bow and arrows. He gave her a sidelong glance, a smile on the fallen-angel features. "But I was wrong."

"Not so wrong," she sighed. "He wasn't the first since—Gifford died," she went on with only a slight hesitation in the naming, "and I don't suppose he'll be the last. The sooner I can get to Leominster, the better," she added, iron resolve in her voice and the set of her generous mouth.

"Aye," he said. "There are many kinds of sanctuary within the Church. Where is your household, Lady?" glancing around the empty hall.

"Hunting," she shrugged. "Boar of the four-legged kind. The weather has driven a small herd out of the deep wood. They're ruining what winter-pasture we have for the sheep, as well as breaking down fences and hedges. The men were talking of it at the meal last night," she added. He'd been there, of course, but all his concentration had been on his harp. Regan knew how he was then. Deaf and blind to all else but the music in his soul and in the white-bronze strings. He had a rare gift, did Gryfyddson, a bard in the ancient *Cymru* tradition, despite his years.

When he'd first arrived, soaked to the skin and half-drowned by the storm, scarecrow-clad and starved to boot, Regan had thought him little more than a child. But dried out and fed and with his wild black hair combed to some sort of neatness, he was shown to be of eighteen or so years, only a little younger than herself. And he possessed a rich tenor voice the like of which she had never heard. So might an archangel sing and with that face to match it was no wonder that most of the women in garth and village were sighing after him. He also had a wicked sense of humor that glittered in his dark blue eyes at ill-opportune moments and that appealed to her nearly as much as the glory of his singing.

Of course, there were those in her household who had not liked his presence. During her years away at Court, she had forgotten the antipathy of the Border-folk to their neighbors across the Dyke. "Welsh," they—mostly the menfolk—had muttered. "Thief at the least. Can't trust 'em. Chancy bastards, the Welsh." But even they had been largely won over by the bard's skill. He knew the Saxon form of poetry and riddling and tale-telling as well as his own. Knew, too, the cut-jewel beauty of Latin, of Ovid and Catullus, knew the legends of Rome and Greece, Brittany and Cornwall and every psalm in the Holy Book. Never had she heard the Song of Songs rendered with such sensual passion. Well, for certain she wouldn't hear that version of it in Leominster Abbey and it was an unwanted reminder that the treasured sanctuary would be obtained at a cost.

Well, she would pay the price and count it cheap, if it freed her of fitzRobert and his like and their "courtship". She'd endure no more of their rough wooing. Her decision was made—and if she chose to go now rather than in the spring who was to gainsay her?

The sooner she was on her way, the better. There was much to be done first, of course and she needed to talk to her steward and reeve, but at least she could have her tiring-maid start on the packing. "Have you seen Morwenna, Dafydd?"

"The Winter Wren?" He smiled. "Most like she is hiding in the thicket, being put in fear by the rutting of fitzSwine. Shall I seek her out, Lady, and send her to you?"

"If you will, Dafydd." Regan ordered her hair and gown as best she could. "I shall not wait until the spring—I'll to the Abbey as soon as may be. But I'll leave all in order here."

Regan had come back to the Marches and her first home to make sure that all was as it should be for the dowering to the Abbey. After eight years away she had been taken aback to discover how much she had missed the place, despite the ever-present peril from the West. But she was not one to break a decision once made. She had set aside the past as she had her childhood toys and taken up the account books and tallies instead.

And there discovered another temptation, to stay and remove the reins from Sigurd Reeve's ineffective hands and run the holding as it should be run, as she knew she could.

For a while that particular seduction had almost been her downfall, until Gifford's brother had come visiting.

She had stood in the doorway of the hall and watched the group of weary men trudge through the freezing mud to the guest-bower. Just before he disappeared inside, Ranulf had turned and waved to her. She'd paused with her own hand half-raised. For a moment he had looked the image of his younger brother and her heart had lurched in shock. Then she saw again the heavier shoulders and remembered that Gifford was dead.

She and Gifford would have been married come the spring.

Her father would have placed her hand in Gifford's with that scowl on his face that hid the love and pride within. Her mother would have wept and scolded and hugged and given much-repeated advice on the managing of men.

Men were not so easily managed and yesterday evening in hall, Ranulf had shown her what an heiress without betrothed or family could expect from those who hunted wife and lands wrapped up in the one cloak. This morning's incident was but another move in that hunt.

With Gifford lost to her, she'd not settle for second-best and since there could be no likelihood of ever meeting one who might be his equal then the Abbey in Leominster would prove a fine haven from the likes of Gifford's brother.

Besides, Regan knew that if she stayed for Christ's Mass in her own hall, then she would never leave.

So, she decided with characteristic abruptness, she would risk the weather and the Welsh and travel to Leominster while she still could. At once. Or as soon as the essentials were packed.

Chapter Two

The horse-drawn litter had leather curtains laced tight against the wind, but the two women within were hardly enjoying a comfortable journey. Regan, bracing herself against the jolting, thought again that she should have ridden, ridden and resisted the impulses to look back at what she was leaving. The curtains shut out view and temptation alike, but the close confines irked her and the cold seemed the worse, for all the furs about her. She supposed discomforts like these would be commonplace at the Abbey. Well, she would get used to them. It was the best course for her, she knew that, the religious life offered peace and security and God knew she felt in need of both. The past year had been a nightmare.

She closed her eyes, whispering a prayer for her dead. Poor Gifford, struck down in his prime by the plague that had ravaged man and beast alike, but not before he had seen his lands devastated by famine and murrain. East Mercia had been sorely stricken. And before she could even begin to think of reshaping her life, unkind fate had taken her parents too. Regan bit her lip in an attempt to hold back the tears that pricked under her lashes. Her dear Mam and Da both, within a day of each other. She had nursed them through the brief sharp sickness to the end and even now had no idea why she had been spared. In the space of two cruel months she had lost all her loved ones. In her grief, she had turned to the solace and safety offered by the Church.

The Abbess of Leominster was a cousin in a distant degree and although Regan knew her only vaguely, still she knew she would be welcomed. She knew well the reason for that was the dowry she would bring — not Gifford's lands, for they had gone to his brothers Ranulf and Geoffrey—but the rich holding given her by her father to be passed on to her children. There were to be no children. The Church would hold and administer the land she had been born in, had spent much of her childhood in, filled with so many happy memories. Memories not stained with grief, for Gifford had never been there and Mam and Da hadn't visited their western holdings for years.

The litter lurched and slid, startling Regan out of her reverie, and Morwenna gave a stifled shriek.

"Oh Mistress, we're attacked!"

"Nonsense," Regan said calmly, resisting an urge to box the girl's ears. "The road is bad, that's all." She tugged at the lacings and the wind tore the curtain from her hands, hurling clots of snow into the litter. "Holy Mother!" she gasped, clutching her hood about her face and leaned out to shout. "Swein! How long has this been going on?"

The man loomed out of the murk of the pelting snow. "About two miles back, Mistress. I didn't say anything then because we could still see the road."

"And now?"

He shrugged, bearlike in his heavy cloak. "Snow's drifting in the wind. We may not get much farther. Shall we turn back—?"

"We've gone too far for that," Regan cut in, squashing her own leaping desire. "Are we near any settlement, do you know? Anywhere we can wait out the storm?"

"The turning for m'lord Leofric's steading was a little way back—the next village could be five miles yet." He waited for her decision. Behind her, Morwenna sneezed.

* * * * *

"Lucca said there was a blizzard brewing, m'lord." Bulking massive in his fleece-lined leather cloak, Godwine chivvied another sheep away from the drifts in the lee of the hillside. "D'y'think she gets much satisfaction in being right all the time?"

His companion grunted, which was no answer, and whistled his hound back to his heel. Snow was already crusting on the dog's shaggy fur, as it was on the younger man's eyebrows, giving him the illusional look of an ancient, though Leofric Edmundson, thane of Staneleigh and a good parcel of other holdings, had seen barely twenty-six winters. Of which this bid fair to be the worst in recent memory, Godwine reflected.

"I think that's the last of 'em," he said, calculating their number in his head. "Seven, was it, that Wat missed from the folding?" He did not need to ask, but he was ready to use any topic to coax the lad into talking. This one failed too.

"The Lady your mam chose a good time to come visiting," was his next attempt. "She'll be here over Yule and into the New Year for sure. Though she'll be missing Christ's Mass at Court, I'll be bound."

Another grunt. Godwine scowled at the lowering slate-dark sky that promised no cessation in the snowfall and probably worse to come. They were fairly sheltered here in the lee of the hill and its crest of trees, but on the open grazing the stuff lay deep and treacherous. Until it was gone, the beasts that remained after the slaughtering of November, the Blood-Month, must be fed from the store of fodder laid by for the winter.

The brief afternoon was darkening into premature twilight that washed everything in shades of gray, a thickening murk that matched the thane's mood, from what Godwine could see of his lord's face. Maybe it had not been such a good idea to get him out of the stifling confines of the hall and his mother's equally stifling attentions, but Godwine's stock of distractions was running low, exhausted over the past months. An idea struck him.

"We could call in on Gyfu. It's barely a step out of our way."

That won him a stare. "We've found Wat's wandering ewes. I'm for home. You may do as you please."

"It'll be you Gyfu would most welcome, m'lord." He tried an ingratiating smile. "Fond of you, Gyfu is. Always has been." She was also a handsome wench, a freewoman these past three years, with a daughter just weaned. Thane Edmund had followed custom and freed her when she had borne the babe, for there was no doubt who the father was and he'd made generous provision for them both.

A pity that the son was not the easy-going philanderer the father had been. Gyfu would be good for him. If Leofric could just be persuaded to visit her. Godwine toyed with the idea of purposely getting the two of them benighted and giving Leofric no choice in the matter.

He was forestalled when the hounds suddenly ceased their quartering and bayed—and he saw, through the gathering murk, the shapes of horses and carts in a baggage train.

"Travelers, m'lord. And heading for our hall, by their look."

* * * * *

"I'm sure Leofric will give us shelter, or his people will if he's not to home," Regan said. "Send a rider ahead, Swein, for courtesy."

"Keep you well-wrapped, Mistress," Swein said briskly. "It's evil weather and we'll be well out of it."

The curtain lacing was difficult for chilled fingers, but at last Regan was able to brush the snow from her cloak and gown. In the gloom Morwenna's face was pale as an owl's mask, dark eyes and reddened nose all the color she had. Regan gave her a smile, knowing she hardly looked much better herself. "Don't worry, child. We'll soon be snug in hall."

Nettleflower

Morwenna's answering smile was wobbly and her eyes still big with fear. Since Gifford had put her into Regan's household, she had never gone farther from home than the village next to the hall and had no wish to go farther afield. Regan felt a twinge of guilt for bringing her. But Morwenna had made her own decision.

Regan smiled to herself at the nickname Dafydd had bestowed. The Winter Wren, indeed — it was the kindest of comparisons, for in truth, the poor girl was small and rounded and brownly drab as that timid bird. Poor Morwenna. It was how everyone thought of her. And truly, she'd had little enough in the way of good fortune in her short life before Gifford had found her on the road to Gloucester and, being a kindly man, taken her up and given her to Regan to train in whatever she thought good. And she, discovering the foundling to be neat-handed, had set about teaching her to serve as a bower-maid.

Starved of affection until then, Morwenna had rewarded her mistress with an almost religious devotion and little by little her story had been told. Her parents both dead and no man ready to offer marriage, she would probably have crept away to starve in a ditch, but for Gifford and Regan. And now Regan could not abandon the child.

Outside, voices were raised above the wind and Morwenna whimpered. But the tongue was Saxon, not Welsh. Regan risked another look — two men were slogging through the knee-deep snow toward them. Leather and fur disguised much of their build and features, but unless she missed her guess one was Godwine Coelson, steward to the thane.

"You come in a good hour, my friends!" she called out. "Are we near Lord Leofric's steading?"

"Near enough, Lady." Yes, it was Godwine and from what little she could see, the years had not changed him. He lumbered closer, blowing the crusting ice from his moustaches and gave her a beaming smile. "Have you sent ahead? Then they'll be waiting. We'll guide you."

* * * * *

The dusk was already deepening the gloom of the snow-clouds before the gates of the steading were sighted, but Swein's messenger had alerted the holding and there was a welcome waiting. The litter halted outside the hall door and Regan, climbing stiffly out, found a steadying hand under her elbow. Godwine's companion, silent during their brief meeting, was no churl or thrall.

It had been at least ten years, she realized with a jolt, since they had last met. Perhaps longer. Somehow, she had half-expected to see the laughing scapegrace who had plagued her youth — a wild tangle of pale bleached-straw hair and a face invariably scratched and bruised from one escapade or another and clothes as torn and muddied as a wolfshead's cub. This tall young man, with an uncharacteristic grimness to mouth and eyes, might have been a stranger.

"Leofric?" She heard her own uncertainty. "Forgive me. I did not know you."

"Lady Regan." The voice was a man's voice, deeper than she remembered, and he bent his head in formal greeting.

"My lord, you offer hospitality in a needy time." She managed a smile for him and saw the solemn face shadowed by the hood lighten a little.

"Lady, to my hearth and my hold you are most welcome," he said, as the situation demanded. "Now come you in, Regan, and thaw out — you're near frozen. And your maid — ?"

"Morwenna," Regan supplied. "In with you, child, or we'll all catch our deaths!"

"Godwine, see to my lady's escort," Leofric ordered and ushered the women inside.

In the murk of the blowing snow, Godwine saw the lady's own man overseeing the disposing of beasts and folk — only one looked out of place. The frosting of snow could not altogether conceal the alien darkness of the hair under the hood of his cloak.

"A Welshling, by the White Christ!"

"Dafydd ap Gryfydd, master." The face was a boy's, though the voice was not—the teeth were chattering.

"What's this you're nursing?" Godwine peered suspiciously at the wrappings of the bundle clutched to the boy's chest and polished carven wood within caught the last glimmerings of light. A harp. "Aha! A gleeman, is it?"

"No, my lord." And pride stiffened the weary backbone. "A bard, so please you."

Beneath Saxon moustaches, Godwine's grin grew wider. "Oh aye? Less beard than a gooseberry and it's a bard? That'll be scanned. Come you then. M'lord's in hall."

He was hustled with rough friendliness toward the dark looming bulk of the hall. The wide door was thrust open and two large shaggy hounds came pushing through peoples' legs to sniff at this other stranger. "Watch yourself, lad," Godwine rumbled. "Trained they are, see, to hunt Welshmen by scent."

"I heard that," Lady Regan cut in. "Pay him no mind, Dafydd. My lord Leofric, I make known to you Dafydd ap Gryfydd, a bard and harper who travels with me."

"Be welcome, indeed." She could hear that it was mere politeness. What had happened here? Then she remembered half-heard gossip about a dead wife. Dear God, was there no end to the grief of this cursed year?

Leofric was as tall as his father had been, though lighter in build. The fair hair, barley-pale, was cut neatly to shoulder-length, snarled now from the confining hood, the blue eyes looked through her, with a remoteness that seemed hold everything at bay. Yet it was still a face she knew, welcome to her own grieving heart, the clean bone structure, the stubborn angle of his jaw. But the generous mouth that had always been ready to laugh was set hard and thin. Here was no more the playmate of her childhood, but a man grown and a warrior bred. Blooded, too, by the scar that cut from hairline to brow. She could have wept for the boy who had been and was no more. And for the girl she had been, so short a time ago.

It had been years since she had sat in this hall and though much had changed, some things had stayed the same. Lucca, the steward's wife, came forward to wrap her in a welcoming embrace that was less that of freewoman to lady than to an equal, but Regan did not resent it. Lucca might be a trifle more buxom than she remembered, but the smile was the same and the simple kindness that enfolded her as surely as the comforting arms.

To Regan's surprise, the Lady Hilde was also present, though the thane's mother was all in black instead of the rich colors that she had favored when her husband was alive, and a gaunt-featured young priest hovered in her shadow. She smiled at Regan and kissed her cheek and made her sit beside her close to the hearth, while one of the women eased off her shoes and rubbed her feet with warm woolen cloths and another brought a bowl of steaming broth and everyone made a gratifying amount of fuss over her.

"I've had one of the guest-bowers made ready, Lady," Lucca said, looking approvingly at the empty bowl. "You'll be better after a night's rest."

"Lucca, I've done naught but sit for most of the day in a litter! I'm not tired."

Lucca looked as if she knew better. "As you say, Lady. But you don't want to take a chill. Traveling the roads in weather like this!"

"Where were you bound, my dear?" Hilde asked solicitously. "Will there be worry when you don't arrive? My son can send to explain, when the weather clears."

"No need, madam," Regan said abruptly. "I shall be on my way myself by then. I am for the Abbey, at Leominster, to take the veil there."

If she was braced for a repeat of the shock her own people had shown, she was disappointed. Hilde patted her hand. "It is the lot of women bereaved," she murmured consolingly. "May you find peace there and strength to endure. I too find my greatest comfort in God."

It was on the tip of Regan's tongue to deliver the kind of retort that had led Gifford to name her his vixen, but she bit it back. Lady Hilde meant all kindly and there was no call to take what she said amiss and it was only that the warmth of the hearth and the food and the spiced ale had all combined to make her suddenly so very sleepy that she could hardly hold her head up. "I think," she said carefully, "I am a little wearied after all. Lucca, if you might show us where we may sleep…?"

Chapter Three

It took a while for the household to settle itself down after the evening meal and the unlooked-for excitement and it was full dark outside when the Lady Hilde kissed her son, made her goodnights and summoned her women to her bower. Things were more relaxed when she had gone. Godwine felt able to stretch his legs out toward the banked fires still burning in the great central hearth and undid his belt a notch while casting an eye around the hall. The influx of guests had necessitated some rearrangement, but it seemed that there would be room enough for them and the hall-folk accustomed to sleep there. Lucca had apparently taken an interest in Lady Regan's harper-bard — she had supplied him with fleeces for his pallet and a deerskin coverlet overall and he was sitting quietly in the dimness, head bent over his precious harp. No doubt there would be a demonstration of whatever skills he possessed on another evening. Though what exactly a Welsh lad was doing with the Lady Regan's household, he could not begin to guess. It seemed odd, to say the least, bringing one of that kind into a Border hold. Well, the lady had been away from these parts for a few years. Perhaps she had forgotten the age-old threat that the Welsh meant to the Border folk.

A scowl crossed Godwine's face. If she had, there were others who had not. He would keep a weather-eye on that lad and his doings. And he grunted softly and unhappily to himself. Not so long ago, he could have confided his unease in the young thane. Now it was unlikely that Leofric would even listen. A grieving silence still held sway, as it had for so much of the year. It seemed that he had locked himself into a windowless prison and lost the key. Or perhaps someone else had put him within and taken the key away. Godwine spat into the fire uneasily. It did not do to think ill of the dead, but there were times of late when he wondered if Leofric's dead Lady had somehow bespelled him, so that without her he would sicken and fail.

Oh but surely that was folly. He glanced sidewise at the unmoving figure of the young man seated in the great chair, firelight deepening the shadows on his face even as it gilded the pale hair.

A glimmer of even paler hair caught his eye—the long braids of his eldest daughter, who plainly thought no one had noticed that she was not in her bed. Where she should be, by the White Christ, especially with so many young stranger-hounds on the hunt. He'd have none of them sniffing around his girl.

"Edwina!" It was a bark and the girl started like a hare. "To your own place and don't tarry."

"But *Da*—"

"Don't you 'but Da' me, my lass! Now, or by the Rood, you'll see you're not too old for a switching!"

Scarlet from collar to hair, Edwina fled, mortification rather than fear speeding her feet, as her Da hadn't raised a hand to her since she was ten. Godwine grunted satisfaction at her obedience, secure in this display of his parental authority until the quickly averted face of the Lady Regan's so-called bard alerted him. The brat was smirking, damn its eyes. He wouldn't be mocked, not in his own hall!

He leaned forward to fix the boy with an eagle's unblinking stare. "A bard, did my lady say?" His disbelief was clear in his tone. "Do they make bards out of bantlings in Wales?"

There was a stir from the man in the great chair, but no word. The guest, however, had no such reticence. Dafydd met the gaze unflinching and smiled. "I do not know how it is among the *Saes*, the Saxon-kind, but among the *Cymru*, the Welsh as you call us, when the gift is given, age is of no account. I have the Lists of the Kings and the Triads and the Great Music, I was trained in the Art by Owen ap Ifor, of Llan Illtud. A name that might not be known hereabouts," and the sweep of his glance implied the barbarism of the place, "but he was Bard and Harper to Kings."

"We are honored then," the thane said quietly before the fulminating Godwine could get a word in. "Will you play for us? Something of Catullus, perhaps?"

One dark eyebrow twitched upward. This was no taunt on the surface, but it might be test. Did this Saxon lordling truly know the Classics? He would turn the test back on them. "Indeed, my lord." His smile had not wavered. He lifted the harp to his knee, caressing the strings. "Tell me your choice and I will sing it."

* * * * *

Regan woke to find the candle still burning, though much reduced. Lying watching the flickering shadows chase themselves over the dimly seen hangings of the bower, she heard a thread of music and realized that it had woven through her dreaming. It had been a mildly pleasant dream, of Gifford in the early days of their courtship, when she had come to see him not as the man she had been betrothed to with hardly a word spoken between them, but as a good friend, a solid, sweet-natured companion. That friendship and respect, each for each, would have been the keystone of their marriage and when he died, she had grieved for the friend more than the husband-to-be. The dream had brought him back for a little, and she cherished the memory as the music drifted through her consciousness. It must be Dafydd. The Lady Hilde's skald was a fine musician, but had not that touch.

Morwenna was a swaddled roll of blankets on her pallet, snoring a little, deeply asleep. Regan decided against disturbing her. She was no longer weary, she needed no help to dress, having lain down in her traveling gown. She pushed her feet into her shoes, pulled her mantle around her shoulders and trod quietly from the guest-bower.

It was not as late as she had thought. Though Lady Hilde's place was empty, many of the household were still in hall, gathered around the hearth. Lucca and another woman were spinning, Godwine the steward working a piece of leather, Leofric sprawled in his chair. They were all of them listening to the skilful harping of the dark-haired young man in their midst, as if he held them in thrall. She moved softly forward, not wanting to break the spell, but Godwine saw her and got quickly to his feet. "My lady, is there aught you're wanting?"

"Only to find the source of such music," she said, smiling at the questioning eyes, and when Leofric stood up and offered her his chair, she thanked him but took the seat next to Lucca's. "But I guessed it was you, Dafydd. Please don't stop. It was so beautiful."

Her harper bent his head. "As my Lady wishes." He took up where he had left off, a haunting silvery drift of notes that conjured a vision for her of dew-starred cobweb on morning hawthorn. His voice joined his music, bell-clear. Here indeed was mastery and not a person listening there but knew it.

For a moment she watched him as he played, lost to the world in his art as a devout man in prayer—dark hair close curled, hidden eyes lashed like a girl's, hands that were narrow and long-fingered and supple with the strength and power of music in their shaping. Then her gaze was drawn to Leofric. Here was another snared by the same net. Her nurse had told her tales of the harpers of the *Tylwyth Teg*, the Fair Folk, whose music could enchant mortal men. Such magic could heal also. She knew herself how grief could be assuaged by this gentle alchemy—perhaps it was lifting the shadow for Leofric, for a space.

The harp strings were finally stilled and there was silence for a few heartbeats.

"Your Lady is fortunate," Leofric said. "This night I have heard music, indeed." Dafydd bent his head in acknowledgment. If he pleased this lord, then he might stay a while. Which would suit his purpose better than journeying to Leominster. The thane beckoned him up to the dais, indicating a seat. "Join me, if you will." It was an invitation, not an order. "My mother's skald has a way of slaughtering the Latin—it was pleasure to hear it so pure."

"Llan Illtud is famed for its teaching, my lord. But you were schooled yourself?"

"At Gloucester. I hated it, until I learned what could be found in books…"

* * * * *

"That voice'll be wasted in the Abbey," Lucca spoke quietly in Regan's ear.

"Oh he'll not stay with me," she answered. "Surely he'll be away to London, or Winchester, maybe the King's court—so best make the most of him while he's here."

"Well, there's wisdom." Lucca smiled at the young musician. "For once having seen the wonders of the city, he may not wish to molder in the country."

Regan did not take the familiarity amiss. Lucca was as much a part of her childhood as Leofric. "He's hardly been with me long enough to let mold grow! All Saints', it was, that he walked into my hall."

Lucca's eyes widened. "A Welshman, Lady? And you took him in?"

"A starveling lad, half-drowned from the storm, chilled to the bone—would it be Christian to turn him away?"

"Perhaps not Christian, but commonsense! Was it not your stock they raided less than a year gone?"

"He's one, not a horde, Lucca! And a bard—he's proven that."

Lucca chuckled. "Oh agreed and he's a bonny lad into the bargain. My Edwina couldn't take her eyes off him. Mind, he's not the only one who'll be wasted behind convent walls."

From anyone else, Regan might have seen that as unwarranted interference. Not from Lucca. "I can be of use there, I think. I have had the running of household and estate—" She broke off, as conscious as the steward's wife must be of the emptiness of her reasoning. "I have a need for the peace of the cloister." She looked pointedly at the combed raw fleece in the basket at Lucca's feet. "If you have another spindle, Lucca, I could help you?"

"For sure, Lady." Lucca shifted the fleece within reach, producing another spindle of carved ash wood. "We heard of your parents' death and your man's. I can't say I blame you for wanting a time of peace."

Regan avoided the sympathetic eyes. "The plague cost me dear." *It took the heart out of my breast.* "Though mine was not the only loss. I hear Lord Leofric's bride was also taken."

"Aye, but 'twas not sickness," Lucca plied her spindle, voice dropping even lower. "Hawiss died in childbirth, St. John's Eve, this summer gone. It was a large babe and laid wrong. We tried to turn it, Anna and I, but…" she shrugged. "We lost them both, mother and bairn. He took it hard. Blamed himself and still does."

"He cannot surely think so!"

"It was his son she died trying to bear and she small-hipped as a child, though for certain a woman grown. As if a man should wed and not bed his bride! The lad's a wittol. But then he ever was." She took a cloth from her waist pocket and blew her nose briskly. "Since then, he's been like a man soul-lost."

"Then that is why Lady Hilde is here, instead of keeping Christ's Mass at the Royal Court. To comfort him."

"Her? As easeful as a hair shirt, that one!" She snorted. "And look you, lass, this night is the first I've seen him smile and that's your harper's doing." She nodded toward the dais. "Perhaps he might be persuaded to stay awhile."

Chapter Four

Come the morning, Regan discovered how uneaseful her hostess could be when she put her mind to it. "So you are set on the cloister?" Lady Hilde asked mildly, as the younger woman sat with her in the perfumed warmth of the solar and shared the work of embroidery. The present occupation was an altar-cloth in penitential purple, though the richness of the design, in brilliant silks and gold and silver thread, would show little of the original color. Hilde was stitching diligently at the figure of the Savior—she had allotted Regan a lesser task, that of the leafy border.

Orphrey-work was not a skill that Regan would claim. She had already had to unpick the length of a stem. Besides, the chamber seemed overcrowded with herself and Morwenna sitting cheek by scented jowl with the two elderly spinsters Hilde had for bower-maids, plus the Lady herself. Heat from the three braziers made the place stuffy. Longingly, she cast an eye at the leaden sky beyond the window-glass and the snow still falling thickly. She could not even envy the men—with weather too bad for hunting, they were all trapped alike.

"If you mean am I called to be a Bride of Christ," she sighed, "then no, I have no deep vocation. But how many do, who seek the sanctuary of the vows?"

Hilde's pink mouth drew together, like a purse when the strings are tightened. "You know your own mind best, my dear, but it seems to me that such a decision should be taken with a whole heart. Perhaps you should speak to my chaplain, who is wise beyond his years. Or wait until your mourning-year is past and then make your choice. I, of course, have nothing left but God, but you are young and the world has yet so much to offer you—and you to offer in return…"

"The world must be content with my prayers," Regan said sharply and jabbed her needle savagely into the fabric, stabbing her own finger in the process. She gave a hiss of annoyance, but the accident at least freed her momentarily from the confines of the solar and Hilde's cloying curiosity. "I would not spot your fine work with blood, Lady. Your pardon."

She fled with as much decorum as she could muster and at the foot of the stair cannoned into the young harper. His hands caught and steadied her. "My lady—is anything amiss?"

The dark blue eyes on a level with hers were kindly and concerned, but she had her balance now and stepped out of his grasp. "No, Dafydd ap Gryfydd, it is nothing. I thank you for the thought."

"At your service, Lady." He made his courtesy. "May I escort you?"

"When you do not know where I wish to go?" She raised an eyebrow.

"My Lady will forgive me, but I do not think you know yourself where you wish to be."

Anywhere, she thought wildly, so it be not here. Aloud, she said, "You are forward, Welshman."

"I claim a bard's immunity for truth-saying, Lady." He smiled at her again. "Be patient. Leominster will still be there. In the meantime, if you would be free of the solar, perhaps the hall-hearth would be more to your liking? Less confining?"

"Yes," she agreed and laid her hand on his offered arm. "The hall-hearth."

The hall-folk were all about their business, but Dafydd set a chair for her, brought Lucca's basket of fleece and a spindle with it and when she was settled, sat at her feet and took up his harp. "My Lord Leofric has had the grace to say I put him in mind of my namesake, who harped before the King of Israel—"

Regan gave a short bark of laughter. "And was nearly spitted on a spear for his pains! He is of Cynric's line, and he a king of Wessex some five hundred years ago. Cynricings are noted for their temper. Did he seek to compliment or threaten, Welshman?"

He smiled and his fingers drew lilting melody from the strings. "I doubt he was thinking of that part of the story, Lady. Perhaps we should remind him, so that he does not forget he has a stranger within his gates and a *Cymru*." Not that the thane seemed in danger of overlooking Dafydd's race, though he showed no hostility. After an awkward, almost stilted beginning—as if he had all but forgotten such things—he had plenty of questions about Dafydd's training, about the depth and range of his knowledge. They discovered a shared love of Homer's *Iliad* and the works of Catullus, though Dafydd had not so much liking for Horace. The legends of Alexander, though, the epic songs of Dafydd's own people and, surprisingly, of the Irish...a complex man, this Leofric Edmundson.

The Lady Regan sat and listened to him play and the thread of wool on the spindle grew steadily. After a while Edwina came, together with Morwenna, a basket of fresh-combed fleece between them and both took spindles too.

"I am surrounded by beauty," Dafydd declared and gave them the pagan tale of the youth lured to his doom by the beauty of the water-nymphs. Edwina was enraptured, her spindle idle.

"There is fine," she whispered, as he finished. "For black Welsh, that is," she added with a sidelong smile.

He was unsure if she was referring to himself or his song, though from her expression, she plainly found him worth looking at—she'd been making eyes at him enough the previous evening, before her father spotted her. She was worth a second look herself—even among the Saxon kind she had a rare fairness. Her braids were wrist-thick, silver-glossy, her eyes, smiling ingenuously into his, as blue as flax-flowers. And there was a faint intriguing scent around her, sweet, but not cloying, like the perfumed air of a summer afternoon in the Abbey garden, where the little clove gillyflowers grew.

There was also the element of challenge in her glance. By the small smile on her mouth, Regan had also seen it and was unaccustomedly amused by the play. The small intrigues of courtship and mating were a facet of life that she would have enjoyed and must now forego—there would be no such pastime at the Abbey.

She was not a beauty by Welsh standards, nor even by the Saxon convention, Aldheim's daughter. Nor was she pretty in the way Edwina was pretty, but there was a clarity and strength to her face that made her strikingly handsome. She would never be plain, or ugly with age, this one. If she had any other claim to rarity, then it was her hair—he never tired of seeing it, hair like dragon gold—or fire… No, like the phoenix of legend, the flame-feathered bird that lives and dies and lives again. It would be a crime to hide that glory beneath a nun's wimple. But she would be safe in the Abbey.

She would never know how he felt about her. He knew that and was resigned. And, God willing, she would never know the part he played. If she thought of him at all, in years to come, let it be with kindness.

* * * * *

The fifth commandment aside, Leofric was rediscovering how difficult it was to get on with his mother. It was years since she had condescended to spend so much time away from the Court—even at the time of his father's death, she had been back at Winchester within the fortnight.

Nettleflower

He had known from previous experience that she would set the household by the ears, antagonizing Lucca and harrying Godwine as if the man was no more than a thrall. He had known that he would be inspected like a seven-year-old and probably found wanting. He had known and braced himself to expect the flood of sentiment she would unleash over the death of Hawiss, whom she had regarded as a most suitable wife for him and had now all but elevated to sainthood alongside Edmund her husband. What he had not guessed at and did not expect was the attack she launched on him when he made his dutiful son's visit to the solar.

"I trust you slept well, Mother."

"As well as ever, in this hold," she sighed dejectedly.

It was an old complaint and Leofric gritted his teeth. "Mother, my father rebuilt this hall for you, in stone and glass to your exact desire and nearly beggared himself to do it. It may not be Winchester but—"

"Your father, God rest him, gave me everything I ever wished for," she said, briefly dabbing at her eyes. Then her tone hardened. "Would that my son was as thoughtful."

"How have I lacked in my duty to you, Mother?" he demanded with some exasperation.

"Not lacked, exactly, dearling, for it was no fault of yours, but now it is time that you put your sad state behind you."

It was like taking a spear in the gut. Leofric stared at her, unable to speak. He had always known that she had the sensitivity of a stone, but this was beyond all forgiveness. "I would remind you, my lady, that," he could not say her name, "my wife has been barely six months dead. Even allowing the briefest mourning, it will be midsummer before I might even think of another marriage. If I should be so inclined. Which I am not."

"Nonsense," she said briskly. "You are a young man, the last of the Cynricings, and these lands need an heir. You have a duty to your line and to your holdings, to the atheling blood you bear through me. I do not expect a love-match, of course—do you think me insensitive?—but something will be arranged. Regan's lands march with yours. I will see to it."

"You will do no such thing—" he barked, but she waved a dismissive hand.

"Off you go about your business, my dear. Leave everything to me."

Leofric knew that if he stayed in there one more moment, he would strangle her. But it was a sin to strangle one's mother, however much she deserved it. He stood outside the door, trying to see past the haze of pure fury that blinded him. *How dare she!*

"Good God, lad, what ails you?" Godwine halted at the head of the stair. "You look half-mazed—I've not seen you look so bad since we brought you home on a hurdle after the battle at Rhyddygroes."

"I sometimes wonder," said Leofric, in a growl, "how my mother has survived at Court without someone poisoning her. Or maybe, like the viper, she's immune to venom. She wants me wed again, Godwine."

"She does?" Godwine said blankly.

"Aye and to Regan, for no better reason than our lands march. Dear God, did I ever come out of her?"

Godwine grinned. "That you did, m'lord, and not in a hurry, as I was told. Best to keep out of her way for a while—she may forget all about it."

"If only it were that easy. Godwine, I need to ride out or I will surely do her a mischief."

"Then I have just the thing," Godwine followed him down the stairs. "The snow has stopped and as I recall, Geadas could benefit from a visit from his thane, though the traveling will be far from easy."

He had expected the apathy of the past months, but the sharp "What has he done now?" gave him hope. God worked in mysterious ways. Even, on occasion, through Lady Hilde.

"I had word that another of his thralls has gone sick. Could be Geadas is up to his old tricks again."

"Which one?"

"Medwin. He was on his feet, by all accounts, but with a face like whey. Geadas maintains it's purely laziness—stubborn willfulness—but Medwin has always been a steady worker with other tenants."

They were into the hall by now and Leofric was stopped in his tracks. Her hair aglow like polished metal, Regan was sitting by the hearth with her maid and Edwina, and Dafydd was shaking his head, laughing as he put away his harp. "I shall be hoarse as a crow, ladies! I need to breathe a little before I sing again."

"If it's fresh air you're wanting," Leofric said abruptly, avoiding Regan's questioning look, "then ride with me. The madness of Saul may have abated, but it could return at any time, so I'll go prepared. Godwine, have the horses saddled. I'll have Lucca make up something for our noon-piece, I won't impose on Geadas' hospitality if I can help it."

That much Godwine could understand. "True enough, his oily ways are enough to sour any man's stomach."

"By your leave, my lady?" Dafydd looked at Regan. It had been a command and he could feel his hackles rising. The arrogance of the Saxons could still sometimes take him by surprise.

"You are a guest here, Dafydd," Regan said, voice expressionless. "You must do your own will. It is not for me—nor anyone else—to compel you."

The gibe was lost on Leofric, already at the hall door, shouting at Godwine to hurry up with the horses. Dafydd shrugged. "He is angry. The company here is more congenial."

"Better anger than dullness," Edwina said suddenly. "And last night he took an interest in your harping, when nothing else had held him so since—"

"Yes," Regan cut in. "Please go with him, Dafydd?"

A request was harder to refuse, so with a smile and a shrug he followed in Leofric's wake.

The thane's long strides had already taken him into the kitchen, where he was upsetting Lucca's orderly domain.

"I'm riding companioned by the harper," Leofric was saying. He sat down to pull on his riding boots, stamping his feet to settle them comfortably. Lucca was drawing out a paddle from her oven, laden with honey-cakes, steaming a little, golden and tempting and slid them onto a waiting platter, returning for the next batch. Leofric reached out and took the nearest, juggling it between his hands to cool it, then tossed it to Dafydd and took another. Lucca caught him at it this time and slapped his hand.

"Keep your thieving fingers away! Worse than a Welsh reiver you are—begging your pardon, Dafydd."

"There are no better honey-cakes in all the borders," Leofric said, taking a large bite and nearly burning his mouth. "Or do you tell me different, *bach* and we will beat a path to that paragon's door. For sure she would not deny us, if you had a praise-song ready." Restless now that his mind was made up, Leofric paced the floor, the flavor of the purloined honey-cake on his tongue reminding him of happier days. "Cheese, bannocks, store-apples, some of these—whatever is to hand, Lucca. I want to be on my way."

"In good time, my lord," she snapped. "There is much else to do here, without your demands! Think you I have more than one pair of hands?"

Things were shaping well for a good fight and it was perhaps fortunate that Godwine chose that moment to come into the kitchen with the news that the horses were waiting.

Chapter Five

The route Leofric chose to reach Geadas' land was a circuitous one for several reasons. Firstly he did not want Geadas to know he was coming, secondly he had not ridden out this way in weeks, perhaps months. Thirdly, the morning was fine enough, if cold, to make the extended ride enjoyable, despite the treacherous footing. The enjoyment did not last past their arrival at Geadas' threshold.

"Why, my lord, what a pleasant surprise!" The man did not show any discomfiture, greeting Leofric with every sign of deference while ignoring both Godwine and Dafydd as if they were invisible. He lacked the Saxon height, Dafydd saw, but he certainly did not lack in girth, for he was almost as round as he was long. Thinning fair hair adorned a round skull and small pale eyes blinked out at the world above a neat-combed moustache and a small pink mouth. He looked for all the world like a pig, Dafydd decided, taking against him on the instant. "Come you in and take a cup of mulled ale with me, sir. It is a cold day for riding."

"I'll see Medwin first," Leofric said. "But I thank you for your offer. Godwine and Dafydd might welcome a drink."

"To be sure, Godwine is ever welcome at my hearth and I'll have a thrall bring the boy out a—" His voice hesitated under the ice-chill of his thane's gaze.

"You are in error," Leofric said quietly and Godwine gave a guffaw.

"Aye, too free with your assumptions you are, Arnelfson. This is no thrall, but a harper guesting with us—Dafydd ap Gryfydd."

"Your forgiveness, I'm sure." Geadas gave a tittering chuckle, the pig-eyes crinkling in a false smile. "It is rare to see a Welshman so honored hereabouts."

"Geadas," Leofric said, still quietly, but with an edge to it that made Dafydd's nape hairs rise, "I will remind you, just once, of the respect due to a hearth-guest in my hall. And I will brook no further delay. Where is Medwin?"

"Gone to fetch the swine from pannage, my lord, before the drifts cover all." The smile had slipped awry and there was fear beneath it. "If you will but wait until—"

A movement at one of the outbuildings caught Dafydd's eye and he looked around. A dark young man was in the act of ducking into a low doorway and seeing the riders he paused and straightened up. His clothing was thin and ragged and the thrall collar was plain about his neck. Leofric saw him at the same moment.

"Coll." He raised his voice in crisp command. "Come here." Sullen, but head up, eyes on the thane's face, the thrall obeyed. "Where is Medwin?"

"In our shed, lord."

"What?" Geadas blustered. "Has he slunk back without the swine? If he has lost my beasts—"

Leofric ignored him. He swung down from Rufus, put the reins into Coll's hands and unheeding of Geadas' protesting cry, he ducked into the dimness of the shed. Dafydd followed him and gasped as the stench hit like a blow in the face. He blinked back tears as his eyes stung with nausea, but then his sight adjusted to the gloom and he saw Medwin.

The man lay in straw sodden with rain that had come through the torn roof, stinking with the filth of his sickness. His eyes were black pits in his drained face and he croaked wordlessly as Leofric knelt beside him. Dafydd moved closer. There were two blankets over the sick man, but they were worn to holes and although someone, probably Coll, had packed straw around him as well, Medwin was racked by shudders. Leofric muttered something that sounded like a curse and the doorway was darkened with figures.

"Merciful God!" Geadas exclaimed. "Is he truly sick then? My lord Leofric—come outside quickly, do not you touch him! Plague!"

"I think not." Leofric got up. "Questions, Geadas. How long has he been like this? Days, if this straw is anything to go by. Why hasn't he been cared for? Given decent bedding? Aye and why are your thralls housed in a hovel I'd not keep a cur in, let alone men?"

Dafydd, trying to breathe shallowly, watched Geadas formulate excuses and hated him for his callousness. Truly these Saxons were but a step up from their reiver-ancestors, with as little care for the folk they had disinherited and enslaved. Even Leofric's anger seemed to him at the moment less that of compassion than the indignation of a man who has found a piece of valuable property made unusable. But no one was taking heed of him or his thoughts, to see what was briefly in his face. None save the thrall Coll.

"He's not been like this before, my lord," Geadas was saying anxiously. "As to the bedding, why, they've had dry stuff for the asking, I cannot think why they did not tell me…"

Softly, in his own tongue, Dafydd said, "Is it sickness?"

Coll's eyes brightened to a hard glitter. "No," he said, in the same language. "Bad food."

"Where?" And when Coll gestured, Dafydd caught Leofric's eye. "By your leave, my lord." He crossed to the darkest corner, brushed back the straw and with distaste picked up one of the bowls there. He had not thought the stench could grow worse, but it did. Holding his breath, he carried it to Leofric, who took it from him and held it under Geadas' nose.

"Well, now we see why your swine are so healthy. You feed the thralls on their leavings, not the other way about!"

Geadas backed out, fast, babbling his innocence, but Dafydd did not listen, nor did he follow Leofric and Godwine out into the clean air of the yard. Instead he unpinned his cloak and knelt to put it over Medwin, tucking it close. The man clutched at it, hands palsied with fever, eyes bewildered.

"You are *Cymru*." Coll made it sound like an accusation. Dafydd sat back on his heels.

"Yes. Dafydd ap Gryfydd, of Llan Illtud, though my father's folk are of Gwynedd."

"Llan Illtud, in the south? You do not look like one of the priest-kind."

"I am not. I am a bard."

"Truly?" It was clear that Coll thought him too young or too priest-led to lay valid claim to such a title.

"Had I my harp, I could give you proof. But I know the Laws and the lists of the Kings and all my master taught me and he had harped for princes. Will this serve instead?" He drew breath and sang the last stanza of Aneurin's great lament for the Companions of Prince Owain, who had died with him at Cattraeth.

Coll stared at him wide-eyed and open-mouthed and even Medwin in his misery turned his eyes to the young man whose voice rang in the hovel as clear and true as a blade.

"We were warriors in those days," Coll whispered into the silence as he finished.

"Owain will come again," he said coldly and deliberately, and heard Coll's caught breath. "God keep you both."

"And you, Dafydd ap Gryfydd."

"Dafydd!" Leofric called him out and he emerged to see Geadas still mouthing protests, face no longer rosily bland. "Coll, come you here." The thrall came out on Dafydd's heels, his face again a closed mask. "Harness an ox and take Medwin to the steading. Anna Priestwife will come to tend him there. Geadas will give you extra blankets."

"My lord, I have none to spare!"

"Then you can give that new cloak you bought at Leominster market," Godwine suggested and Geadas choked on his objections, hurrying back to his house.

"Do I return here after, lord?" Coll made bold to ask.

"No. You'll stay to care for Medwin until he's able to look after himself, then Godwine will find another place for you. Geadas will be without thrall-labor until such time as I judge he has better learned responsibility. He can hire freemen, if he can find any willing." Leofric mounted Rufus, signing for Dafydd and Godwine to follow him. "Take it steady with the cart." And he clattered out of the yard and back up the track.

Leofric reined in to wait for them and his face was pale with fury. He gave a bitter laugh. "Well, Godwine? Am I my father's son? Did I put the fear of God and the Cynricings into that slimy toad?"

"You did, lad, and not necessarily in that order," Godwine beamed. "Will I put the word out with the free laborers that they should ask a quarter again of their usual wage from him?"

"Make it a third," Leofric said. "He's wealthy enough. Some of the best land in these parts and he penny-pinches like a miser! Lord above, what was he feeding them? It reeked like week-old offal!" He grimaced and spat. "They must have a good placing when they are well—Coll did not look in much better shape than poor Medwin! By The Tree, I'll have Geadas summonsed to the Moot for this abuse!"

But Geadas was not the only one at fault, he acknowledged. Part of the blame was his. Since Midsummer he had turned away from his responsibilities, ignored his own duties to his people. His mother was right in part, he had a duty to his holdings, to the people who looked to him for care and justice. If he had been fulfilling those duties as he should, then Medwin would not be ailing and Coll would not be little more than a ragged scarecrow. That much, at least, would change from now on.

*****

The track down to the village was fairly clear of deep snow, but it was icy underfoot and Edwina picked her way cautiously over the frozen path. She had no legitimate errand for braving the inclement weather for this visit to the Priestwife's cott and prayed that she would be unrecognized, if not unobserved, gossiping tongues being what they were and with Lady Hilde's household underfoot.

Father Edric had had the benefit of a sturdy and well-built cottage next to the little church and his widow had retained it. The Lady Hilde had often said that married clergy were not approved of by the Church, but no one else had thought to object. Father Edric had been a good priest, as well as a good husband and father and from stories she'd heard, Edwina thought that an unmarried one would have been a far worse bargain. The half-blind and stone-deaf old dodderer they had now was better than Lady Hilde's kind of priest. She'd not have felt so safe at her Confessions if the priest had been single—maybe even young—whereas even if Father Edric had the inclination to stray, Anna kept him firmly in line. Anna had a reputation of her own. As Wise Woman she had doctored them all at one time or another, as midwife she had had most of the young through her hands. Edwina herself had been brought into the world by Anna's skill and there was no one more knowledgeable in the mysteries of womankind. But there was something more important she needed to ask of Anna than the infusion of Lady's Mantle. For Anna also followed the The Old Way.

Edwina tapped on the door before pushing it open and stepping inside. It looked like chaos, Anna's three youngest were chasing energetically in circles, together with two dogs who were unsure exactly what the game entailed and took sidetrips into the pen where a goose was setting her eggs, which resulted in yelps and hissing and the family cat trying to doze at the hearth was adding to the turmoil with an occasional well-aimed claw. The noise was incredible, but Anna sat imperturbably on her stool in the midst of it, a half-plucked hen in her lap, and crooned as she worked.

She greeted Edwina with a smile. "You make the day bright, lass," she said comfortably. "Sit down, child, and warm yourself."

Edwina moved the cat carefully to one side and took a seat, stretching out chilled fingers to the fire. She glanced a little shyly at Anna's plump bulk, at the kindly brown eyes in the weathered face. "I come for counsel, my Mother," she whispered and Anna gave a nod, though her fingers never paused in their plucking.

"Aye, well, I did wonder. When a maid has trouble with her courses, it's most like for one reason or the other. Astrid! Take your brothers out to see the piglets." And when the children were gone, "So, my Daughter. You've not the look of a breeding woman, so it must be the other. There's no need to conceive if you—"

Edwina felt a blush scorch her cheek. "Oh no! It's not...I mean, I would that it were, I'd bear his babes joyfully, but he doesn't...he hasn't...Oh Anna," she wailed finally, "I'm mad with love for him!"

Anna's hands paused. "Well," she said softly. "Well. And does your Da know?"

"Mary Mother, no!" Edwina was horrified. "He'd never agree!"

"Then what's to be done, Daughter?" The feathers began to fall again. "Eh, dear old Gudrun...if tha'd not stopped laying, I'd not be having to pluck thee for the pot... You're mad for this lad, but he's not spoken for you. Is he like to?" Shrewdly, she studied the flushed young face. "Has he tupped you?"

"No!" Edwina's cry was half outrage and half regret.

"Aye, but has he tried?" Anna gave a rich chuckle. "Did you put him off and then think the better of it?"

"No, Anna…He only arrived yesterday. I don't think he's like that."

"Ach, child, all men are 'like that', though they be sprung from hedgerows or princes. In fact," she mused, "I'm not at all sure the princes aren't the worst of 'em. So, Daughter, what shall Anna do for you?"

"I want him to love me," Edwina whispered. The blush deepened. "And Mam won't let me dye my hair red, I thought there might be a charm or a potion…" Her voice trailed off under Anna's amused look.

"Oh there could be," the priestess agreed. "But consider — suppose it worked. You'd never know if it was yourself he loved, would you, or something the magic made him believe he loved. Hark, 'Dwina dear. If he's for you, then the Good Goddess Herself won't come between you and your heart's desire. If he's not, then you'll get over him and be thankful when you find your true man." She smiled into the disappointed blue eyes. "And you will, dear. I tell you this and I do not lie." Then, because she was kind and did not like to send any suppliant away unsatisfied, she got up and went to her herb cupboard, sorting through until she found what she sought. "Here now. Wear this around your neck, under your gown, so it lies against your skin and between your breasts. Hold it each night when you pray and ask the Holy Mother and St. Brigid for their blessing. You've no need to be changing the color of your hair. Dearie me, I never heard the like."

Edwina took the twist of linen eagerly, tied the thread at her nape and tucked the thing under her shift. "Oh thank you, Anna! I knew you'd help!"

Anna gave her a hug. "It'll only work if he's the right one, mind," she cautioned and watched her safely down the path before going back to her stool and lifting the fowl back onto her knee. The dried flowers of meadowsweet and lavender, together with a pinch of other oddments, would do no more than scent the girl's linen pleasantly, whereas the power of prayer was something she did not take lightly. Anna, like many others, worshipped the Old Powers of Corn King, Spring Queen, the bountiful Earth Mother, with an equal reverence given to the White Christ and His Mother Mary and all the saints. There were times, in fact, when she wasn't at all certain that the Holy Names weren't just that—mortal labelings for the Unnamable.

But that was something she kept to herself.

"Dear old Gudrun," she sighed, shaking her head over the hen. "A bonny layer in your day…Dye her hair red, indeed. So it's one of Lady Regan's household she has a mind to." She gave a quiet chuckle. "Well, Gudrun, it won't take a scrying to find out who it is and that's for certain."

"Mam!" Astrid poked her head round the door, blonde elflocks teased wild by the wind. "Leofric Thane's coming!"

Chapter Six

Leofric reined in beside the small cottage next to the church. The ride back had leached away some of his fury and the cold air had cleared his head, so that he no longer wanted to throttle anyone. Well, a swift kick might suffice for Geadas, though what he could legitimately do to his mother was still a puzzle.

"No need to wait, Godwine. Go and have a place prepared for Medwin. I'll talk to Anna. Dafydd, I think Anna knows more of the old legends than you and I together and knows what they mean into the bargain. Come you in and meet her, if you've a mind." He swung down, ruffling the fair curls of the child who grinned gap-toothed up at him. "Astrid, will you hold Rufus for me?" He flung his mantle over the animal's back as it steamed in the still cold. "And keep your brothers from under his hooves and him from out of your Mam's herb-patch." He ducked under the lintel, Dafydd silently on his heels. "Blessed be, Mother," he said quietly.

"And thee be blessed, Son, and shut the door. You were ever born in a byre." She pulled his head down for a kiss on both cheeks then pushed him toward a stool by the fire.

"Anna, this is Dafydd ap Gryfydd, bard with Lady Regan's household." Somehow it still felt strange to give her the title — Trout, he'd called her, many years ago, for her freckles and that she could swim better than he.

"Sit down and warm yourself, boy, you're welcome here," she smiled. "I'll wager you'll both be glad of some mulled ale."

"Always," Leofric said with a wry smile. It had been months since he'd visited Anna's cott, but nothing seemed to change. That in itself was a balm to his spirit. He breathed deep of the herb-scented air, redolent of rosemary, tansy and rue. Anna's cat blinked up at him, purring when he scratched behind its ears. "But it's not on our account I'm here. Medwin is being brought to the steading. He's ailing and he'll need your skills, Anna. Probably Coll as well. Will you come to him there?"

"That Geadas!" she snapped, pleasant face suddenly and unsettlingly grim. "Something will have to be done about that man and if you do not do it, Edmundson, then by the Lady, I will."

"It will be done," he promised.

"Your Da protected him too much," she went on, bent over the fire with two beakers set ready. "And all for Aeditha's sake. What did the man do but take advantage! I know she's your half-sister but—"

"But now my people are coming to harm through his greed," Leofric finished for her. "Yes, Anna. He and I will both pay compensation to Medwin and to Coll."

"I know you will," she nodded. "Now, bad food and the cold, by my guess? Tell me what you found."

Dafydd accepted the earthenware beaker she offered him and looked curiously around as he sipped at the hot spiced ale. The house was trim and neat, everything craftsman-made and mended, from the clay beehive shape of the bake-oven to the black iron of the cooking-spit. Just then a weight descended on his shoulder and a raucous voice squawked "Jack! Jack! *Da Bach,* Jack!" in his ear, so that he nearly choked.

"Don't mind Whitewing," Anna said, chuckling. At her voice, the bird—a large jackdaw with odd white flashes to his wings—flapped from Dafydd's shoulder to perch at her side, head cocked hopefully. "Ah, you're a scold and a thief, but a good creature for all that."

Dafydd was fascinated—he'd never come across a bird that talked like a Christian. Leofric held out a hand and the bird hopped onto it, dipped its beak in his ale and wiped it after on his sleeve. "*Da Bach*, Jack!" it said, approvingly and Anna laughed.

"Good boy, is it? For shame, you wanton!"

"For shame!" The bird echoed in wicked mimicry, raising his wings, then clucked like a hen.

"Your family grows all the while," Leofric said, amused and as intrigued as Dafydd was. "When did this fine fellow arrive?"

"I mended his leg this summer, and now he chooses to live here and eat scraps rather than go back to his wild brothers, lazy thing that he is."

"Lazy, maybe, but daft he is not," Dafydd commented. "He sleeps warm and eats fat winter-long."

"Ah well, he has paid for his keep," Anna said quietly, looking with satisfaction at the grin on Leofric's face.

* * * * *

Although the Hall was no longer a haven, filled as it was with the come and go of the household, Regan was already regretting her retreat back to the solar. Lady Hilde had apparently forgotten that they were lonely, bereaved sisters joined by the solace of God and had launched in with an inquisition on her lands. The reasons for this were clear enough, though Regan could not guess at the man Hilde had in mind. She answered as politely as her fraying patience would permit, but eventually set down the embroidery. "Your forgiveness, my Lady, but this is a fruitless exercise. I have no wish to marry any of your Court lordlings. I shall be continuing my journey to Leominster in a very few days. The roads should be clearing by then, according to Godwine."

Hilde's reaction was not what she expected.

"Oh my dear…!" Pale eyes brimmed. "Please stay a little! I shall miss you so!"

"I cannot," Regan said firmly, keeping her gaze on her lap. "They will be expecting me at the Abbey." This was not strictly true. She had sent no word of her coming.

"Then send word that you are delayed. Regan, I beg you, stay and keep a poor widow company. There is no one here who can comfort me, I am so alone these days, with naught but my memories—in Christian charity, stay!"

Thunderstruck, Regan gaped at her. The Lady Hilde was imperious, insensitive, totally without tact—and yet her grief over her husband was genuine if little else was and it was this Regan responded to. Almost as if the words were torn from her, regretting them even as she spoke, she said, "I shall stay awhile longer."

Hilde dropped her needle and clasped the younger woman to her, eyes overflowing. "So kind!" she murmured brokenly. "So kind…!"

Regan murmured a few platitudes and eased herself from the scented embrace, giving Hilde into the care of the two elderly bower-maids. "I'll fetch you something to restore you—some spiced wine, perhaps?" and ran down to the hall, leaving Morwenna slack-jawed on her stool by the fire. Once there Regan indulged herself with closing the door with a crash loud enough to turn heads.

"I am a fool!" she stormed. "A-a moon-led wittol!"

"My lady?" Dafydd was instantly at her side, frowning. "If there is one here who has threatened you—"

She knew he thought of Ranulf fitzRobert. "No, no, merely that woman!" She was too nerve-taut to wonder where he'd sprung from.

She dropped her voice to a whisper, aware of interested ears all about the place. "I said I'd stay awhile longer, like some bespelled witling, because she wept and begged me to and all the while she would marry me off to one of those combed and swaggering louts she has for housecarls! Stay and keep a poor widow company, she said!—poor, do you note it,

Dafydd?—poor? Well, yes, if you overlook the estates and holdings she has, scattered over Mercia, Essex and Wessex and not visited for years because she is bower-woman to the Queens. Not to mention the jewels she wears about her—enough to sink a war boat! Old? If she is five years older than Lucca I'll be amazed. She'll not see fifty for some years yet. Widow…yes, that she is, for almost two years now for all that she wears the black as if it's a mere se'ennight and she adored her Edmund. But I can name you six high lords she could have had for the taking, not to mention any of the younger men in her own household! As for alone—" She saw the amusement in the dark blue eyes and realized her indiscretion. "Dafydd ap Gryfydd," she said sternly, "you are deaf and I have said nothing."

"Your pardon, Lady? My hearing is something lacking…"

"Ah the tact of the *Cymru*. I swear, by God's Blessed Mother, if ever I get as bad as that, I hope someone throws me in the river." And she heard her own pain and was surprised at it until the soft voice broke her thought.

"I shall bear that in mind, Lady."

She stared at him for a disbelieving moment, then laughter bubbled up.

"Insolent Welsh pup!" She cuffed his ear gently. "Ah but I needed that. Bless you for your ready tongue!" He was, she abruptly noticed, still in muddied boots and cloak. "How went your ride?

His smile did not change, but something behind his eyes did, making him suddenly a stranger. "Well enough, my lady, considering the state of the ground. Is her skald with her? If not, I could take my harp to the solar. It might sweeten her tongue a little."

"That'll take bardic skill indeed," she sighed. "Along with skeps of honey. Now I had best get that spiced wine, or I'll hear nothing but carping from her."

She did not have the opportunity. Before she had even finished speaking, the stair door banged back on its hinges and Morwenna almost fell into the hall. She was weeping gustily, her headrail was gone and one cheek was fiery red. "Oh m'lady…"

"Heavens, child, what ails you?" Regan held her upright.

"I didn't mean any harm, m'lady, truly I didn't, but the threads got in a worse tangle however I tried and she said I was a cow-handed slut and—"

"Who did?" Regan demanded, coldly, but she already knew the answer.

"—not fit for a byre, let alone a lady's bower!"

"Hilde." Regan did not need more. "Morwenna, bide here. Here's Edwina to comfort you. Witch-hazel on that cheek, I think, 'Dwina. I," and the tone was of one arming for battle, "will deal with my Lady Shrew." She did not notice Dafydd behind her as she mounted the stairs two at a time. Skirts bunched in her fists, she stalked into the solar.

Hilde was having rosewater applied to wrists and temples by Thyra, while Constance chafed her hands. "Regan, my dear," Hilde said feebly. "That clumsy—"

"Under no circumstances and at no time will you or either of these ever raise a hand to one of my maids," Regan cut in. "You are fortunate that your rings did not cut her, or I would claim the blood-gild."

"My dear—!" Hilde's eyes widened in shock.

"I am not your dear anything, Lady, and if I am to be in your company again, for however long, then we must understand each other."

To Regan's astonishment, Hilde smiled. Pushing aside the fluttering maid, she rose to her feet with all the regal bearing of the queens she attended. "My dear," she said deliberately, "I believe we already do. You are exactly what this steading needs." Which so effectively cut the ground from beneath

Regan's feet that she was halfway down the stair in full retreat before she was aware. So. It was to be war. Regan rallied her defenses and moved in for a flanking attack.

*****

If Leofric had any doubts that his newly reborn interest in his holdings and his people was more than a little overdue, these were swiftly dispelled. His brief expedition to Geadas fast became common knowledge and folk from both the village and outlying farms were beginning to arrive at the hall, bringing stored-up problems for the thane's attention. It was also an effective antidote for the never-ending ache of loss within him. Not that it cured it, of course, merely blanketed it.

Since he'd grown up knowing most of the people on his land and having an excellent memory, Leofric rarely needed Godwine's somewhat irritating prompting to put names to faces or place them about the map. Within the hour, he had dealt with and resolved disputes over the ownership of stock, the establishment of bounds and whose responsibility it was to keep certain fences in repair. At some point, Lucca brought half a cold fowl and a dish of savory porridge and he ate as he worked, barely tasting it.

"Right. Who's next?"

"Sifrith, m'lord. Thrall with—"

"Thank you, Godwine, I do know where Sifrith is placed. How goes it, man?"

Sifrith, mired to the knee with red mud, grinned at him, hooking a finger under the iron collar almost hidden in his tangle of blond hair. "I'll be a free man come Yule, m'lord. Reared a runtling pig Oswy gave me because he thought it wasn't going to live and sold it on in Blood Month."

"Glad to hear it! I've won my wager then—didn't I say you'd do it within five years? Pay up, Godwine."

Godwine grumbled good-naturedly, chewing his moustaches, but he gave the thrall a wink. "So what's Oswy sent you here for?"

Sifrith became abruptly serious. "His brindled heifer is gone. Not strayed—I've fixed his fences so that Sleipnir himself couldn't break through. No, this was reiver's work. She was taken out the back of the farthest byre. We found tracks going into the forest. Two men."

"That's Intake," Leofric said, glancing at the map to remind himself. The forest was the southern edge of his land, a wide sweep marching with river and border. South of it was a strip of no-mans-land and Guthlac Thane's land, to the west was the river and the Welsh.

"The sooner it's cleared, the better," Godwine said. "That was ever a favorite bolt-hole for the damned Welsh. Trying to flush them out of there is like fetching a stoat from a thicket." He consulted his tally-sticks, though he had the figures all in his head. "We've lost eight beasts overall these last two months," he announced.

"Wolfsheads," Leofric said.

"Welsh," Godwine insisted.

"You see the Welsh in every shadow."

"Aye, we even have one in hall, don't we?" Godwine countered and Leofric rolled his eyes.

"Use your brains, man. When did they last attack us in winter? They're too busy staying alive and preparing weapons and men for the spring raids. They don't winter their war-bands this side of the Dyke—if they did, we'd be losing a sight more than eight beasts, that's for certain. Wolfsheads, Saxon, Welsh or heathen Dane."

"Wolfsheads," Sifrith put in. "There were no horse-tracks, just the cow and men."

But Godwine would not be persuaded. "There were a lot of raids to the south of here last year," he reminded them, "though they didn't bother with us this time. These could be a rag-tag left behind to harry us."

"I don't think so," Leofric said grimly. "But either way, there's little that can be done until the weather changes. Sifrith, as soon as you've rested and eaten, you'd best go back to Oswy. Make sure all the stock is kept as close as they can be and that the house is well-protected. I'd sooner lose beasts than lives. And be back here with your man-price at the Yule-feast."

"Aye, m'lord."

"Next," said Godwine, "is—"

"Regan Aldheimsdaughter," she announced, shutting the stair door behind her and walking toward the impromptu moot. Her head was held high, chin and mouth set in a way Leofric recalled from years ago. Regan was angry. Then the child had often come at him with flying fists, now the woman advanced like a warrior-queen, tall and stately and not to be gainsaid.

"My lady," he said formally, rising to his feet.

"The Lady Hilde has requested that I stay awhile to bear her company." Her voice was clear as a bell and without expression and he knew that his insufferable mother had spoken to Regan as callously as she had to him. And no doubt on the same subject. "Since the roads to Leominster are impassable and likely to remain so for some days, I have decided to postpone my leaving until after the Yule feast. Then, as soon as it is possible to travel, I will be away to the Abbey. That being so," she went on before he could speak, "I ask leave to approach Godwine Gunnarson for his daughter Edwina. I wish her to join Morwenna as bower-maid to me while I am here."

Battle lines, then, had been drawn between the women. Through his own anger, Leofric acknowledged it with some amusement. Knowing Regan of old, Hilde could find herself routed before she could comprehend it. He felt the warmth of remembered friendship and felt an ache of regret. This woman-grown was something of a stranger, but enough of the old Regan was still there for him to know how much she would hate being mured up with his mother and the bower-women, for convention dictated she could not escape it without aid. He should have asked her to ride with him to Geadas as well as Dafydd—if his mother had not opened her viper-mouth, he would have done so without thought, because it would have been right and fitting, if only for friendship's sake. And that would have been all it was. Friendship's sake.

"You are welcome in my hall for as long or as short a time as you wish to stay, my lady," he replied. "When you leave it will be with an escort befitting your station and I would ask only that you remember us in your prayers within the convent. Well, Godwine, what say you?"

"Of course, my lady! You do the lass much honor. I don't doubt she'll leap at the chance."

Edwina was sitting on a bench consoling the still sobbing Morwenna and leap she did to her feet with a joyful shout when Regan approached.

"My lady," she began, but Regan held up her hand.

"How brave are you, girl? How much Lucca's daughter are you?" She did not need to say more. Edwina's chin jutted and a martial light glowed in her blue eyes, she understood well enough. Bower-maid she was and companion-protector to the vulnerable Morwenna.

Chapter Seven

൪

The weather was changing. Dafydd could sense it, though little could be heard through the bulky weight of thatch and the heavy shutters over the high windows. He huddled a little closer to the hearth.

Most of the hall-folk were already wrapped in their fleeces and asleep. Some still sat in groups, Leofric' people and Regan's together in easy camaraderie, dicing and talking in hushed voices while the smoke rose and torches guttered in the ever-present draughts. No one minded the quiet ripple of sound from the harp-strings, would probably have requested it if he were not playing.

But this was for himself alone, an attempt to soothe the unease and restlessness that was steadily growing inside. He'd stayed too long and the snow was not reason enough. This weather-change was omen and goad, he should leave and soon, lest he be snared…

A man came back from his journey to the midden, cloak clutched around him and dripping to the rushes.

"Raining," he reported in a low voice as heads turned. "Heavy as Sleipnir pissing. The snow's loosening, but if it keeps up for long the fords'll be flooded and there'll be no ride to Leominster for the Lady for weeks."

"The longer she bides," another grunted, "the more she's likely to take the east road homewards."

"Not Aldheim's lass," Swein, Regan's man, drew the covers closer about him. "Once she's made up her mind she'll not change it. Stubborn as a rock, that one. Now get back to your bed and let us as wants to sleep."

Dafydd smiled. Not complimentary, perhaps, but said with affection. She was well-loved by her folk and they had no mind to see her behind Abbey walls. But there could be no other, better, place for her.

Raining. The snow-melt would add to the run-off over the frozen ground and the rivers would be rising fast. To the south the road ran along the top of a raised bank, he could travel that way easily enough then turn off—

"Son of Owain," a voice whispered, the *Cymru* tongue liquid and soft as a breath in the hall. Dafydd looked up to see a hooded thrall carefully piling more logs on the hearth fire. Coll, his drawn face grimly determined in the shadows, crouched at his feet and stretched out his hands to the flames, as if he were just warming himself for a while after his task. His wet clothes steamed in the heat. "A few days of this and it'll freeze again, with more snow," the man murmured. "There'll not be a better time for Medwin and me to be away from here. The Hounds of Annwn would have trouble tracking us. But we need your help. For Owain's sake. We must have food to take with us."

"It's too soon," Dafydd hissed. "Medwin is too weak. Let Anna's potioning work first."

"No! He wants to be away. Swears he'll take his own life rather than stay another day in a *Saes* hold." Coll's face took on a grimace that might have been a smile. "Me, I'll take *Saes* lives before I'd take my own."

Dafydd nodded. He could well understand the hatred and need for revenge. "Fetch Medwin and wait for me behind the kitchen midden," he said. "I'll bring what I can."

Dafydd took a swift glance round as Coll disappeared. No one had noticed the exchange, no one watched him now. He waited for a while, then yawned and stretched and slipped the harp back into her bag. He picked up leather coverlet and cloak together, swung both round his shoulders so that the deerskin was out of sight beneath and moved silently to the door. Just another man making the walk outside to relieve himself.

The rain struck him like a falling wall, its force staggering him. He nearly fell on the slick ground and ducked into the lee of the hall for shelter. The freezing bite was gone from the air. In its place was a raw damp chillness that was somehow worse, eating into his bones and catching at the back of his throat as if he was trying to breathe water like a fish.

This was madness, he knew. Medwin was going to his death as surely as a man to the scaffold. But as the songs had it, better to die a free man than a slave and as one of Owain's many Sons, it was his duty to give what aid he could.

Lucca's kitchen store was full to bursting with supplies set by for the Yule feasting. The little the two men could carry would not be missed. Dafydd found a leather sack and filled it with cheeses, store-apples and a half-leg of smoked pork, then let himself out into the rain. He could see little more than an arm's length ahead and was certain that none of the gate guards would see the thralls leaving.

Medwin and Coll were crouched against the rear wall, the sick man smothering a coughing fit with both hands clamped over his mouth.

"Will you not wait?" Dafydd asked. Both shook their heads. "So be it then. Here is food. Will you go to the Sons?"

"Aye," Coll whispered fiercely. "Just tell us where."

"Follow the south road out of this holding until you come to the Intake woods. Quarter of a mile farther on, there's a double-trunked oak on the right, beside the way. Turn off left there. The trees are blazed just above head-height by a small arrowhead mark. Be watchful, they aren't easily seen in daylight, let alone in a wet night. Follow them due east. The Sons will find you. Tell them," and he paused. "Tell them the Falcon sent you. Tell them 'too many swords, not yet'."

"Too many swords, not yet." Coll nodded, understanding and a kind of hunger glittering in his dark eyes. He accepted the sack and wrapped the deerskin about Medwin, then turned back to Dafydd. "I don't know what to say to you, ap Gryfydd," he whispered in a hoarse voice. "You've given us more than freedom—we have our pride back as well, even if we die for it."

"Aye," Medwin wheezed. "We'll not forget this and if ever we can repay—"

Dafydd gave him a smile. "No need for that. My Da used to say that if a thing wasn't worth fighting for, it wasn't worth having. Come on now, I'll open the gate a crack and you can be gone."

It was easily done. Almost too easily, said a small, unwelcome voice at the back of Dafydd's mind. The great hinges were kept well-oiled and made no sound at all when he'd slipped the bar and swung one gate barely wide enough for the men to slide through. They vanished at once into the torrential rain and he shut and barred the gate behind them. He could have opened it to a horde and none would have known until the blades were at their throats…

He hurried back to the hall and his place by the hearth.

"Best see Anna Priestwife," said a sleepy voice not far away. "She'll fix you with a potion if you're blocked."

"I might do that," he muttered and rolled himself up in what was left of his bedding.

* * * * *

In the room that had been his father's, Leofric lay in the large bed and listened to the rain hammering on the thick glass panes. "Norman contrivances," Edmund had sneered, but because Hilde had wanted it, he'd agreed, more from wishing a quiet life than to give a beloved wife her every whim. So Hilde had her solar, also glazed, she had her little chapel-room set between the chambers. She had her own Norman priest to say Mass, since she had not approved of Father Edric and had nothing but contempt for poor Father Egnoth—and then had not spent more than a few months of the year at Staneleigh. Which did not displease her husband. Or her son.

That had been a political marriage, Leofric knew. Anyone less like a saint than his cheerfully pagan and profane warrior-sire would be hard to imagine and Leofric could not understand why Hilde had chosen to elevate him to such lofty rank once he was dead. His own marriage, on the other hand, was an entirely different matter. He'd fallen in love with Hawiss the moment he'd seen her, the first time Hilde had brought the girl to Staneleigh as a bower-maid. Kentish-born, she was, with high-ranking kin, according to his mother, but he was more interested in the bright mantle of curling gold hair and her huge smoky-amethyst eyes and high apple-round breasts. She was beautiful beyond any man's dream and if she giggled a lot it was because she loved life—and loved him with a passion and sensuality that matched his own.

"Your mother has a mind to see you wed," Edmund had said to him toward the end of that winter.

"And I've a mind to be wed," he'd replied, "But it will be my choice, not hers. Hawiss or no one."

"By the One Tree," his father had groaned. "I'd hoped you'd have more wit than balls. She isn't the one I'd match you with, boy. I know you're hot to bed her, you don't have to wed her into the bargain."

"Hawiss," he'd repeated. "Or no one." They were married within the month and for Leofric it was as if he had entered into Eden. Not even the death of his much-loved father less than a month after the wedding could overshadow his joy for long. Hawiss took no heed of the running of hearth and hall, leaving that in Lucca's capable charge. All her attention was given to him, teasing him away from ledgers and tally-sticks, from tenant-visits and moots and into their bed at every opportunity and later, riding out through the long summer days to find bowers in the woods and lie together in the grass.

There was one place in particular they'd often search out. He had found the clearing years ago, when youth and a yearning for adventure had had him riding these wooded hills throughout his boyhood. When he had described it to Godwine, he'd been told to avoid it. His father had merely grunted and warned him of pitfalls. His mother had crossed herself and uttered a pious prayer. But none of them had ever seen it. Once, long ago, before his race had first invaded these shores, there had been a building here. The walls still stood knee high in places, fine dressed stone though overgrown now with grasses and herbs and tree roots had pushed up through once-level paving. But it was still possible to trace the outline of the place—three times the size of his own hall in length, enclosing a court with jutting wings. Molehills dotted the area—in past years he'd found red tile and glazed colored fragments.

In summer the spaces between the walls became suntraps edged with dappled shade, heavy with the scents of wild herbs and flowers, thyme and marjoram and mallow and meadowsweet and bees wavered drunkenly from flower to flower until almost too laden to fly. He had woven the blossoms into a coronet for Hawiss, purple and cream-white and pink on the corn gold of her unbound hair and the flowering hawthorn was not whiter than her breast.

It was there, with autumn putting copper and golden glory to the leaves and an exhilarating zest of frost in the air, that she had told him of the child to come. Throughout the winter and spring they had rejoiced as her body swelled with the infant. She had laughed to feel it kick—had held his hand over the place so that he might feel the thrust of life within her.

She was dead by midsummer, murdered by the monstrous fruit he had planted in her womb.

The pain of the memory stopped his breath and he crushed it with reckless strength. No. It was not to be thought of. Looking back he could see that for months he had been like a man stunned and sinking deeper into a morass. Yesterday he'd found a foothold, but if he let the agony and loss overwhelm him again he'd slide beneath the surface and be lost. He could not let that happen. Not now. He had finally seen how his people looked to him. He was needed here and if he shirked that duty he was little better than Geadas.

Rain began a slow drumbeat on the windows then became a waterfall roar as the deluge struck in earnest. Leofric welcomed it. Tomorrow the tracks would be awash but passable. There would be dykes and sluices to inspect, tenants and cottars to reassure and repairs to be ordered, scattered stock to be traced and returned. More than enough to fill his days and form an impenetrable barrier to the past.

Medwin and Coll, for instance. He was to blame as much as Geadas. That could be set right. He would pay their man-price and Geadas would give them coins or kind. Enough for them to stay and farm rented land, or go their way as they chose.

Eight beasts. He should have asked Godwine who had lost, plotted them on the map to see if all led back to the Intake. He must send a rider south to Guthlac as soon as the weather permitted, to see if that thane had lost stock as well. Leofric frowned. He had a vague memory of someone telling him that Guthlac had been hit hard by a Welsh raid and he should send men — but that had been just after Hawiss —

The trees of the Intake clothed rising, broken land. There would be places where men could hole up and survive the winter, if they had stolen animals to feed on. Time it was flushed out then and before the summer growth had thickened up and provided cover. With his men, Guthlac's and Regan's and his mother's if — God forefend — she was still at Staneleigh, there would be more than enough to beat through the woodland for a gaggle of wolfsheads.

For the rest of the night he lay open-eyed, staring up in the darkness and listening to the storm, planning the day ahead.

Chapter Eight

From the walkway above the gatehouse, Dafydd could see much of the steading's immediate land. After his troubled, dream-racked night, it was almost pleasant up here, with the stout palisade keeping off the worst bite of the wind and the pale sun warming the wood under his hands. For the first time he could get a good look at this garth, mark its strengths and weaknesses before the weather closed in again.

More than twenty feet, the walls reared, solid tree trunks bedded in the earth. A man's height below the top edge of the palisade was a walkway, wide enough for three men to walk abreast and with many narrow gaps so that a defending archer or slingsman could create havoc in any attacking force. Not that they'd easily get close to the walls. There was a narrow level space at the foot, then a wide deep ditch, filled now by slush and sharded ice. The gates themselves were guarded by small watchtowers to each side and a covered walk across the top. Luck as well as the weather had been with him last night. This was another steading that could not be taken by force. Well, these *Saes* barricades may not be the walls of Illium, but he did not need a hollow horse to gain entry. Just his harp.

Behind him, the long hall lay like a drowsing giant beast, furred with bulrush brown thatching pied in places where the reeds had been replaced, with the smaller guest-bowers not far from it. The byres and barns huddled around within the stockade like piglets around a sow, all safe behind the massive fence.

Beyond, to the west the reed and turf-thatched cottages straggled downhill toward the road and the water-meadows with the river beyond. Each cott had a patch of ground for herbs or kale or pulses, each with bee skep or tethered goat or handful of scratching hens. And to either side of the track, the strip lynchets, lord's and tenant's side by side, so each had shares in good land and bad. He'd seen the pattern before, of course. One Saxon holding was much like another and all of it stolen. He picked out the shape of the little village church, identified by the cross atop. Tomorrow, no doubt, he would be going with the household to Mass.

He turned south, glancing out over pasture and rising land to the lip of the Intake wood, and wondered if Coll and Medwin had been found by the *Meibion Owain*. Quickly he turned half-circle, gazing due north. Here, too, the land rose gently toward wooded slopes, but here the highest top was cleared, as if the hill had been tonsured like a monk. A good place to keep a beacon. They or the folk before them might have lit the fires when the invading Vikings came up the Severn in their Dragon ships, before great Alfred raised up the Fyrd and met and defeated them so that England should lie no more under the yoke of Danelaw. Well, so the song said. There were, as England had found, other ways of invasion than the sword and stronger alliances may be made in a woman's bed than in a burning city. The Old Queen knew that when she widowed one king and wed another.

And that was another song entirely. Dafydd leaned on the rough rail, chin on fists and dreamed of another age, when the *Cymru* rode victorious under the Dragon banner and drove the *Saes* back into the sea...A roll call of great names, of heroes out of old time, Artos and Gwalchmai and Bedwyr and Cei and Owain... An age that would surely come again and soon.

He knew the tales and the songs. Tonight he would spin such a web at the feast that they would still be talking of it come the next Yuletide. If any of the *Saes* would be alive then to recall it.

The sun slipped behind a bank of cloud, fringing the unpromising slate-colored bulk with bullion. Dafydd shivered in the sudden chill. He thought abruptly of Regan, soon to be safe in the Abbey at Leominster. Thought, too, of plump, plain little Morwenna, whose only beauty was the blue-black glory of her unbound hair. And the gentle sweetness of her nature, he reminded himself. She too would be safe. But then there was Edwina. Somehow he could not imagine that one kneeling meekly before the High Altar, robed in a nun's habit. *Duw Mawr*, but he had not thought to ever have these difficulties— she was *Saes*. They all were. Land-thieves and worse. He must never let himself forget that.

*****

Leofric was up before dawn, heavy-eyed but restless. He was by no means the first. Lucca and her women were already in the kitchen and the smell of baking bread was beginning to drift across the garth.

Regan's man Swein was about as well, sitting by the hearth drinking a beaker of ale and scratching at his ribs.

"You were in-hall yesterday," Leofric said quietly, sitting beside him. "You heard about the missing stock? The eastern edge of the Intake Wood runs on Regan's border. Has she lost any beasts?"

"None that can't be accounted for, one way or another," the man answered. "We're well-forward with the tallying, for the Abbey's books. If you need spears for a hunting band, m'lord, just send word to us."

"Thanks," Leofric smiled and stood up, feeling the need to be out of the confines of the hall.

The rain had stopped, he discovered, though by the look of the sky it would not be long before more fell. At least it was not cold enough for snow. Thankful for small mercies, Leofric started across the garth then saw the figure up on the pallisade-walk.

Regan's Welsh harper—for a brief moment suspicion stung him and his hand went automatically to the hilt of his dagger. But that was stupid. He was letting Godwine's carping get under his skin. The Welsh honored guest-right as much as the Saxon and besides, bards were men apart and not just for the skills they possessed. He'd heard it said that they'd been priests once, back in the old days, and something of that still hung about them.

"Dafydd," he called and saw the man start as if his thoughts had been adrift. "Have you eaten this morning?"

"Aye, my lord." He came down the nearest steps and joined the thane. "I was looking at the river. I swear it's wider than it was."

"She floods fast," Leofric said. "I'll be taking a closer look shortly. You're welcome to come along, if you wish." Now he looked closer he could see signs that the harper had not passed an easy night either.

"I'll be glad to." Dafydd welcomed the offer. The more he could learn of this man and his holding the better he could plan their downfall. "There were plenty who snored all through the storm last night, but I wasn't one of them. This morning my head feels like a drum."

"I want to see how Medwin is before we go," Leofric went on. "If he's no better, Anna will want him brought down to her cott where she can keep better watch over him."

"You have a care to your possessions then," Dafydd said politely.

"Yes, I do." Leofric said shortly, aware that that care had been recently lacking.

"My lord!" Godwine stood in the byre door, beckoning them in. Anna was beside him, dwarfed by his bulk. "Coll's disappeared. What's more, the dolt's taken Medwin with him."

"In this weather?" Leofric reacted with patent disbelief.

"I thought they'd at least have the sense to wait until the spring!" Godwine said disgustedly. "Will I send out a search-party?"

"How long have they been gone?" Leofric demanded. "Have they been seen this morning?"

"Lucca brought stew for them last night," Anna said worriedly. "At least for Coll. Medwin could have nothing but arrowroot in broth, poor man, and I settled them down last thing with nostrums for them both. Lord Leofric, Medwin has the bloody cough. He is spitting red for all I could do."

Dafydd saw the thane's face change from incredulity to grief. "Damn," he said quietly. "He won't last the week in weather like this. Yes, Godwine, put the word out and send men north and south, see if you can find any trace of them. Though if they left in the storm, there'll be no tracks to find, nor scent either. We'll ride east, they might have headed back to Geadas' place to collect things left behind. And Godwine, let it be known that they are to be treated like freemen if found, not escaping thralls."

Godwine gave a snort through his moustaches. "Aye, my lord," was all he said, but the tone spoke volumes. The harper too was staring at him as if he'd suddenly sprouted another head.

"Well?" Leofric barked. "Why are you both standing around gaping at me? We've a sick man to find."

"Surprised you don't flap after him, m'lord Bladdud," the steward grunted and stamped off toward the hall. "Daft as a bloody broom…" came drifting back.

Leofric gave a wry chuckle and headed for the stables at a near-run. The bard sprinted to catch up with his longer legs. "What—?" Dafydd began, fetching saddle and bridle to his dappled mare, "um, my lord? Bladdud?"

"When I was seven," Leofric was busy with his own mount, "my mother brought a new skald to hall. He told us the tale of King Bladdud, who built a tower and a pair of wings and tried to fly from the top? You know the one. Well, the next day I gathered some feathers—for which the geese did not love me—and climbed Anna's apple tree. It was your

Lady's fault, as I recall," he mused, pausing to remember with a fond smile on his face. "Four she was, or thereabouts. All legs and scratches and burrs in her hair. She told me I could do it and I believed her, so I did. Took my biggest leap and broke my arm. At least I'd had the good sense to do it by Anna's cott. Godwine's never let me forget it."

"Yes," Dafydd said weakly, "I can see how he wouldn't. But—my lord, you said 'freemen'."

"Yes, well, I decided last night I'd pay their man-price." Leofric was concentrating on tightening Rufus' girth and avoiding the disgruntled horse's teeth and did not see the utter confusion on the bard's face. "So even though their collars haven't been struck off and the manumission scrips given, they were free men from that moment, as far as I'm concerned. We have to find them, Dafydd, and swiftly for Medwin's sake. Besides, if another thane finds them, how is he to know they're thralls no longer?"

"You would have told them this morning?"

"Yes. And Geadas will be paying recompense as well. He can still pay it, for that matter and I'll hold it for them and pray we find them before the cold kills Medwin."

"I see," though it was clear from his tone that he didn't.

"Geadas won't like it, of course," Leofric said with some relish. "Very tender in the purse is that man and a bully when he thinks he can get away with it. If he wasn't my brother-in-law, I'd have had him off this land years ago."

"I did not know," Dafydd began and Leofric gave him a grin,

"How should you? I forgot you're a stranger in these parts."

"Ah, but bards are always interested in family trees," he smiled back. "This sounds the stuff of sagas to me."

"Not much of one, unless it be something of a comic tale. Geadas is wed to my half-sister, Aeditha. My bastard half-sister, I should say—she and I were born in the same year, with but a few months between us. My father looked elsewhere for his pleasures when Mam was with child." The grin widened wickedly. "Before and after, into the bargain. Well-known in these parts, my Da, for putting himself about. Not that I blame him. I'd do the same were I wed to someone like my mother."

Dafydd gave a whoop of laughter then a spluttering apology. "I'm sorry. Please go on, my lord."

"Well, I've a handful of siblings in the village that I know about—Anna's eldest daughter for one and little Astrid." He paused as they led the horses out of the stable and mounted. "Anyway, when Geadas' first wife died, he courted Aeditha. He must have been different then, that's all I can say. It was while I was at Gloucester, so I never saw it. She agreed to wed him and Da gave her dowry, which didn't hurt, but if Geadas expected sons out of her, he's been disappointed. His first wife was childless too, by God's grace. He wanted Gyfu, Sifrith's sister, Lucca told me, but neither she nor Godwine would hear of it—she was old enough, but barely. And it would have gained her her freedom. But I thank God she refused him. She might not have borne Yseult for my Da else. Have you brothers and sisters?"

"Oh yes," Dafydd lied blithely and spun tale after nonsense tale about the mythical doings of his supposed kin, until the thane was bent over his horse's mane, helpless with laughter. Deliberate falsehood to mislead or harper's creation to heal grief, Dafydd was no longer sure and for now he did not care. The feeling of companionship had sneaked up on him before he could guard against it and slipped past the carefully constructed defenses.

* * * * *

They crested the rise and Geadas' house was visible through the bare black trees, hazed with a thin veil of smoke in the still air. The snow lay in shrinking piebald patches on the land, leaving naked red earth or green growth and the ever-growing sheen of standing water.

Leofric called a greeting as they approached the house. Aeditha came out, wiping her hands on her apron and blinking a little in the light. Leofric swung down from his saddle and went to her. "Little sister," he said with teasing affection and kissed her.

"My lord brother—bless us, I did not expect—the house is not prepared—we did not know you had come yesterday, until Coll—oh but we were so ashamed! But come you in out of the damp…"

There was little of the family look about her, Dafydd considered, following. She was tall, yes—by a hand and a half taller than her husband, he would judge—and maybe the leanness of her now had once been slenderness. But her skin lacked the clear pink and white of the true Saxon maid, being sallow, and the wispy hair escaping her headrail was as dark as his own. She seemed a gentle creature, easily flustered, and he did not think it was her doing that the house was as well ordered as it seemed. Rather it lay to the credit of the older woman who sat spinning at the hearth, one eye sharp on the baking bannocks.

"Was it my man you came to see? He is up at the high pasture, mending the fence—we did not know, you see—and all this way for nothing…"

"I came to see you, sister," Leofric smiled at her, settling himself in the master's chair. "And Wyn, how are you? This is Dafydd ap Gryfydd, bard and guest." The serving woman set down her spindle unhurriedly, got up and fetched two cups and poured ale, then inspected her bannocks to select two that were done and offered food and drink to her thane, all without a word given or spoken.

"Thank you, Wyn," Leofric said politely and received an unsmiling acknowledgement before the woman returned to her spinning.

The bannocks were excellent and the ale and Dafydd complimented his hostess.

"Ah that is Wyn's doing," she said and smiled at the unspeaking woman. "What else, when she learned under Lucca's eye? For sure this would be a sad household without her skills. But tell me, how is Medwin? We've been worried about him, Wyn and I. If we'd known what was about, we would have put a stop to it… Somehow… Ah but we should have guessed!"

"He is sick with the bloody cough," Leofric said quietly and Aeditha covered her mouth with her hands, eyes showing pain. "But he and Coll have fled the steading. I've men out looking for them and it's possible they might come by here. Did they leave anything with you?"

"Aye, with Wyn, as usual. Medwin's savings and keepsake from Megan, but nothing of Coll's. He—he is a bitter man, brother."

That was a truth he should have remembered and Leofric cursed himself for letting so much slide away for so long. "Yes," he said, "and because of that I would like you and Wyn to come and stay in-hall for a while. Just in case. They've no love for Geadas, Aeditha."

"Ah, poor souls, I know it…" she wrung her hands. "He would not let me near them, nor Wyn either… He took against Coll from the first, I think, when the lad would only speak Welsh to him—and Medwin—why, I said to Wyn, that man isn't strong… But leave here?" she continued doubtfully, looking at Wyn. Who shook her head, firmly and decisively. "No, my dear, we couldn't possibly do that."

"Well, be on your guard and warn your man. I'll give him no more thralls to abuse, but I'll ask the neighbors to keep an eye out for here as well." He stood up, taking Aeditha's hands. "If you change your minds, there's a place in-hall for both of you. But don't fret, sister. If they should come, then tell them it is my word that they are free men from last night forward and they have broken no law that I know of. But more than likely, they'll be away across the Dyke." And as Dafydd joined him outside, "At least, that's where I'd head in their shoes."

Aeditha had a handful of crusts for Rufus and Dafydd's mare and a flurry of messages for the hall-folk. "Do not you forget now," she commanded and Leofric smiled down at her.

"Dafydd is a bard, remember, and what he hears, he does not forget," he assured her. "God guard you both, sister."

They rode on their way in silence for a while, then, "She is a good woman, Wyn…" Leofric said abruptly. "Her saga is short and sad. She's Geadas' sister. Her man farmed a piece over by Pyon. There was a raid—Welsh or wolfsheads, we never knew, and she saw her man and bairns killed before her eyes. She's never spoken a word from that day to this. Geadas likes to pretend he gives her a roof over her head out of charity, but she runs that household as my sister never could. She may not have the tongue to scold her brother, but by the One Tree, I've seen him quail at a look from her."

Dafydd was silent. He had learned much of these *Saes* today and was now wishing he'd stayed behind and remained ignorant.

Chapter Nine

The household had already begun preparing for the feast of Yule, though Lady Hilde, with Father Odo's support, had decried it for a pagan festival, pointedly referring to Christ's Mass. No one, however, was taking much notice of their objection. Even her son, Hilde discovered, blatantly turned a blind eye to the heathen practices.

"You will be wishing I had not detained you," she said to Regan, as boughs of winter greenery were brought in to deck the hall. "At the Abbey, be sure all will be fittingly celebrated. We will go to the chapel and pray."

"Your pardon, lady, but I must speak with Lucca—you will excuse me." It was blatant untruth. For every Christ's Mass of her life, Regan had seen the beginning of the celebrations with the Yule brought in and she did not intend to miss it on the whim of the pious Hilde. Summoning Edwina and Morwenna from their spinning, she waited until Hilde was gone from sight then sent the girls for cloaks and pattens, for it was snowing again. The big feathery flakes caught and clung like goose-down and the crowd of women who waited at the gate were all caped and capped in the ermine of it, like so many queens. Regan and her maids were just in time to see the men of the steading take the place of the straining ox-team that had brought the tree that was to be the Yule Log from the forest—now two teams of four on each of the ropes, they heaved at the weight of the naked giant lashed to the sled, drawing it steadily up the slope, while boys ran behind to wedge stones under the runners. Peering, Regan could see Leofric at the head of one team with Dafydd, while Godwine headed the other and their voices rose in the chant of a work song as they pulled. In spite of the snow, Leofric wore no mantle, only a leather jack over his brown woolen shirt and he was bareheaded, the fair hair damp with exertion and the thawing flakes. He was laughing breathlessly, probably at his own attempt at song, and something within Regan melted, though she could not have said what it was.

So the Yule came within and Lucca met the men at the hall doors, demanding to know their business.

Leofric snatched off his cap, twisting it between his hands. "So please you, Mistress, we do bring in the Yule," he said broadly. Lucca laughed.

"Enter then and with God's blessing!"

The hauliers were offered mulled ale with the froth of burst baked apples like lambs' wool on the top and the talk and laughter rose like bubbles in wine. Regan found Leofric at her elbow and accepted the cup of ale he offered her.

"Pagan or no," he said, smiling, "could it be Yule without the Log? Or Midwinter without Yule? I can understand the old fear that the sun might neglect to return if men did not kindle the needfire."

"Your Lady Mother would have it neither Yule nor Midwinter, but solely Christ's Mass," Regan pointed out.

"So she never ceases to tell me. Let us thank God that she finds this all so offensive that she takes herself off and doesn't stay to sour the ale. *Waeshael*!" He raised his cup to her.

"You should be shamed, my lord," she said primly, but could not hide the sparkle of amusement in her eyes.

"So I should," he agreed ruefully. "And worse, for she hadn't been here more than an hour before I was wishing her gone."

This Regan could understand, having endured the Lady's company for longer than she would have wished. But it ill became her to say so. "For shame," she said again, softly.

"I am incorrigible, I know it." He did not sound in the least repentant. "Ah they're starting the dance—come dance with us, Trout!" The circles were forming, the beat of bodran linking with the skirl of pipes and her foot was tapping out the rhythm already and his hand was warm on hers. Oh surely this could have no wrong in it?

Well, Lady Hilde was not there to see or scold her for it, if there was. "Trout, is it?" She aimed a gentle buffet at his head "So long as you do not tell your mother," she warned and he laughed and drew her into his arms.

It was a fast-stepping measure and her feet remembered it well. Which was fortunate, for she was becoming more and more aware of the man beside her. His eyes were locked with hers—gray-blue, they were, expressive, though now they showed a kind of puzzlement, as if he was seeing her clearly for the first time. Gifford would have been heavy-set beside his lean height and dark of hair and eye. "Stocky as a young bullock," her Da had said of Gifford, "but a good man." Leofric was like a hunting-wolf, lithe and light and handsome as— They both missed a step and nearly tripped the couple behind.

Dafydd, used to a different kind of measure, found this romping circle dance wasn't as easy as it looked. Edwina seemed to find this extremely funny. Well, maybe she had the right of it—surely one who could sing and play a carol should also be able to make his feet do as they should? But no one cared. Indeed, he was not alone in his disability. Swein and Godwine were both grinning and sweating as they stamped and stumbled. The primary purpose was enjoyment not skill and there he could not be faulted. He took Edwina's hand during a break in the pattern and drew her to one side.

"Laugh at me, would you?" he whispered under cover of the music. "Glad I am to be the cause of such mirth, mistress."

"Oh but Dafydd," she leaned against him, smiling. "How should you know our dances, Welsh that you are? But I am sure you could learn. Morwenna, do you take his other hand. Let's teach this reiver how it's done!"

* * * * *

With the coming-within of the Yule log, the season was truly begun and the celebrations went on into the night. Come the next morning, however, Lucca was in a harrying mood and no one was safe. Leofric determined to get out from underfoot as quickly as possible and with the weather clear and frosty, thought he might take one of his hawks out. If it came to that, he would lay any money that Regan would enjoy the outing as well. He grinned reminiscently. Last night, she'd boxed his ears because he called her "Trout". It had been just that way when they were children. Well, the old nickname was not so appropriate now. She was a wildcat. And he could well feel her claws if he tried to ride out without her. He caught Dafydd's eye.

"A favor, *bach*—go you and ask Lady Regan if she will ride out with us. As pretty a request as you can devise, mind. And—"

"Don't tell your mother!" Dafydd finished for him and sprinted off. Leofric called a thrall to saddle up Arianrhod, Dafydd's dappled filly, and make ready Emer, Regan's wheat-colored mare. He attended to Rufus himself and was barely done when Dafydd reappeared, a wide grin on his face. "The Lady begs you wait while she dons her riding boots. Your Lady Mother was with her," he paused, with wicked glee, "but when she heard my errand, she was quick to agree that a morning hawking was just what her dear Regan needed."

"Did she indeed. She grows ever more subtle, my mother." Leofric's eyes narrowed, but at Dafydd's questioning look, he laughed. "Come, we'll fetch out Macsen my goshawk and the merlin for my lady."

The birds were excited and short of temper, but that was as nothing to Regan's mood when she stormed across the garth to the stables.

"Mary, give me patience!" she said fervently. "If I had to spend one more hour in that—woman's—company... Would God I were a man! She'd not be trying her matchmaking with me then!"

"Would she not?" Leofric gave her a wry look, helping her mount. "My mother would not be gainsaid by the King himself. Forget her, Regan, for at least this morning."

It was a fine day for their sport, crisp and cold and clear, without a breath of wind to stir the wine-sweet air or disturb the heaped confections of snow on every exposed branch and twig. They kept the horses to the hard-packed tracks, not risking the white-gleaming expanses where a horse could be mired belly-deep between one step and the next, until they reached the high tops where the snow lay lightly, scoured from settling by the winds out of Wales. The hounds put up a hare, winter-clad in white, and Macsen took it in one swift deadly swoop out of the pale cloudless blue. It was the first of several, though small game was scarce so high and Regan cast the little merlin after a pigeon and soothed her when she returned unsuccessful.

It was good to be out on the land, unconstrained by walls. Leofric drew a deep breath, relishing the clean cold bite of it. Things were always so much clearer out here, where he could see his lands spread out before him, hazed and blanketed now under the coverlet of snow. And over there, beyond the ridge, Regan's holding from her father. Suddenly he knew she would not go into the convent at Leominster. She loved her lands too much—it was in every word, every inflection and gesture. She could no more gift them to the church than he could. Regan, in the somber homespun and coif of a nun? He looked across at her where she sat her mare, slender and straight-backed, head high, profile gem-clear in the cold air, a small unremarked smile on her mouth. With something of a start, he suddenly saw her as she was, the image not overlaid by the memories of the tomboy hoyden. She had none of the Saxon beauty of Hawiss—but it was as unjust to compare them as to compare the rosette of the wood-violet with the tall orchid-like blossom of the nettle flower.

It made him smile.

"Is it a jest for sharing?" Dafydd said, reining in beside him.

"A private thought. We have had all the hunting I think we are likely to get. Will you sing us home?"

It was an inappropriate choice, a *Cymru* raiding song, but both Regan and Leofric knew the words and for once Leofric did not care that his voice buzzed tunelessly under their merry caroling. Neither did they.

It was dusk before they rode in through the gates and as thralls came to take the horses, Leofric held up his arms to lift Regan down as naturally as if they had both still been children and just as naturally she came into them, light and lithe under the layers of wool and fur. "Thank you, Leofric," she said simply. "I enjoyed the hawking and the company. It will be a sweet memory for me when I am behind convent walls."

Leofric restrained his curse of annoyance until she was out of earshot, but Dafydd caught it and cocked an eyebrow at him as he went into the stables to see to the care of the horses. "Women!" Leofric said, which raised the other eyebrow.

"There I cannot help," Dafydd admitted. "They never behave like this in the songs."

"I'm none so well-schooled in their ways myself," Leofric told him. "In fact, I've yet to see the man who is. You heard her talking of her lands, Dafydd—you saw her face. Can she really mean to give it all up?"

The bard's face smoothed of expression. "I was taught the greater the sacrifice, the more pleasing it is to God."

"You're no comfort," Leofric groused, then relented. "No, I didn't mean that. At least I can talk to you, friend to friend."

Friend to friend. It was casually said, but suddenly Dafydd knew that it was true. This man, this Saxon thane, the ancient enemy, was his friend. And his host, to whom he owed guest-right. He had eaten his bread and salt in the most sacred of traditions of both their peoples. And at a word he could change it all, bring red death down on every soul within these walls.

A scant few days ago he could have done it without hesitation, as he had done so many times before. For the first time, the enemy had names and faces and he was no longer certain they were the enemy.

* * * * *

With the darkness came a further snowfall, though Lucca said she doubted it would be much. However, it intensified the sealed-in atmosphere between walls and Dafydd found the Lady Regan in an introspective mood when he disposed himself nearby as she shared spindles and fleece with her two bower-maids. He and Edwina traded smiles as he played, fingers light on the strings, and finally sang a snatch from the legend of Culhwch and Olwen.

"…*and her eyes! Their look*
Was lovelier than the thrice-mewed hawk…
…her breast was softer than the sun!
Where she trod, four white clover flowers
sprang up behind her feet…"

His mind's eye saw her, the Princess of the story, with her fair white skin and yellow hair and now he gave her the face of the silver-gilt girl who span in the firelight.

"*All were longing-filled when they beheld her*
And therefore was she called – Olwen…"

The sweet dying chord hung in the air and the Lady smiled at him. "It is a while since you gave us that tale, Dafydd. The Saxon skalds sing of Arthur, but not of his cousin Culhwch."

"Then there is yet something we can teach them," he said, "and I will sing the whole story for you, Lady, if you but say the word."

"I shall hold you to that." The spindle was idle in her hands. "Does it still snow outside?"

"When last I looked, Lady. Thick as swan's-down."

"Ah well. At least there will be no raiding this weather." Dafydd stared. That was the last thing he had expected her to say. "You know how my lands lie. They raid these parts more often, perhaps, because the forest runs unbroken between and they have good cover for their ambushes. My lands are more open — the coppices do not offer such concealment."

"You are bound to miss it, Lady. For a while." He did not want to encourage her homesickness. "The life of the Holy Sisters will offer you diversion, you may be sure." The settled round of the religious life, the canonical hours, the holy festivals in their seasons — *Duw Mawr*! As well break the wings of this she-hawk. And if she remembered, after, that he had persuaded her into that cage… She would damn him and he would deserve it.

But he could not have her anything but safe. Here, behind the Lord Leofric's walls, it was true that she would have a fit place and a strong defender. But surely the Abbey would be safer still?

The Sons waited on his word. If he did not give it, or if he exaggerated the numbers of the fighting men, then he could keep her and Edwina from harm.

"Your home is near, Lady. Leominster is farther off." Edwina dared a comment.

Regan's eyes rested upon her. "It might be in Cathay, but still I would go there, Edwina Godwinesdaughter." *And no need for you to add your ladle to the stirring either*, was unsaid.

"I claim a bard's immunity for truth-speaking, Lady Regan," Dafydd found himself saying, despite the confusion within. "She has the right of it. The Abbey is no place for you."

"You may claim it, but I do not promise to hold to it," Regan snapped. "A Welsh custom it is, not Saxon."

"Then answer me a question, Lady?" Once started, he had to continue. "Why would you go? What is it that you think to find there?"

He thought he might have trespassed beyond the mark, for Edwina's eyes were wide with concern. But Regan sat quiet and at last lifted her hands, twisting the spindle into its spin. "Have I not made that plain to you? I thought you, of all people, understood me. I go because it is in my mind that I wish to make my own decisions for my life." The long strong staple of the woolen fibers twisted into a fine, even thread.

"In the *Abbey*?" Dafydd queried, all emphasis on the last word. "I was schooled in an Abbey. Once you are within, there will be no decisions at all!"

"But at least I will have peace!" Twisted too hard, the thread snapped and the spindle fell to the floor to roll at his feet. He bent to retrieve it. "Peace from men like Ranulf and that damned Hilde's machinations! I will not wed any of her choosing—"

"Then choose for yourself, Lady."

"Have I not said?" she spat, snatching the spindle back. "You go too far!" The holly-green eyes snapped with anger and Edwina gasped.

"Yet not so far as you would," Dafydd said softly. "So far from those who love you—or who might come to love you and not as children love."

The spindle flew at his head and he was just in time to duck its flight. The Lady Regan was on her feet. "Immunity or not, one more word and I break your jaw, boy!"

He knew she would do it too. He stood up, made her a deep bow and left the hearthside, all in submissive silence. Let the Lady think on what he had said. The germ of it had been already in her mind, he was sure—he had merely fostered it a little. For himself—at least he would be able to live with his conscience.

* * * * *

It was a time for gifts. Edwina, who had worked a length of orphrey with a high-summer mixture of ripe ears and poppies and cornflowers, presented it rather shyly to Lady Regan that morning as Morwenna set about dressing the lady's hair.

"'Dwina, it's beautiful!" The praise was sincere. "You have a rare skill, but you know that. Thank you—I'll treasure it."

"I'm glad it pleases you, my lady," Edwina smiled. "I feared for a while I would not have the threads to finish it, my store of silks is thinning fast and Hod Packman isn't due here for weeks and weeks, round about Lady Day. See, the panel is meant to be worn thus," she went on, holding it up to fall from throat to hem, "on the front of a holiday gown, perhaps…"

"Such as seldom worn by the Holy Sisters?" Regan looked at her with irritated affection. "Don't you start, Edwina. I have it from all sides."

"Lady Regan—"

"You, Dafydd, the Lady Hilde, Anna's geese for all I know. Let it rest, child, for pity's sake."

"Your pardon, Lady…"

Morwenna, hovering behind her. advanced.

"Shall I comb your hair now, my Lady?"

Regan dragged her fingers through the mane of fiery copper that fell past her thighs unbound. "Yes. But first—" She put her hands to her nape and unfastened a chain. "You have both served me well. Edwina, a gift should be made for a gift. Wear this, or put it to your dowry." It was a delicate chain of gold links and Edwina had never owned anything so fine. "After all," Regan said to the girl's mute and dazzled eyes, "I shall have little need of such gauds in Leominster. Morwenna, this brooch is for you." It was a Celtic twisting of silver bands, set about with moonstones. Both girls were effusive in their thanks until she lost patience and dismissed them.

Edwina told it all to Lucca when she went to fetch the lady's breakfast. Her mother admired the chain but tutted over the donor's reasons.

"Not need it at Leominster, indeed!" Lucca said. "From all I hear of that place, she could go clad in silk and not be thought worldly. Stubborn she is, not to have seen what lies here waiting for her to stretch out her hand and take it…"

Edwina's eyes stretched. "Mam!"

"Aye, lass, I know I've said too much, but what's out cannot be recalled. It's *his* word she'd listen to, no one else's and he's too addled still to speak it. I could crack their heads together sometimes!"

She gave a snort of impatience and would probably have said more, but Dafydd came into the kitchen and was greeted by sudden silence. Edwina gave him a smile and thought to show him the chain but then decided against it. There would be a better, more private time for that. She already had plans concerning the Lady's harper and privacy was a vital part of them.

Chapter Ten

ೲ

"I wonder," said the Lady Hilde, as she broke her fast in her solar, her son summonsed to her side to share the meal, "if it might not suit me to go into a nunnery."

"No," Leofric said, around a mouthful of cheese. "It would not."

"Regan is too young, of course," she went on as if he hadn't spoken, "and far too alive, for all her grief. I, on the other hand, have nothing left but God…"

Leofric pried a piece of cheese rind from between his teeth. "If I had a gold piece for every time you've said that since you arrived, I could buy you the damned nunnery," he said indistinctly, ignoring the frigid glare that was intended to freeze him into abject apology. "Let it be, Mother. You know it would not suit at all. No court gossip, no silks or fine linens," he checked them off on his fingers, "no jewels, no feasts, no lords to give flattery—"

"Do you think such things are important to me?" she demanded, voice throbbing with outrage.

"Yes," said her son, unrepentant.

"Oh Leofric! Do you care so little? Know me so ill? To be as a stranger to my own son…"

"Oh Mother, have done!" He gave her an urchin's grin. "I know you well and I love you well for the most part—and I know you grieve for my father. But I also know that you're very much a part of the Royal Household, and you wouldn't give that up to be Abbess of a dozen nunneries. Besides," he added, cunning, "would the queen look kindly on such a decision? To lose one of her senior bower-women?"

"I was Emma's bower-woman," she corrected him coolly. "This Editha of Wessex is a poor queen. She's no more than a pawn, to bring the King within Earl Godwin's guidance."

"Well, if Edward's as priest-led as they say…"

"He is most devout," she said, with an unspoken codicil that a little more devotion here might not come amiss. Then, in a confiding fashion, "He would be happier in a monastery, the dear man. Or a hermit's cell. Sweet-natured and gentle as he is, he is no ruler…"

"Then thank God for Godwin of Wessex," Leofric said feelingly. "And for my part, I'm glad I'm out of it."

"Nonsense. You do very well at Court. When you're there," his mother pointed out acidly. "You would do even better if you spent time with the household. Haven't I told you before? We could easily find you a permanent place at the King's side! You are my son, you are of noble blood and you have all the family looks—"

"What, is Edward another Ethelred, to fill the court with," and he swallowed the term "catamite" quickly, "personable young men? Poor Editha!"

"Leofric!" his mother exclaimed. "That was not at all what I—"

"God give you good morning, Regan," Leofric said cheerily, cutting his mother off in mid-scold. Regan gave him a smile, accepting the seat he offered her. "Mother, since Regan is here to bear you gentle company, I will go about my business. Ladies…"

He made his bow and took himself out of the warmth of the solar, whistling. His "business", as his mother knew, was just an excuse to be out of the hall—his father had been wont to do the same thing. He made his way across the garth and up onto the catwalk beside the palisade. The view was a white wonder after the new snowfall and on the slope just below the steading the village children had constructed the shape of a Winter King. He grinned, remembering his own childhood games. And in an echo of that time, there was a snow fight in progress nearby, punctuated by squeals. Leofric squinted across at the combatants. Familiar in his blue cloak, Dafydd was dodging a veritable hail of missiles from a pair of children, who were led by—could that be Edwina? Leofric's grin widened. His guest was grossly outnumbered and it behoved the courteous host to come to his aid.

He headed down the steps and out of the gate, arming himself as he went.

* * * * *

Something was on Regan's mind, Hilde decided. The child had barely spoken two words that morning and her attention was obviously wandering.

"You have been a great comfort to me, my dear," she said, laying gemmed fingers on the young woman's arm. "I shall miss you, you know. And I shall not be alone in that. To see my son at peace and finding joy again—ah that has eased my heart."

Regan flushed. "You give me too much credit, Lady," she said stiffly. "That has been the doing of a harper out of Wales, with a rare talent."

"Oh I grant you Dafydd helped," Hilde said dismissively. "But—I have seen it—Leofric's heart lightens at the sight of you."

"Does it so?" Regan stood up quickly, disengaging herself. "Then for the good of both our souls I should be from here as soon as may be. It would not be good for a man to lose his heart to one bound for the Abbey."

"Regan, my child—"

"No child of yours, Lady Hilde. If you have forgotten, let me remind you that I am in mourning for my parents and my betrothed. I have no thought but to seek solace with God. By your leave, I will seek my steward and instruct him."

Lady Hilde was left alone, displeased. *I must be losing my touch,* she thought. But it did not matter. There was time yet…

Regan's steward was nowhere to be found. She hunted him in hall and garth and only finally tracked him to the smithy, where Padraig the smith cheerfully informed her that she had but that moment missed him.

"Gone out with Godwine, m'lady, to check the condition of the roads. Not be back before noon, I'd say."

"If you see him before I do then, tell him I wish to speak to him?" Regan turned away. "Oh and you might look at Emer's off-fore, if you would. I do not want her lame and delaying me here any further."

That should put a stop to the running gossip, she thought, moving away. Padraig Smith was as voluble as a church bell. Word would be all round the steading—aye and the village— before the day was out.

She had intended to return to the guest-bower, or to sit in-hall and spin, but now she hesitated. Neither place would be safe from the attentions of Lady Hilde. A surge of anger shook her. Why would they not let her be? Had she not made her decision clear right from the start? Why must they seek to turn her from it? She thought of the Abbey, the peace of the cloister and the ordered round of prayer and devotion and surprised herself by the intensity of her own longing. To shut out the world and the hurt and all the well-meaning scheming of her friends, to shut out memory and pain and the grief that tore at her sometimes when she heard children playing. *If I had had bairns…*

She pushed the yearning back behind the walls of her self-control. Where was there here that would provide her with sanctuary from the intentions of the Lady? She thought, then made for the weaving sheds. But no—all too well she knew the thread of rumor that was enriching the weft and the clacking tongues that accompanied the clacking looms.

The stockade, however, was deserted save for the watchmen on duty and the steps were too steep for Lady Hilde's climbing, as well as slick with ice. Hitching her gown up, Regan picked her way to the catwalk, where spread ashes crunched reassuringly under her boots. The wind was stronger up here but not as cold as she expected. There was a softer feel to it, the sense of the coming thaw. The river was already turgid with the melt-water and had burst its banks. She should have Sigurd watch out for that on her lands. And if the grazing was not all sere, the ewes-in-lamb could benefit, though Shep must keep his eye on them…

She caught her breath at the sudden pain of loss. These things were no longer hers to oversee, or would not be once she was within the Abbey.

A shriek distracted her, the excited screams of children. She did not falter or turn away but made herself stop and look over the wall.

There was a battle going on below, two against three and the larger war band, led by the truant Edwina, was forcing Dafydd and Leofric into ignominious retreat. As they took shelter behind the snow-mounded Winter King, Regan found herself smiling. Childhood is not merely a matter of years after all and Leofric looked to be reliving his. He was laughing and deadly with the snowballs, well-plastered with the stuff for good measure. Envy struck at Regan then. He had lost his bride, but he was forgetting grief already, while she, bereft, had nothing left her but the Abbey—

She gave a sudden choked laugh at herself. Nothing left but God? How often had she heard that from Hilde and despised it? Holy St. Bride, was she turning into another drooping female, sodden with self-pity?

With a surge of resolution, she hurried back down the steps, nearly slipping in her haste. By the time she was at the gate, Leofric and Dafydd had retreated behind a huddle of hurdled sheep and she scooped up a handful of snow and allied herself with them by foiling Edwina's flank attack.

Nettleflower

Within seconds, battle was joined again in earnest, three against three, until Dafydd launched himself into the hail of snowballs to capture the enemy war-queen and Leofric and Regan between them thwarted the attempt at rescue. Astrid and her brother drew off to confer. The leadership was at issue, for shortly the two were hurling snow at each other and Edwina, giggling, remained a not-unwilling captive in Dafydd's arms.

Leofric looked at his cohort with mock sorrow. "Theseus snared by Hippolyta," he said. "There's a song you should give us, tiercel."

"Tiercel?" Regan echoed, seeing sudden shock in Dafydd's eyes and wondering at it.

"Fierce as a falcon, he is," Leofric grinned, "and so I've named him. You'll never make a fitting baresarker, lad—you're entirely too well-mannered."

Edwina dropped a curtsey to her lady, a little shame-faced now, since she had absented herself without leave. Regan laughed. "I am truant myself, Edwina. Take your lad off and get dry—I cannot have you down with a chill."

And as the two of them made for the gate, Leofric chuckled quietly. "I imagine you know how they'll be warming each other. For shame, my lady. Contributing, you are, to their mischief."

"The sooner your lady mother leaves here, the better for you," Regan said mildly. "She's having the most dreadful effect on you."

He laughed and drew her into the lee of the wall, his hand slipping down her arm to close on her fingers. His were as cold as hers, but she did not heed.

"She'd scold if she knew what I'd been doing," he confided. "I should know my place better and not consort with the lower orders… Do you remember when we were children and we all played together, careless who was free and who was thrall?"

"Good times," Regan murmured. "I can remember you telling Gyfu I had put the frogspawn in her bed, when it was you—didn't I break a crock over your head for that?"

"Oh aye, I had my first battle-scars from you, vixen!" he grinned.

"Holy Mother, I remember how you bled!" She frowned up at him and raised her fingers to touch the scar under the snow-wet hair. "Is that it?"

"No, the Welsh gave me that, at Rhyddygroes. But I bear the mark of your teeth yet, where you bit me after I put burrs under your pony's saddle and he bucked you into the river-mud."

"Really?" She was enchanted. "And what of the time Gyfu let the bull loose and said it was us and you and Sifrith stirred up a bee-skep and both Gyfu and I got stung. I don't think I ever paid you back for that, Edmundson—and it's long overdue!"

She pulled free of his light hold, filling her hands with snow, but he caught her wrists, laughing, and they struggled for supremacy like the children they had once been. But the man would not let her win, any more than had the gangling towheaded boy he had been then, even if she pitted all her strength against him. Now, as then, she used cunning to defeat him. Hooking a heel behind his ankle, she threw her weight forward. He staggered, caught off-balance, but twisted as he fell so that when they landed she was half-pinned by him in the snow bank. The impact and his weight combined drove the breath from her lungs and her shout of protest died in her throat. His face was inches from hers, the wet hair falling forward to touch her cheeks with its coldness. Her skin felt hot. There was a look of surprise on his face, an almost comical expression that suddenly made her want to laugh. Or cry.

For he was going to kiss her. Regan knew that, it was as certain as sunrise. The refusal shaped by her brain would not come to her tongue. Then his lips were gentle on hers and deep within her something that had been frozen began to thaw. She let her mouth open to share the kiss and for one sweet moment was aware of nothing but the strong length of his body pressing her down and the taste of his mouth.

Sanity came back to Leofric with a sickening lurch that quenched the rising heat in his loins. He pulled back a little. "Regan…" His voice sounded thickened to his own ears. "God help me, I'm sorry."

He could see the reflection of himself in the wide startled green eyes, but no condemnation at all.

"There is no need, my dear," she said. "It is too soon. For both of us."

Leofric nodded and stood up, face carefully schooled again, blue eyes guarded. But when he held out his hands to help her to her feet, she saw the slight apologetic smile she remembered from their youth. She accepted his steadying grasp and did not let go.

"Are you so set on Leominster?" he whispered, the words almost dragged from him.

"I—don't know," she said honestly. "Not anymore." She owed him the truth at least—the truth, she now saw, that Dafydd and probably everyone in the steading had known before she did. "I'm not sure, Leofric." Then, taking a deep breath, "Ask me again tomorrow."

"If you do not go to the Abbey…" He hesitated and she guessed that he was as confused as she was, unsure both of himself and her.

"The future… Only God knows." And she begged him silently for understanding.

"If you decide to go back home—" His eyes were steady, earnest, caring.

"Oh Leofric. Do you know why I wanted to go there? To Leominster?" She was unable to prevent the break in her voice.

"Yes," he said softly. "I tried to find a safe haven too." He lifted her hands to his lips and kissed them. "Until tomorrow and your answer, my Lady."

Chapter Eleven

Long after the bower-maids' breathing had settled into sleep, Regan lay wakeful, gazing up at the invisible ceiling. The rest of the day had seemed inconsequential. Lady Hilde had been no more irritating than usual, no one had made any untoward comments and even Leofric appeared unchanged by what had happened between them, save that perhaps his eyes dwelt on her more frequently. She was as guilty of that as he was. She smiled in the darkness. He was so much the young Saxon thane, yet clean-shaven as a Norman, or the boy he had been so long ago. The snow battle had been such fun. It had felt so good to be happy and free of care for a while. Another jewel of memory to take with her to the Abbey — if indeed she was going to the Abbey.

Regan sat up in the big bed, drew her knees up and wrapped her arms around them. It was time she gave her situation some serious thought. Leofric had the right to his answer.

It seemed that they understood each other. If she turned from the convent and went back to her own lands, then he would come and court her. There was a warmth in the pit of her stomach, a small shivering flame that she knew for desire and suddenly the bed was too big and far too empty. "Ah Gifford…" she whispered. "My sweet friend…"

He had been a good man, would have made a good husband. But he had never romped in the snow with her like a six-year-old, never brought that urgent ache to her belly at the thought of his arms around her, his body pressing her into the bed. And he had never looked at her as Leofric had, with startled wonder and abiding tenderness and need.

Too soon, she thought desperately. *It is too soon, for either of us. I am no Hawiss. He is not Gifford.* And yet, and yet… *Perhaps there might be a future for us together.*

The choice was hers alone. On the one side, the Abbey and the shelter it offered away from the world, her path laid out for her. On the other, a man in her bed, one particular man and maybe children, by God's grace. Her heart ached for a child and unconsciously her arms curved as if she held a babe at her breast. Joy and grief shared, pain and comfort, anger and laughter, snow fights in the winter.

Too soon, too soon! But—later, when the time of mourning was over and they had both had time to think.

* * * * *

It was yet another wakeful night for Leofric. He watched the window graying toward dawn with relief. In a little while he could with reason be up and busy enough to quiet the voice in his head that repeated over and over what had been said in the unexpected moment of intimacy. She had been startled by the kiss, of course. It had come as somewhat of a surprise to himself that he could feel desire. For six months it had been as if that part of his life was in the grave with Hawiss. Regan had shown him that he was wrong.

He had loved Hawiss with all his heart, with the single-minded passion of his youth. He would never love again with that intensity. That being the case, did he need a wife? A woman in his bed, should he feel the need, was easily found. Gyfu, for one. Heirs? He remembered the child of his that had killed its mother and itself and a sick coldness damped down the growing warmth in his loins. No heirs from him, then, but there were his sisters' sons to carry on the bloodline and hold the lands.

So did he want a wife?

Regan, as his Lady, would grace this hall. She could be as elegant as any courtier when she chose, with presence and authority. She was well able to stand up to his mother. Then he recalled how her body had leapt to his touch and his own flesh had responded. As it did now at the mere recalling, and despite the blight of darker memory. He wanted her, ached for her. If he wed her, if she would agree to wed him, if she did not grow a child in her womb to threaten her life.

It all added up to a future no longer gray and bleak and empty, but with the possibility of *something* that was almost too bright to look upon. The thaw had come to his grieving winter, he realized. And to hers, for she too had her sorrows and like him had tried to run from them. He tried to think of her in a nunnery. Regan, who had climbed trees as agile as he, who could ride as well and as fast, who could wield a spear or draw a bow like a Welshman. Regan, who loved life with a passion that matched his own.

That was the key. He swung from his bed and strode to fling the shutters open. "Ask me again tomorrow," she had said. The light of the new day flooded in, tempting him to put aside the dread of what-might-be.

*****

It was not in Lucca's nature to stint a feast and this Yule she cast her eye over the preparations with a certain pride. Two whole venison, two boar, a variety of fowl, roasted and stuffed, pastries savory and sweet, breads, cheeses and apples and pears. No one went away hungry from any table of Lucca's.

Edwina, in her best kirtle and gown of holly green and russet, stood meekly while her mother finished twisting the bronze bands onto the ends of her braids. It was for her to carry the Guest-Cup, since there was no Lady of the household yet, save Hilde, who would consider it beneath her. Also, it was time she learned. "The Lord first and then his Lady mother, the Lady Regan, then the harpers," her mother said again. "Then each man by rank. Do not you forget now."

"No, Mam," Edwina sighed, having received this instruction too often already. The Guest-Cup stood ready, a great mazer of turned white lime wood, carved with flowers and fruits and leaves as if all seasons were one on the curving sides. It was full almost to the brim with the honey-scented mead liquor. Lucca lifted it and gave it into the girl's hands.

"Now don't—"

"Spill any. I know. I won't."

She moved across the hall to the lord's seat as gracefully as a young swan over water. Lucca could not hear what was said between the thane and the girl, but there was nothing to complain of in her demeanor, at least not until she brought the cup to the Lady Regan's bard. Lucca's sharp eyes did not miss the change of attitude.

He was well, even richly, clad in dark blue with discreet embroidery, with the looks and bearing of a prince, albeit a Welsh one. Edwina, in her feast-day finery, was a pretty lass whom any young man might speak sweetly to. As, it appeared, he did, for Edwina ducked her head shyly and glanced up under her lashes and generally acted the flirt until Regan caught her eye and with a gesture reminded her of her duty. Lucca dug an elbow into Godwine's ribs where he sat beside her.

"It's time we started thinking of a husband for that one," she said warningly. "She's grown bonny over the last year. Leave it too long and she'll be no better than she ought to be."

"What, my little flower-face ready to be a wife?" Godwine looked fondly at his firstborn. "She's years yet. She's like her Mam, God bless her." And he gave Lucca hug.

Lucca elbowed him off with a snort. In her youth before she decided on Godwine Coelson, she had been a wild lass herself. She knew well how it was for a girl with awareness of her womanhood and a train of young bucks all hot on her trail. Edwina might be lucky. If her Mam had anything to do with it, she'd wed well. *Mary Mother, but it hardly seemed like last month the girl was Astrid's age and here she was, a woman grown, bearing the Guest-Cup.*

In the immemorial way of all mothers, Lucca wondered where the time had flown. She gave herself a shake. *You're not in your dotage yet, Thorkilsdaughter, so less of the woolgathering. With folks no longer eating, Dafydd'll be singing soon.*

She had heard his voice often enough and thought she could never tire of listening. He seemed to have an endless store of songs, because he hadn't repeated one yet unless asked to. She wondered what he would have for them tonight. He settled the harp on his knee and touched the white-bronze strings like a lover, waking a rippling lilt. The hall hushed to listen.

"By your leave, my lord, my ladies —good folk—I will sing of the Christ's Mass Court of King Artos—Arthur, when the Green Knight came to challenge them."

His voice and harp together wove magic, transporting his listeners to the palace of Camelot, to Arthur's hall with the knights and their ladies in brilliant array. The Giant entered— the young Sir Gawain accepted the terrible challenge…

The tale unwound to its heroic conclusion and Regan smiled into her cup as the hall-folk applauded. Hilde's skald would be hard put to match that. Dafydd ap Gryfydd had a gift for giving people just what they wanted.

Leofric gestured him to the dais. There was a formula for these occasions, but the warmth of his smile gave it added sincerity. "For the gift of your artistry, Dafydd ap Gryfydd, a gift in return. Drink *hael!*"

The cup was two hands high and of finely chased gold. Dafydd blinked in amazement, managing to stammer a thanks before Lady Hilde pressed a silken bag of coins into his hands and murmured that she meant to offer him greater rewards yet. And Regan smiled at him and gave him a cloak-pin of red-gold, in the shape of a dragon, with garnets studding its scales. "You'll sing again?" she asked.

"In my turn, Lady," Dafydd gave her a smile in return, bowed and took a seat in the shadows, allowing Sigurd, Hilde's skald, pride of place. He found himself beside a most unusually clean and combed Sifrith.

"Drink *hael*!" The thrall toasted him. "By God, man, that was a good song! Poor old Sigurd, having to follow that! I do love the old tales myself." He took another long drink. "Thor's Hammer, will you look at my hand shaking…"

"Why?" Dafydd asked. "Should you not be here?"

Sifrith gave him a nervous grin. "Thane told me to bring my man-price to him this night, Gryfyddson. Padraig Smith took the collar from my neck this afternoon."

"Then you're a free man."

"Aye, soon as he says so."

"You'll be away from here, I suppose."

"What?" Sifrith stared at him. "Why ever should I?"

"I thought, since he'd enslaved you…"

"Got things ass-about-face, Dewi! 'Twas my Da sold us into thralldom himself, when our farm failed ten years since. It was that or starve, see. This way we were clothed, fed and housed—and my sis, Gyfu, she took Edmund Thane's eye and got with child by him, so he freed her. That's custom. I couldn't take that way out, could I, so I've been saving instead."

"And your Da?"

"Lazy sod was too busy drinking what he saved. Three years back, he buggered off, God knows where, like that stupid fool Coll." He spat expressively into the rushes. "Well, he could do as he liked, but he might have left Medwin out of it. He'd have been freed before long, the way he was putting bits by and away back to his Megan. Or Thane'd give him a piece of land and he could have fetched her here."

"Perhaps," Dafydd suggested, "Coll had his reasons."

"Working for Geadas? Na, he was sour enough before that. Not saying I'm surprised he's gone, look you. Only that he's a stupid bugger like my Da."

Sigurd's retelling of the Journey of the Magi was drawing to a close and the man was called to the high table for his reward. Then Leofric thumped his fist down and called for silence. "Sifrith Snorrison! Are you in-hall?"

Sifrith gulped, spat again for good luck and lurched to his feet. "Here, m'lord!"

"Then do you come forward."

Very tall and magnificent Leofric looked, in his festival tunic of deep blue, thickly worked with gold thread. The band about his brow was chased gold and he looked like a prince out of a story. Like King Arthur perhaps, Dafydd thought, standing ready to grant a boon at the Pentecost feast.

And Sifrith, on one knee before him, could have been a knight about to swear allegiance. Indeed, it was much the same thing.

"Sifrith Snorrison," Leofric said, "what do you ask of me?"

"Lord, I bring my man-price," the thrall croaked, the leather bag in his hands.

"And what would you do with your freedom, Snorrison?"

"Lord, if you grant me leave, I will ask permission to be your tenant and to be your weaponsman in time of need."

"Willingly I grant it." Leofric raised his voice. "Bear witness all, Sifrith Snorrison is hereby a free man." Leofric held out both hands and Sifrith put his between them, palms together as if in prayer.

"God All Father hearing me, I Sifrith Snorrison do swear I am your liegeman of life and limb and earthly worship and faith and truth I shall bear you all the days of my life. Your friends shall be mine, your enemies mine—I shall be as your shield in battle, your spear in war."

Leofric smiled down at him. "And you are my liegeman, Sifrith Snorrison. I uphold your honor as my own and should you die untimely it shall be mine to claim the full weregild of your slayer." He loosed the man's hands, took a ring from his own finger and put it into Sifrith's palm. "From this day, you are of my household, with all the privileges and duties thereto." And, the formalities over, he pulled Sifrith to his feet and into a bruising bear hug. The hall-folk raised another cheer and under the noise of it, Leofric pushed the moneybag back into Sifrith's hands. "That'll start you off," he said. "Godwine will show you your land tomorrow—there's a cott already, though it'll need work."

"Lord Leofric—" Sifrith's eyes were overflowing.

"Rent to be two cheeses at Michael's mass, a bull calf or wether and a set of horse-harness in the colors of my house. Dafydd! Sigurd! A song to honor the occasion!"

Sigurd had a fine rousing piece that pointed up the sacredness of the bond just made between lord and liegeman and his strong voice filled the hall. But Dafydd, with his eyes on Leofric, did not need to be told that.

"I wish my lady could wear other than those dark and somber stuffs," came a whisper in his ear and he knew from the scent of her that it was Edwina.

"She looks very well to me," Dafydd said and she gave a most unladylike snort.

"So she would, to you, if she was wearing sackcloth the pig had slept in! Men!"

He gathered he had been tactless. "But she's no fairer than you, cariad," he said quickly, to redress the balance.

"Morwenna looks fine, does she not?" He supposed she did. She was in a red gown he'd not seen before and indeed, she had seemed to gain a new confidence.

"The Winter Wren has become a Robin," he smiled.

"The gown was mine, but the color never suited me and poor Morwenna had so little… My lady gave her a lovely brooch-pin for a Yule-gift." Her breath was warm in his ear as she sidled closer. "Do you want to see what she gave me?"

Dafydd's chest felt unaccountably tight. He'd had offers before and some he had taken up, but always he had managed to stay heart-free. This was different. He hesitated too long and she drew back a little, chin high to hide her hurt. Quickly, he put a caressing hand to cup her cheek. "Do you know a place?" he whispered.

The two of them slipped unnoticed out into the snowy garth and across to the largest of the outbuildings, store for winter fodder for the beasts. It was dark inside and smelling fragrantly of the hay, a ghostly scent of summer past. Edwina led the way up the loft-ladder, kirtling up her skirts and climbing nimbly as a squirrel to the upper level. There was more light here, through the wider slats and louvers necessary for ventilation and they found they were not alone. A big golden tabby had made her kits a nest in the loose hay. They were nursing as Edwina bent over them — four kits, two of their dam's color, one stark black, one smoky gray. The hearth cat fed her litter with queenly pride, purring a response to Edwina's crooning praise.

The dam was licking the kits, an indiscriminate tongue laving whatever came in reach, and the kits were squeaking objection. Their eyes were just open, Dafydd saw, a wandering hazy blue and each triangular mouth showed the tiny ivory points of teeth. Edwina had the gray one in her hands, stroking it with one finger.

"Oh Dafydd… Feel how soft…" She held the kitten to her cheek, waking an amazingly large purr in the minute body and obediently he stroked it. It was very soft, indeed — but no softer than the cheek nestled to it, so he kissed both. The kitten squeaked, but Edwina set it back with the others and wound her arms around Dafydd's neck. "Kiss me again?"

It was dim in the hayloft and he had to make his hands do the work of his eyes. Her skin was silky, save where gooseflesh roughened it where the cold air found her warmth and she smelled of rosewater and another more elusive scent. It was intoxicating as wine and went as quickly to his head. She was honey and spice, silk and swan's-down and before he knew it her fingers had unfastened his belt and they were flesh to flesh. Edwina gave a gasp and then a small sound of pleasure and he was moving in her. If the roof had fallen in neither would have noticed it at all.

The short day had darkened. In their nest, the kittens squeaked and suckled and slept and the two lying clipped close beside them finally stirred. "I am all over hayseeds..." Edwina said, a little shakily.

Dafydd pulled her back into his arms. He felt very peaceful and content.

"*'How fair is thy love, my sister, my spouse...'*" he quoted softly. "*'How much better is thy love than wine...'*"

Edwina's eyes were very large in the dimness. "Oh you are wicked, Dafydd... That's from the Holy Book!"

"I'll say it in Welsh then, shall I?" The practiced words came smooth to his tongue. "*Calon fy, anwylyd,* I love you, you are my life, my hope of heaven, my—"

She laid her fingers over his lips, smiling. "Oh hush. Such foolishness."

He kissed her fingers and her mouth and would have gone on, but she held him away. "My lady will be wondering where I am."

He had not noticed the passage of time. "Tidy yourself then, sweeting, and I will take you back into Hall."

"No." She was decisive. "Best we go separately. You first—and I will follow in a little while." She clung her mouth to his for a moment. "You truly love me, Dafydd?"

"By Him that died on the Rood, I swear it." And he hoped he lied.

She let him go, sat feet tucked under her hearing him cross the barn floor and go out into the snowy dark. Even then she did not stir, sitting dreaming with the soft sounds of the she-cat mothering her kits for company. She reached for Anna's charm and held it, thanking the Holy Mother for granting her wish—then caught her breath as another thought struck her and she laid a palm on her flat belly. But no, that was unlikely. Her courses were due and her Mam had instilled that knowledge into her when she first came to womanhood. Besides, everyone knew it was rare for a virgin to conceive from her first time. Edwina smoothed her hair and gown as best she could, took several deep breaths to calm herself and followed her lover back to the hall.

Chapter Twelve

At the dais table, Leofric and Regan drank *hael* to the new freeman, their childhood friend, and rediscovered more old escapades to laugh over. Their reminiscing was interrupted by Hilde.

"That girl's vanished again," she observed beadily. "Really, my dear, should you not keep better control over your bower-maids?"

"Morwenna's right there," Regan pointed out hopefully.

"Well, the other one isn't. Neither," she added, "is your harper."

Before Regan could speak, Leofric gave his mother a nudge. "Speaking of harpers," he said with a wicked grin, "was that not a tryst we heard you make with young Dafydd? Greater rewards, you said?"

"What do you mean?" the Lady demanded. "Edwina—"

"Oh for shame!" Regan stretched her eyes wide, trying not to laugh.

"Well, you hear such stories about the goings-on at Court," Leofric went on. "And he's a pretty enough lad. Eh, Mam? Sweeter meat than old Sigurd, I dare say."

"What are you talking about, Leofric?!" Hilde's voice became shrill.

"Yes and no wonder," Regan said, studying the oblivious skald. "For myself I would certainly prefer a man clean-shaven. Never did see the attraction of whiskers a yard wide."

"Me neither," Leofric agreed solemnly. "So do not you grow any, my girl."

"I shall make shift to remember," she agreed. "And hide my disappointment. Let us drink *hael* to whiskers!"

"You're mazed, both of you," Hilde said repressively, "and if you won't search out and chastise that baggage, I will." She started to get up from her chair, but they grabbed an arm each and sat her down.

"Trysting with a Welshman, Mam," Leofric said sternly. "I don't think I approve. Sainted Da would be turning in his grave."

"Like a top," said Regan.

"Tryst?" Hilde picked out the one word that seemed to make some sense. "A *tryst*? Don't be so—as if I would! He's young enough to be my—"

"Son?" Regan put in.

"Grandson?" Leofric suggested. "Drink *hael*."

Hilde drew herself together with all the dignity she could muster. "I'll deal with you later," she informed her son coldly. "How dare you infer I would dream of such—dalliance—"

"Why not?" Regan asked. And smiled sweetly at the basilisk glare that came her way.

"It is, of course, no business of anyone what I intend," Hilde announced, "but if you must know, I will be taking the harper into my household, to advance his talent with noble and possibly even royal patronage." She watched their faces change and savored the victory. "For such a gift as his is sadly wasted out here in these God-forgotten borders," she declared soulfully. Leofric stared at her.

"That decision should surely be his to make," he said. "Dafydd is no thrall to be ordered will-he nil-he to follow at your call."

"Tch!" she said dismissively. "How should he refuse such an offer? See that you say nothing to him, mind. You have as much tact and subtlety as a charging bull and I don't want the boy put off or over-awed. When he comes back, send him to me." She rose to her feet and swept from the hall and Leofric watched the stair-door close, a scowl on his face.

"She wouldn't," Regan said anxiously. "She couldn't."

Leofric leaned across to fill up her cup then slid into Hilde's vacated chair beside her. "I know my mother," he said. "She would and she could. And she almost certainly will. Unless."

"Unless? Where is he, by the way?"

"Trysting," said Leofric. "With 'Dwina. Saw them slip out of hall some while ago."

"It's no small thing, to sing for a King's Court," Regan sighed. "Leofric, it could be the making of him, but—he has become dear to me."

"Has he, by God."

"Oh foolish!" And gave him a clout about the ear, knocking his circlet askew. He took the thing off and hung it from the corner of his chair, scrubbed his fingers through his hair until it was an untidy mane that fell partly over his forehead.

"Damned thing always gives me a headache," he grinned. "Look at it in this wise, Trout, if you were a red-blooded young buck and had to choose between my mother and Lucca's daughter, which would you pick?"

"If I were that young buck," she said, unable to resist the urge to caress a blond lock from his brow, "I'd find a way to have both."

"Oh," he said, blankly. "Then I hope Dafydd hasn't got your guile."

"We should warn him," she went on, "so that she cannot take him off-balance."

"My thought also. Hah, there he is." He stood up and beckoned then poured wine into another cup and gestured the harper to a seat.

"Dafydd," Regan said earnestly, "I want you to know that I have never before heard such skill as yours."

"Nor I," Leofric said. "Nor, Dewi, has my Lady mother."

"I am honored," he said politely.

"You are likely to be even more honored," Leofric smiled ironically and reached out to remove a wisp of hay from Dafydd's hair. At the harper's other side, Regan began a similar service. "She has a mind to take you with her when she leaves. She is bower-woman to Queen Edith and would give you entry to the Royal Court. You could harp before the King, Dafydd ap Gryfydd."

"*Duw Mawr!*" It was a shocked croak and Dafydd took a deep swallow of wine. Regan fished a small comb from her girdle and put the curling black tangle to rights, while Leofric removed more of the hayloft from his clothing.

"There," he said. "You're decent to be seen in the presence of fine ladies. My mother wants a word with you, up in the solar."

"Your mother?" Stunned still, Dafydd stared at the thane as if he had lost his knowledge of the *Saes* tongue.

"Yes, you remember her, the lady with a liking for black?" Leofric said tolerantly. "Jesu, Dafydd, she'll think the Fair Folk have stolen your wits, as well as rolling you in the hay." He brushed solicitously at the last wisps adhering to the back of the bardic tunic, then turned him around to make sure all was seemly "You'll do. Best fetch your harp as well, she's bound to want you to play."

"Oh Dewi," Regan sighed as the stair door closed on him. "Bemused as a pollen-drunk bee, poor wight. Well, she shan't have him. 'Dwina and I will see to that, if need be. And 'Wenna." She glanced around and saw to her surprise that Morwenna was whispering with Sifrith, her round face flushed and almost pretty.

"Ah but," Leofric leaned closer, his fingertips warm on her cheek, turning her back to face him, "nuns are not permitted to keep harpers in their cloisters. So what then, Trout?"

"Do not you call me that!" she said crossly and made to box his ears again. But he caught her wrist in a gentle grip she could not break. Not that she tried very hard.

"What shall I call you then?" he murmured. "Freya is not more fair, nor Sif, for whom the Dwarves fashioned marvels. Her hair was merely living gold, while yours is surely fire given mortal form. Hearth-fire, wild-fire, dragon-fire—"

"Leofric," she said unsteadily, "you're drunk."

"Yes," he whispered, "and you are more intoxicating than any mead…"

To Regan's intense disappointment, the stair door crashed open behind them and Dafydd stood there, eyes glittering and mouth set with anger.

* * * * *

Groomed and neat-combed, Dafydd had presented himself to the Lady Hilde in the solar.

She was alone there, save for Constance, and seemed displeased. She greeted Dafydd with a smile, however, gestured him to the stool beside her chair and requested a suitable song for the holy season. When he had obliged, the last notes of the harp falling into an appreciative silence, she breathed a contented sigh.

"Truly balm for the troubled or sorrowing spirit," she said, her ringed hand patting his head absently. "I have heard that you've spoken of a wish to see Winchester and London and other of our cities."

Of course he had, since it would be expected of him. "So I did, my lady."

She did not notice his qualification. "Then you shall. You do not need me to laud your skill, nor to tell you that this poor place is not the proper setting for it. There are those who will honor your gifts for what they are, Dafydd, and know you for bard, not mere singing boy. I knew," she went on, "from the moment I first set eyes on you, as I told Sigurd, that you were meant for higher things. Soon I shall be returning to Court and you will come with me. You shall not lack for patronage there, I promise you. You shall sing for his Grace the King, Dafydd. What have you to say to that?"

He thanked God and Leofric for the warning. If he were what he claimed to be, it would be a wonderfully generous offer and few could dream of such good fortune. But he was of the *Meibion Owain*, the Sons of Owain, his allotted task pre-set and half-completed. Last but not least, he did not want to go with her. Ten minutes in her company would have him howling mad for her blood were she *Saes* or *Cymru*.

"You are destined for great things, Dafydd," Lady Hilde said kindly, taking his muteness for gratitude.

"I thank you most humbly, my lady…" Uncharacteristically, he groped for the right words to refuse without offending.

"Time for that later, when you are fittingly clad in fine silk and linen, your harp gilded—"

"My harp needs no embellishment, my lady!" he objected, jolted by the suggestion.

"I know just the craftsman to do it too. A master of the art, for me he will gladly—"

Dafydd stood up. "My lady, I am more grateful than I can say for your kindness. But I have no wish to leave here."

She stared at him. "Nonsense," she said brusquely. "You have given no oath, surely?"

Only to Edwina, he thought, but the lady did not mean that sort of vow. "No, lady, but—"

"Then it is settled. Be sure no one will stand in your way. You shall be part of my own household."

She was not listening, Dafydd realized. Having set her mind on a thing, she was incapable of countenancing refusal. He tried again, more firmly this time. "Lady Hilde. You do me great honor and I thank you. But I cannot leave Staneleigh. As yet there is something that binds me here."

The bright eyes sharpened. "That chit? You can do better than Edwina Godwinesdaughter, boy."

Dafydd took a steadying breath. "Lady, I stay here at Staneleigh while Leofric Thane gives me his hospitality. I look for no higher station. I do very well here, lady — I neither need nor wish for more."

Hilde had known defeat before, but she had never taken it well. Now she sat silent, her eyes fixed on him like a stoat trying to intimidate a young hare. Dafydd ap Gryfydd, bard and Son of Owain, stiffened his proud spine and met her gaze levelly.

Finally, she bowed her head in a gesture of martyred submission. "I see I cannot persuade you, child. So be it. But," and the gray eyes sparked again, "should you ever see fit to change your mind, come to me. I shall not count this rejection against you."

"Lady." Dafydd made his deepest bow and backed out of the room, letting out his breath in a gasp of sheer relief as the door closed at his back. He took the stairs fast, in case she found cause to call him back and cannoned into hall before he could stop himself.

* * * * *

Startled, Leofric turned in his chair and gave him a smile. "So what was your answer, Dewi?" he chuckled. "Or can I guess? You came out of there like a bung from a barrel!"

Dafydd collected himself and went to sit at Leofric's side. "I think," he said slowly, "that I have insulted your lady-mother."

"Think you so?" Leofric said, grinning. "Somehow I doubt it."

"Oh yes. She said I should have my harp gilded—"

"By The Tree!" Leofric choked. "And she said *I* have no more tact than a charging bull!"

"That is beyond jesting," Regan snapped. "I hope you told her so."

"She does not listen well," he said carefully.

"Not when it's something she doesn't want to hear," Leofric said mournfully. "Very deaf then, my sainted mother." He sat forward, chin on fist. "So tell us the tale, bard."

"There's little to tell, my lord. Perhaps some day I may go to a king's court and seek advancement there, but not yet." He caught Edwina's eyes as she sat in the shadows behind her mistress. "I fear the Lady Hilde was offended by my refusal."

Leofric gave a crack of laughter. "Don't fret, Dewi, you're not the first to say her nay in this hall! She'll survive it. Oh it'll be martyred sighs and mournful glances until something serves to distract her, but she doesn't bear grudges. I for one am glad you'll be staying with us for a while longer. And I'm sure I'm not alone in that. But don't plan in haste," he went on quickly. "Listen, come the spring I go to do my service to my liege-lord, Earl Godwin of Wessex. Have a thought to coming with me. It'll be for three months and by the end of it you'll have offers a sight more to your liking than this of my mother's, I'll warrant. The Earl keeps a rich household—richer than the King's, it's said and Saxon to the core, no Norman ways there. Of course, it might be too *Saes* for your stomach. Don't decide now, but think on it."

"Take him to the Old Wolf's court?" Regan bristled with sudden anger and Dafydd stared at her, startled. "Well, it'd teach him to cheat, anyway."

"I don't know what you mean." Leofric twitched an eyebrow at her calmly.

"Taught you fast enough," she claimed. "Honest as noonday you were before he snared you. Look at you now!"

Fascinated, despite this second shock, Dafydd waited to see where this was leading. But Leofric only gave a chuckle. "Aye, look at me now. Scheming to keep this harper out of my mother's clutches. Say nothing to her, mind," he warned Dafydd, "or we'll neither of us hear the last of it!"

"I'm glad you're staying, Dafydd," Regan said quietly, "if only for a while. Good night, my friend." She leaned forward, gave him a hug and a kiss on the cheek. "'Dwina, 'Wenna, we'll away to our beds and let the men drink themselves senseless." Then, "Good night, my lord," to Leofric, but she did not embrace him.

"Wait," he said suddenly. "Regan, my answer—"

"Tomorrow," she smiled. "When we are both sober."

Chapter Thirteen

※

"Leofric." The voice had an edge to it that would do credit to a scraemasaex. He winced and dragged at the covers, tried to heave them over his head. "Leofric. Get up." His mother's voice, sharpening by the second. "Leo-*fric*!" Acknowledging defeat, he sat up, moving as carefully as he could lest his head fall from his shoulders and bounce—a beaker was shoved into his hands and he drank without thought, until the foul taste of the liquid sank into his awareness and he choked.

"Anna's most potent cure-all," Hilde said with satisfaction. "Are you awake now? Sensible? Or is that too much to expect?"

"What time is it?" he asked. His tongue felt too big for his mouth and strangely numb. As if it belonged to someone else. It tasted like it belonged to—

"Leofric, pay attention. It is an hour past dawn. I want you up and dressed. In your best clothes, mind, and not the ones you were wearing last night because they are ale-soaked."

"Why?" he demanded, wondering if this was some drunken nightmare. It would be like his damned mother to invade even his dreams to carp at him.

"Because I tell you to!"

"By Odin's Tree—" Her hand connected with the side of his head and he fell over.

"You will not use those foul heathen oaths in my presence," she snapped. "I am leaving and you and your household will make a suitable farewell. I'll send Godwine in.

He's no more sober than you, but at least he's dressed and moving."

"Leaving?" he echoed, not daring to believe his ears. He forced his eyes open and squinted at her. She was a silhouette in the dimness of the shuttered room. A silhouette wearing her favorite fox-fur-lined mantle. "Leaving?" Hope burgeoned, singing in his voice like a summer chant. He managed to focus on her face. At first it was no more than a pale blur, but gradually he could make out that she was smiling. A rather fond and gentle smile.

"Yes, dearling. All that talk of Royal Courts and Queens, it quite unsettled me. I have been away from it far too long. There is more snow coming in the next day or so and if I don't leave now it'll be too late. Don't be long now."

She disappeared and he gazed owl-like at the place where she'd stood.

"Leaving…" he whimpered prayerfully and then remembered that she was capable of wrapping a drunken bard in a sack like a purloined pig and taking him with her whether he wished it or not.

He half-fell, half-crawled from the tangled bedding and talked himself into his clothes. All went well enough until he got to the boots. Or rather, the boot. The right boot. The left one seemed to have taken itself off somewhere. He crawled round in a circle, looking for it and asking himself with increasing irritation where it was. Then he thought he'd found it, but unfortunately, Godwine was already wearing it. "She's leaving," he told his steward's knees. "Where's my boot?"

"Here, m'lord." Godwine did not bend down to give it. Obviously his head was also loose at the neck. "Better not let her see you like this."

"Too late. Already has. Thought I was dreaming—can't let her have Dewi in a sack."

"No, m'lord."

"Trout wouldn't like it."

"No, m'lord. Drink this."

"Anna's?"

"Aye. It's for the best."

"Nnggh," said Leofric, but drained the beaker put under his nose.

Once he'd thrown up, he felt a lot better. As if he might possibly live.

By the time Leofric walked gingerly down the stairs and across the hall, he was able to take in the pale sunlight without more than a wince and a moan. Dafydd was propped against one door jamb, starkly white under the unruly raven-black hair. He looked, Leofric decided, more like a barrow-wight than a bard. He said so and received a glare laden with venom.

Then Leofric saw Regan, tall and slender as a Valkyrie-maid, her hair drawn gently back in one loose-woven braid beneath her headrail. Kirtle and over-gown were immaculate, her face pale, calm and composed. He joined her, painfully aware that for all his care he looked not unlike the bed he had so recently left.

"How do you look so neat?" he demanded accusingly.

Without turning her head, she shot him a glance that rivaled Dafydd's for poison.

"Women," she breathed, "are bred to endure pain…"

He gave a crack of laughter and groaned, clutching his throbbing skull. "You had that from my mother," he whispered.

"Who else? Her Grace will be making her entry now you're here."

As if she'd heard a signal, Hilde appeared and a passageway opened up in the throng to let her through. Her litter was in place out in the garth and she stepped toward it dainty as a cat over the frozen ruts. Then sat in state and beckoned Leofric to her.

"I thought Hawiss was the perfect wife when I brought her here for you," she said, her voice clear and carrying. "I am not so small-minded that I cannot admit when I am wrong. For all her breeding and the dower-lands that came with her, she had no more wit than Anna's hens. You need a wife with a mind and a will to match your own. Well, you know my wishes. God keep you, my son." And she twitched the leather curtain closed between them.

"Damn you, Mother!" Leofric hissed the curse through clenched teeth as the train moved ponderously out of the gates. Then Regan's hand was on his shoulder.

"Be easy, my dear. She aimed that dart to hurt you."

"And succeeded."

"So I see. I think," Regan murmured, "that I will let it be known that I will run off across the Dyke with my harper before I will wed you. Just to annoy her, old toad that she is."

"From his looks, Dafydd isn't going to be running anywhere, unless it be to the midden." Leofric had not thought his pain could grow worse. He was wrong. "Is that your answer, lady? You'd sooner wed a Welshman?"

"I wish there was some way of doing what I wish without your mother crowing like a dunghill cockerel," she muttered. "Leofric, my answer is this, I do not go to Leominster but back home. And if you wish, you may come to pay me court there. What we decide after that will be as our hearts dictate." Her voice gentled. "Now let us get out of this painful daylight before my head splits open."

"You're going home?"

"Soon. Tomorrow, if the weather continues to hold." She linked her arm through his and they walked back toward sanctuary of the hall. People gave way for them, their muttered comments showing indignation, pity and a kind of perverse pride in the Lady Hilde's parting statement.

"An outrageous she-dragon, but our own," Leofric said wryly. "Perhaps we could return the favor and wed her to a Danish Prince. Or Welsh," he added thoughtfully.

"Or one of those Norman lords she's so fond of?" Regan suggested, glad to see the shadow lifting from his eyes. "Well, will you come to visit me?"

He stopped and looked down at her. Eyes of summer-green gazed at him, proud, affectionate and perhaps a little anxious,

"Yes," he said quietly. He wanted to put his arms around her, hold her close, kiss her — he was also aware that every pair of eyes in the steading were fixed on them as if they were performing bears on a feast-day. Regan smiled and nodded and walked into the hall.

* * * * *

As soon as the bustle of Hilde's departure had settled down, Regan collected her maids and retreated to the quiet sanctuary of the guest-bower. Not yet was she ready to face the hurly-burly of hall-life, not while her head still pounded like a war-drum. Morwenna's gentle fingers unraveled her braid — every individual strand of hair seemed to have its own ache — and Edwina brought a cloth dampened with rosewater for her brow.

For a long time Regan lay on her bed and drowsed, the quiet whispers and occasional giggle from the two girls a comforting reminder of companionship without obligation of polite conversation. She'd done right to pick Edwina and not just for her needle-skill. Morwenna had found a friend and the new confidence that brought with it was a joy to see. She fell asleep, smiling.

Some time later, Edwina brought her a platter of cold meats and honey-cakes and though she had not thought she could face food, Regan picked at it in a desultory fashion until it was mostly gone. By that time, so too had her headache.

She sat by the small hearth and sipped the mulled wine, stared into the flames and thought, not of Gifford, but of her parents and one other.

"That Leofric," her Da would grunt, smiling under his moustaches, "wild as a hawk. But Edmund's right to let him run free, especially with that scold-wife of a Hilde trying to Norman the boy."

"That Leofric," her mam used to say, when she'd traipsed home all scratched and muddy, with the sling-shot he'd made for her and taught her to use. "Mad as a March hare and more mischief to him than a boggart!" But she never could pretend to be angry for long, there was almost always laughter under her words. "And how did you get into such a state this time?"

"Hunting," Regan had said proudly. "Leofric and Sifrith said I'm almost as good at it as they are and I nearly brought down a pigeon." They'd also scattered Anna's hens, fought a running battle with Mildberg's geese, let loose (accidentally) Oswy's milk-cow and fetched her back again, lost one of Gyfu's new shoes in the river and she had fallen out of the willow tree into the duck pond. Lucca, of course, had not let her go home across the fields until she'd put all four children into the large tub and scrubbed them indiscriminately, thrall- and thane-brats together. Then, with Anna's green-salve lavishly daubed on the worst of the scratches, she'd bounced onto her pony and headed for home, whooping like a marauding Viking.

Why was childhood seen always in a golden glow of things lost, never to be regained? Oh she'd been one of the fortunate few, with doting parents, a privileged life—she had never gone hungry or known want. She wanted to offer that same kind of life to her children, when God saw fit to send them. Until now, she had only seen them in her daydreams, vaguely as if through a mist, without definitive features. Suddenly, they were before her, fiery-headed and barley-blond, with Leofric's grin and her eyes, his height and her slenderness and she ached for them with a sharp longing.

"Dear me," she told herself sharply, in unconscious imitation of Lucca, "this will never do! Pull yourself together, woman!"

"Lady?" Morwenna whispered and she realized she'd spoken aloud.

"Take no notice," Regan smiled, "I'm maundering on to myself like an old biddy. Where's 'Dwina? Off with that Dafydd?"

"N-no, lady, she's fetching our needlework from the solar. Lucca is giving the chamber an airing."

"More than an airing," Edwina came in to hear the last few words, a covered basket clutched in her arms. "Mam's going through it like a storm-wind," she laughed. "Wants to get the old-maid smell of those two bower-cats out of it, she says, so she can put it back the way Leofric likes it. He, of course," sounding very much like her mother, "is nowhere to be seen. Men!"

"Indeed, men!" Regan smiled. A sudden urge to be up and doing swept her to her feet. "I've been idle long enough," she announced briskly, "and if Lucca's started the spring-cleaning this early, no doubt she'll welcome more pairs of hands."

"Oh she will, my lady," Edwina said. "Shall you sit here or in-hall while we're away? I can fetch your spinning—"

"Neither, 'Dwina, we'll all go."

Regan changed into an older kirtle but did not bother to re-braid her hair. She twisted it up and stuffed it into a snood, tied an old headrail over all and wrapped a mantle around her for the short dash to the hall.

It came as something of a surprise to discover it was not long past noon, dull but dry and bitterly cold. The hall, though, was warm, while the solar, windows and shutters flung wide, was not. It smelled of beeswax, with the green scents of lemon-balm and meadowsweet among the fresh rushes. The perfumed frowst was gone. "Ah you're here to help?" Lucca said with pleasure. "You come in a good hour, Lady. If you will, take these and bestow them in m'lord's coffer across the way." A great cushiony mound of feather pillows was heaped into her arms.

"I'll help—" Morwenna began, but Lucca cut her off.

"I've hangings to be brushed, lass, and they need your gentle touch. Edwina, you show her how."

Chapter Fourteen

෩

Smiling at Lucca's suborning of her bower-maids, Regan hefted her burden and carried it across the landing, kicking the door open. The room was shuttered and warmly dark and in any case her vision was restricted by the shifting load—she made blindly to dump them on the bed so that she could open the coffer.

The bed gave a startled grunt.

Regan dropped the rest of the pillows. "Leofric?" she squawked. "What are you doing here?"

"Sleeping!" he retorted. "Or trying to!" He sat up, shoved the hair out of his eyes and glared at her, bare chest and shoulders making him no more than a pallid wraith in the gloom.

"It's afternoon!" she snapped.

"What of it? And what are you doing here?"

"Working! While the menfolk lie idle like swine in a wallow!" And neither of them noticed the hand that silently drew the door closed.

He threw a pillow at her and fell back with a groan, one arm over his eyes. "Jesu, I thought it was my mother come again, like some molting harpy—"

Regan hurled the pillow back at him. Her aim was better than his and he sat up again, spitting out a feather. "Slug-a-bed," she jeered and strode to the window. "Well, we'll have none of it." She opened the shutters and turned to see the pale daylight wash in a swathe across the bed and her victim ducked under the covers with a yelp.

"Regan!" he bellowed. "Light hurts!"

"I don't find it so," she shrugged. "Lucca will be airing in here next. You'd best be up and about, my lord, or you'll be hung out of the window with the bedding." She made to drag at the deer hide coverlet and he clutched it back, determined to return to his interrupted rest. But she was equally determined that he should not.

There was a short and unseemly tug-of-war that, along with the extravagant and dearly familiar threats being thrown at her, took Regan back to their shared childhood. A bubble of mirth awoke and became breathless chuckles that lost her some ground in the fight for the bedding.

"Laugh at me, would you," he growled.

"Well, if your mother could see us now…"

"Most improper behavior."

"Yes, indeed." She got a double handful of the supple cover!et, hauled—staggered as his greater strength pulled her off-balance and only his swift reaction saved her from an ungainly tumble. She found herself held close, his arms tight around her and her hands braced against naked shoulders that were hard with muscle.

The shape and form of him had been unseen in the snow, bundled as they both were in layers of thick wool. Once his body had been familiar to her—all tendon and slim bone and the gawkiness of a colt. The intervening years had put layers of strength on him, had brought a seal-sleek pelt of fine gold hair that spanned his chest and now there was a hunger in his darkening eyes that she had not seen in him before. It awoke a need in her own body and the yearning that had been half-asleep since the kiss in the snow became an ache of desire that was almost painful. She needed his touch, needed his lips on hers—needed *something* only he could give her. His hand moved up her spine, igniting a fiery path even through the layers of clothing and his fingers closed on the snood, pulling it from her head. Her loosened hair flowed down in a river of copper silk and he whispered her name.

This time, Regan knew, there would be no retreat, nor did she wish it. Then her mouth was under his, his tongue probing gently for entry and she welcomed him, her body involuntarily arching closer.

Awareness of the outside world fell away and all time stopped. There was only the two of them locked close on the bed and Regan knew that the pulsing wonder of the moment would last in her memory forever. Her man. The first time he had truly held her.

Leofric's skin felt hot under her hands, the play of muscle satiny smooth as his hand stroked up her leg, pushing aside the skirts of her kirtle. Yes, get rid of it. Regan did not want anything between them, least of all fabric, she needed to feel the length of his nakedness against her, the weight of him, solid and male and hungry for her—

Leofric drew back and she gave a wordless cry of protest, reaching for him. He laughed quietly, a breathless sound almost drowned by the wind outside, buffeting at the window. Then he got a double handful of kirtle and shift and hauled them over her head together, threw them across the room.

For a moment he knelt by her side, gazing down at her with an expression of bemused wonder on his face. She thought he would speak, but he didn't. In any case, Regan doubted if she would have heard him. The hair that glinted gold on his chest narrowed to a thin line down to his groin, where it widened into a thatch of bright curls around the base of his erect manhood. The sight of him caught the breath in her throat and she felt as if she was melting into liquid fire. Slowly, without conscious thought, Regan parted her legs, hips moving in sensual invitation that was as old as time and entirely instinctive, arms raised to summon him to her.

The shock of pleasure when their bodies met at last drove any pretense of restraint from them. His erection was hot and slick and urgent at her belly and she lifted her knees to grip his lean hips, gave him entry to her body. The moment of penetration made her gasp—she had not known it would feel like this, alien and yet totally a part of her, stretching and filling her nearly to the point of pain and the source of the most amazing waves of pleasure. Instinct drove her now and she rode the pulsing tide until the world broke into a sparkling cloud and she cried out, hearing him groan her name as his body convulsed.

She stirred in his arms, nuzzling the hollow of his throat and relishing the weight of him. "Most improper..." she whispered in giddy delight, not wanting to let him go.

"Mmm. Shall we do it properly next time?"

She tweaked at a blond hair near his right nipple and he yelped.

"Only if it feels as good. Mam never said. She sort of hinted about the delights of the marriage bed, but she didn't go into detail." She paused. "Just as well, really. I wouldn't have waited this long."

"Oh shameless," he drawled, grinning down at her.

"Oh yes," Regan smiled. "Why, I'd probably have half-a-dozen bairns by now—" and felt the shudder that ran through him, the tensing of his muscles that somehow took him away from her. "Leofric?" Then remembered how Hawiss had died and cursed herself for a fool. But maybe not. Better it came out now than later, perhaps. "Tell me?" she whispered, stroking the tangled locks back from his brow. "Leofric, dearling, tell me."

He lay back on the pillows and stared up at the ceiling, not looking at her at all. His face was pale under the gloss of sweat from their lovemaking, his mouth a grim, unforgiving line.

"I'm sorry," he muttered. "Best see Anna—"

"Why?" Regan kissed the corner of his mouth and he flinched.

"In case I've got you with child. If any harm came to you through me I couldn't—"

"Where's the harm if you have? You're coming to court me, aren't you? Although I have to confess I'd just as soon not be big for my wedding. My finest gown wouldn't fit."

"No!" He pushed her away and sat up, wrapped his arms around his drawn-up knees and stared anywhere but at her. "This is wrong. I cannot risk you—"

"How will I be at risk?" she said, as gently relentless as Anna lancing a festering wound. "Tell me, Leofric."

"Hawiss," he whispered. "I killed her and the child I gave her."

The pains had started one morning. He had been out with Godwine overseeing the wool clip and had not known until a thrall came panting with their noon-piece and the news that the Lady Hawiss had taken to her chamber, with Lucca and Anna Priestwife in attendance. Leofric had ridden back to the hall, though aware that he would most like be underfoot and superfluous to requirements. "You could have saved yourself the trouble, lad," *Anna said brusquely, sweeping past with an armful of linen.* "It'll be a while yet."

"How is she?" *He made for the stairway, but she forestalled him.*

"As well as any lass about her woman's business for the first time. No, my lord, you may not see her. Bide you and we'll care for her, you may be sure."

The afternoon had passed into evening, into night and still Hawiss had not been delivered of her burden. Leofric slept in snatches in his chair by the hearth, rousing each time a sound came from the birth chamber, but the hours crept on to dawn and full day and there was no word. Gyfu attended to the young thane's needs, even though he would not eat—food was so much sawdust in his mouth—and reassured him as best she could.

"It is often so with the first, my lord. I was a night and a day with Yseult."

But the day wore on. It was mid afternoon when Anna came hurrying down to the hall, pale and grim-faced. "The babe will not come," *she murmured to Gyfu and, to Leofric,* "Would you send for my man? He may be needed."

Leofric felt the blood leave his face and his belly clenched into a sick knot. "Hawiss…?"

"She is sinking, sir," she said gently. "The child is large for her and lying wrongly."

But he heard no more. Pushing past her, ignoring her protests, he went up the stairs three at a time, thrusting open the door. The heated air struck him like a blow. For all the balmy summer warmth outside, the windows had been shuttered, the fire basket kept stoked, for it was well-known that fresh air could be fatal for the newborn. The room reeked – of sweat, of herbs, of blood – and the lamplight showed him a Hawiss transformed. She was propped on the birthing stool, supported by Lucca, and the linen shift that was all she wore was plastered to her body by the sweat that was running from her like rain. They had unbound her hair – there must be nothing of knots about her – and it clung in dirty tow-colored elflocks to her tortured face. As he watched, her body twisted, head thrown back so that the tendons of her throat stretched taut and her mouth opened on a scream that she was too weak now to voice. Leofric fell to his knees beside her. "Hawiss – Jesu, what ails her, what's wrong? Hawiss!"

It was Lucca, herself flushed and glistening with exertion, who told him.

"You should not be here, lad. You can't help. Your lady cannot birth the child. The effort has torn her, inside. We need Father Edric, for the Sacrament."

He heard her words, but they made no sense. This was Hawiss and she was bearing their child and this could not be happening.

"Hawiss…!" It was disbelief, anguish, denial. But she did not hear, too far sunk in the extremity of pain and as he knelt, gripping her hand in both of his, she gave a choking wail and blood splattered the floor beside his knees, a gushing stream. When he looked again, her eyes had set in her head. Lucca's hands were on his shoulders then.

"Out," she commanded. "We have one chance to save the babe."

He only comprehended what she meant when he had stumbled out into the stairwell and his belly revolted, but there was nothing to come up. He crouched there, shuddering, in a sick daze and after *some little time, Father Edric came up and Anna opened for him, sorrow etched on her face. The door closed again. Then Lucca came out, carrying something wrapped in a cloth – paused, shook her head gently at him and went on her way.*

So there was no child either to cherish and care for as he had cherished and cared for his bride.

They told him it had been a son – perfectly formed – and it had been baptized for his father, though it had not drawn breath outside the womb. It was buried along with its butchered mother, while everyone wept for the wasted lives. Leofric had not. He had no tears in him anymore.

Nor did he weep at the telling of it. The flat, unemotional voice told without words of the iron control he had over himself and Regan needed all her strength of will not to cry enough for both of them.

What to do though? What to say? This was not a man you could mouth platitudes to and have them accepted. But had his people done any different? Oh no. Gentle words and sweet reason could not break through barriers of guilt and grief, no matter how much you love the man imprisoned within.

Regan got up from the bed, stood in the shaft of light and shook back the silken wealth of her hair.

"Leofric Edmondson," she commanded. "Look at me."

Slowly his head turned. She saw his eyes widen, his lips part a little and knew how he saw her. Hair a glorious mantle to mid-thigh, breasts firm and proud, nipples flushed and peaked from their lovemaking. Narrow of waist yet wide-hipped to match the width of her shoulders and long slim legs to give her height above that of most women. "Look at me," she repeated. "Hawiss, may Mary Mother bless her, by all accounts had no more height and bone to her than a half-grown lass, for all she was a woman in years. Most like any man's child would have killed her. I, on the other hand, am the mare to your stallion. I will give you sons and daughters and make no more work of it than any brood-mare. I love you, Leofric Edmondson, and I won't have you torturing yourself over a tragedy that wasn't your fault." She opened her arms to him and he came to her, wrapping her in a tight embrace and was held as securely.

"Ah, lady, I love you." His voice was hoarse, muffled by her hair. "Do not forget that, ever…"

Chapter Fifteen

☙

Lucca set her empty bowl down and sighed contentedly, "Did I tell you?" she asked complacently and not for the first time. "It was nigh on three hours before that Regan slipped away to the guest-bower. There's a good day's work we've done, Godwine. 'Dwina played her part well and when I shut the door on them I knew all would be as it should."

Godwine smiled and took another bramble-cake from the depleted dish, stretching his booted feet to the warmth of the fire. "So when do you think they'll wed, Mistress Know-All?"

"Well, it'll be a year come Midsummer that Hawiss left us, poor sweet lady, God rest her. So he won't speak of it before then. It wouldn't be seemly. I'd say—Lammas. That would be about right. Besides, he'll be off to do his liege-service this spring, he'll not do aught until that's over. Lammas. Or after Harvest." She nodded, well-pleased with the prediction. "And next summer at the latest, with God's grace, a babe… Cynricings never waste time."

"Aye, don't we all know it!" Godwine hooted. "Though he's not the randy tup his father was, thank the White Christ. The wonder was there was a maid left hereabouts while that one lived!"

"True enough," Lucca said, her smile one of fond memory. Godwine launched into one of the wilder tales of the old thane, but she scarcely listened. Edwina. If that daughter of hers was still a maid she'd be surprised. At least she'd told the girl what she needed to know and there was always Anna… No need for Godwine to know it though.

* * * * *

Leofric leaned his elbows on the palisade and gazed out over his land. His breath was a white cloud in the air and the few stars that were beginning to show in the purpling sky told of a hard frost to come. But the days were lengthening and despite more bad weather to come, spring was not so very far away. New life, new growth—a new beginning for him and Regan—

"My lord?" A familiar voice, rich with music and the Welsh lilt. "I have a boon to ask of you."

"Then ask it, Dewi," he smiled, turning to prop a shoulder against the seasoned wood. "I'm in the mood to grant you anything you could wish for. Except the moon and stars, I've promised them elsewhere."

"Yes, my lord. I—was a guest in the Lady Regan's hall and I have been a guest here…" He sounded uncharacteristically stilted, ill at ease and Leofric raised an eyebrow.

"So you are and glad I am of it. Has anyone offered you insult?"

"No, my lord, not that. On the contrary. I ask leave to stay here awhile longer. You see, there is a…" and he hesitated.

"A lass you're courting," Leofric prompted and watched the color rise in the harper's face.

"Yes," he admitted. "She has become more to me than— but I have little besides my harp and my horse and I'm *Cymru* besides. Her Da has no cause to trust me—"

"Rein back, Dewi," Leofric interrupted gently. "Hear what I have to say first, then think if you would ask longer guesting elsewhere. Though this does not go beyond the two of us, mind. The Lady Regan does not go to the Abbey but back to her own hall tomorrow. By midsummer we will be wed."

"My lord, that is—great news. You and she were fashioned for each other. But how—Oh. Edwina goes with her as bower-maid," and he frowned, thinking fast.

"I'll be riding with the escort tomorrow—ride with me?" Leofric asked. "We'll all three of us be glad of your company."

"Thank you, my lord, but I'll bide back." The dark head came up, resolution in the set of the expressive mouth. "I ask again, may I stay in your hall awhile longer?"

"For as long as you wish it," Leofric said. "Weeks, months, the rest of your life if you choose. You have friends here, Dafydd ap Gryfydd." To Leofric's surprise the man flushed red, then the blood left his face and he was chalk-white.

"I—I thank you for that," he stammered.

"But why remain when you could be under the same roof as 'Dwina?"

"Because her Da doesn't trust me, black Welsh that I am. If I am here I have a chance to prove to him that I am worthy of his jewel."

"A good thought." Leofric nodded gravely. "And when I ride to visit my lady, what more natural that you should ride with me?"

"Indeed, my lord." Dafydd's smile was that of an archangel beholding the Grail.

"And that's another thing," Leofric said, grinning back. "I've heard more 'my lords' from you this eve than Geadas at his most unctuous. I have a name, Dewi, and friends use that rather than the rank. You'd best go find your *Saes* jewel—and remember, no word to anyone else about Regan."

* * * * *

"I have something to ask you, 'Dwina."

Edwina looked up from her embroidery—a particularly complicated patterning of clover-flowers that she had worked out after hearing the Song of Olwen—and studied her mistress. The sheen about the Lady Regan, that had not been there before the spring-cleaning of the solar, showed no sign of fading. If anything, it was enhanced by the glow of the candles surrounding them. "Yes, Lady?" hiding a smile that was in danger of becoming a smirk.

"I leave here tomorrow, Edwina. Swein and Godwine agree that the roads will be clear enough by then. I would have you tutor Morwenna in orphrey-work. She has needle-skill but I cannot train her, having little. Would you come with me?"

"Oh yes," Morwenna leaned over to lay a hand on her arm. "Please say you will?"

Edwina swallowed hard. Leaving tomorrow? Why so soon if all had gone well? And was it to Ashford steading or to Leominster and the nunnery? Oh surely not! She would rather die, she thought melodramatically. "Lady, you do my poor skills too much honor—"

"Nonsense. No one embroiders as finely! Besides, it would be a shame for Morwenna to lose a friend so new-made. I've other maids to my bower, of course, so the duties would not be onerous." And she hesitated, seeing Edwina's expectant eyes. "I'm going home, 'Dwina," she said and happiness bubbled in her voice. "Not to Leominster. Say you will come with me, just for a while?"

Entirely forgetting her place, Edwina dropped her embroidery and threw her arms around the other woman. "Oh my lady!"

Regan laughed and hugged her back. "Well, it seems that you are pleased by my decision!"

"Oh my lady, no one could mislike it! We all thought the nunnery was no place for you—I mean, none of us wanted—we hoped you and…" she broke off, flustered and blushing, but Regan merely smiled.

"I'm well aware of what everyone thought, my dear, and maybe I've changed my mind. Go and ask your Mam if I might speak with her—if you do wish to come with me, that is?"

"Oh yes, my lady!" Edwina gathered her skirts in one hand and ran to the door and was out into the thin gloom. It was only as she was forced to slow her pace by the slushy puddling underfoot that she thought—*Dafydd*.

It stopped her in her tracks. As if conjured by her thought, he appeared, crossing the garth toward her with a smile.

"What a face, sweeting, for such a fine evening! What's wrong?"

"Dafydd—the Lady Regan is to go home and I have said I will go with her and I did not *think*!"

"Hush you." He put gentle fingers to her lips. "It's not for all ears, that news."

"You knew?" She stared at him.

"Leofric has just told me." He gave her a secretive grin. "And no one is to know it yet, but he and Lady Regan have reached an—understanding."

Edwina realized her mouth was open and shut it. Then, "What do you mean, no one is to know it?" she snorted. "Dewi, the whole of Staneleigh knows how they spent the afternoon! But Dafydd, if I go…"

"My lord plans to ride to visit the lady. Frequently. I might ride with him."

A host of possibilities blossomed in Edwina's mind, not all of them concerned with Dafydd, though to be fair most of them were.

Many of the same possibilities came to Lucca's head when Regan broached the subject. It would be a good thing for 'Dwina, her mother thought. Firstly, it might well-come to her Da's notice how much she was seeing of the Welsh lad and he would not be in the least happy about that, being under the Lady Regan's eye and at a distance from this steading, could not do aught but good for the girl. Also, while a steward's daughter may make a good match, a lady's bower-maid may make a better and who knows but there might be more than one likely lad in those parts? And if the girl's mind was set and the harper's likewise, why then a short separation would do them no harm and would even make them appreciate each other the more.

"I can see nothing against it, my lady," she said firmly. "And may I say how pleased we all are? That you have decided to go home, I mean," she added quickly, lest Regan should think gossip had already married her to Leofric. It had, but as Lucca herself had so often said, counting the eggs before the pullets had started to lay only invited disappointment.

"Yes," Regan said calmly. "Seeing how much like home this hall is, I was too stricken by—how does Dafydd put it? *Hiraeth*?—to go to the Abbey as yet. I may wait until the spring to make my decision. And you need not fear for Edwina. I shall look to her as if she were my sister."

"God bless you, Lady." Lucca hugged her. "I hope she repays your kindness."

"She is a dear girl and a credit to you. We shall leave tomorrow, Lucca, if you could help her with her things?"

* * * * *

Any speculation the steading might have over Regan's swift departure was set aside when it became known that Leofric would ride with her. Dafydd, though, hung back. Despite their requests that he accompany them, he had refused. He'd already made his farewells to Edwina, he said. To ride now and have to make them over again at Ashford would only prolong the pain of parting. He'd tried to make a joke of it and failed.

So now the convoy and its armed escort moved out of the gates and down the hill and it seemed as if all of Staneleigh and the outlying cotts had come to cheer them on their way—as if it was a marriage-party in truth.

The celebrations lasted until Lucca ceased waving her farewells and turned back to the hall. Then she barked a series of instructions and the bustle started. The guest-bowers were to be made ready for whoever might next arrive. The thane's own room would be aired while he was safely out of the way. The hall, as well, she said, looked as if Danes and Welsh together had marauded through it and would also be set to rights.

Dafydd got under her feet until she clouted him about the ears and ordered him from her sight. "You should have ridden out with them," she told him, "instead of biding here like some lovesick wittol, plaguing the wits from me with your sighs! Go after her!"

He gazed earnestly at her, eyes wide and dark with doubt. "But they'll be long—" he began and collected another buffet.

"Go!" Lucca snapped. "How fast do you think they'll be traveling, fool?"

"You're right," he said, brightening visibly. "It isn't too late, is it? What with the litter and the bad roads—"

"Then get on your way," and she gave him a shove toward the stables. "Just don't break your neck chasing after."

It was all the impetus Dafydd required and exactly what he had been playing her for.

* * * * *

With ribald jokes at his expense ringing in his bruised ears, Dafydd sent his mare out of the gate at a fast trot. The going was treacherous and did not improve once he reached the road and turned south. The tracks left by Regan's people was clear to be seen in the mud-churned snow and he kept Arianrhod to the ruts of the litter.

The wind had heaped great drifts in some places, scoured the wet earth bare in others, but among the trees of the Intake it lay thick and deep. Dafydd took frequent glances up at the sky. It was leaden gray and low with clouds and there was an almost damp smell to the wind that spoke of more snow to come by nightfall. The brief respite would soon be over, both the Lady Hilde and Regan had left Staneleigh at a good time, though he wished bitterly that one of them had stayed.

The road dipped into a hollow, flooded now by both the rising river and a widened stream that flowed out of the trees. Dafydd kicked the reluctant horse into the water and reined left, splashing hock-deep into the wood.

The footing was dangerous with rocks and potholes and hidden tangles of fallen branches. But no one could track them here. The mare lurched and slipped and struggled on, ears flattened and eyes wild while he encouraged her with hand and voice. Once past a certain brake of holly, he could leave the water and travel more or less direct to his destination.

Chapter Sixteen

The ground was rising in a series of wide natural terraces climbing toward the crest of the tree-cloaked hill. Thick undergrowth, rocks and snow did not make the going any easier or safer than the stream-path and by the time Dafydd reached the twisted beech, he was cursing himself for a fool. He also had the itch between his shoulder blades that warned of eyes watching. Far too late to turn back now. He gave the high, whistling call of the falcon, again where hazel grew among an outcrop of massive boulders and heard the answer come shrill on the chill air.

The mare picked up her stride, ears pricked forward. She knew where they were going now. Then their destination was before them, a shape like the up-turned keel of a longboat scarce to be made out under dead bracken and briars and snow.

Iorweth had discovered and chosen this place to be their base—had used it years ago when one Gryfydd ap Rees had ridden with the war band. And only the force of their leader's will, coupled with the fear and respect he had from his men, held them to acceptance of it. For such places were hung about with ancient songs and legends and wise men stayed well clear of them lest at the very least, their souls might be snared when the *Tylwyth Teg* rode out…

Iorweth himself feared neither God nor Devil nor any man. For him, this long, low mound with its lintels of weathered stone set in at the northern end was the ideal badgers' holt. They could lie here in all seasons, right in the heart of the stolen lands, and strike at will. Inside, the small cells off the passageway gave ample storage space for provisions, while the large chamber at the end of it made ideal, if cramped, living quarters for some ten men. Furthermore, in the unlikely event of the *Saes* hunting them through the woods, the fear of barrow-wights would ensure they kept well away from the place. It certainly would not occur to them that the living dwelt within. Not that anyone would be hunting Welsh in this weather, of course.

His unconscious pressure on the reins had brought them to a halt on the edge of the clearing. Dafydd liked the mound no more than the rest of the men. Each time he approached it, unease tightened his belly and made the flesh creep along his spine. If he were a cat, he acknowledged ruefully, every hair would be on end from whiskers to tail-tip.

"Dewi." The voice had him reaching for his knife even as he recognized it. Iorweth stepped out of tree-shadows and caught the mare's bit-ring. "You're unlooked for, if overdue paying us a visit. How goes it, *bach*?"

"Not so well," he said, swinging down from the saddle with a grimace. He made another when Arianrhod's head snaked round and her strong yellow teeth took a hefty bite of fabric at his hip. "Poor beast," he smiled, fetching out a honey-cake kept for her in his belt-pouch. "She knows well who to blame for taking her away from her warm byre. But I tell you, Iorweth, what with the floods and the snow and more *Saes* swords than I've seen in a while, it's been difficult to get away."

"They are gathering?" the man frowned. His face, starkly handsome under the shock of white hair, might have been carved from weathered ivory and his deep-set eyes were coal-dark and unreadable. A warrior's face, pared down to the fine bone-structure, commanding and proud. A hero's face out of legend—Arthur come again, Gryfydd ap Rees had maintained, Bedwyr the Hundred-Handed. Dafydd saw no reason to doubt his father's word.

"No, not for any purpose," he said. "Merely households combining. I sent two to you before Yule. Did they reach this far?" *Duw*, but it was good to hear again the singing lilt of his own tongue.

"Oh aye." Iorweth's smile was grim. "There's a fierce wolf, that Coll. But come you within—there's a fire and drink to warm you and this beauty will be glad to reach shelter."

"I can't stay long," Dafydd said and felt those black eyes fasten on him, cold and considering. "The task is not yet done," he went on under their pressure. "Not until the households lessen."

"That sounds as if it needs some untangling, Dewi," Iorweth said mildly. "Bran," raising his voice only a little, "take the mare and see to her care."

It took a while for Dafydd's eyes to become adjusted to the darkness of the chamber. The only light came begrudgingly from a fire in the center and a feeble spill that managed to reach in from outside. It was cold and the place stank with unwashed bodies and stale food. Well, Dafydd told himself, niceties were not for a war band living off the land within the enemy's borders.

Half a dozen men lounged in the dimness. Some slept, some repaired weapon- or pony-harness. Those who were awake greeted Dafydd by name, including Coll. He would have asked after Medwin, but Iorweth was wanting explanations and he was not one to be kept waiting.

"Ashford steading has two households within," he reported. "Its own and the company the Lady Regan brought with her. She was supposed to have gone to the Abbey at Leominster, which would have lessened the sword-count enough to give us the victory, but she changed her mind and has returned home. Staneleigh had three times its usual count, for the Lady Hilde was staying and she always travels with half an army—Coll will know that," he added with a wry smile. "She's left this last day or so, but Leofric is gathering his men for his liege duty to the Earl of Wessex."

"Coll told us that might be so," Iorweth said. "But a surprise attack in the night has given us the victory before and over twice our number."

"True, but not against men already on their guard," Dafydd said. "The killing of his stock has made him wary." It was not always wise to criticize Iorweth, but he said it anyway. "Since Leofric was to have been a target, the cullings should have been from another's fields, not his, as it always has been our way in the past. Unless there are others preying on the *Saes*? No? Then I counsel he be left untouched until the next year, when he will no longer be looking for us."

"No!" Coll barked, pushing between them. "He has to pay!"

"And so he will," Iorweth said coolly, "sooner or later. Dafydd speaks sense. On the other hand, these *Saes* are swift to grow complacent in their strength and with him inside to distract the wall-guards and open the gates for us… Perhaps our fine thane won't have a steading to come back to when he's done his stint with Godwin of Wessex. I'll think on it. Break your fast, Dewi-*bach*, then be on your way."

"Here," said Coll, pushing a horn-beaker of muddy ale at him. "I don't know how you can stomach it, living under their roof, smiling-polite at them every day."

"He is my Falcon," Iorweth smiled, one arm draped across Dafydd's shoulders. "And he flies where I will it. Be thankful I sent him to Staneleigh, or you would not have found us."

"How is Medwin?" Dafydd asked before Coll could answer. There was something unsettling about the man's eyes, a kind of hunger that had nothing to do with food or the lack of it.

"Dead," Coll said shortly. "He did not last the week. At least he died a free man."

"I'm sorry he did not live longer," Dafydd said quietly. It was on the tip of his tongue to say that Medwin would have been free before long in any case, man-price saved and paid in accordance with the law, but common sense told him that would be plain daft. Coll would be at his throat the moment the words were spoken and most like, the rest of the band with him.

"The thane killed him," Coll was saying, "sure as if he put a spear in his gut. Him and that Geadas, may their souls rot in hell. They'll pay, Dafydd. Blood-price, they claim for a man—weregild. I'll claim such a price there won't be enough blood in all their bodies, not if they died ten times over—"

Dafydd could not bite back the words this time. "And if you'd let Medwin bide just a few weeks longer," he snapped, "Anna's healing would have given him the strength to enjoy his freedom for a good few years to come and there'd be one less death to mourn! A healing owed him, Coll! A *Saes* to sicken him, a *Saes* to cure. That's justice, man, by anyone's laws, theirs and ours!"

"What do they know of justice!" the man shouted. "Stealers of land, lives and freedom—justice is a blade in the night, a fire in the thatch, until they are all driven out or slain!"

Suddenly Dafydd felt sick. "Aye," he said heavily. "When Owain shall come again."

"That's my Dewi," Iorweth purred in his ear. "Go you back to the thane and when the time is right—give him to me."

Dafydd nodded and turned away, needing to be outside in the clean air and the light. Iorweth went with him and did not speak until Dafydd was mounted and about to rein away. Then he leaned forward a little and held his gaze with eyes as black and soulless as polished jet, eyes that could surely read the thoughts in a man's head. "Dewi-*bach*," he murmured. "Don't get too comfortable in yonder hall." It was a warning, stark and unmistakable as a drawn weapon.

* * * * *

The difference between Regan's last journey and this one could not have been greater. She looked back on that other Regan as if she were a stranger, some poor creature bespelled by circumstance so that she had neither courage nor common sense and knew that she would never take that road again, come what may. Very little was certain in this world, least of all life itself, yet she had an utter certainty that the man riding beside the litter was her true life-mate, that she loved him and would always love him and that he loved her in the same degree. A mighty revelation to have come upon her so quickly—in the space of a day or so. Or had it been growing between them all their lives?

Regan studied his profile, finer than those young gods on the old coins, his hair a pale gold, wind-tangled about his shoulders. He was a handsome man by any standards. Her man. Warmth grew in her stomach and, as if he had sensed her gaze, his head turned. Their eyes met with an almost physical jolt and without volition Regan leaned toward him, one hand raised as if she would catch him to her. Leofric leaned from the saddle and his gloved fingers closed over hers.

"Are you weary of the litter already?" he smiled.

"Yes," she said. "I don't know why I let Lucca arrange it thus—I'd sooner be riding."

"Easy done," he chuckled and nudged Rufus closer to the litter. "Ride up-by me, Trout, only don't make him throw us off into the nearest midden." It was an old quarrel, that and made her smile.

"It wasn't me who made Patch buck," she objected. "Gyfu poked him with a stick." But she used the strong grip on her hand to step from the litter to sit astride behind the saddle, arms locked fast about Leofric's waist. It was colder out here, but she did not care. Horse-warmth and man-warmth were comfort enough.

"You can still change your mind," he said quietly.

"What about?" she frowned. "Marrying you?"

"No. Never that. About going back to your steading. Say the word and we'll turn back. You need never leave Staneleigh."

"I know." Regan closed her eyes and leaned her head on his shoulder. His hair blew in silk strands across her cheek, reminding her of the afternoon spent in his bed and her arms tightened around him. "Which is why I can go away for a short time. There are things to arrange, my folk need to be told by me that I do not go to the Abbey. And why. Oh my dear, I wish you could have seen 'Dwina's face when I asked her to come with me and she thought I meant to Leominster. You'd think I was Grendel come out of the fog to eat her!" She felt his laughter as well as heard it and hugged him closer.

Following the roads, the fourteen miles or so to Regan's holding of Ashford took hours, slowed as they were by the state of the going. Then the litter stuck fast in axle-deep mud and it took strong shoulders to the wheels and horses roped to aid the team to free it. The bower-maids were taken up behind the riders—Edwina with sparkling-eyed delight, Morwenna with trepidation—but the day was more than half-done and there were three miles yet to go.

"When the weather eases," Leofric said, "I'll be able to cut across-country and more than halve this trek—" He broke off as a shrill whistle cut through the air. At the same time Swein barked an order and they were surrounded by drawn blades. "A rider behind us, m'lady, Lord Leofric."

"Rest easy, man," Leofric smiled. "It's Dafydd," and Edwina gave a crow of pleasure, pushing her hood back and craning round to see him through the crowd of armed men.

Sweating and mired to her belly, the gray mare slithered through the fresh-churned mud toward them and Regan began to laugh quietly. "Poor beast," she murmured. "I'll wager she'll make Dafydd sorry for this as soon as she gets the chance. Look at her, cross as a goose. But 'Dwina will be rejoicing, she took it hard that he would not ride with us."

"He had a good reason," Leofric grinned. "So good, I'm surprised he's here."

"So she told me and that was wise of him. A shame he did not remain so wise."

"Wisdom is a cold bed-fellow. Are you certain you won't turn back to Staneleigh?"

"Quite certain, Edmundson," Regan said primly. "I hope he has not done too much harm to his standing with Godwine."

"I doubt if it's altered at all," Leofric said. "It'll take more than a few hours for that one to change his mind about a Welsh wolf tupping his precious ewe-lamb. Well-met, Dewi. What brings you riding this road?"

"Escape, my lord." The harper gave him a jaunty salute and a grin, but his eyes were on Edwina. "Lucca is set on turning hall and bower inside out. All those of us who could found business elsewhere than the steading. Besides, she said I was under her feet."

"Escape or driven out?" Leofric snorted. "Embroider that into a saga, song-smith!"

"Driven?" he said with a laughing twist to his mouth. "Indeed not. Routed, more like. She'd scatter the Wild Hunt itself with but a broom in her hands. Now there's your saga!" He heeled the mare close to Edwina and held out his hand. "Ride with me, *cariad*?" and she changed mounts with swift agility.

The rest of the journey passed in a kind of a dream for Regan. Eyes closed, she was distantly aware of the muted sounds as Dafydd and Edwina whispered together, the harper occasionally singing quietly. But the center of her immediate world was the man in her arms and the steady beat of his heart close to hers. It seemed to her that the two rhythms matched and became one, like a never-ending song.

*****

Celebrations broke out anew when Regan entered the gates of her steading. All her people were there to greet her, from the youngest babe to the oldest crone and all were rejoicing as if at a wedding feast. So pleased were they that she had returned to them, that there was no chance for her and Leofric to make private farewells. Which was as well, she decided. She might be tempted to bid him stay the night and travel back in the morning and if he did stay then it would be in her bed and come the morning she would be even less inclined to let him ride away.

One thing Regan did insist upon was that Dafydd should have a fresh horse. His mare had been ridden hard and was limb-weary—but not so tired she could not manage a swift bite as he dismounted, nor a kick when she was led away to a warm byre.

A cup of mulled ale and a bowl of steaming broth were all Leofric would stay for, or else there would not be enough daylight for their return journey, even though they would be traveling faster without the litter to slow them down.

Regan and Edwina watched them from the top of the gatehouse, waving until a turn in the track took the two men out of their sight. It would be a lonely, empty time for all of them, a testing time, perhaps.

That night, the snow fell again, freezing as it did so, and winter closed its fist on the land once more.

Chapter Seventeen

༶

Lonely nights passed slowly. So too did dull days made worse by a smother of freezing fog. January was done and Candlemass came, but there was no relenting from the weather for another week. Then the skies finally cleared, the thaw set in and the lengthening of the days could clearly be seen.

The weeks had crept by like years, though it was time enough for Regan to be certain she was not pregnant. On the one hand, her best gown would fit her well on her wedding day, on the other was a feeling of hollow disappointment. Which was foolish, she told herself sternly. There were years ahead of her for bearing children.

"He'll come soon," Edwina said on that first bright day—and it was a moot point as to which "he" she referred.

"Your man might," Regan sighed, "but mine won't. There'll be too much to do, what with the thaw-floods and more rain certain to come, the spoilt grazing. If the water-level doesn't drop quickly, he'll have problems with the spring plowing."

"He'll find a way to be here," Edwina predicted.

Regan shook her head. "A thane has responsibilities to his people, 'Dwina. He can't up and ride off when the whim takes him. Unlike a certain Welsh bard."

Edwina blushed and chuckled, but the arrival of Sigurd Reeve saved her from trying to find a response. The man came to the hall-door, making a great deal of noise about scraping the mud from his boots before coming farther in.

"How goes it, Sigurd?" Regan smiled. "Are the ewes stolen or strayed?"

"Three stolen, m'lady, though the reivers were the four-footed kind. Pulled down by wolves, they were, a bitch and a pair of half-grown cubs by the sign. The other five we found up by Deerleap, lame and hungry but nothing past curing."

"So then. All our beasts are accounted for."

"Aye, mistress. No sign of reivers on our lands."

"Thank God," she sighed. "I've no wish to try our defenses against an attack, should they be desperate enough to try it."

"Never think it, lady!" The reeve made a swift warding sign against the ill luck. "Besides, Swein has the steading as secure as the Royal Hall."

"Yes, I know," Regan said. "But even so... I wonder if Staneleigh has been as fortunate. They had lost animals to thieves before Yule."

"We'll know soon enough." Sigurd's moustaches lifted in an avuncular grin. "Leofric Thane'll be here as soon as may be now the weather's eased."

"Well, I don't look to see him yet awhile," she said briskly and turned the conversation to such mundane things as grazing and field-drainage.

* * * * *

Regan might not expect her thane to come riding in, but Edwina certainly waited on her bard's arrival with all the stoic patience of a cat on a hot griddle. Anna's charm had undoubtedly brought the bard to notice her and become her lover, Edwina was almost certain it would now draw him to her side and she frequently touched the small sachet and whispered his name, just to remind it. Besides, she missed her family as well and her friends. He would be a welcome link.

Not that Edwina neglected her duties, but when left to her own devices, once she had visited Dafydd's mare with the odd store-apple or honey-cake, she would find business that took her to the vicinity of the gatehouse and the watch-walk above it.

So it was that she was the first to see the rider come into view round the curve of the track, but her cry of delight became a spit of disappointment. The distant figure was a round-shouldered slouch on a stocky bay pony and love was not blind enough to let her mistake the man for Dafydd. More animals came into view, four mules walking in line, all laden with panniers. A second man brought up the rear.

Edwina's mood swung back to delight. "It's Hod!" she called down to Morwenna. "Tell my lady Hod Packman is here!"

* * * * *

Hod was more than just a footloose pedlar. He, along with his son and four mules, traversed most of Mercia, Wessex and a good part of the lands across the border into the bargain. He had a phenomenal memory for names and faces and the minutiae of everyday life and spoke the Saxon dialects and the Welsh with equal fluency. As well as trading goods, for the many folk of both races who did not travel farther than the next village, he was the main source of news on events in the wider world.

His visits were infrequent, rarely more than three times in a year, but it was unusual for him to arrive at Ashford so early in the season. The cause of it was grim telling, villages and steadings already suffering from previous bad winters and poor crops the previous summer, struck now by floods or murrain or both. Once thriving farmers were having to sell themselves and their families into thralldom merely to survive the coming year — and some not even able to do that because the thanes and landholders were in little better shape. Many, thinking to find a haven from starvation in the towns, had joined the beggars on the streets. And always there were wolfsheads ready to prey on the weak and undefended — especially of late down south toward Hereford — while the Welsh were only waiting on the spring to send war bands across the border.

"Will it never end?" Regan muttered, refilling Hod's ale-mug.

"Oh aye, it'll end, right enough." Hod spat into the hearth-fire. "But if God Himself knows when, I'll be surprised. Believe me, m'lady, there are *Cymru* like yourself and these folk of yours who'd as soon live in peace with their neighbors. But there are too many young hotheads who believe the old songs, too many old war hounds who won't let go of past grudges, too many who can gain power by keeping the wounds red-raw. And that's as true of the Saxon as it is of the Welsh. Until they're all muzzled and silenced, there'll be no end to it."

But Edwina was not interested in politics. "What of Staneleigh?" she burst out. "We've had no word from there for weeks!"

"That's no wonder," the pedlar said wryly. "I heard along the way that north of here the river's risen higher than it ever has before and there are great stretches of road swept away. Ashford is as far north as I can travel, but don't fret yourself, lass. I'll wager there'll be a way across country for them as knows the lay of the land, so I'll be leaving the Staneleigh goods here. I'll come back and collect the trade from them later on. In the meantime, I've got your gold and silk threads in my special pack and if you've brought your fine stitchings, we can bargain while you tell me how you come to be at Ashford, Edwina Godwinesdaughter. Married, are you? Who's your man?"

"Not yet and he's Dafydd Gryfyddson, bard and guesting with Leofric Thane," she said with a lift of her head. Tears stung her eyes but she would not let them fall.

"Now there's a name I've heard before," Hod smiled, "what say you, Bran?"

His son nodded. "Been up and down the river last year, by all accounts," the young man said. "Sings like one of God's own archangels, it's said, and knows the *Oran Mawr*, the Great Music."

"That's a fine thing," Hod sighed. "Haven't heard a true bard since I married Gemma over by Llaniltudd."

"What about when you married Olwen at Caernarfon?" Bran put in.

"No." Hod shook his head. "That one wasn't what I'd call a true bard. Well, if he's set on you, lass, then he'll still be guesting with the thane and I'll hear him and judge for myself when I visit later in the spring. I'll have Sifrith's dyed leather by then. Has he raised his man-price yet?" And so on, exchanging news and trade-goods in equal measure and if there was a certain cynical twist to the pedlar's mouth, Edwina did not notice it.

"Her bard'll be long gone," he said quietly to Regan when the girl had gone to fetch her finished pieces of orphrey-work and silk embroideries. "A fine-looking lad, they say, most like he'll have a wife in every town. "

"Much like a pedlar, you mean?" Regan smiled sweetly. "Ah but he left his horse here and he'd no more go off without that mare than he'd take an axe to his harp."

"Well, if you say so, m'lady. But what's this I hear about you and Leominster Abbey?"

"Old news, Hod. I may yet change my mind."

"So I should hope. I've watched you grow up from so high and you are not suited to the cloister. What's more, I'll wager the Abbess will be glad if you stay in the world."

"Why?" she demanded. "She is my cousin and invited me."

"To stay a while maybe, but take the vows? Oh no. You'd have the reins from her hands and be managing the Abbey within a month and that would be as welcome as a baresark at a wedding feast."

"You," she said, laughing, "go too far!" But she knew that he spoke the truth.

* * * * *

The pedlar stayed until the next day, giving all of Regan's people who wished it a chance to barter and catch up on his news, but he would not stay longer. Hod was heading east into the heart of Mercia, where weather and murrain had hit less hard.

Edwina took up her vigil again, though now she watched from the west wall more than the gatehouse until rain beat up from the southwest and drove her into the hall.

Come the dawn and it was still raining, a solid downpour that looked set to last the day out. The afternoon was drear and bleak, as if winter had come again to blight them all. Morwenna was hatching a cold and her red-eyed misery did nothing to lift the gloom in Regan's bower.

"He isn't going to come," Edwina said abruptly, throwing down her spinning. "Not even for Arianrhod. He's changed his mind and gone after that Hilde to be bard to the King—"

"'Dwina, do you want your ears boxed?" Regan snapped. "How could he possibly ride over from Staneleigh in this weather?"

"I expect he's got a cold," Morwenna suggested, coughing into her nose-rag. Regan gave her an acid glare.

"Yes!" Edwina pounced on the idea. "He could be sick— the ague—"

"'Dwina, one more word and you'll be sorry!" Regan interrupted. "I swear you have more imagination than he does! And as for you, Morwenna, if you can't think of anything helpful to say, then for pity's sake, be silent!" She would have said more, but a thrall-boy pushed open the door and stuck his head into the room.

"Riders coming, m'lady," he announced. "A dozen and Swein says it looks like the lord Ranulf."

"Oh no!" Regan surged to her feet, her spindle following Edwina's to the rushes. "That's all I need!"

"He said you wouldn't be pleased," the boy grinned. "Swein says if you wish it, Mistress, he can hold the gates against him, tell him we've got the pox in here, or the sweating-ague."

"Oh that's temptation," she sighed. "No, I can't deny guest-right this weather, not even to fitzRobert. Have the fires lit in the guest-bower and see there's byre-space for the horses. You two, make sure there's hot food and mulled ale and keep out of Ranulf's way as best you can."

"But—why?" Edwina protested. "He might have news of Staneleigh."

"I very much doubt it," Regan snorted.

"Dafydd doesn't like him," Morwenna said. "Calls him fitzHog. Or was it fitzSwine?"

"That's enough, the pair of you. Just do as you're told."

She knew the curtness was unjustified, but the arrival of Ranulf fitzRobert came very close to being the last straw.

"M'lady?" the boy was back, this time, round-eyed and pale. "Swein says there's been trouble. They're coming with a couple of men riding double and bodies slung over saddles."

* * * * *

Regan gave the man formal greeting in the hall, her bearing ice-cold and distant.

"You are an unlikely and unlooked-for guest," she said coldly, avoiding the embrace he would give her.

"And unwelcome?" he asked wryly.

"Yes. Do not presume on custom or my patience, fitzRobert. What brings you here?"

"To see how you fare. The winter hit hard in the Marches, I was worried about you. Justifiably so — we found murder done not ten miles from here — a Welsh raid, I'd say."

"As you see, we fared well. Better than most and the Welsh have not raided here in several years. Now your mind is set at rest, you have no reason to stay."

"An Ice-Maiden still?" Ranulf drawled. "I had heard otherwise."

"What does that mean?"

"That you'd changed your mind about the Abbey and were thinking of marrying."

"Hedgerow gossip!" Regan said scornfully. "And you believed it?"

"When it came from the sainted Lady Hilde and concerned her son, yes. Leofric has enough land, what with the hideage he holds from Wessex as well as owns outright. Why should we let Lady Spider spin Ashford into the web?"

"Ashford is mine!" Regan snapped. "And will remain so! I do not need you to protect it or me!"

"So you are not taking vows then?" His smile was very close to being a smirk and Regan's hand itched to slap it from his mouth.

"What vows I take," she said, "are none of your concern, fitzRobert, nor will they ever be. If you have come all this way on the strength of a viper-tongued harridan's daydreams, you have had a wasted journey. Gifford was by far the finest man in your family and I will not marry one of his lesser kin. You I would not marry if my life depended on it. Do I make myself clear?"

"Don't speak in haste, sweeting," he purred. "Is it a proper courtship you're wanting? You'll have it. All the gifts and honey-words—"

"Which you can take and throw on the midden! Guest-right you have for this night, fitzRobert. It ends with the sunrise. You will leave here and not come back."

Mournfully, he shook his head. "I cannot, in all conscience. You were hand-fasted to my beloved brother, so for his sake I must do all I can to protect you. It was the Welsh. Killing done for killings' sake. They slaughtered even the pack-mules and destroyed the goods. Wolfsheads wouldn't have done that, now would they? I do have some experience in these matters, girl."

"Five mules and a pony?"

"Yes. You knew the men?"

"Hod Packman and his son. They left here yesterday."

"As I said, they didn't get ten miles. The mud was too loose for us to make much of the tracks, but there must have been up to a dozen and most of them mounted."

"We have been alert for trouble since before Yule," Regan said, outwardly unmoved. "We know there are wolfsheads in the area."

"You aren't listening to me, woman. There is a *war band* close by, perhaps even over-wintering this side of the border—God knows the woods are dense enough to shelter an army! You will need me and my household!"

For a moment Regan hesitated. But only for a moment. "No," she said, shaking her head. "Any help we may need will be found close enough at hand. You will ride on come the morning."

"From Staneleigh? By the time Leofric gets here you'll be raped and dead and your steading in flames around you!"

"You insult my household," Regan flared, "and you insult me! Do you think Ashford is so easily taken by the Welsh — or by you? No, fitzRobert!"

"By Christ's Blood," he said thickly, "I don't know whether to shake you or kiss you —"

"Try either, my lord," Swein said from the doorway, "and I'll take your head for it. Have you heard, my lady? It was Hod and Bran."

"Yes, may God rest them. We'll see them fittingly buried, as for our guests, they will be leaving at dawn, Swein. See that they are provisioned and safely on their way."

The man nodded and bowed, a feral smile under his moustaches for Ranulf.

* * * * *

The meal that evening was a tense affair and Hod's death was only a part of the cause. With Regan at her coolest and Swein watching with the expectant watchfulness of a mastiff set to guard, Ranulf momentarily turned his attention to the silver-gilt beauty of the new bower-maid.

But Edwina had taken a dislike to him and was doing her utmost to match her mistress for winter-chill toward the unwanted guest. Morwenna soon pleaded a growing ague and left the meal for the refuge of her bed.

"A coward's retreat!" Edwina hissed with a mock scowl as the girl hurried past her. If Ranulf heard, he gave no sign but leaned a little closer to Regan.

"So tell me," he said quietly, "do you intend to marry this Marcher-thane? There are those who might oppose it and not just for love of you."

"And what does that mean?" she snapped.

"He has lands aplenty and his first marriage brought him more. A grief and a pity the lass died so soon after. Opportune, some might say. Now he seeks more land and looks to gain it through—"

"I will not have my friends slandered by you, fitzRobert," Regan cut in scornfully, giving Edwina a hard kick under the table before she could burst out with the words that were clearing boiling on her tongue.

"I meant no insult," he protested. "I merely warn you what might be said. Regan, I love you, I only seek to protect you—"

But Regan interrupted again. "Horse-shit," she snorted. "You care nothing for me, only Ashford. Well, I don't fault a man for being land-hungry, but I might have respected you more if you'd made no pretense of wanting me as well. Not that it would have made any difference. I've already told you. Ashford is mine and will remain so to my deathbed."

"As you wish." He gave her what he obviously thought was a fond and indulgent smile. "It can be written into our marriage contract. I still would have you to wife, Regan."

"No."

His smile faltered a little and became strained. "Then if I can't persuade you, another shall do so," he said with a certain smugness. "I have standing with powerful lords, Godwin of Wessex will be glad to grant me the boon of your hand—"

"Enough!" Regan came to her feet. "First of all, fitzRobert, no man can compel me to marry against my will, be he Earl, King or Pope. Secondly, I look to Mercia as did my father before me and Wessex has no command over me whatsoever. Edwina, to me. Good night, fitzRobert. My steward will attend your leaving at dawn."

"You're a stubborn woman, Regan." Ranulf still had his smile, though his teeth were clenched behind it. "But I am an equally stubborn man. By the year's end, you'll be my wife and glad of it."

The look she gave him would have scorched metal and it said all that she did not bother to voice as she swept past him to the door.

Chapter Eighteen

❧

"The boy's getting as devious as a Welshman," Godwine grumbled, feeling hard-done-by. "'Just going riding'. Hah! In this weather? And will he tell me where? Don't we all know?"

"Then why ask?" Lucca snapped, manhandling a wodge of dough into her kneading trough. "You know how he is—too much curiosity from folk who should know better and he's off like a green colt."

"And that bard—going to collect his filly, he says and he rides east, while our Cynricing turns west to the river-road and never a word about riding to Ashford—"

"Just because he doesn't spill his guts to you the way he did when he was green-sick over Hawiss?" she jeered. "Have done, man. You're not his confessor."

"Aye but—"

"He's learning to keep his own counsel and it's about time." She punched again at the dough in the trough. "That open face of his showed his thoughts clear as fish in a chalk stream, which was never a good thing to my mind." She cast her eyes heavenwards. "God send the King many strong sons and many years to reign! For should he die untimely and without heirs, we all know who's poised to step into his shoes." And she thumped the dough again.

"Hush you, woman!" Godwine huffed. "To speak so of our thane's liege-lord—you don't know what you're talking about!"

"Do I not then?" Lucca demanded. "Well, God preserve us from ambitious men, I say. Now get from under my feet, or I'll not get this batch of loaves in the oven today and my lord must needs go begging his bread. Out with you, man! Haven't you got anything better to do than gossip like an alewife?"

And Godwine, who had, stomped from the kitchen into the hall to take his temper out on the dogs, who would only look up at him mournfully when he grumbled at them for a circumstance that was none of their choosing.

*****

The hazel coppice was greening fast, the catkins blowing free on the willows and here and there in the shelter of bramble or hawthorn, the first shy flowers of spring were beginning to show their heads. Dafydd, who had heard variations on country weather-lore throughout his life, knew well that winter could yet grip sore. But spring was flourishing in his heart and he chose to ignore that chance. He sang as he rode and Olwen of the White Track was not lovelier than his Edwina, though the song had been a pretty compliment to the Lady Regan.

Dafydd chuckled and his horse's dark ears flickered back to listen. Certainly Leofric had it easier than Culhwch, though — no terrible Ysbaddaden Chief of Giants to conquer before he could win his lady's hand, only the lady herself and their joint contrariness to thwart the Lady Hilde's plans. Leofric would probably have preferred a straight fight with Ysbaddaden, it being something he understood. Still, unless Hilde interfered again, there would be a marriage before many months. Hilde or Iorweth. He shook off the chill that last name put down his spine and lost himself in the music again.

Culhwch and Olwen — Culhwch who was cousin to Artos, Arthur the High King, and Olwen who no longer had hair of dragon-fire but of moonlit gold. For in the tale it was Artos who aided Culhwch in his quest and without the king's help, Olwen would never have been won. As was Olwen, now also was Artos changed and fixed in his imagination, tall and gilt-haired, with an atheling's circlet on his brow, because Dafydd knew that without Leofric's friendship he would never be able to claim Edwina.

Friendship—more than that, surely? He had never known what it was to be part of a family, unless it be the *Meibion Owain*. These last weeks he had learned how unlike a family the Sons were.

He drew rein as he topped the rise and emerged from the wooded track, looking for the plume of smoke from Geadas' roof hazing in the still air. The man himself would still be in his fields, but Aeditha would have food at the hearth—some of Wyn's oatcakes, with sheep-cheese to crumble on and a cup of ale to sustain him—and he would chat with her, Wyn watching silent but sometimes smiling. It was a prize, to win a smile from her.

He wondered briefly if the thane would be there before him and decided it was unlikely. Leofric would not skimp the check on the river banks. But they had plenty of time. After all, if they reached Ashford after dark, there would be no question about them returning until the next day.

Ysbaddaden thundered his challenge to his daughter's suitor, naming the conditions that must be fulfilled before her marriage, the thirteen treasures of the world, each more impossible than the last. But Dafydd did not finish the catalogue. He could see the neat cluster of farm buildings now. There was smoke, right enough, but darker than it should be, thicker. He stood up in his stirrups, as if a few extra inches could give him clearer sight. There was movement down there. A tight huddle of cattle in the yard and a figure sprawled nearby.

Too far to see who it was who lay there, but whoever it was needed help. Dafydd kicked the bay gelding into a gallop down the track.

The fall of the land cost him his vantage point, so that he could see nothing further until he reached the level and rounded the byre into the yard and there his mount squealed and fought for his head, wild-eyed and sweating at the smell of death. It was Geadas who lay there and he was past any mortal help. The thin blond hair was all that was left to identify him—his face was gone—and he lay in a wide pool of blood, his guts spilling in a grotesque tangle from his ripped belly.

Annwyl Crist! Dafydd choked on his own nausea, swallowing the bile that rose in his throat at the sickly rich stench of blood. The smoke eddied, thicker now and carrying with it the ominous crackle of fire. Even as he dragged his horse's head round he heard a scream and another sharply cut off. Aeditha, he thought desperately. She and Wyn, trapped—

The shadows came alive and there were men facing him, ragged and filthy, weapons gleaming in their hands. One stepped out and drew his bow, the arrow unwaveringly trained on Dafydd. He knew in that instant that he was going to die, because at this little distance the man could not miss. It was as if he suddenly had the preternaturally sharp vision of his namesake, because he could see the very tendons in the archer's wrist tighten, the man's teeth bared in a grin…"

"Hold!" a voice cried, in his own tongue. "It's the Falcon!"

The arrowhead dropped.

"Dewi!" Maelgwas stepped out. "Dressed so fine, we didn't know you!"

Dafydd reined the gelding in hard. "What—" He cut himself off, realizing that questions were superfluous. What they did here was murder and why—they were the Sons of Owain. As was he.

"Didn't expect to see us, eh, *bach*?" That was from Coll, a long knife in his hand, bloody to the elbow. "Neither did *he*!" A gesture at the corpse, a harsh chuckle. There was, if anything, even less flesh on Coll than when Dafydd had last seen him, but now there was a difference. He carried himself with a kind of arrogance. His gaze raked over the gelding and he snorted and tried to back as the man came forward, carrying the rank smell of blood with him. "Doing well out of the *Saes* bastard, are you? Don't blame you—bleed him white while you can!" Hatred rasped in his voice and it came to Dafydd that Coll would serve Leofric exactly as Geadas had been served, whether or no it was deserved, simply because Leofric was Saxon. Like Aeditha and Wyn.

Under the mask of drying blood, Coll's face was exultant. "Come with us! We'll strip all we want from this place, fire the rest—they'll know we're a force to be reckoned with then! And we'll drive the cursed *Saes* from all the lands of the *Cymru* and the good old times will come back, like the prophecy! Owain will come again!"

The others took that last up in a baying cry—a cry insanely echoed, for a moment, by another and one of the raiders gave a yell and pointed back up the slope. Dafydd swung round to see the horseman coming straight down across the fields toward them, the big red horse at full gallop, clods flying from the hooves like spray.

Leofric, Dafydd thought, having forgotten him completely in the stress of the moment. And, *there are too many of them. He won't stand a chance.*

The raiders forgot Dafydd. Here was new danger, but one man and easily dealt with. Dafydd wrenched the bay round on his heels, drawing the scraemasax from his belt. "No!" he yelled, amazed that his voice worked. "No, he's mine!" And kicked his horse into a standing gallop before any of them could think to stop him. He distinctly heard Coll's howl behind him but didn't stay for it. They would be on his heels, hungry for their prey. He had to head the rider off somehow.

He saw Leofric's recognition and the surprise that checked Rufus' pace. And he saw the arrow strike and the instant of disbelief, blond head flung back as he fought for control and failed and almost fell, slumping over the stallion's neck. By that time Dafydd was close enough to snatch Rufus' rein, seeking to turn him, but the raiders were upon him as well, hands clawing to drag them both from the saddle.

Desperate, Dafydd slashed down at them, not knowing or caring what damage he did so long as they let him be. Coll's face, twisted with fury, was at the bay's shoulder. "Are you gone daft, man? Kill the bastard and have done!"

"The Fyrd, damn you! The Fyrd ride with him!" Dafydd snarled and, when Coll reached for the bridle, slashed down with the blade. Coll howled and fell back and Dafydd kicked his mount again, crowding him close to Rufus, forcing the big horse away and back up the slope.

They were both clear targets for the archer's deadly skill, but no arrows came and when Dafydd risked a glance over his shoulder he could see the men running not in pursuit but for the shelter of the woodland. God be thanked, they'd believed him—or if not, had at least withdrawn to regroup, which should give him enough time. Beside him, Leofric seemed to be more or less balanced in the saddle, even if it was only that he was too good a rider to fall off. Dafydd thanked God for that too, knowing that if the man fell, he'd never have the strength to haul him back up. He drove the horses on with heel and voice until the thicket of trees ahead embraced and absorbed them and he was forced to a slower pace.

Dafydd spared a moment to look at the injured man. The arrow had taken him below the right shoulder and the slender bodkin point stood out a full handspun from his back, with a wet blackberry stain spreading all around it. Leofric's eyes were closed, skin grayish and chill to the touch, but Dafydd found the pulse in his throat—rapid and not too strong, but steady.

At any moment, the raiders could be hunting on their trail. He had to get Leofric to safety and as fast as possible, before Coll and the others realized that the Fyrd were not out and the man did not look likely to stay in the saddle unaided. Well, Rufus would have to carry two. Dafydd dismounted, knotted the gelding's reins with the stallion's and swung up onto Rufus' back behind the saddle. He reached around to gather up the reins, urging both animals to a walk then, as the way cleared, into a canter. He nearly lost his hold on Leofric as the first lurch jarred the heavy body, but he tightened his grip and leaned farther forward. "Go on, Rufus! Run, damn you!"

* * * * *

Torchlight flaring in the dusk, the familiar bulk of the steading, gates standing open and shouts as men came running—Dafydd saw it in a blur of exhaustion. He ached in every fiber from the strain of keeping the two of them in the saddle. His arms were numb, he did not even know if it was a living man he was bringing home or a dead one. He could no longer feel the reassurance of a heartbeat against his wrist.

Whichever it might be, he had done all he could. The thought brought little comfort, either then, or as people crowded round. Hands reached to take Leofric's body, Godwine and Padraig Smith between them carrying him inside. Awkwardly, Dafydd slid from Rufus' broad back and almost sat down in the mud because his legs wouldn't hold him. Then someone was there, steadying him and he managed a somewhat garbled account of what had happened. It must have made some sense, for Sifrith clapped him once on the shoulder and then swung away. Dafydd limped slowly into the hall. Everything seemed to be in chaos, people milling around like a disturbed hive of bees. He sat down on a bench near the hearth and wished vainly for his head to stop spinning.

I did all I could. It was a barren thought. What if it had not been enough? Lucca came hurrying past and he caught at her. "Is he—?"

She gave him a fleeting smile. "He'll do well enough. Hard to kill, the Cynricings."

The hall and Sifrith and Lucca all blurred out of focus into a glittering gray fog and there was a discordant thin high singing in his ears... Something hard jarred at his teeth and he swallowed the mouthful of liquid automatically and nearly choked on it. Padraig Smith's water-of-life. The second mouthful was better and he opened his eyes to see Lucca bending over him, holding the cup and looking concerned. "Be easy, lad. You did well. Are you hurt?"

That hadn't occurred to him. "I...don't think so," he said uncertainly. "No. No, I'm not. Lucca, are you sure he—"

"He's survived worse," she said tartly. "But come see for yourself. Sifrith, I want you to go for Anna, we will need her." Dafydd didn't hear any more. He pushed himself to his feet and made his way to the stairs.

The big room was brightly lit and Leofric lay in the center of it, stretched out like a corpse on the big bed. They had stripped mantle, tunic and sark from him—the bloodied heap lay discarded on the floor—and now Lucca supported head and shoulders as Godwine examined the arrow still protruding obscenely from his breast, high on the right side. It moved a little with each faint breath. Dafydd hesitated, sure that when they noticed him he would be sent away, but when Godwine glanced up and saw him, he merely gave a nod and turned back to the bed.

"Now?" Godwine said.

"Best so," Lucca answered and lifted Leofric into her arms. The arrow had punched clear through him, Dafydd saw, the head showing dark against his bloody skin.

Lucca held Leofric securely. Godwine took hold of the arrow and snapped the shaft just below the fletching. Then he took hold of the point and drew the broken thing slowly and steadily through the wound and out. The split flesh gaped for an instant before blood filled and flooded out, bright as holly berries. So much blood. How much could a man lose and still live?

Lucca did not seem alarmed. She merely pressed a pad over the wound and when that was soaked, wadded another over the first. Then Anna came in and without a word took Leofric's wrist. "My box, Godwine," she said calmly. "Dafydd, there is a flask of barley-spirit by there—tip it into the bowl and bring it here." The opened box revealed a roll of soft leather, which unfolded on an array of sharp-honed instruments, delicate-bladed knives, tongs, wicked little probes. Before she used one, she dipped it in the fiery spirit. Dafydd could remember Leofric telling him that the stuff was good for cleansing wounds. She was shortly as bloody-handed as a butcher, but she worked fast and expertly as any barber surgeon. Throughout the surgery, Leofric made neither sound nor movement and Anna paused once or twice to watch the shallow rise and fall of his ribs. "I don't think the lung is touched," she said at last. "Was the arrow tainted?"

"Can't tell." That was a growl from Godwine. "Best put the iron to him in any case."

"I don't need you to tell me my business," she said shortly, watching as he laid the cautery in the heart of the coals, swabbing the injury with spirit as she waited. "What happened, Dafydd? Tell us how it was."

Dafydd, who had seen the cautery used in Llan Illtud's Infirmary when a wound was dirty or turned sick, was grateful for the distraction. He managed some kind of account, desperately edited, from the moment he had seen the body in the yard to the heart-stopping gallop of their escape, with reasonable coherence, only faltering to a stop when Godwine took up the glowing iron. Anna said, "Help me hold him, Dafydd." He did as she instructed, holding his breath as the wounds in chest and back were seared, smoking like burned meat. Even unconscious as he was, some message of pain must have registered with Leofric, for he made a sound like a groan and tried to twist away from the torment. But when it was over, he lay like the dead again, closed eyes sunken and bluish. Lucca crooned at him, calling him her cubling, telling him it was all done with…

There was a cold sweat broken out on Dafydd's brow and a slow churning in his belly. The reek of scorched flesh caught in his throat. He hoped he was not going to shame himself by fainting or vomiting and managed not to do either, though it was a close thing. He stayed in the room, trying to make himself unobtrusive when he could not actively be of help, and people came and went. Young Astrid, with more of her mother's herbs, Padraig to report that the raided farm was now deserted. He had doubled the watch on the walls, as well as sending warning out to tenants and neighbors. Sifrith came with food that Dafydd could scarcely touch. Even though his belly grumbled, his throat closed up at the first bite.

I did all I could. He watched as they passed and re-passed and the window was gray with dawn although he had not noticed the night creeping past. He dozed where he sat.

In the dark before dawn, Dafydd rose up and left the hall, leaving the doors wide to the cool spring night. The silence was absolute—no sound of man nor beast nor waking bird. Even his careful footfalls were silent, ghost-silent. He reached the gates and lifted the great bar, set it down out of the way, then put his hands on the metal-girt oak and pushed. The massive iron hinges made no outcry at his act, the great gates swung open at a finger's touch and in slow seconds the steading stood defenseless. Iorweth slipped past him, wolf-lean, with a smile and a wink for Gryfydd's son—Maelgwas was close on his heels with a silent laugh and a long knife bright in his hands. Others followed, dark shades that passed him without a word and all of them Cymru, *their faces familiar.*

He did not look after them. He gazed out instead over the spring-scented night-dark world toward the village and the church, seeing in his mind's eye the hearth fires and the well-known faces. When he turned back it was to a garth filled with fire and death, though he had heard no sound, nor heard any now. He might have been struck deaf. He wished to God he was blind. But there was no escaping the sights. Leofric was standing before the door of his hall, arms outstretched. It took Dafydd a moment to see that he was pinned there by blades through hands and naked breast. Like the White Christ on the Rood, or Odin on the Tree. Instead of dancing wolves, his hounds lay gutted at his feet. Godwine was near him, head half-severed from his neck—Sifrith, with no face but a mass of flesh and splintered bone. Edwina, legs asprawl, skirts up around her waist, a knife standing between her breasts. Lucca and Anna — all stretched out at the threshold of the burning hall…And Regan, lying in her own blood, with his father standing above her, blood-masked features laughing with a terrible delight. "**Mab fy!** *My son, my beloved son! What, boy, do you weep? Is it a good* **Cymru** *heart that beats in your breast then, or that of a Saes changeling?" And Maelgwas' long knife drove in and twisted and his father reached in and drew out something that pulsed in his two hands.* "**Saes…**" *The hissing whisper ran through the watchers like a soughing wind.* "Ssssaaeeesssss…"

He woke with a jolt, shuddering and sick. Daylight had begun to gray the square of window. Nothing else in the room had changed.

No. One thing had and that was his own heart. He had not stopped to consider, before, why he had saved Leofric's life, why he had lied and lied again to the *Meibion Owain*. He had known, of course he had, of the bloody carnage the Sons left behind them. But until that day at Geadas' yard, he had never seen it. The noble tales, the songs that stirred the blood — they were thin webs to hide the ugly reality. The Sons of Owain might believe, as he had once believed, that they fought for freedom and all those other fine-sounding ideals. But they lived on blood and took a vile joy in killing — *Saes* or no, innocent or no, they did not stop to ask. He had given them his loyalty because he had known no better and had not wanted to know.

The knowledge had been forced on him.

What was he to the butchering Sons of Owain? The Falcon, the son of their martyred Eagle, Gryfydd. Who had recognized the gift his son had and set him to be schooled in the art — not for the art's sake, but because it could be used as a tool, as yet another weapon again the hated *Saes*.

They had called him from the quiet life of the cloister and told him his father was murdered. And they had begun to use him as Gryfydd had planned.

He had known no better. It was only when he had ridden into Lady Regan's steading and fallen in love with her that he had even thought to question his role. Then had come Yule and Edwina. And he slowly realized that his loyalties lay in an altogether different direction.

For the first time in his young life, he had made his own choice.

Time ceased to exist. Day passed into night again and Dafydd broke his fast there at the bedside only because Lucca stood over him and watched him eat. He was not aware that he slept at all, between dreaming and waking there is a seamless state of being where fantasy and reality are one. All his will was concentrated into one wish and he prayed to every saint he could think of for the life of the thane.

He had sat vigils before of one kind and another during his time at Llan Illtud. Those times were set in his memory, finding an echo now. The long nights broken by the measured piety of the canonical hours, but seemingly endless none the less. Did Leofric know he was there? Did the soul remember anything of what passed while it was out of the body, hovering between life and death? Leofric had called him friend. Perhaps, then, a friend's hand could draw him back from the abyss.

Palm down on the brindled wolf skin, the right hand lay slack and unmoving. Dafydd locked his own fingers around it, feeling the dry fever-heat of the skin, the racing pulse. "Leofric." He whispered the name into the stillness. "My lord, come home."

Chapter Nineteen

The void of unknowing thinned only gradually, like a November fog, sometimes thickening into oblivion but always thinning again, each time a little more. With returning awareness of self came pain, which was interesting after the nothingness of the void and he spent awhile examining it. He was no longer a discorporate entity, he was alive and therefore possessed of a body that felt and needed and hurt. There were voices, though he could not hear them clearly, and hands that touched and lifted and did things that brought temporary ease. He wanted to reach out to them, to make himself understood, but the effort was like trying to lift Padraig's anvil single-handed and quite beyond him. It was easier to let himself drift back, let go of the pain that anchored him, go free…

…except that there was something he knew he should remember. It kept hovering just out of reach, as hard to pick up as the moonlight on water. He forced his mind back… Riding out to meet Dafydd at Aeditha's, then to go on to Ashford and Regan… All the things he loved most about his land, the richness of it, the beauty and the peace… Smoke from the thatch, thick and roiling, the first glimmer of flame. He urged Rufus into a canter. The sight of men in the yard and the lone rider and the lurch of shock that drove his heels into Rufus' ribs, a wordless yell of rage on his lips. Rufus' stride lengthening into a full gallop, the rider breaking through the men around him, crouched low over the black-maned neck, riding as if the Wild Hunt were on his heels…

Nothing more.

If they had killed Dafydd, then by Christ's Blood, by Odin on the Tree, he would take such a blood-price as would be talked of from Chester to Bristol!

He tried to move and the flash of pain that ignited in his shoulder made him groan. A hand touched his brow, a voice said, "Anna, he's waking." And he got his eyes open enough to see dark blue eyes shadowed by sleeplessness and worry and the dawning of a grin in the unshaven and haggard young face. "*Duw*, man, don't make a habit of this, will you? I think I've aged ten years!"

And Anna, calm and competent and very much in command, taking charge and shepherding Dafydd out of the way while she and Lucca tended their patient, made sure he was kept too busy to think straight until, their ministrations done, they settled him back on his pillows and let him rest. Lucca had made him drink something that had a thick aftertaste and he knew he'd probably be asleep before long, in spite of the fire consuming his right shoulder. He could feel the heaviness creeping through his limbs already. But first—

"Dafydd," he said, stretching out his left hand and the young man came to kneel beside the bed. "You saved my life."

"What else could I do?" Dafydd said simply. "I am your man. And hers."

"God knows, you have proven that." It cost him, but he managed to close both hands around the long fingers and in that instant, something unspoken was understood. Softly, the singer's voice giving the words depth and meaning, Dafydd recited the ancient Oath.

"I Dafydd ap Gryfydd hereby swear I am your liegeman of life and limb and earthly worship and faith and truth I shall bear unto you in all things. And if I break faith with you, may the green earth gape and swallow me, may the gray seas roll over and overwhelm me, may heaven's stars fall on me and crush me out of life forever. God and the Holy Mother witness this, amen."

Leofric tightened his grip. "You are my liegeman, Dafydd ap Gryfydd. Your honor is as dear as my own and your life, and I shall bestow upon you all that is your due, in peace and in war—" He caught Godwine's astonished eye as his steward walked in. "Godwine, bring me the small chest. Quickly, man! Dafydd, in exchange for your oath, it is for me to gift you with a ring. God knows I should give you a bushel of rings for what you have done." Godwine had brought an ash-wood casket banded with silver and now held it open for Leofric's searching. "None of these will fit you. But—yes!" It was finer than the plain gold or silver circles usually given and smaller, and the wide band was chased with a pattern of ivy leaves. Godwine gave a grunt of surprise.

"But that was hers—" he began. Leofric smiled, putting it into Dafydd's palm and closing his hand around it.

"She would not grudge it," he said and leaned back on the supporting pillows. "Dafydd—Regan has to be told."

"I'll see to it," Dafydd promised. "Rest you now."

"And *that's* good advice," Godwine said gruffly, taking the casket away. Lucca caught Dafydd on his way out, holding him by the shoulders to look at him straight.

"Before you go anywhere, you'll eat something and clean yourself up," she advised, with a small catch under the stern commands. Then she pulled him into a hug, kissing him firmly on both cheeks. "God bless you, lad, for all you've done. Go down—Gyfu will feed you and there's water hot for washing."

It was full day by the time he was done and the garth was full of people. The tenants from the more remote cotts had brought their goods and families to the safety of their lord's walls until the alarm was over. On his way to the stables, Dafydd saw Sifrith looking grim. His face lightened at the sight of Dafydd and suddenly Dafydd decided to ride companioned.

"Dewi!" Sifrith pushed through to his side. "I heard my lord was hurt, maybe dying—"

"So runs rumor," Dafydd gave him a grin. "I'm for Lady Regan's hall, to quell it. He'll live, man—Lucca has her mind set on it. Will you ride with me?"

Padraig, consulted, outfitted them both with scale-sewn leather byrnies, short swords and a bow and arrows for each. "And ride cross-country," he advised as a thrall brought the horses.

"I know the best ways," Sifrith said confidently. "Better than Lord Leofric, most probably. His Da wasn't the best poacher in these parts!" He clambered into the saddle and Dafydd let him lead the way out and down the track.

The route Sifrith chose was not an easy one, cutting through thickets and over rough country, but with strong horses under them they made good time. By noon they were outside the gates of Regan's steading. She had taken the warning well—the walls fairly bristled with men—and Dafydd saw that her tenants, like Leofric's, had taken shelter within. He dismounted outside the hall, giving his reins to Sifrith, and Swein took him straight to his lady's bower. She was sitting at the window as he entered and stood up, letting spindle and fleece fall to the floor, holding out her hands.

"I knew it would be you who would come to tell me," Regan said, voice tense and brittle. "Tell me quickly, in God's name. Is my man dead?"

"No, my lady." Dafydd bowed over her hands. She knew the route they have to take to come to Ashford. It was a short step to believing Leofric and Dafydd both slain. "He was wounded, but he recovers. His first thought was of you." God would forgive him that small exaggeration.

"Mary Mother…" She gave a shaken sigh. "I have been thinking him gone these past two days." And she tried for a laugh at her own folly and nearly got it right. Her fingers tightened on Dafydd's. "Tell me what happened," she commanded and he obeyed, making it as brief as he could. "So Aeditha and Wyn are both dead." She signed herself. "God rest them both and Geadas too. And Leofric—how bad is the wound? Is he fevered? What does Anna—oh this is foolish, how can you give me the answers I need? I shall ride back with you, Dafydd. Unless Leofric has changed amazingly, Lucca will need help with him and Gyfu is too soft."

"My lady!" The idea appalled him. "There are but two of us, Sifrith and myself. You should ride escorted even if there were not wolfsheads on the land!"

"And do you tell me that two of my lord's sworn men are not escort enough?" she countered. "You did not get that ring from me, my dear."

Much to his own surprise, Dafydd found himself blushing.

"Lady, even were I not sworn to my lord, still I would give my life for yours. But I would rather not have to."

"Go you and eat, Dafydd ap Gryfydd. My mind is made up."

At a loss for any immediate argument, he went down to the hall-hearth, sliding onto a bench beside Sifrith, who was eating his way through a dish of roasted fowl under Morwenna's doting eye. "Good fare here," Sifrith said around a drumstick. "Dig in, Dewi. What does she say?"

"That she rides back with us," Dafydd told him. Morwenna squawked in shock. Sifrith put down the drumstick.

"She can't."

"Do you go tell her so," Dafydd said. "She'll not listen to me. Says your sister is too soft to deal with Leofric and Lucca will need help."

"Well, that's true enough. Even when we were bairns it was always Gyfu who gave in to him and Regan who blacked his eye." Sifrith leaned conspiratorially closer. "I'll tell you something, *bach*, that I'd not say back home—Hawiss was a beauty, lovely as a May morning, but she had less brain than one of Anna's geese. They were besotted with each other, or he'd have seen it himself. Once he started to see straight, she'd have driven him mad with her maunderings. His Mam wanted the marriage—Hawiss had lands in Kent—and once he laid eyes on the maid… But I shouldn't be saying this."

"Leofric has his memory of her. He should be allowed to keep it."

"Ah, but if it stops him seeing another lass, one better fit to be his bride?" Sifrith's voice had dropped to a whisper. "You know how he's been these last weeks? Barely a mention of her!"

"You want to keep your ideas behind your teeth, man," Dafydd advised. Never having seen Hawiss, he was unable to comment on Sifrith's frank slander of her and as for her memory blinding Leofric to others, he knew his lord's mind. Equally, he could keep his own counsel. "But if you know how we might dissuade the Lady Regan—"

He did not have time to finish. She came into hall, dressed like a man for hard riding, her hair bound up under a cap and a sword at her hip. She flashed him a smile, grimly amused by his astonishment. "Oh I know how to use this, Gryfyddson. And Sifrith can tell you of my skill with a bow, which has not lessened since last he saw it. Edwina is packing what little I need until Swein can bring her to join me. You have until the horses are readied to let her see for herself that you have a whole skin yet."

Edwina, folding linen for her mistress' saddlebags, came into his arms wordlessly and clung for a minute. "No one said, no one knew," she whispered. "If you had been killed, I would have died as well…"

He kissed her gently. "I came as soon as I could, *annwylyn*."

"They said you saved his life." Her hands in his, she felt the alien touch of the ring and her eyes widened at the sight of it. "Ah, Dewi, you are sworn!"

He gave a shy grin. "It seemed as well to make it clear. He is my lord. And he'll most like skin me for bringing the Lady Regan to him, but she has her mind set, I think."

"She has. I'm to pack what else she may need and follow in a while, to be her bower-maid while she stays with him."

"Then one good thing comes out of this coil, my honey-sweet." To Dafydd's eyes she was as fair as one of those Folk who live under the hills and in the wild places where men seldom go. The shining hair was less severely dressed, escaping the single fat braid in soft feathery curls against her brow and neck and her skin looked as delicate as the windflowers that had yet to bloom in the woods. The gown was true Mary-blue, embroidered in green, and she was wearing a cobweb-fine silken veil he had not seen before.

The bower was similar to Lady Hilde's solar, pleasantly furnished and large enough to house all the maids, should the need arise. Now, however, it held only one person beside themselves, a crone of some incredible age who sat close to the fire basket, teaseling wool.

"That's Brytha," Edwina said softly. "She was nurse to my lady's mother. She says she was born the year the blessed Saint Edward was martyred and Ethelred became king, but I don't believe anyone can be that old, do you? Maybe her mind wanders. She hasn't any teeth." That was evident from the smile the ancient creature bestowed on them. "And she can't hear very well and she can hardly see at all, poor old lady. Are you comfortable, Brytha dear?" she added, pitching her voice just below a shout. Brytha nodded. Dafydd could see that her eyes, in their wrinkled, nearly lashless sockets, had a pearly film over them. But if Brytha's claim were true, those eyes had seen the rise and fall of four kings and the accession of a fifth, for all they saw very little now.

"I must go," Dafydd said. "Lady Regan is waiting. I ask a small boon of you—care for Arianrhod for me and bring her home with you? I shall count the hours until you come to me, until we are together again, *cariad*."

"Of course I will. Ah, Dewi. Promise you will always speak such pretty things to me? Even when I am old and bent and gray as Brytha?"

"For sure I hope you are not as deaf then," he said, "for sweet words are not so sweet if shouted rather than whispered in your ear."

Edwina giggled, seeing it clearly — she and Dafydd, aged and grayed, sitting bellowing love-words at each other. *God grant it!*

The Lady Regan was waiting impatiently in the garth, mounted on a big-boned bay mare. The woman seemed to pass some of her mood to her mount, for the animal put back its ears and snaked its head as if to bite, had not Regan's hands been firm on the reins. "Morrigan and I are eager to be off," she said shortly. "Make your farewells, Dafydd."

"They are made, Lady." He mounted, fell in beside Sifrith and followed the lady on her Morrigan out of the gate.

If anything, they made better time on the journey back, for Regan did not seem inclined to check her pace for anything. It was three lathered and muddied horses that finally cantered up the track to the steading as the sky grew golden with evening and the open-mouthed amazement that greeted them was exactly what Dafydd had expected.

"Take me to my lord," Regan said, swinging her leg across her mount's withers and tossing the reins to a gawping thrall. Dafydd, on her heels, was waylaid by Lucca.

"What are you thinking of?" she hissed. "With the hills full of wolfsheads, to bring the lady from the safety of her own hall!"

"She would have it so," he said shortly. "It is not my place to nay-say her. She feared him dead, Lucca."

Her expression softened. "Aye, poor lady…"

"How is it with him?" Dafydd thought it might be politic to leave them alone and he could use the time to get some of the mud off.

"He's fevered, but that's to be expected. Anna brought one of her brews, but we could not make him drink it."

"Lady Regan will see to that, I think." Dafydd decided that if he had to be nursed by anyone, he would choose Anna or Lucca. The Lady was altogether too forceful, whatever Sifrith thought.

Sifrith, Dafydd discovered when he went to look, was telling the tale of their ride to a group of admiring tenants and thralls as if it were an epic adventure. "But I am not a bard, to make a song of it," he was saying as he saw Dafydd. "Dewi, do you sit and say how it was!"

It was a good way to pass the hour and good company, and he forgot the time until one of the hall-folk came to look for him. Leofric wanted speech with him.

"I'm to answer for bringing the Lady here, for sure," he told his audience, getting up. Sifrith clapped his shoulder.

"We share the blame, Dewi. Do you tell him so."

Dafydd had no intention of doing that, even if Leofric was inclined to listen. He could hear, as he climbed the stair, the mayhem above. He pushed open the door just in time to duck as a bowl hurtled past his head, splattering its contents over the wall. Leofric, looking wild as a bating hawk, was sitting up in bed, Regan standing just out of his reach, still in her riding clothes, equally angry. But with a new target, Leofric changed his aim.

"I told you to take her word, man, not bring her here!"

"The word I took, my lord. Bringing the lady here was not my will but hers."

"Are you Welsh ruled by your women then that you cannot say them nay? Before God, I would send her back, if it were not to risk even more!"

"And if I would go," Regan cut in, "which I would not. Dafydd, my lord mislikes the sops he was to eat. Do you go and ask Lucca to put honey in the next bowl? If he will act like a babe, then I will treat him like one."

"Sops!" Leofric spat. "Tell Lucca I want meat! Damn it, I lost blood, it makes sense to replace it!"

"Sops," Regan said again. "In milk. Later, in wine." She left the bedside and stalked to Dafydd. "And tell Lucca we need more of Anna's fever drink. I'll get that down his throat if I have to kneel on his chest to do it!"

She did not need to resort to such drastic measures. The rage born of the rising fever did not last—the man was too weak to sustain it. By nightfall, he had sunk into a stupor and his nurses were able to do what they would with him, though as Lucca said, that was not a good sign. "He's a bad patient, that one, as soon as he's on the mend. This meekness is unnatural in him."

Regan, who had allowed Dafydd to take her place in vigil, was taking the opportunity to change her clothes and refresh herself, sponging arms and throat with warm water at the kitchen hearth.

"I know it. Well, we have the wound poulticed to draw out the infection and Anna's fever drink will help him sleep. I fear I was short with you, Lucca, when I arrived. I'm sorry."

"Bless you, Lady! You were worried. We knew that. Will you eat a little?"

"Some bread and cheese and then I'll go back. Dafydd will be asleep where he sits."

Chapter Twenty

It was three days before the fever broke in a drenching sweat and during that time none of those who had the care of the injured man got much unbroken sleep. The days and nights seemed one long round of changing dressings and herbal packs and vile-tasting draughts that Leofric sometimes took and sometimes peevishly refused. Toward the end, Dafydd, made stupid by tiredness, discovered himself talking his mother-tongue as he tried to coax his baulky patient to drink. Oddly enough, it worked. He went thankfully to change his clothes and to sleep, but did not manage to do more than pull off his boots before dropping onto his pallet and into oblivion too deep for dreams.

No one came to rouse him. He woke by himself, with something of a start, to discover the morning well advanced and Lucca and Regan sitting at the kitchen hearth, talking drowsily. He greeted them, took a bowl of porridge and laced it with honey and cream and took it up the stairs with him.

Anna smiled at him from her seat beside the fire-basket. "I told them to let you have your sleep out. You feel the better for it?"

"Much," Dafydd agreed. "How does he?"

"He'll mend." Anna sounded pleased with herself. "The fever broke before dawn and he's sleeping now. And the wound isn't seeping so much. Of course," she went on thoughtfully, "he'll be even worse to tend now, as soon as he starts getting his strength back. It'll be a struggle making him keep to his bed. He'll be itching to be up and about."

She knew her lord all too well. If he could not leave his bed to be about his business, it seemed, then all the business must come to him and there was a steady stream of visitors through the hall, up the stairs and into his chamber. At least, until Regan put a stop to it.

"Will you fret yourself into another fever?" she demanded tartly. "Godwine has your affairs well in hand. There has been no sign of wolfsheads since the raid. Yes, Father Egnoth has given your folk Christian burial. Is there aught else itching at you, Leofric, or will you rest awhile now? And eat your broth? If Dafydd plays for you?"

"You're worse than Lucca and my mother put together," he grumbled, but let her settle him back on his pillows and feed him broth. Dafydd was well aware that love-songs were not appropriate and battle-songs unwise. He drew instead on the wealth of Celtic myth and legend, the tales of Old Time that Owen ap Ifor had taught him in his years at the Abbey, unashamedly pagan though they were. Some of them were stories Leofric knew, but there were many he did not and the newness of them often kept him quiet and listening instead of restless and fretting to be up, so Regan was pleased with them both.

"But you cannot sit and harp for us and take no time for yourself," she said rightly, after a morning had passed with the retelling of the Pigs of Pryderi. "It is a spring day and the air is mild. Go you and breathe some of it!"

Which meant, Dafydd reasoned, that she wanted Leofric to herself. Or at least, she wanted his attention, which she knew was elsewhere when Dafydd was story-weaving. He set his harp to one side, gave her a bow. "As my lady pleases."

"And ask Anna if she will attend me, if you will," she added. Leofric grimaced, because that meant more herb drinks or—worse—a probing at the wound. Dafydd shot him a look of sympathy and went to do her bidding.

It was spring and mild as she had said, but the air was misted with a thin fine rain and did not inspire him with any wish to go out in it. He leaned on the door post of the hall and one of the hound bitches came pushing her nose at his hip. No doubt she missed being with her lord, he thought. The hounds had been forbidden the chamber. His fingers found the pleasure-place where the soft fur of the ear met the harsher pelt of the skull and she leaned her weight against his leg with a sigh. Rain or no, he might go out riding and take the hounds for a run with him. Now that Sifrith had gone back to his cott—as had most of the people gone back to their own places, the threat of wolfsheads passed—then he might enjoy a visit.

Over at the gate someone gave a shout of welcome and Dafydd glanced up to see a rider in the garth. The bitch pushed herself up, ears pricking. The horse was a big brute, solid with bone and the man on its back was a massive hulk in a dull brown cloak as mired as the horse, shabby and worn ragged at the hem. But this was no beggar, Dafydd realized, seeing the lines of breeding under the muddy winter-coat of the heavy stallion. No beggar would be riding a horse as good as this one, unless he'd stolen it.

The rider pushed back his hood, revealing a ruggedly battered face adorned with straggling beer-stained moustaches and framed by an untidy mane of graying fair hair. "Hey, boy," he boomed. "Is the thane to home?"

The note of authority in his voice made Dafydd stand straight. "He is within, master," he said. "Shall I take your horse?"

"So long as it's not across the Dyke." Teeth showed under the moustache, square and yellow as the horse's. "Who are you, cub? Guest, thrall or hostage?"

"I am Dafydd ap Gryfydd, bard and harper to this hall and the thane's sworn man." There was still a sweet thrill of pride in the saying of it.

"A bard, is it?" Interest sparked and the man swung down from his mount. "Then I'll guest in-hall, for I've a mind to hear a bit of harping. Godwine!" A bellow of greeting as the steward appeared.

"My lord!" Godwine stopped in his tracks. "And you come without warning! Leofric'll be that pleased to see you!" Then he glanced at Dafydd. "Did you tell my lord Wulfstan?"

"Tell me what?" The demand was a growl and even Godwine's size was dwarfed by the newcomer.

"There's no need for worry," the steward said ingratiatingly. "That is, the lad's well on the mend. Dewi, go tell him his uncle Wulfstan is here."

"On the mend from what?" followed him as he sprinted back into the hall and up the stairs, skidding around Lucca at the door.

"Your uncle has come," he announced breathlessly. "Wulfstan."

"Wulfstan!" Lucca screeched, voice horrified but eyes alight. Leofric struggled to sit upright.

"Wulfstan!"

"That is all we need," Regan sighed. "Unless perhaps we can arrange for a gaggle of geese and a pair of bullocks to join us. But I'll not stand by and see him chivvy you into another fever—" She had time for no more. The room seemed to shrink as Wulfstan strode in.

"So this is where you've laired up, boy! Great Odin, haven't you managed to grow hair on your face yet?" Beaming, he advanced on the bed with the clear intention of giving his nephew either a slap on the back that would probably knock him senseless in his present weakened state, or fold him in a bear hug that would fracture ribs. Lucca forestalled him, insinuating herself between them. "Lucca!" Wulfstan bawled, grabbing her into a hearty embrace. "My little partridge! As toothsome as ever too!" He kissed her smackingly on the mouth before letting her go, flushed as a maid and with her headrail awry. Wulfstan caught sight of Regan then and that young woman drew herself up and fixed him with a glare that would have felled a charging Dane, so he merely captured her hands and wuffled his moustaches over her knuckles. "Eh, lass, I always said you'd grow to be a beauty. Grown too fine to sit on an old man's knee and buss him a good one, are you?"

"If you know of an old man hereabouts, my lord Wulfstan," she raised her eyebrows at him, "we might try and see." And she kissed him decorously on the cheek. "You are well-come, indeed. But please don't tire Leofric out. He still has some fever."

"Aye and what's all this about, lad?" Wulfstan turned on his nephew. "I come to remind you of your service to the Earl and I find you lazying about in your bed!"

"It's nothing, Uncle," Leofric said quickly. "A scratch. By the end of the week—"

"We'll be laying out your corpse if you don't do as you're told!" Lucca snapped. "He took a Welsh arrow through the shoulder, my lord, just days ago." And she went on to give an abbreviated account of the attack and Dafydd's part in the rescue. When the tale was told in full, Wulfstan pounded Dafydd mightily on the back in approbation.

"By the Tree, boy! A true shoulder-to-shoulder man you are—and before you were sworn too! Leofric, nephew, you always had the gift to gather good men about you, I see you've not lost it. And Welsh, by Thor's Hammer! A race that would as soon stab you in the back as spit in your face—and no offense meant, boy—"

"None taken, my lord." Dafydd kept his face straight somehow. It was impossible to dislike this aging reprobate of a Saxon. Within the space of a few minutes he had reduced the ordered sickroom to chaos, confounded and charmed its guardians and brought vitality like a fresh breeze. Hilde, Dafydd decided, would not like this man. He kept no better state than a down-at-heel freeman, dressed in coarse unbleached linen and wool, though there were traces of old embroidery showing threads of gold and the belt slung under his belly boasted a clasp finer than anything Leofric owned. No, Hilde would not approve of her husband's brother.

"Good! Good! So you'll harp for me tonight! And none of the milksop-and-maid wailings that my sister's skald calls music, mind! What's-his-name—Sigurd—I'd think Hilde'd had him gelded for all the fire there is in his songs! Lucca, there's a brace of wild duck at my saddlebow, just crying out for your sharp sauce. That'll tempt your appetite, eh, nephew? Been fed naught but slops, I'll wager!" He gave a derisory snort.

Dafydd blinked at him. This frankly pagan old warhorse was *Hilde's* brother?

It was true though he came to realize that there was no love lost between brother and sister. They were complete opposites in all but one thing. Yet the appalling tactlessness that was so hard to accept in her was, in him, somehow redeemed by his attitude to people. Wulfstan did not regard them as pieces on a board to be moved and mated for one's convenience. If he spoke his mind, it was with a good heart. Maybe it was his blunt honesty that had placed him high in the councils of the Earl of Wessex, though he, like Leofric's father, was a Mercian born.

Saxon politicking went over Dafydd's head so he was not paying much attention to the discussion Wulfstan was beginning over the dish of wild duck and the savory mess of nettle-tops braised with onion and bacon that accompanied it. How Wulfstan managed to eat and talk in equal measure was a matter for wonder. After an initial interest, Leofric only picked at his share, so Dafydd found himself and Wulfstan finishing the dish. The man had shed his heavy tunic and one expansive gesture swung a gold ornament free at his throat, a rune-patterned pendant in hammer-shape.

"Not seen one of these, lad?" Wulfstan interpreted his curious gaze. "Hammer of Thor, this. My lucky-piece. Got it of old Cnut himself, when I was a weanling. Leofric cut his teeth on it, for all Hilde had him half-drowned for the White Christ. Didn't do him any harm."

"Mother would hardly agree with you, Uncle," Leofric said, with a shadow of a grin. "She thinks I'm altogether influenced by you and my lord of Wessex."

"Can hardly do better than that!" Wulfstan boomed. "But I can't see him being happy about you, nephew—you'll not be fit to do your liege-service this spring. Come autumn, though, he could be in more need of you. I'll tell him the way of it anyhow." He took a draught of ale, wiped a hand over his moustaches and bent an eye on Dafydd. "Well, boy? What are you going to sing for me?"

"With your leave, my lord," Dafydd settled his harp on his knee, "I will sing of the Three Hundred at Thermopylae."

"Never heard of it. Welsh, eh? Or in the Danelaw?"

"In Greece, Uncle," Leofric supplied.

"Oh. Foreign. You're not going to sing it in foreign, are you?"

"No, my lord. I will Saxon it." Dafydd exchanged a smile with Leofric. It was a song to appeal to the *Saes* battle-ethic, this—the valiant army who had died to a man defending the pass, the doomed warriors noble and undefeated in death—and by the end of it, the last harp-note falling soft from the spoken epitaph *"Tell them in Sparta…"*, unashamed tears were sodden in the long moustaches as the old war-horse wept like a child.

"By Odin's Eye, boy, that was good!" he choked out, snuffling. "Sing it again!"

Chapter Twenty-One

On the same day that Wulfstan left in the morning, Edwina and Morwenna, with their Lady's belongings and Arianrhod, arrived in the afternoon and Dafydd, lifting Edwina down from the seat of the cart, felt that spring had finally come.

"I wanted to come sooner," she said breathlessly, when his kiss let her, "but there was so much to be done and Swein would not hurry himself and—oh Dewi, I have missed you!"

"And I have missed you," he said loyally, though in truth he had been kept too busy to feel her absence. "My lady has all things well in hand here, as you will see."

For a little time, the greetings of the household had to be endured, as Lucca exclaimed over her new finery and quizzed her as to the ordering of the Lady Regan's household and generally enjoyed herself. There was the bower to see to then and the lady's instructions and it was evening before Edwina was free to seek out her lover, finding him in Leofric's company, seated near the window where the soft honey light of the spring evening touched the strings of his harp. Unwilling to disturb his music, she slipped into the room and sat on the footstool beside Regan's skirts, where she could watch and fill her heart with how he looked and moved and sounded, as if she had been empty a long time and needed to store all these things against a lean time to come. The shadowed hands were gentle on the strings, as caressing as when they touched her, and the look of tenderness on his face, beneath the curling cap of dark hair, was for no mortal lover. He was smiling, eyes half-lidded and unseeing and for all his awareness of his hearers he might have been alone. But alone and happy as she had never seen him before. She drew a deep careful breath and felt Regan's hand on her hair as the Lady spoke into the silence after the harp-song.

"Beautiful, Dafydd. But sad. Does the Wanderer ever find peace, think you?"

"I do not know, my lady. Owen told me that we of the harper-kind are footloose too and destined to wander in many lands, as indeed he did. But there is a reason, he said. We seek always the source of music."

Leofric stirred against the propping pillows. "Did he find it, your Owen? Is it for the finding of any man?"

"I cannot answer for him, Leofric. If we are fortunate, he said, fortunate beyond belief, then yes, we find it…" But his eyes met Edwina's and after a moment he bent his head again to the harp and began to play once more. But this was wordless. It did not need words. His music spoke more clearly and told of it all—the magics that lie at the heart of all things, the flame in the log of apple wood at the hearth, the white-briar-rose in the withered rose-hip, the music lying sleeping in the harp for a touch to waken. And love, sang the music. The love of brother for brother, of sworn man for his lord, but most of all, of man for maid. It was a braiding of light and shadow, as life is a braiding. A lovely insubstantial web that caught and held and lifted the heart so that when at last he stilled the singing strings the absence of it was almost pain.

"The source of music," Regan whispered. "Look no further, my dear. For sure you have found it and I thank you from my heart for sharing it with us."

"Music is barren if it is not shared, Lady." He always seemed to know the right things to say, the graceful turning of a compliment. Edwina supposed it came from being a bard. She was too full for words and must let her eyes speak for her, and she knew from Dafydd's smile that he read her message. He set his harp carefully aside. "But my lord Wulfstan's visit has wearied you both. If I have your leave?"

Leofric sighed. "You're too damned observant, *bach*. Yes, I'd best get some sleep, I suppose. No, Regan, I doubt I'll need any of Anna's brew, honeyed or no."

"Well, if Wulfstan has made you tired enough to sleep the night through, we have that to thank him for. Edwina, I'll settle my lord, if you will ask Lucca to come up. And then take time for yourself, child."

Edwina bobbed her curtsey to her and her lord and Dafydd followed her out of the door, taking her in his arms in the darkness of the narrow passage. "It was for you, my music," he said softly, holding her close. "It has been growing in me all this time you have been away. Oh 'Dwina, *brialla*…"

She knew his need and shared it. But with no privacy, there was nowhere in hall where they could safely be alone, even in his own place. Then she had it, though it was risky enough.

"My lady's bower," she said breathlessly. "She will stay with my lord for a while, will she not?"

"She does so nearly every night," he said. "I will wait for you there, my heart. Be swift."

* * * * *

He had kindled a light by the time Edwina had delivered her message, managing to give her mother the erroneous idea that she wanted to visit Anna before retiring to her lady's service. With luck, no one would think to look for her. And Dafydd, she already knew, was known for doing as he willed. Before the door was closed behind her, she was in his arms, giving kiss for hungry kiss. Tumbled on the fur-covered bed, too impatient for each other to do more than pull her skirts aside, they came together with the wordless need of wild creatures, prompted by the same instinct born of the rutting spring and Edwina had to stifle her cry against his shoulder as he stiffened, shuddered and reached his peak.

"Say you love me," he begged, breathless, still in the embrace of her body. "Say it, *cariad*."

"Do you doubt it, Dewi? I love you. *R'wy'n dy garu di.*" The Welsh sounded sweetly exotic. She could feel him softening within her and tightened her thighs to hold him, careless of the risk.

"*R'wy'n dy garu di…*" he murmured, rubbing his face against her hair, heavy on her now, wanting to rest there, to sleep. She did not want him to go from her arms—she had been too long without him. "*Am byth, cariad…*"

"Forever," she said, easing his head into the hollow of her shoulder. The aftermath of loving was like drowsy honey in her veins. She could feel the come and go of his breath on her throat and one hand lay slack on her breast, the long fingers curled to the curve of it. Half-dreaming she held him and at last he stirred and kissed her, disengaging himself.

"Tomorrow?" he demanded.

"Tomorrow," she promised, sitting up and straightening her skirts then smoothing the bedcover. It was just in time—the moment after he had snatched one final kiss and she had pushed him out of the door, she heard her lady's voice saying something in a light and slightly amused tone and then Regan was in the bower, still smiling.

"He has a ready tongue, that lad of yours," she said. "And a ready wit as well, which he is like to need if you two are not more careful." The smile did not fade, but there was concern in the fine eyes. "'Dwina, come here. And sit. Did you truly think we did not know where you would be and what you would be about?"

Edwina bit her lip, feeling a hot tide of blood in her cheeks. "My lady…"

"No apologies, child. I am not your mother, nor your confessor, to take you to task for dalliance. Just—be more careful? Your Da would not take this kindly. It isn't easy, I know only too well, with a place this small and eyes and ears everywhere, but do try." She paused and her voice softened. "You do love him, don't you, Welsh though he is?"

"Yes, lady. He could be a—a heathen Moor," this being the most outlandish thing she could think of, "and I'd still love him." She would have gone on, delighting in the freedom of talking about the beloved, but Regan held up a hand.

"And does he love you?"

"He tells me so, lady."

Regan sighed. "Far be it from me to warn you of the dangers that lurk in a handsome lad's honey speeches and fair-weather promises… For what it's worth, I think he does love you. Now show me what of mine you brought with you."

Advised by Morwenna and using her own good taste, Edwina had selected everything she thought her mistress would need and they had added a few things that might not be strictly needed but could be relied upon to please. All in all, Regan conceded that the girl had discharged her duties excellently.

"Tomorrow," she said, "I shall attend on my lord. If he is well enough, it will be his first day out of bed and trying his legs. It'll do him good to realize just how weak he still is."

From which Edwina surmised that Lord Leofric was living up to his reputation as a very awkward patient.

It was no more than truth. With the strengthening spring, all the business of the estate was accelerating and he felt that he should have charge of it. As it was, everything came to Godwine, who was kept occupied from cock-crow to sunset but found time to keep his lord informed. This, Leofric decided, was not good enough.

"Holy St. Martin!" he burst out, watching the women make his chair ready for him. "I swear you are a flock of hens with but one chick between you!"

"It's only to be sure that we get a little peace from your temper that you're being allowed this much," Regan told him shortly. "Dafydd, stand ready."

"And I'm perfectly capable of standing on my own feet—" Leofric began, starting to suit action to words and abruptly finding that his legs had less strength in them than an hour-old foal. Regan had stepped to his side, getting her shoulder under the thane's while Dafydd steadied him.

"You've been abed too long," he said tactfully. "A few steps, just to the chair. Later, a little farther."

"You're as bad as the rest of them," Leofric grumbled, but by the time he was lowered into the padded embrace of his chair, set where he could see out of the window and take the air, he was the color of curd, face glossed with a fine dew of sweat. He made little of it. "Right. Now send for Godwine."

"He is gone to the sheepfolds," Dafydd said. "Wat sent for him. They are taking the tally of the ewes not yet lambed. Wat thinks the old ram is past his best."

"Oh does he? And what does he think to do about it? Tup the ewes himself?"

The sour comment brought a vivid picture to Dafydd's mind and he grinned. "For sure he knows them all well enough," he said lightly and won a chuckle from Leofric, even if Regan was trying to look scandalized and almost succeeding. "I can ride down and give any instructions you think cannot wait," he offered. "And ask Godwine to attend on you as soon as he can."

Leofric gave a grunt. "So long as you tell him not to leave it too late. The women will have me back in my bed again, else and I will not discuss my flocks while on my back."

Over the next few days, it was discovered that there were a number of other activities that Leofric would not countenance while bedridden. The periods spent sitting in his chair grew longer and the women felt easy enough with his progress to leave him alone there for a short time. So it was that Dafydd walked in with a message from Padraig one afternoon to find Leofric not dozing in the chair as expected but standing by the window, left hand clamped on the edge of the shutter.

"My lord!"

"Don't stand there 'my lord'ing me," Leofric hissed. "Lend me your shoulder!" And he released his grip on the shutter to lean on Dafydd. "I got there well enough, but my legs gave out before I could get back."

"As well it was not the Lady Regan who found you," Dafydd said, helping him back to the chair. "Was there anything you needed?"

"Only to have the use of my legs again." He gave Dafydd a narrow grin. "But it's improving. I didn't make it as far yesterday. Tomorrow I'll get there *and* back." He rubbed at his shoulder. "Damn this bandage. It itches."

"Lucca says that means it's healing."

"I know." He heaved a sigh. "Dafydd, I'm bored. Play chess with me?"

But his mind was not on that either because Dafydd managed to beat him.

"Shall I fetch my harp?" he asked gently, wondering as he said it what music might serve to salve Leofric's chafing spirit.

"Dafydd, your music is fit to soothe King Saul's madness, but it cannot compensate me for being mewed up in here." He flexed his right hand, wincing as he did so. Further movement was impossible due to the strapping that held his arm immobile. "This is the time I should be out on the land, not relying so much on Godwine. Does he think I don't know he's under orders not to fret me?"

"There is nothing worth your fretting." Dafydd laid the chess pieces back in their box. "If there was, I would know of it."

"And you'd tell me?"

"I am your sworn man."

"Yes, you are." He laid his hand briefly over Dafydd's. "And I thank God for that."

*****

The few steps from bed to chair to window and back were soon no longer a problem and Leofric prevailed upon his nurses to move his chair down into the hall. This, giving him far more freedom as well as access to his people, came as a great relief to all. Enthroned by the hearth, with plenty to occupy his mind and space enough to try out his increasing strength, Leofric was easier to deal with. Quite shortly the worst of his grievances had shrunk to the wearing of a sling to support his arm and prevent the wound from tearing open. He would rather have been exercising it and said so. But no one, not even Dafydd, backed him up on this, so he conceded defeat with bad grace and took every opportunity to dispense with the hated restriction.

He was wearing the thing in hall, however, being under scrutiny and scratching surreptitiously at his shoulder while trouncing Regan at chess, when Donal Padraigson came panting in. His heavy face was flushed to a dull red with excitement. "'S a rider from the Earl!" he announced.

"Who?" and "Which Earl?" came together as the game was forgotten. Donal, flustered, stared from one to the other. "Take your time," Leofric advised. "Now. Who is the rider?"

"Thorfinn Wulfstanson, my lord," Donal managed. "From the Earl of Wessex."

"That's better. Thank you, Donal. Go bring my cousin in and then warn your mother. I've been expecting this," he added to Regan, "ever since my uncle was here. He doesn't believe in wasting any time."

Thorfinn strode in as if he owned the place, grinning a greeting at his cousin. "How do you go on, man? Fit enough to guest the Old Wolf, are you? I hope so, for it's a devil of a ride on to Shrewsbury, where Leofric of Mercia awaits us! Regan, my beauty! Da said you were here! Do you hold her for me, cousin, and I'll try for a kiss without her cracking my jaw."

"That you will not," Regan told him, smiling. "Welcome, Thorfinn."

He was a handsome man, Wulfstan's eldest son, with perhaps more of a likeness to Hilde than to his father, being lighter-boned. But he had the same lack of tact, even if a large measure of natural charm took some of the edge off it. Leofric regarded him with affection.

"You are well-come indeed and my lord of Wessex also. I'd need to be at death's door before I turned either of you away. Regan, would you warn Lucca?"

Thorfinn took her vacated seat and grinned. "Aye, well, from what Da said, you weren't far off that. And you don't look so much better now. Harrying you into an early grave, is she? Da said she had you well-trained and you not even wed to her yet."

"For God's love, man," Leofric winced, "Keep that behind your teeth! There's nothing been said yet. We're both newly bereaved."

"Well, but her year is up come Easter and yours in May." Thorfinn looked mildly astonished at the thought of delay. "Or is it my dear aunt Hilde you're keeping in ignorance? That I can credit!"

"My mother is all for the match," Leofric put him right. "At Yule she did everything but throw us into each other's arms."

"So soon after her sweet Hawiss?" Thorfinn was now quite scandalized.

"She wants me wed and breeding sons," Leofric said shortly, shifting a little to ease the ache in his shoulder. "Like any mother."

"She shouldn't have bedded you with little Hawiss then," Thorfinn gave his opinion. "She ought to know that Cynricings always get big foals. I mind Da said she was a night and a day bearing you and fit to scream the roof off, though that was more from the indignity of it all." He was interrupted by Lucca, bearing the guest-cup brimming with ale. "Bless you, mistress, I was parched voiceless! Hilde should have known," he went on, regardless of the company, "that fairy-hipped child could never birth a Cynricing—"

"Hawiss' babe was laid wrong in the womb," Lucca cut in. "And begging your pardon, Lord Thorfinn, size had naught to do with it." *So keep your ill-framed opinion behind your teeth,* went unsaid, but Thorfinn chose not to heed her warning, or the strained white look to Leofric's face.

"Warriors or war-horses," he went on, "it's the dam that bears them and Hawiss wasn't made to bring your seed to harvest, man. The Lady Regan now," and his free hand sketched a shapely curve in the air, "has hips to carry an army…"

Lucca's mouth had thinned to a tight line and she might well have broken guest-right by upending the crock of ale over Lord Thorfinn's head, had not Dafydd and Edwina arrived in that moment, distracting the man from his subject.

"Dafydd ap Gryfydd, bard and harper and my sworn man," Leofric said quickly. "Dafydd, my cousin Thorfinn Wulfstanson, come to warn us that my liege-lord will be guesting with us this night."

"My lord," Dafydd made his bow and Edwina curtseyed.

"The skald!" Thorfinn sprang to his feet. "I hope you're in good voice, lad, for Da has talked of little else but your Song of the Spartans and my lord Earl will wish to hear it. And I too. Also, I owe you my thanks, man, for I hear you saved my cousin's life and I'll not forget that. I like him better than most of my brothers."

"How are they all?" Leofric asked, gesturing Dafydd to a seat beside him.

"Oh attracting trouble, as usual. Hereward has sworn to Tostig, Ranulf and Osric to Harald, Coelred and Cernig to Sweyn. Eadnoth finally followed the old tradition and swore for Leofric of Mercia—we should see him tomorrow."

"And Beowulf?"

"Don't mention his name to Da. He won't even hear the old saga." Thorfinn pursed his lips. "Took himself off to the Abbey at Gloucester, didn't he, and sent word that he'd pray for us all."

"He's taken Orders?" Leofric sounded as though he found that hard to believe.

"Aye, lost to us in the cloister, would you credit it? Da's favorite, he was and the likeliest, and then he ups and turns monk. Da went nearly purple," he added reminiscently. "Oh and don't tell your Mam. Da thinks she'd crow louder than any midden-cockerel in the kingdoms."

"She probably would," Leofric agreed. "Well, I'll keep silent on it, if you will on the other matter." He got to his feet. "We'll talk further in my chamber, cousin. Lucca wants us out from underfoot, if she is to prepare for my lord's coming."

Chapter Twenty-Two

૭૦

Regan joined Lucca in the near-impossible task of preparing for the visit within the hour of one of the first men in the realm under the king himself. She set the house-thralls scurrying, sent Edwina to raid the linen-presses and Morwenna to see to the ordering of the bowers and herself lent a hand in the hall. Lucca found her supervising the placing of tables and benches, manhandling Leofric's great chair, with Donal's help, onto the dais.

"Gently, my lady," she advised. "It were well if you retired now to change your gown. You can safely leave the rest to me."

"I had forgotten," Regan said, leaning on the table, "that Leofric, like his father before him, follows on Wessex like a well-schooled hound. And why should I change my gown? You do not think the Godwin will notice what I'm wearing?"

The scorn in her voice raised Lucca's brows.

"Whether he does or no, be sure my lord Leofric will notice if you do not dress to do him honor, my lady." She cast a swift glance around—no one was within earshot. "And why so sour on Wessex, my dear? For sure there are far worse Earls than the Godwin."

"And there are better. Mercia, for one. Him at least I would trust!" Gifford had been a Mercian man and Regan had found much to admire in both Leofric of Mercia and his Lady. "I have heard things—aye and seen for myself!—but what use to tell of them when there are those who will believe only what they wish. Wessex cares for no one, Lucca. His thanes are no more than pieces on a gaming board and women even less than that."

For a moment, she and Lucca were in absolute agreement, but it was not for Lucca to say so. "He is still first Earl in the realm, my lady, and in this hall he will be treated as befits his rank. Shall I have Gyfu broach the imported wine?"

Regan gave a small smile. "Thank you, Lucca. I needed the reminder. And I will go and make myself fine, for Leofric's eyes if not for the Godwin's."

It did not take her long to change one dark gown for another and to have Morwenna dress her hair, but she did at least allow Edwina to select some jewels to set off the somber stuffs of mourning. Thus armored, she swept to Leofric's chamber.

Thorfinn was sprawled in a chair by the window, booted feet propped on a stool and a full cup balanced on his belly, while Leofric was struggling into his holiday tunic unaided. From the look on Dafydd's face, he had offered assistance and been refused. The language issuing from the richly embroidered neck of the tunic as Leofric managed to get his head through it was colorful, heathen and obscene.

As her father had never minded his tongue in front of his daughter, Regan had heard worse than this, but she slammed the door to alert them and enjoyed the result enormously. Thorfinn jerked in shock, spilling most of his ale down tunic and breeches, and Leofric got his lame arm trapped in folds of cloth and hissed a new stream of curses.

"For shame," Regan said tartly. "Dafydd, do you help my lord before he scorches all our ears. Thorfinn, you can hardly sit down to eat with your lord in that state—shall you borrow from your cousin? For sure there is little to choose between you." She was not talking of height or width of shoulder. Dafydd shot her a glance of amusement as he eased Leofric into the tunic.

"I've fresh clothes in my saddlebags," Thorfinn mumbled, coming to his feet. "By your leave, my lady."

It was a retreat and they all knew it. "One routed," said Regan with satisfaction. "Now, have you wrenched your shoulder with your boy's pride, Leofric?"

"No." But he still looked white and was carrying the arm awkwardly. "And I'm not wearing the sling," he added, forestalling her.

"You must do as you please, of course," she rejoined coolly. "If you are shamed of a battle wound—"

"I'm not shamed! I don't need it! Dafydd, my belt."

"And when your right arm fails you because you put strain on it too soon, what then?" She had him there and she was well aware of it. "You're in pain now, man. The sling will ease that."

"My lady speaks truth," Dafydd said quietly and took the sling from where it lay. Leofric made no protest as he slipped it on, gently arranging the afflicted arm in the support. Regan came to free the blond hair from the pressure at his nape, but let her hand lie for a moment.

"You're a fool, Leofric Edmundson," she said softly. "But, God help me, I love you for it."

* * * * *

For all his rank and power, Earl Godwin traveled in no great state, his immediate household consisting of a mere dozen men and no baggage train at all. But among those dozen men was a face that Regan found too familiar for her liking.

"Pox take the man!" she hissed from her place at Leofric's side.

"For pity's sake," Leofric snapped, "don't start on my liege-lord before he's even drunk the guest-cup!"

"Not him—fitzRobert. Gifford's brother." She caught Dafydd's eye across Leofric, saw the growing scowl on the black brows. "And my would-be husband."

"Your what?! That's the first I've heard of this! Which is he?" Leofric's eyes had narrowed and his jaw was set in a way that boded ill for the evening.

"The man on the sorrel-spotted gray at Wessex' right hand," she said, her mouth tightening. In his holly-green cloak pinned with the great brooch of gold and carnelian, Ranulf fitzRobert plainly knew he looked like the answer to a maiden's prayer. But not this maiden. "He sets himself high in Wessex' favor and thinks so much of himself that he cannot conceive of my continually refusing him."

"We'll see about that," Leofric growled. Regan thanked God that his right arm was still immobile, or he might have gone for his sword on the instant. But there was no more time to warn him that Ranulf would have been seeking Godwin's boon.

Dafydd, standing at the thane's other side, found his eyes drawn away from fitzRobert to the man at the head of the party, mounted on a finely trapped black stallion and knew without being told that this was Wessex. He sat his horse like a centaur and the leonine mane of red-gold that crowned his head was untouched by gray, yet he must be well past his fortieth year. He swung down from his mount, lithe as a boy and strode to greet his liegeman with an embrace that made Leofric seem like a stripling in his arms.

"What's this, boy? Holding the Welsh off single-handed, I hear!"

"Hardly that, my lord," Leofric said. "I think my uncle may have exaggerated the case."

"If not the injury, eh?" And with his hand familiarly on Leofric's good shoulder, the great Earl allowed himself to be led into the hall. Regan herself offered him the guest-cup, with Lucca, Gyfu and Edwina serving the household in the same manner. Dafydd, whose curiosity had been piqued by the ambivalent attitudes of the thane and his lady, not to mention the rest of the steading folk, set himself to study Earl Godwin and like many a man before him, failed utterly to remain even-handed. Earl Godwin of Wessex would either be worshipped or hated. It was not in his nature to inspire lukewarm affection. Beside him, all others looked colorless. He filled the hall now with his presence and Dafydd fell willingly under his spell. To bask in this great man's good humor was to enjoy the warmth of the summer sun. Dafydd did not need telling that the reverse would also be true, that his displeasure would be colder than midwinter. One glance from the steel-gray eyes had told him that when Leofric had presented him.

"I have heard much of you, Dafydd ap Gryfydd," the Earl said, "and I trust I will hear this song that my good friend Wulfstan esteems so highly."

"It will be my privilege, my lord," Dafydd said, making his deepest bow. Well, it was time now to make good Wulfstan's boast and do his lord honor.

The hall stilled as he settled the harp on his knee, drew the familiar dear shape of her to his breast and tested her strings. Her clear sweet voice sprang from beneath his fingers, joined by his own. He had learned the story and the form of the song in Welsh, from Owen, but had Saxoned it and adapted it until it was his own and with half-closed eyes he saw what he sang as clearly as if he stood with the doomed Three Hundred on the Greek shore.

"*...hard the sun beat on the helmed heads,*
On Immortal gold and purple!
Bright on blade and mailed corselet,
Furnace-hot the Spartans forging
Into adamantine valor!"

It could not fail to please the Saxon mind, the Spartan battle-ethic being similar to their own.

"*'Throw down your arms!' the foe demanded –*
'Try and take them!' Sparta answered...
Brave as boars and fierce as falcons,

Fell the Fyrd upon the foemen!
Black with blood the ground beneath them,
Black with blood of proven warriors…"

And now Dafydd had a model for the Warrior-King, for surely Leonidas had a fit successor in Godwin of Wessex?

"*Lion-led and lion-hearted,*
Never would they flee the battle,
Never leave a foe the victor,
To Death alone would make surrender…"

The harp sang of spear-clash, the ring of blade on blade.

"*…when blades were broken, spear shafts shattered,*
Still they fought with teeth and fingers,
'Til like fallen leaves in autumn
Lay they dead upon the seashore…"

The harp mourned their loss, sighing like a small crying wind over the slain heroes.

"*…Three hundred men had held the gateway,*
Three hundred died ere night had fallen.
Not defeated, never conquered,
Sparta's sons won fame undying…"

His fingers stilled the strings one by one and, over their silence, spoke the epitaph. "*Tell them in Sparta, passer-by, that here, obedient to their laws, we lie…"*

Into the hush, Godwin of Wessex rose to his feet. "Now by Him Who hung on the Tree, I swear I have not heard better!" He blinked as if to clear a moistness from his eyes. "Dafydd ap Gryfydd, stand here before me. A drink for the bard, someone!"

It was Leofric who pushed the cup into Dafydd's hand, his grin wide with unspoken congratulation. And the Earl pulled a great gold chain from around his own neck and dropped it over Dafydd's head and the household echoed and endorsed his approval with a hammering of cups on the tables.

Dafydd raised the cup in salute to the Earl and drank, hardly tasting the good wine and the Godwin smiled broadly and gave him his hand, and Leofric gestured for him to sit at the high table. The Earl's skald had the unenviable task of following Dafydd's triumph, while Dafydd was called upon to retell the story of the ambush in which Leofric had been injured.

"Hmmm," said the Earl. "Any further raids since?"

"No, my lord. And no reported sightings of them."

"And they were wolfsheads, not armed soldiery?"

"One at least was an escaped thrall," Leofric said. "For the rest, I could not say."

"Wolfsheads for certain, my lord Earl." Dafydd spoke up. "But maybe part of a larger group. They spoke of an uprising, to drive out the *Saes* and reclaim their own. But I doubt there was much organization behind them. This was a vengeance killing."

"So. Blood-feud?"

"Of a kind, maybe. Though Medwin's death can hardly be laid at Geadas' door, he must have hastened it." Leofric was at pains to explain the circumstances and the Earl listened and nodded as if the fate of a couple of thralls mattered to the security of England.

"And you, Welshman," he said, turning the sharp keen gaze on the youngster at his side, "What's your word on this? This king of yours—what's his part in it? Eh?"

Dafydd, who had had more wine thrust upon him than he might otherwise have drunk in a week and without the wit to refuse it, gave him an owlish stare. "If he has a part in it, my lord Earl, what would I know of it? I was not raised at his court. The affairs of the world hardly trespassed on our Abbey."

"Then it's a rare place, lad, in this land." He turned a casual shoulder and waved away the men of his household who had crowded close and they fell back, Ranulf among them. "Hmm. Well, Dafydd ap Gryfydd, with a talent like yours, I wonder you were not sent to sing for him…" And he smiled. "Or is that your next desire? You have sung for the Earl of Wessex, why not the King of Wales?" He swung round and faced Leofric. "Eh? Why should he not?"

"No reason," Leofric agreed, bemused.

"I am sworn to my lord's service," Dafydd said quietly, but Leofric cut in on that.

"Dear God, tiercel, you fly where you will! I'll not hold you back from rightful advancement!"

"Well said," the Earl approved. "But no need for this air of sacrifice, liegeman. I have it in mind that you shall go with him."

It was Leofric's turn to look owlish. "What?"

"Listen, both of you." He drew them confidentially nearer, though the noise in the hall was such that he could not have been heard an arm's reach away. "You are a gift from the gods, you two. I have been minded, all this year, to find a way to mend this ancient enmity between our peoples. God's blood, but it costs us dear enough in men and money and to what end! An acre of land gained that may fall in the next attack—a settlement that may wake any morning to find their throats cut. You, harper, you are honored in a Saxon hall, sworn man to a Saxon thane. Are you Welsh still?"

"God made me so," Dafydd said, indignant. "My blood is *Cymru* and my heart!"

"Peace, lad, I did but ask. And you were bred up in an Abbey—can you read?"

"In Welsh, Latin and Saxon," Dafydd said proudly. "And I can write them too and in a fair hand. I can speak the Norman French also."

"Good! Good! And you, liegeman, what Welsh have you?"

"Border Welsh only." Leofric shrugged. "My Norman French is better."

"Save that for Edward's court. You'll need to improve your Welsh. Maybe your man here can aid with that. Now I'm told that a bard is held in high honor by the Welsh. Is that true?"

"Yes, my lord Earl." Dafydd gave an unwise nod and clutched at the table as it seemed about to swim away from him.

"And guest-right is respected? A Saxon given hospitality in a Welsh hall is safe from attack?"

"*Duw Mawr*! Of course! Are we savages? A guest is fed and sheltered and has a place at the hearth—he eats first and of the finest, even if the host must go hungry after! And he has the best bed and lies in it as safe as if it were his own!"

"I see why you have named him your tiercel," the Earl grinned at Leofric. "He's fierce enough to fly at an eagle, is he not? Heed me now, the pair of you. What if I should send a Welshman and a Saxon to the court of this king of Wales, two men joined in friendship, respect and sworn loyalty to each other?"

"Then both races might call their own a traitor," Leofric said, voicing Dafydd's unspoken thought.

"But if there were to be benefits to both kingdoms? A settled peaceful border, aid against enemies—I hear he has trouble with the southern tribes, as we do with the Danes— sworn alliances binding on both sides! Think on it! Is he wed, this king?"

"I—don't know." Dafydd was having trouble following the quicksilver brilliance of the Godwin's plan.

"Well, if he's not, I have daughters yet unwed, I'll offer one of them. If he is and has children, why, we'll betroth his eldest girl to one of my boys. D'y'see? Alliances close as blood-bonds!"

Thane and harper both gazed at him, speechless. It was an amazing idea and stunning in its daring and—if it went awry—would cost the Earl nothing but the lives of a minor thane and an itinerant musician. If it succeeded, on the other hand, it would make his name sing down the years as Godwin the Peacemaker—and his grandchildren would be kings.

"Think on it," he commanded.

Chapter Twenty-Three

ಬ

Regan took a few moments from pouring mead at the end of the dais table to stare across the hall. She tried to will Leofric to meet her eyes, but the concentrated glare had no affect. He and Dafydd sat there like bumps on a log gazing at the Earl with the wide and worshipful eyes of a pair of heifers at a bull. How could otherwise intelligent men be so—besotted? And she wondered what was being said that held the two men so rapt.

"He's very handsome," Morwenna sighed, taking the empty flagon from her.

"Holy Mother, not you as well!"

"He's old," Edwina sniffed. "And not so fine looking as Dafydd. Or our own thane," she added as an afterthought.

"Oh dear," Morwenna said suddenly. "I think I'll go and see if Lucca needs help with anything—" and ducked out of sight among the press of people.

The cause of her retreat approached Regan with a confident smile beneath his moustaches.

"Well, my lady?" Ranulf said smoothly. "Did I not say to you I have the Godwin's ear? I've spoken to him and he has promised—"

"I have no interest in the promises of Wessex," Regan interrupted and turned her back on him. As a snub, it had all the subtlety of a battering ram and those around them of both households did not bother to hide snorts of laughter.

Scarlet-faced with fury, Ranulf took a swift pace forward and grabbed for her arm. "I'll take no more of this willfulness of yours!" he growled. "You're mine and that's the end of it. Come, I'll have the Earl's seal on it this instant!"

"You'll have my seal on it first!" Regan hissed, whirling to snatch up in both hands the great platter of broken meats swimming in a congealing mass of grease and gravy. Ignoring the mess that splattered her skirts, she swung it around with all her strength to bring it down on his skull with a satisfactory thud. "No! And no! And no!" She emphasized each word with another impact. "Is that finally clear enough for you, fitzHog?"

Semi-stunned and off-balance, he staggered back and tripped over a questing hound. He landed with a jarring crash on his rump in the rushes, the erstwhile contents of the platter slithering down hair and face and moustaches, to the intense interest of a gathering pack of dogs.

The scrape of Leofric's chair was loud in the sudden silence and he came across the dais in a lunge, left hand reaching for his belt-knife. The Godwin was quicker, grabbing a handful of tunic and hauling him back with one hand and capturing Dafydd with the other.

"Hold!" he roared and the force of his will struck like a wall, freezing every man where he stood. "Woman, what goes on here?"

Regan drew herself up to her full height and met his angry stare with eyes that flashed she-wolf-fierce. "A rutting swine thought to break guest-right and insult both yourself and me, my lord," she said with a coolness that did not match the rage in her. "He actually had the gall to tell me that you had promised him my hand in marriage—I who hold from Mercia. A true man should not lie so."

"Indeed, he should not," the earl snapped and his gaze did not waver from hers, "for I promised him no such thing. You, fitzRobert, take yourself out of my sight. We'll discuss this matter when I see fit. Hold still, man," to Leofric, who was straining to be free like an ill-trained hound. "Do you want to re-open that wound? I'll take care of this insult to your lady, my word on it. And you, Gryfyddson, put up that blade and remember you are a bard. Harp us peace, man, and put this to one side."

Men of the Earl's household came to help Ranulf to his feet and their grins were imperfectly hidden. But the man did not see them, dazed as he was and half-blinded by the greasy stuff streaking his face. For a moment Regan stood at bay, then relented and came to Leofric's side.

"Let be," she said quietly. "If I have the word of the Earl of Wessex, foremost in the land, shall I not be content?"

* * * * *

With the morning Dafydd woke to be reminded once again exactly why the Holy Book enjoined the faithful to "look not on the wine when it is red". There was an anvil in his skull with hammers pounding at it, light hurt his eyes and his mouth tasted as if a fox had laired in it. From Leofric's look, he was feeling the same and should by right have been in his bed. The duties of a host, however, demanded his presence.

By contrast, the Earl was as spry as a colt. He broke his fast with appetite, made cheerful conversation and referred to his revelation of the previous night not at all. Dafydd began to wonder if he'd dreamed it, but Leofric's transparent bewilderment told him otherwise.

Godwin kept them waiting until his household—a sullen Ranulf among them—were mounted and waiting in the garth and Thorfinn was taking some protracted farewells of the womenfolk. Then he drew off his gauntlet and gave his hand to both thane and harper, smiling benignly on them.

"I will not look to see you until this autumn," he said. "Liegeman, learn well from your bard and when you come to me I shall expect you to be as fluent in his tongue as he is in ours. Dafydd ap Gryfydd, you shall delight my court as you have delighted me with your music—and this Yule you shall both keep in Wales!" He set his hands on their shoulders, looking at them proudly. "Yes, by the gods, you stand well together! Shoulder-to-shoulder men!"

Dafydd knew the phrase from the old sagas. The sword-brother, the spear-brother, sworn comrades in peace and war. Headache forgotten, he copied Leofric's obeisance to his lord, knowing himself dazzled by the man and not caring. For if the Earl's design worked even a little, the consequences were unimaginable. To have a part in it was honor undreamed.

Farewells taken, the Godwin swung up onto his stallion and the household fell in behind him, Thorfinn coming running to mount and take his own place. Only when the riders had gone from sight did Leofric let out a quiet breath and lean on the door jamb. Dafydd knew how he felt, feeling more than a little frail himself. He turned to offer a shoulder, getting Leofric back inside and settled in his chair by the hearth.

"Imported wine," Leofric said shakily. "In future I'll stick to good Saxon ale. Jesu, but my head aches!"

"So it should," Regan told him. "You should have kept to your bed this morning. How does the wound?"

"It aches, nothing more." It also itched as if a legion of fleas were at it, but he forbore to mention that. "And I know what courtesies are due my liege-lord."

"Wessex." She looked as if she would like to spit. "Risen high for a fatherless man, that one!" And she turned on her heel and stalked away. Leofric pushed himself to his feet.

"One moment, my lady!"

"A fatherless man?" Dafydd repeated questioningly and Lucca spared him a glance from clearing the tables of the broken meats where the household had eaten.

"Sired by a swineherd, some folk say," she murmured. "Which could account for much."

"Lucca!" Leofric had overheard that. "You will not speak so of my liege-lord. Whatever his birth, he has made himself what he is today!"

"Aye!" Regan shouted from the stair door. "And would make himself more if he could!"

"Holy Saint Martin!" Leofric howled, clutching his head. "What is it with you women? He's done nothing to harm you, yet you rail against him as if he had spat upon your virtue!"

"He could hardly do that, when he never even sees us!" Regan included the entire female population in that statement. "I swear Leofric of Mercia is worth ten of that one. He does not treat women as witless whores or broodmares!"

"This is foolishness!" Leofric went after her, following the angry swish of her skirts up the stairs to his chamber, glad to put closed doors between this quarrel and the inquisitive ears of the folk in hall. "Did he not speak for you in hall last night? Earl Godwin has nothing but the highest regard for women."

Regan snorted. "He did not. He spoke only to protect his own honor. Oh and if he has such high regard for our sex, why did he treat his own daughter so?"

"He made her Queen!" Leofric stared at her as if she'd run mad.

"He has little respect for queens either, or he'd not have treated the Old Lady so shamefully." Leofric had no answer for this. His own mother had wept as she told him how Lady Emma, the Queen Mother, had been stripped of her rights and her lands and even of her jewels at the orders of her son the King, and his three most powerful Earls, Godwin first among them. "As for poor Queen Editha—she'd be better wed to some simple country thane—"

"Like me, I suppose?"

"Aye, like you!" Her mood had softened a fraction and the green eyes no longer glittered with anger but were dark with pity. "A man who cares not who shapes the world, who'd give her children to hold in her arms and cherish. But instead he weds her to that Norman-bred puppet-king who spends more time on his knees than in her bed. Which is as well, for she'll get no sons by him. If by some miracle she did, I'd wager they'd not outlive the cradle. Is this a loving father?" She caught her breath and he seized his opportunity.

"This is fancy, Regan! How can you know all this?"

"I kept my ears open at court, that's how! Oh what do you know, planted down here like an oak in a meadow. I can guess how you are when you're in the Royal Household—the making and shaking of the realm going on about your head and you with your mind full of drainage ditches and last year's harvest!"

She had cut too close to the bone and he felt himself redden. "That is slander, Lady—"

"It is truth! Holy Mother, I think the women have more care for this land than the men who either bring it to ruin with their ambition or ignore it so they can sit content on their own middens."

"Now you go too far! No proper woman has such things in mind! My poor Hawiss would not so have meddled—"

"No, she would not, no more than does the ewe-lamb at grass! Gifford, God rest him, at least had respect for my opinions and didn't plan to keep me tied to bower and bed!"

Leofric drew breath sharply. "How often," he demanded, "are you going to throw that man at my head?"

"As often as you throw Hawiss at mine!" Battle lines had been drawn. "But do you not try to lure me off the scent. It's the Godwin who's the contention here, him and his ambition to put his sons on the throne, if he can't sit there himself!"

"Now that is madness!"

"Do you tell me he does not seek to rule?" she shot back.

"Enough, Lady! I've had enough of politics rammed down my throat by my mother and my uncle! I'll not have it from you! When you are my wife, I—"

"Wife?" Regan cut in. "Wife? Are we hand-fast then? Or even promised?"

"What?" Totally taken off balance, Leofric gaped at her. "But we agreed—"

"But nothing, Leofric Edmundson." Regan folded her arms. "As I recall, you asked me if I was set on the Abbey. I said I was no longer sure. You asked if you might visit and I told you yes, but how many times had you come to me? Oh yes and neither had Dafydd come, though we expected him daily, Edwina and I. Can you blame me if I doubt your intentions, man?"

A pounding headache is no aid to coherent thinking. Leofric rocked on his heels. "But—"

"Well? Can you deny you have—assumed my consent? As Ranulf fitzRobert found, to his cost? No, Leofric. This time I will have a choice in the matter." And her mouth softened into a smile. "Oh you dear fool! I think it is time we ceased this game of pretense and made our intentions plain. After all, didn't your beloved Earl say it? 'Your Lady', he named me."

"So he did," Leofric said warily. "And are you? Will you take instruction from Godwin of Wessex in that, if naught else?"

"Never!" she snorted. "But I'll follow my own heart. Your Lady I am, if you will have it so."

"No question of 'if'," he whispered and forgot about throbbing head, aching shoulder, forgot everything but the woman standing before him. He drew her to him with his good arm. "You fill my heart like no other, my lady and my love."

"Your wound—be careful—" she began, but he silenced the words with his mouth and with a small moan of pleasure she melted against him. It had been long weeks since the afternoon she had spent in his bed and now her body awoke to sudden hunger. His lips moved across her cheek and down her throat, leaving a lava-trail of fire in their wake and his left arm slid down her spine to her buttocks, pressing their bodies closer. Common sense fought a rear-guard action. "No," she managed. "We cannot. Your shoulder—and someone might come in—"

As if summoned by the words, the door opened and Godwine stood there, hand on latch.

"My lord," he began, "the—"

Leofric lifted his head. "Out!" he barked. "And keep all else out! I'm busy." He freed his arm from the sling and took the headrail from Regan's hair and neither of them noticed the widening grin on Godwine's face as he quickly shut the door.

"If your wound opens," Regan said breathlessly, "Lucca will gralloch us both."

"It won't," he said, voice husky with need. "Ah, Regan, I've dreamed of you—"

Well, so had she dreamed of him, of his hands moving over her body, gentle and sure and setting every part of her alight with their touch. "Take care then," she whispered. "Let me…" and moved away from him long enough to step out of her shoes and take off kirtle and over-gown together. He had taken the great sheepskin that cushioned his chair and spread it on the rushes by the fire basket. Now he kicked off his boots, but she stopped his hand when he reached for the ties of his shirt and undid them herself. "Let me," she repeated, smiling up at him and got a laughing assent.

It was not the first time she had taken the clothes from him, but then he had been out of his head with his wound, an injured man to be cared for and no thought of the fine body naked to her gaze. Now, despite the bandaging that darkened the moment with might-have-beens, this was her lover and he was splendid in her sight, proudly male and in the prime of his strength.

Their mouths met and joined, tongues caressing, bodies moving together in a slow sensual glide that carried her away from reality. There was only Leofric and the hard pressure of his erection at her stomach, the pulsing need deep within her that only he could fill. His mouth moved to her breasts, teasing and suckling at each nipple in turn and Regan cried out, fingers locked in the blond mane to hold him there. But his head moved down and she felt his kisses on her belly, tongue dipping into her navel as his hands cupped her buttocks, kneading the firm flesh. She gasped his name and felt the warmth of his breath as he chuckled, then he was kneeling at her feet and kissing the bright triangle of copper at the join of her thighs. His tongue probed deeper and she gave a sharp groan as the sweet sensation lanced through her, bracing herself with hands on his shoulders when her knees threatened to give way.

Then Leofric was urging her down and the softness of the sheepskin was under her shoulders and Regan had no clear idea of how she had got there—then as he bent over her the starkness of the bandage across his chest and shoulder brought back some measure of sanity.

"Wait," she whispered, "this way—" and pressed him to one side. For a moment he was startled then went with her insistence and lay back, still with his good arm about her hips. Regan leaned over him, mantling him with her hair and kissed his mouth while her hands caressed down the planes of his body to the hard shaft of his manhood. He gasped and arched into her grasp as her fingers closed around him, quivering tension in every muscle. Ancient knowledge told her he could not hold out long against such an assault on the senses. Well, neither could she. This was more than need, more than hunger—she swung astride his hips and guided him into her hot slickness, muscles tightening to draw him and hold him deep within. Leofric shouted his pleasure, body surging beneath her, and Regan rode the powerful thrusts with an abandon that matched his own. Until the waves of completion took them both and left them spent and breathless and at peace.

Chapter Twenty-Four

The blackthorn buds broke into white stars, the primroses clustered in the woodland banks, and the violets showed royal purple within their rosettes of new green. Lady Regan settled into the guest-bower with Edwina for company, since Morwenna was now hand-fasted to Sifrith and the household rearranged itself to fit. It was now openly acknowledged that she was to be their new Lady as soon as the proprieties had been met. Lucca was smugly pleased. The wedding, she told anyone who would listen, would be at Lammas for sure, if not Midsummer. Neither Regan nor Leofric bothered to contradict her, since she was right.

But there were other things to think of besides weddings. The shoulder healed, sling finally discarded, Leofric set himself to recover his strength and suppleness, making Dafydd a partner in his training program.

"For you still handle a sword as if it were a meat-knife," he said truthfully if unkindly, testing the new-healed muscles carefully. "You ought at least to look as if you know how to use it."

"I learn fast," Dafydd assured him. "How if we speak only in Welsh as we practice?" he suggested smoothly. "Your accent is terrible."

Leofric, who had not expected to be pupil as well as teacher, grunted. "I don't need a polished accent, dammit, just an understandable one. How if we concentrate on weapon-play this morning and have our Welsh lesson when we ride out with my lady this afternoon?

It was not such hard work as he feared. The pattern of the language was already in his head, from hearing it spoken around him over the years. Most of his people were bi-lingual, if more fluent in one tongue than another. As Dafydd said, it was more a case of opening his ears to how it was being said rather than teaching him anything new.

Also, Dafydd and Regan together made the learning enjoyable, since Regan had decided that she should regain her knowledge of the tongue. Dafydd spiced the lessons with song and story. "I wish my Latin teacher had been as good a companion," Leofric said idly as the three of them rode abreast through the water meadows one afternoon. "Brother Barnabas had but one method of instilling learning and that was the rod."

Regan chuckled. "There are advantages to being female then."

"I benefited from Owen's teaching," Dafydd said. "I think he thought in song and rhyme and meter were his meat and drink. Though I had my share of discipline. It was reckoning, with me and Brother Huw. Though once I had the trick of it, I did not merit many beatings." He drew rein abruptly, head cocked. "Listen."

Clear above the murmur of the water, the sweet double note of the cuckoo came to the ear.

"That's early," Leofric said. "We'll have to ask Lucca what it means, weather-wise." Dafydd, letting the filly's rein lie loose, cupped his hands and mimicked the cuckoo-call so perfectly that the bird itself appeared confused.

"*Croeso, meistr cwcw!*" Regan offered, laughing and Dafydd joined in and the affronted bird left them to it. "You should make a wish, Dewi, on hearing the first cuckoo."

"That's easy done." He closed his eyes to make the wish more potent.

"Edwina?" Leofric guessed.

"Ah, but if I tell, it won't come true."

They turned for home. "At least you look as if you could fight now," Leofric said consideringly. "Though if the Godwin's Grand Design is successful, we may never need to. Or not on these borders, anyway."

"He is a great man," Dafydd said seriously. Regan snorted but did not speak. "Do his sons have his vision, do you know?"

"That would be scanned," Leofric said with honesty. "I've met them all. It's true enough that the Old Wolf has bred up a pack of young wolves to follow him, though it's my guess he has them all on a tight leash. Sweyn—he's hot-headed, acts before he thinks. Tostig I'd guess is most like his father in the way of ambition. To be sure, they don't agree. And Harald…" He turned in the saddle to face Dafydd. "Harald is like someone in one of your songs," he said abruptly. "He has all his father's fire and it burns with a steady flame, unlike his brothers. He's a man of his word—known for it, not only in this country. A good overlord to his people. When the time comes, it'll be Harald I declare for." His voice had become introspective with memories. "I met him first when the Godwin came to visit my father. I was about eight summers and I took an instant dislike to the man, because I knew Da wouldn't be taking me out hunting with him! But he had Harald with him. A tall tow-head, with eyes like amber and a smile—dear God! Even then, it was a smile to woo women!" He gave a short, self-conscious laugh. "He swung down off his pony and walked up to me where I stood behind my Da and he said—I can still remember how he said it—*'I am Harald Godwinson. When we are grown, you will be my thane, as your father is my father's and we will go to war together.'* And I followed on his heels like a hound and we spent the day out blackberrying and I was his man from then on, though I took my oath to his father when it was time for me to do so." He fell silent for a moment, lost in his thoughts. His description of the child had painted the man in Dafydd's mind's eye. A tall Saxon lord, with a mane of barley-pale hair and eyes like an eagle, golden-fierce, a hero out of legend, like Leonidas. It was easy to imagine him standing with his Fyrd against overwhelming odds, his roar of defiance out-shouting the war horns…

"The Earl looks hale enough to live long," he said, dismissing the image, because Leonidas' fate was an unlucky thing to wish on Lord Harald.

"The higher a man climbs, the more uncertain the footing. And the harder the fall," Leofric said somberly. "Dafydd, you haven't spoken of your wishes in this. You are not a warrior — and I do not know what dangers there may be on the road to the Welsh king's court."

"I thought that was why you were teaching me to fight?" Dafydd said innocently. "Oh no road is without its dangers, but perhaps Earl Godwin thought to provide you with a sure safe-conduct." He caught Leofric's puzzled frown and grinned. "I'll have my harp at my back. And a bard travels where he will, unhindered. Indeed, there are those who hold to the Old Ways who would think it cursed to lay violent hands on a maker of songs!"

"Self-interest, would it be?" Regan murmured. "Lest you make a parody on them?"

"Surely! Though Owen thought it was older yet, from the time when bards were also Druids and therefore sacred. To kill one was to be death-cursed, he told me. And in all his wanderings, no man had ever offered him violence. I may have to harp for our suppers, but I doubt we'll go hungry!"

"And my lord Earl knew it…" Leofric gave a short laugh. "There's wily as any wolf! Why am I teaching you weapon-play? It would be more to the point if you taught me to sing!"

Dafydd gave him a very straight look. "A bard may also be a Druid, Leofric, but I never heard it said that even Druids could perform miracles."

* * * * *

The austerities of Lent passed and Eastertide came and Regan put off her mourning.

"We will honor the Holy Season," she told Edwina and Morwenna, smiling, "in new gowns. Garnet for you, 'Wenna—green and blue for you, 'Dwina."

"And you, Lady?" Edwina had first-hand knowledge of the stuffs carefully folded away in the cedar-wood dower-chest under the window in the bower. There was a dark chestnut brown wool which would look very fine, if enlivened with a little embroidery, but it was hardly springtime wear.

"Shall we see?" She led the girls to the chest and unlocked it, lifting the heavy lid. The fragrance of the wood had permeated the fabrics, released as she lifted them out, considering. The brown? She considered it, head on one side. Yes, it was fitting for one widowed and 'Dwina's skill would enrich it but… Was it betrayal of Gifford and her parents to long for the bright colors they had loved to see her in? There at the bottom of the chest was a length of silk Gifford had bought her, at great expense, from the mercers who supplied the Queen herself. She drew it out, her fingers stroking, loving the heavy softness of it, the color that was halfway between rich cream and light gold in the sunlight.

"Oh my lady…" Morwenna sighed. "That is fit for the queen of Heaven."

And there was a tawny, in light wool, for the tunica, the over-gown. Regan held the two together and her eyes met Edwina's. The two colors would marry together with perfection, they knew.

"My lady will shine like a flame." Edwina said softly. Regan, estimating the amount of sewing that would need to be done if they were all to be suitably gowned afresh, laughed.

"I hope you will consider the effort worth the trouble!"

"What matter, so long as Lord Leofric finds my lady fair? And surely he will!"

"Leofric…" Regan, having made her decision, shut the lid and sat back on her heels. "The dear man would not notice if I went clad in sackcloth. No, this indulgence is for myself, 'Dwina. Though I am vain enough to hope that my lord's heart will quicken at least a little." She sighed. "Ah, 'Dwina, I envy you! That lad of yours eats you with his eyes and you bloom like a lily whenever he's near! Well, we must be about our stitching, if we are to dazzle our menfolk at the Easter feasting!"

Morwenna and Edwina both insisted that their lady's gown should be completed before their own finery was begun and it seemed to take no time at all before the silk was being fitted to her, smooth as water against her skin, trimmed extravagantly with bright bands of embroidery, as was the tawny-gold overdress. Edwina adjusted the woven cincture, with its bullion tassels and stood back in pride. "If my lady would but wear her hair loose."

"I am not sure it would be fitting," Regan said, smoothing the fabric over her hips. The combination of colors, toning and complementing each other, had worked as well as she had hoped. She knew what Edwina meant—to loosen her hair would be to add a final dazzling richness. Well, why not? She would no doubt scandalize everyone who saw her by going without her veil save for a wisp of gauze and wearing her hair like a war-banner. She was, after all, no widow to hide it.

"Lady," said Edwina firmly, "we could walk beside you in our shifts and none would notice. Does the candle flame challenge the sun?"

"You have learned pretty speeches from your Dewi," Regan laughed. "We shall see where his eyes light, my bird."

And I was wrong about Leofric, she admitted to herself as she saw his face when he stood at the hall dais to greet her. "Freya witness, but you are fairer than the morning, Lady," Leofric breathed as he took her hand.

"I owe Edwina an apology," she smiled up at him. "I did not think it mattered to you what I wore."

"If you went clad like a beggar-maid," he said, returning her smile, "I would love you still. And if I am stunned, Dafydd will be inspired. The joy of the season to you, my lady!"

"And also to you, my lord!"

Leofric might be restricted to colors that showed his mourning state—though the muted blue-gray he wore was embellished with rich embroidery—but Dafydd was as finely dressed as any prince. From Lucca's proud gaze, Regan could guess whose work that had been. Shirt of natural silk, tunic and breeches of russet bright as a ruddock's breast and Earl Godwin's chain of heavy gold as ornament, he almost glowed as he stepped to the dais and made his bow,

"Lady, at Yule I began to make a song for you. Now you have my thanks, for the sight of you has been the making of my song."

It was a pretty speech. She smiled at him, inclining her head, and he stroked the first notes from the strings. The music was *Cymru* in form—the words and meter Saxoned. He had married the two conflicting styles into one, yet neither had lost its beauty, as a goldsmith may marry gold and silver and the luster of one will complement the other.

"*Phoenix immortal, bright bird of fire*
Rises from ashes to ride the winds' gyre
All scarlet and crimson, tawny and gold
Flame-feathered, glorious in ancient tale told…"

Leofric's hand closed over hers as she listened and she leaned a little toward him. The music soared with the phoenix flight, each string singing harmonies to swoop and lift and check as if they too rejoiced in the mastery of the sky.

"*Peacock and kingfisher, popinjay rare*
For all of their beauty cannot compare
Like a spark of the sun she burns in the sky

Acknowledged the empress of all things that fly!"

Instead of calling him to her, Regan stepped down from her chair and, taking his face between her hands, kissed his brow. "I cannot claim that song, my dear—it is too rich for my wearing. But from my heart, I thank you!"

He was blushing. "Lady, when my lord smiles at the sight of you, all here owe you their thanks."

"The Godwin chose his embassy well, I think," she said lightly. "You who could sing the very stars out of the sky, as Gwydion did to make a necklace for his favorite sister, you will have the Welsh court in the palm of your hand!"

Chapter Twenty-Five

The Welsh lessons progressed, as did Dafydd's skill with weapons and Leofric's recovery of the full use of his right arm. Anna, on one of her visits to the steading, found the two of them sitting by the well, sluicing dust and sweat off, laughing and paused, basket on hip.

"Almost healed, I see," she said with satisfaction, nodding at the puckered pink scar beneath the right shoulder. "It doesn't catch you at all?"

"I've fast-healing flesh," Leofric grinned at her, using his discarded shirt to towel his wet hair. "It's good as new, Anna, thanks to your magic."

"Tch. Get on with you, making fun of your Anna. Dewi, that's a fine bruise you'll have there!"

"That was my doing," Leofric told her. "Dafydd thought I was holding back, you see, and so he fetched me a buffet to rock me off my feet and I lost my balance and missed my stroke and nearly brained him."

"I'm fast on my feet." Dafydd gave Anna a reassuring smile for her concern. "And you weren't trying your hardest, Leofric. Admit it."

"Well, maybe I wasn't. But you're lucky I didn't crack your head open. If those blades hadn't been blunted, I'd have taken your arm off at the elbow!"

"And been spitted like a chicken on my sword too, so you wouldn't have lived to boast about it, *Saes*!"

"Fierce, isn't he?" Leofric said to Anna. "He's a better practice mate than Godwine or Padraig—they're always so careful. But my tiercel has the makings of a baresark!"

"That wasn't what you said at Yule. You said I was entirely too polite."

"With snowballs, you're polite. With sword or spear or your hands you're not." Leofric tossed his shirt aside and stood up, stretching. "So, Anna—who's ailing?"

"Thank the Good Goddess, no one. I've but brought some of my new marigold salve for Lucca. Her flowers are late this year, or mine are early." She paused. "But I would have come to see you soon, my lord. Beltane is near."

"So soon." He gazed at her solemnly, all levity banished. "I had forgotten."

"She has been kind to us," Anna said softly. "The land has suffered, these years past, but we have felt it hardly at all here. Murrain and plague have passed us by and if the harvests might have been better, still we have not known want. And you—has not your shoulder healed clean? The Lady is gracious."

"I know it," he agreed. "But—to take my father's place… Anna, I don't think I'm ready yet."

"No one will force you, my lord. She understands grief, the dear lady. Did She not mourn the Son mankind hung on the cross? If Edmund's place is not filled by you, then it must be another. Godwine, perhaps? Steward is better for the health of the land than just anyone, I'm thinking."

"But Edmund's son would be better yet?" Leofric voiced her unspoken thought. "Even untried, unprepared as he is?"

"He is still accountable," Anna said. "And you do yourself a miss-service if you think yourself unfit, my lord."

Leofric drew a deep breath. "I will come to the Fires, Anna. That much the least of my people can do, in thanks to the Lady of Plenty. But as to the other… I must think on it."

"She asks no more," Anna beamed and touched his brow. "Blessed be." And she moved away, a placid and rather dumpy figure, to complete her errand. Leofric sat down again and met Dafydd's questioning eyes.

"She's right, of course," he conceded. "It's just that I hadn't thought that I would take my father's place for many years."

"You have been all that he could have wished, surely," Dafydd said, plainly puzzled. "You inherited because he died untimely — is that not so?"

"Yes. It seemed almost as if I was cursed. Him and then Hawiss and the babe."

"They are with God." It was a standard response, spoken to comfort, but Leofric laid his hand on Dafydd's shoulder for a moment.

"And God's ways are not always as we would wish, is that not what Holy Church would tell us? Dafydd, you were raised in the Faith, I should not be speaking to you like this."

"Whatever you say, it is between us alone," Dafydd said staunchly.

"Oh I know you will keep your counsel. What do you know of Beltane?"

"Only what I have heard here." He gave a grin. "We did not keep it at the Abbey."

The image of the Abbot and monks dancing with due stateliness at the Fires brought a smile to Leofric's mouth. "No, you would not. But there are older faiths than that of the White Christ and older gods, also — and I do not think the priests of Hereford would look kindly on those of my people who hold to that worship. We are pagans at heart in these lands, Dewi. So we have always been, so we always will be, whatever constraints Holy Church may put upon us. Fires have been kindled on Old Top in the name of the Threefold Goddess since before the *Saes* came to this island, before the Caesars came, before Jesu died on the cross… People have short memories, but the memory of the Land is long. You've made up my mind for me, Dafydd. I will take my place this Beltane. I hold this land from the Lady and I will do Her honor. We'll ride down past Anna's cott later and tell her so."

Beltane. Dafydd reviewed what little he knew. It was kept in his own country, he knew that—he could remember seeing the flames leaping upwards into a kingfisher-blue evening sky and the brothers hurrying their young charges inside, away from the evil influences of the devil-worshippers. But Owen had talked of the Lady Rhiannon, of Don the mother of Gwydion, of proud Arianrhod in her castle of the Silver Wheel, as if they too were goddesses the equal of the Olympians in the stories of the pagan Greeks. And there had been whispered tales of a young monk who had professed a devotion to the Holy Mother so intense that he had argued with the Abbot himself that She should be held the equal of Her Son and God the Father. No one knew what had happened to him. Some said he had run mad and left the Abbey—some, that he had been sent to St. David's, for that great saint to restore his reason. It was more likely, Dafydd thought, that he'd been sent there to have the taint of heresy beaten out of him. He found himself hoping that the first story had been true and the young man had cast off the homespun habit, grown out his tonsure and spent his life in solitary worship of his Lady, by whatever name he called Her.

Well, Beltane was undoubtedly a pagan thing. And as a good son of Holy Church, he should not attend. However, could he rightly condemn a practice he had not witnessed? As the days grew longer and the time approached, he knew that when Leofric went to the Fires in celebration of the fertility of the land, nothing would keep him away.

Edwina sought him out on the last day of April, daring her father's disapproving eye, to ask him if he would be there.

"Da says I'm to stay home and help mind the children because I'm still too young. But I'm not. I'm a woman grown and old enough to marry! So I'm going to wait until everyone else is gone and I'm going to follow. Even if Da sees me, he'll not turn me away once I'm there." It was clear she wasn't sure of that. Dafydd stroked her cheek. "He wouldn't—would he? Not in front of everyone?"

"It's a long walk to the Top and in the dark," Dafydd said softly. "How if I wait and walk with you?"

"You would do that, Dewi? You would miss the start of the dancing for me?"

"How not, when you are the only girl I want to dance with?" He kissed her, taking his time about it—here in the lee of the hall, the hanging eaves of thatch drooped over them like sheltering wings and only the garth geese were watching.

"Mam says that Cuthbert Coelrigson has been talking to Da," Edwina whispered, reaching up to brush a curl out of his eyes. "He holds half a hide of the Lady Wulfgive's land over to Pyon. Mam thinks he'll offer for me soon."

"And you'll have no choice in it?" This was an unlooked-for problem.

"Oh if I'm given a choice..." She smiled. "You know where my heart is set, Dewi."

"And mine, *cariad*. You cannot wed this Cuthbert. How if I go to your Da and—"

"Holy Mother, no! Coelrigson holds land and you have none."

"I could speak to Lord Leofric," he hazarded, not sure what this might avail him but not willing to consider even the possibility of losing Edwina.

"But Coelrigson is Saxon," she said. "And you are not, my heart."

There was nothing to be said to that. "I will carry you off across the Dyke," he promised rashly, "before I see you wed to another, were he a Prince of the Blood himself. We would go to the court of the *Cymru* King and I would be harper there and everyone would marvel at your beauty."

Which led to more kissing. Finally, reluctantly, she held him away.

"Mam will be looking for me. I must go."

"I'll wait for you tonight," he said. "By the hawthorn thicket where the path steepens."

* * * * *

Lucca was the last to arrive at the church, looking harassed and rather annoyed. "The girl's not to be found," she grumbled. "I'll fettle that man of mine, telling her she was too young for the Beltane Fires. She'll be off sulking and it's all his fault."

"Not to worry," Anna said calmly. "If the Good Goddess wanted her here, be sure she would be." She bent in genuflection to the little statue of Mary the Mother. "May we do Your will, Lady." All the women in the place, from hall or cott, thrall or free, were of bearing age, maids or matrons and here there was no distinction of rank. Regan sat beside Lucca, a thrall-woman she did not know at her other side. Orderly and without undue haste, Anna took up the covered basket and each woman took an oat-cake. "May the Mother of us all make her Will known by this token," Anna intoned and as they all murmured an Amen, they each broke their portion in half.

"Anna," said Regan into the silence, "did you plan this?" In her palm lay the Goddess' sign, a tiny clay figurine of a gravid woman.

Anna smiled. "Go against the Goddess? Would I? It is fitting and right, my dear—as you are Lady of this steading, so He is your Lord. Sisters, let us make ready."

* * * * *

The shadows lay deep and black around the tangle of thorn and Dafydd crouched on the dew-damp grass and watched the last stragglers pass up the track to where the new fire was already sending showers of red gold sparks up into the starry darkness and snatches of song and laughter came faintly to where he waited. It had been easy to absent himself from the hall—Leofric was abstracted. His mind no doubt on whatever his duties were that night and everyone else had preparations to be made, a kind of effervescent current of anticipation sweeping them up. No one saw Dafydd slip away, or marked his empty place.

He had watched them pass, talking and laughing, light of foot and heart and the flare of the torches they carried had driven him closer to the thorn until he realized they would have to fall over him before they would see him. Anna had been one of the first, her older children with her and all of them garlanded and crowned with flowers. In couples and groups the people of the village were joined by those from outlying farms. The hall-folk had been among the last, though Dafydd had not seen Leofric with them.

The fragrance of the may-flower was heady on the night air. On the hilltop, dark shapes passed and re-passed in front of the red-gold heart of the fire and there was music now, the compelling thud of drumbeat and the skirl of pipes and it drew him as nothing else could.

Something flitted up the path toward him, moth-like in the dim, and then Edwina flung herself breathlessly into his arms. "I thought they'd never go," she breathed. "But Aelfwine has the little ones and she's telling them stories, so as long as I'm in my bed by the morning, no one will be the wiser. Oh Dewi, do you hear?"

Voices had joined the music, though he could not make out the words. He took Edwina's hand and they slipped from shadow to shadow beside the track until the brow of the hill lay before them, the bare top and the great need-fire, leaping like a live thing as torch after torch was thrown into it and the people raised a cry. A naked figure was standing in the glare of the fire, Dafydd saw, straight and tall, made taller yet by the twin branches of a king-stag's antlers.

Edwina caught her breath in a little whimper of awe. Dafydd felt the short hair on his neck rise in prickling wonder. He gripped her hand tighter and as the people sank to their knees in a ripple of movement, Edwina pulled him down beside her, to do reverence to the Horned One as He came to His worshippers.

The figure raised his arms, lifted his voice. The language was the ancient speech of the land and yet Dafydd understood.

"Erce, Erce, Erce, Eordan Modor…
Hail to thee, Earth, Mother of All!
Be thou fruitful in God's embrace,
bringing forth food for the use of men…"

So the Consort, Son and Beloved, invoked the Goddess and the people echoed his prayer and She came out of the darkness into the firelight, tall and stately and clad in scarlet, with flowers crowning the mane of bright copper hair that rippled around her like a cloak. The proud stag's head bowed in homage and the two joined hands, God and Goddess incarnate, turning to face their people.

The crowd began to move toward them, forming a sinuous single-file line that seemed like a dance as they bent and turned away and circled the fire again. Without quite knowing how, Dafydd found himself and Edwina part of the moving line. The singing and the drumbeat worked in him like yeast and when he bent the knee before the Horned One and looked up, he hardly recognized the familiar face beneath the antlers. Oh the voice was Leofric's voice and the hands that held out a piece of honey-cake were the hands that had enclosed his during his oath-giving, but the eyes that gazed down at him without recognition were like Macsen's eyes, the iris a thread of color around the dilated blackness of the pupil and what looked out of them was nothing human at all…

"Eat of Her bounty," the voice commanded. "Blessed be!"

And the flame-clad Lady smiled at him and held the cup to his lips. "Drink deep of life, Dewi. Blessed be." And her eyes were fully human and more than human.

The honey-cake was sweet and moist, the wine laced with something else that he could not identify. Taken fasting, they went straight to his head. Edwina's fingers were twined with his, her face dazzling in the firelight, and her hair hung free in a pale flame-gilded mane, flicking at him as she whirled about him in the dance. The hot light of the fire backlit her body through the fine linen of her gown, teasing shadows of the substance within. From somewhere she had found or been given a crown of flowers and further garlands looped her shoulders, cinching her narrow waist. *Olwen*…he thought vaguely and knew he would have dared any giant to possess such a treasure. Or was she Blodeuwedd, mage-made out of flowers?

It did not matter. She was warm breathing flesh in his arms as the dance drew them close, her mouth tasting of honey, the scent of her more potent than the wine. He held her when the dance would have parted them, drew her a little aside from the throng and buried his face in her hair. He could feel the swift beating of her pulse under his mouth as he kissed her neck and his own heartbeat was louder than the drum in his ears. Her hands moved over his shoulders and back, caressing, and she purred pleasure at his touch.

"'Dwina…" His voice sounded thickened and strange. "*Brialla*, I must have you…"

It did not matter that the hilltop was alive with people and almost as bright as noonday. He would have taken her there on the bruised sheep-cropped grass if she had not pulled away and led him, like a sleepwalker, away from the firelight and into the verges of the forest that tonsured the hill. From short turf the footing changed to leaf-litter and the fresh uncurling fronds of bracken, yielding under their joined weight like the finest goose down. There was no pretense at courtship. He dragged at her skirts roughly, bunching them up, and her parted thighs received him.

* * * * *

Regan became aware that she was sorely out of breath, her scarlet gown was sticking to her back with sweat, she had a painful stitch in her side and she had never been happier in her life, a joy that ran elemental through her, body and soul. "I think I've got a thorn in my foot," she whispered to the Horned God as they came together in the figures of the dance and saw him grin.

"Hate to tell you where I've got thorns, sweeting." Regan heard herself giggle and wondered just what was in the sacramental wine. She let herself lean against him, ignoring the spiraling pattern that continued around them, feeling the heat of him and the hard strength.

"I could help you get them out," she offered, her hands feathering teasingly down the length of his back. He gave a stifled groan and his body arched involuntarily.

"Witch…"

"No. Goddess. For this night."

"Every day and every night, in my heart, Lady." The fires were dying and the darkness creeping in and it was not difficult to slip into the shadows of the trees. The moss beneath the oaks was cool and moist and softer than swan's-down underfoot and she drew him to her. His hands came up to loosen the drawstring at the neck of the gown and it slithered from her like a sloughed skin to pool at her feet. In the light of the risen moon, her body was glimmering pale as the creaming blossom of meadowsweet, tender as hawthorn flowers. Threads of blue veining traced her whiteness here and there and her full breasts were rounded and high and pink-tipped in the cool. "Before God, you are fairer than the moon and stars—" Prayer and invocation both and for the mortal as well as the Goddess within. She cupped his face in her palms and looked into his eyes. Leofric gazed back, his soul his own again and she kissed his mouth, tasting the last vestige of the wine.

"My Lord, my love and my lover," she whispered. "I swear Dewi has been lessoning you in sweet words."

"No." He took off the horned headdress and wedged it in the branches above them. "You are inspiration enough to give a dumb man speech." His hair was matted into sweaty elflocks from the close-fitting cap and Regan ran her fingers through it before pulling his head down for another kiss.

"I know that by custom we cannot be church-wed until Lammas," he said huskily, "but if you will consent, this night shall be our hand-fasting and marriage—vowed before the Lord and Lady of the Beltane Fires, no matter what we must swear to for earthly witness at another time."

Which seemed perfectly logical and right to Regan.

"Let it be so then, dearling," she whispered and pulled him down with her onto the yielding moss.

Beside the Old Gods of the land, even the Horned One is a newcomer. She is Corn Queen, Life-Bearer, He is the Green King, Seed-Sower. And the Land remembers and makes their Sacred Marriage with each renewing Spring.

Chapter Twenty-Six

The crushed bracken gave off a wet, wild scent, the leaf-litter sweet with slow decay. Dafydd lifted his head from Edwina's breast, the urgency of the first mating past, the fire in his blood no longer scorching. She was smiling up at him, eyes shadowed, languorous.

"'Dwina…" he breathed her name. "*Cariad*, let me see you?" Gently, he loosed the lacing of her gown, drew it from her, slipping shoulders and arms free of the hampering fabric. The chain Lady Regan had given her was a slender golden serpent coiling between her young breasts and naked and unashamed as Lady Eve before the Fall, she let him look at her, seeing in his eyes that she was fair indeed.

"Now you, Dewi." Less complicated this, for he wore only shirt and breeches and soft boots. He was spare still—would always be so, she judged, not having the build to carry weight of flesh or fat, but strength does not rely on weight. Muscle flowed smooth under the satiny skin, brown where the sun had kissed him. He was good to look at, interestingly male, and she drew him back down to enjoy the feel of him. Hands and lips had leisure and license to explore and they investigated each other like children until children's games were forgotten in adult passion once again.

They slid into sleep curled together in their hidden nest, waking to the shivering chill of dawn and the first impudent piping of birdsong. Dazed, Edwina sat up and Dafydd stirred and blinked. "*Duw*… A nymph, a fairy maid…" he whispered and reached for her, but she pushed him back. The garland of blossoms, tangled in the sheet-silver of her unbound hair, shed petals like tears.

"Dafydd, it's morning! Oh if they miss me, Da will take a switch to me! I must go!"

She struggled into the crumpled gown, trying desperately to smooth it and make herself neat and failing. Dafydd tried to help by pulling bracken and flowers from her hair, but however fast they worked, the morning advanced faster. Flushed and near to tears, Edwina was about to knot her hair loosely at her nape when Dafydd caught her hand. "Listen!"

Mingling with the birdsong, voices, singing. Young voices, children and not far away.

"Ooooh…" Edwina moaned. "Now they'll *know*…"

"They won't," Dafydd said quickly. "Here—" He reached up and cut a branch of hawthorn laden with white and green. "They're bringing in the May, are they not? So, we rose even earlier, to be here before them. Dry your eyes, sweeting. There, you're tidy. Do you carry and I'll cut."

The hall children greeted the sight of Dafydd and Edwina with shrill delight, accepting Dafydd's explanation without question. The sun was clearing the trees before they all trailed homeward, laden with flowers and singing a song Dafydd made up on the spot, involving summer and cuckoos and growing things. If anyone thought it odd that he and Edwina had been found together, no one spoke of it.

* * * * *

Anna was singing softly to herself as she drew the wooden paddle from her oven, the loaves risen and brown upon it. Shielding her hands from the heat with her apron, she lifted each, tapping the underside to test it for the hollow sound that meant it was done and set it to cool. Whitewing flapped down from his perch on the dresser, hopeful for crumbs. "*Da bach,* Jack?" he wheedled.

"Later, greedy one." She ran a finger over his glossy head and he preened at her touch. "My lord," she called, not looking around, "come you in. You make the day bright."

"How do you do that?" Leofric said, ducking his head under the lintel. Anna chuckled.

"Lucca sent word you would be visiting, of course. Do you think I have eyes in the back of my head? Or that Whitewing here tells me secrets? For shame. There is fresh bread and honey and ale—or would you prefer milk?"

"Milk, Anna, thank you." He moved, she saw, as if his head hurt him. It probably did. Those not used to the Beltane drink often took more of it than was needful and though the Good Goddess saw they came to no harm by it, still the headache was fair warning for the next time. But she did not have it in her to scold. She poured milk and spread honey on a warm crust of bread and watched fondly as he ate. Just so his father had come to sit at her hearth the morning after his first Beltane, a little dazed, unsure, but well-pleased with himself. But this was the son and he was troubled.

"What bothers you, lad?" she asked gently. "It is that the Lady chose Regan? Better a woman grown than a green girl when the god is on you. And she is most fit to be goddess to your god."

"But Anna—what will Regan—I mean, there might be a child—"

This she should have expected, that Hawiss should come to haunt him. Well, only time and Regan could exorcise that unhappy ghost. For here and now, guilt had no place in the joy of May-time. "You are hand-fast to the lady," she said calmly. "You will soon wed. And even if that were not so, what is done at Beltane is the will of the Goddess, as you well know. Your Da certainly did!"

And took advantage of it, she added silently, remembering Edmund with affection. *But no wonder, wed to that pious bitch.*

"Do you think I don't know my own half-brothers and sisters?" He gave her a wan smile. "It's just that I don't want to

Nettleflower

hurt Regan—" He hesitated, choosing his words with care. "Anna, is it true that you can see the future?"

"Lady bless us, lad, what a question!" She stared at him, genuinely nonplussed. "If that were so, if I could see what the years ahead hold, would I have wed my Edric, knowing he would die untimely?"

"I don't know. Would you?"

"Ah, most like I would, for true." She smiled. "No, Lord Leofric, I am no seer. Sometimes I have a—feeling—about things, that is all. I mind when you were a youngling, I felt it would be you and not your Da who would choose to live here. But I did not foresee your father's death, nor would I wish to. It's not a kindly gift nor a gentle one when She gives it to mortals. What did you want to know, my dear, to ask such a thing?"

"I'm not sure." He looked confused. "So much has happened. I thought there'd be peace here, so far from court, with no intrigues and plotting. But even here…"

"My Edric used to say that men find peace only in the grave and women only when their men are in the grave. He was joking, bless him, but it was a sore jest to me. Leofric my lord, when the tide is running, it's wise to go with it. So my grand-da said and he was a seaman out of Bristol."

"Seer you may not be, Anna, but you talk sound good sense." He set down his plate and Whitewing fluttered down to peck at the sweet crumbs. "Thank you." And he paused on the threshold. "Blessed be."

"Blessed be, my dear." She watched him out of sight as he strode across to the churchyard. Hawiss was chested there, under a flowering tree. A year it had been, come the next new moon, since she had died. "Goddess send you peace…"

* * * * *

Dafydd's experience of the morning had been entirely different. After bringing home the May in armfuls to decorate hall and bower, he and Edwina had left the children and slipped away to walk by the river. No one had questioned his invention that they had risen early, rather than having been out all night and now, in full view of any who cared to look, they strolled the meads hand in hand and did not talk, content to be in each other's company and nothing more. Edwina would not wed Coelrig's son, Dafydd had determined that. He would speak to Leofric and offer for her hand himself. There was no doubt in his mind that she would accept.

Duw, but she was lovely! There were still flowers tangled in her hair and on her neck a mulberry-stain mark where he had bitten her in their love-play and her eyes were violet-shadowed, mouth silken and scarlet as a poppy. Blodeuwedd, indeed — maiden of flowers, designed and fashioned for love.

The glossy golden cups of the marsh marigold were a cluster of vivid yellow on the riverbank — he scrambled to the edge and leaned to pick them for her.

"Dewi, be careful! Don't slip!"

He gave her a reckless grin, handing her the flowers with a bow, and she wove them into a chaplet as they walked and would have crowned his dark curls, but he said they would be fairer on her head and no queen was ever lovelier. It was flattery, of course, but sweet to be courted so, none the less and she did not welcome the summons from her mother, delivered by Aelfwine, to be about her chores. "I hope my lord weds the Lady Regan as quickly as may be," she said fiercely, clinging for one more kiss. "Then I shall be bower-maid again and no more my mother's drudge!"

This was blatantly unfair on Lucca, but Dafydd did not argue. "You will be bower-maid and my wife," he told her. "I shall speak to my lord tonight. Your father will heed his command, if he will not hear my suit."

"God grant it!" she whispered fervently and went reluctantly with the girl.

Dafydd watched them up the track, the two fair maids hand in hand. He had been wrong to name her Blodeuwedd, he thought. The Flower Maid had proved false to her wedded lord and brought doom upon them both. Edwina would keep troth. She should have a song for her own, no more borrowed finery of Helen or Olwen, but a song that bards and harpers yet to come would sing to a hushed hall and make men wonder that such beauty had ever existed. He might not have gauds to give her, jewels or gold to gild her, but he could grant her another gift—fame undying, her loveliness a legend, her faithfulness rivaling that of Penelope.

Words rioted in his head, fighting for precedence. To calm them and to give himself a rhythm to work with, he began to walk, constructing phrases, rejecting or polishing them, fitting together and taking apart, spinning the song as the spider spins a web from her own substance. His feet, undirected, carried him away from the steading and the new-tilled fields, across rough pasture peopled with fresh-shorn sheep, looking strange and ungainly without their thick woolly coats and into the fringes of the forest. The young sunlight glowed like largesse scattered by some lordly hand over the ground, lighting the fresh new leaves with almost translucent green. Sun and dappled shadow, tender warmth, the smell of growing things.

He sat at the base of a great beech, on a cushion of moss between humped roots like the knuckles of old age and put his head back against the smooth bark. Closing his eyes, he let the shifting sunlight paint his inner eyelids in brilliant colors—crimson and royal purple, gold like the sheen of the flowers he had picked for Edwina.

Lulled by the warmth, weary from the events of the night, he let himself slide into a doze and dreamed of the Beltane Fire, of the stag-horned god and the flame-headed goddess who had presided. She smiled at him, a smile full of wisdom that was old before the mountains were made, and held out a hand. He took it and was drawn into her arms.

"A fair dream, Dewi?" said a voice and he jerked awake to see the goddess of his imaginings standing there before him, the sun kindling her hair to a coronet of fire. That and the smile were the only similarities to the goddess, fortunately. The Lady was clad as simply as Edwina in a plain gown and kirtle, the skirts raised and tucked into her leather belt, stockingless and in old shoes. He blinked at her. "I saw you from the meadow," she said. "I've been with Wat, overseeing the wool clip. I've sent to my shepherd for my best tup—we're going to put him to Leofric's ewes."

It was an odd sort of conversation to be having with a goddess. Or maybe it was not so odd—the deity of the Beltane Fire would certainly be more concerned with the welfare of the flocks than with niceties such as dress or proper deportment. Dafydd gave her a grin.

"And you caught me sleeping the day away. Do you claim a forfeit, lady?"

"I'll think about it. Until then, you can share my noon-piece if you will and bear me company."

That was no hardship. She knelt beside him and they unpacked the scrip she had carried over her shoulder. There was more than enough for the two of them, bannocks and bacon and hard-boiled eggs, a handful each of dried fruits, washed down with clear sweet water from the brook that ran past toward the river. He had not realized how hungry he was until he began to eat.

They carefully talked of unimportant things, neither wanting to waken the memories of last night's happenings. The magic of Beltane was of firelight and darkness and things done then had no place in the sun. Yet Dafydd could not forget the sight of her, robed in crimson with a coronal of flowers on her unbound hair. Truly, only a god was fitted to be her mate.

Something tickled his hand, and he looked down to see a humble-bee, as big as the top joint of his thumb, crawling up from the moss. It was almost too laden to fly, furry as a bulrush and splotched with pollen and it buzzed intermittently like a scolding woman. Slowly, carefully, he lifted his hand until the creature felt the warm breeze and launched itself once more into erratic flight.

"You owe me honey for that good deed!" he reminded it and Regan laughed.

"Walk with me back to the flock, Dafydd," she suggested. It was pleasant to stroll through the dappled shade in no particular hurry and they joined their voices in one of the nonsense songs he had invented for the Hall-children. They came out of the woods' verge, at last, on the brow of the slope—below, the river swept a shallow curve down towards the mill—across it, the road was a dust-pale ribbon through the green of the water-meadows. And there on the road, a solitary rider, fair head bare to the sun.

Dafydd grinned. Even on this fine May afternoon, the thane was about his business. Probably he was planning to join Regan in checking the flock and to speak to Wat Shepherd of Regan's offer. Wat, being Wat, would ponder the suggestion until it was too late to implement it unless his lord chivvied him along.

He waved an arm, called, but the distant head did not turn until he stuck fingers in his mouth and whistled like a merlin, keen and shrill. Leofric reined his mount back, half-turned, shading his eyes to search out the source of that summons. Regan laughed and Dafydd raised a hand—and his wrist was seized from behind, an arm wrapping about his throat like a bar of iron, cutting off his voice. He kicked back out of instinct, drove an elbow into the bulk of whoever held him, heard a wheeze of anger and was almost free—

"Hold them fast, damn you!" came the yell and something hard clubbed down. He did not quite lose consciousness, but the gray fog stole all coordination from him. He was dragged upright, a hand tangling in his hair, pulling his head back, and the ice-touch of a blade was at his throat. Blinking desperately to clear the fog from his eyes, he saw as if in a dream the red horse fighting the bit as Leofric hauled it to a plunging halt at the river's edge. Someone laughed, soft, behind him.

"There is sensible," came the murmur. And, pitched to carry, "*Saes*! Do you value these lives, come no farther. And listen well. You have no Fyrd at your back this time, *Saes,* and we're minded to take a blood-price for betrayal. But you can buy them both, if you care to, like any other thralls. Twenty head of cattle, at the ford below the spring, by noon tomorrow. And come you alone, mind, and no shirt on you to hide a weapon, or we leave you their heads." Something hissed past Dafydd's ear and he saw the arrow impact between Rufus' fore hooves. "The next one will be in your heart, *Saes*!"

Dafydd did not see Leofric's response to that, for something thick and rank-smelling was dropped in muffling folds over his head, his wrists pulled back and tied and a halter was tight around his neck, leashing him like a recalcitrant hound or a tethered beast. Or like the thrall they had called him.

Well, he lived yet. It was small comfort, remembering the bloody shambles they had made of Geadas' yard, to know that the men who held him were the *Meibion Owain* who had thought him one of their own until his betrayal. He did not want to think what they might have in mind for him on that score. Or for the Lady Regan. Blood pays for blood.

The uneven footing, the impatient jerk of the leash, had him stumbling, sometimes falling, as his captors hurried him along. When finally he felt a too-close brush with some spiny bush rip into shirt and breeches, his own anger came boiling up and with it an idea. He leaned against the pull of the leash, cursing.

"*Annwyl Crist!* Will you take this thing from my head before I break my neck for your foolishness?"

"Soon enough, *bradwr*," came the growl and a hand between his shoulder blades thrust him forward, losing his balance completely so that he fell and all but rolled down a steep incline before he managed to catch himself and get his legs under him again. And there was a difference now—cooler on his skin, no sun-warmth and a feeling of being closed in. Where? The howe?

The hoodwink was pulled off. He shook his head and spat and glared about him at the hostile faces that ringed him in the dimness. "Owain would weep," he said scathingly. "A flock of sheep have more brain. A herd of donkeys!"

* * * * *

After the initial shock of the attack, Regan had tried to fight the grasping hands and encircling arms, kicking as hard as she could and making some impression, if the muttered curses were anything to go by. She had bitten someone as well, before a foully smelling something had been thrown over her head, all but smothering her, and she was hauled off her feet and dumped ungently over a pony's back. That was when she first had leisure to feel fear.

They were Welsh, she knew that from the accents and the lilt of the language that filtered through to her ears. She had heard the shout, understood some of it, enough to know this was no random assault. If it had been, both she and Dafydd would be dead. Might yet be dead soon enough. She breathed a prayer for them both as best she could, trying to take her mind from the reality of what was likely to happen to her before they killed her. She did not intend to suffer the indignity of rape if she had the least chance of avoiding it— just let one of them leave a blade within her grasp and she'd see herself out of life. Holy Mother, grant it!

The pony halted and she was dragged to unsteady feet, stumbling down a slope and falling at last to bruise her knees on stone. The hoodwink was pulled off—in the smoky flare of torchlight, she saw Dafydd's furious face and could have cried aloud with the relief of him being alive. Like her, he was bound and filthy and bruised—but if he was afraid, he did not show it. Nor did his voice betray him. Anger burned white-hot through it as he berated their captors—the tongue was Welsh, but spoken so fast and in an unfamiliar dialect that she understood barely one word in ten. But they—they were laughing and one of them came with a knife and cut Dafydd free. Shock held her rigid as realization came, but before she could find her voice to curse his betrayal, his hands were on her bound wrists, his eyes intent on hers.

Chapter Twenty-Seven
༨

"*Ma Dame,*" Dafydd whispered in accented but fluent Norman French, "Trust me and do as I say and we will both come safe out of this. I swear it. I will die before I let them harm you." And, as she gaped at him, he switched again to Saxon. "You are not hurt?"

She shook her head. "No. Dafydd, what—who are these—"

"*Meibion Owain,*" he said with a smile that did not touch his eyes. "The Sons of Owain, which makes them my kin, since my Da was one of them before the *Saes* hanged him. My sorrow, lady, that I could not tell you all before this, though surely it changes nothing between us."

"Between us…" Regan echoed, feeling a little like Anna's talking jackdaw.

"You'd have us believe she'd choose you, this fine *Saes* bitch, over one of her own kind?"

With a start, Regan recognized the speaker as one of Leofric's thralls.

"Guard your foul tongue, Coll," Dafydd snapped, "or I'll have it out of your head by the roots. She is—"

"No, let's hear it from her own lips, shall we, boy?" A silkily gentle voice, the speaker came into the light. He was lean, with a shock of hair white as a dandelion-clock and he moved with the grace of a stalking wildcat.

"All *Saes* are liars, Iorweth!"

"Peace, man. We shall see. Well, lady—what is he to you, our Falcon?"

They called him the Falcon—and Leofric's nickname for him was "tiercel". Regan stifled a bubble of hysteria in her throat.

Dafydd's eyes, agonized, pleaded silently for her comprehension. And Regan, going on what little she had heard, guessed wildly. "Maybe Coll will have heard me say that I would run off across the Dyke with my harper. I was for the Abbey, before Dafydd stole my heart. He said," and she embroidered on the idea, seeing his small grin of encouragement, "he would take me to Gwynedd and the king's court and there be wed."

"Did he so?" Iorweth smiled widely. "Well, he's a pretty lad, our Dewi, with a smooth tongue. Promised her marriage, did you, boy? We'll not make a liar out of you—after our business tomorrow, we'll have a wedding, yes?"

Watching Dafydd's face, Regan did not for the moment realize what was behind that innocent-sounding statement until Iorweth's grimy hand came out and fastened on her breast. Dafydd hissed a curse and struck out and earned himself a blow that dropped him gasping to his knees. "Dear me, the bridegroom doesn't seem to want to share his good fortune," Iorweth crooned. "What do you say, sweeting?"

Regan gave him stare for stare, meeting his gaze unflinching. "I'd sooner lie with a rutting hog," she heard herself say steadily.

"Do you say?" He looked at her consideringly while his hand weighed her breast as if it were a ewe's udder. "We shall see, shall we not? You may change your mind before we're done." His hand dropped and he turned his back on her. Dafydd climbed shakily to his feet, holding his jaw tenderly and after a moment turned his head and spat blood.

"There was no need for that," he snarled. "Before God, haven't I earned a share of your spoils? And have I ever asked for anything? So now I claim my right. The woman is mine!"

Iorweth swung to face him. "As to that, Dewi *bach*, we shall have to wait and see, won't we? Let's say that there have been doubts voiced as to your loyalty since you interrupted our raiding—we could have finished that bastard if you hadn't interfered."

"If I hadn't interfered, you'd have had the Fyrd on your scent within days! Man, the Earl Godwin, Wessex himself, was set to visit! If you'd killed his liegeman, he'd have hunted you down like vermin, if he had to scour the borders to do it. I saved your skins that day and you're dafter than I thought if you can't see that!"

"It's true," Regan said coolly. "The Earl is hot to clear these lands of wolfsheads. The murder of one of his thanes would be all the reason he'd need."

They were uncertain, she could sense that. Taking advantage of their confusion, Dafydd came to her side and began to work on the strips of rawhide that bound her wrists. The long fingers were deft on the knots—she caught the glint of gold from the ring he wore and felt comforted by it. Against all sense or reason, she did trust him to fulfill his promise to her and abide by his oath to Leofric.

The picture of the solicitous lover, he drew her to sit on a pile of heaped bracken, massaging her numbed hands. "You are the bravest lady I have ever known," he said, with a smile, "as well as the most beautiful." Someone muttered and Dafydd fixed them with a glare. "Where is the famed hospitality of the *Cymru*?" he demanded. "A drink, at the least!"

"Where are we, Dafydd?" Regan whispered. Now that her eyes had grown accustomed to the dimness, she could make out crudely dressed stone arching up from the walls in the darkness of the unseen roof.

"A fine house this, *merch,* and of the kind that all men come to, soon or late." A grinning man came to set a bowl down before her, along with a cup. "I'm Maelgwas, second to

Iorweth. Dewi here knows me. Me and his Da were like brothers. Make her comfortable, *bach*, eh? Most like she'll miss her soft bed in the *Saes* hall."

Regan made herself smile, though the man's sour body odor made her want to retch.

"We'll miss the honey-cakes from the kitchen," Dafydd said wryly. "For sure I don't smell any such cooking at your fire, man."

"Nor will you." Maelgwas gave a grunt and sat back. "But there's mutton from the flocks yonder. Eat up. While you're our guests, you'll not starve to death."

The mutton in the crude bowl was not appetizing to the nose and it tasted worse—seared on the outside, but raw within and none too fresh. If it was one of Leofric's beasts, it was no recent kill.

One bite was enough for Regan. The coarse stale heel of bread was better, was at least palatable and there was ale in the cup to wash it down. Neither sat easily in her belly.

Nor did Dafydd eat much. He tried his best for her, asking for something to wrap her against the chill of the stone, but the thin spread of bracken was not enough to cushion the hard earthen floor and the blanket Maelgwas tossed to him was thin and verminous and stank. It provided little warmth for her comfort.

Neither did her thoughts. Leofric must guess that the exchange would be a trap. Would he risk that for the chance of rescuing the son of a wolfshead? No—but for his hand-fast bride, he would walk through fire. The man relished danger. Well, he would be walking straight into it if he came to the meet-point. What would he do? Counter the ambush that he must know to expect with some plan of his own? One thing was sure—the morrow would see bloodshed. Regan could only pray that none of it would be Leofric's, or Dafydd's for that matter. She knew that if there was any way that Dafydd could prevent it, Leofric would not fall into Iorweth's hands.

"You are shivering," Dafydd said softly.

"Mmm." She nodded, aware that if she tried to speak, her teeth would chatter. He shifted closer to her, slipping an arm about her shoulders, and she was grateful for the warmth of him. There was a lewd comment from the hunkered group by the smoky fire, but no one interfered and she let her head drop to rest on his chest, closing her eyes and willing her body to relax. She could feel the steady rise and fall of his breathing, the beat of his heart. Against all sense and reason she slept.

* * * * *

Leofric did not move until the band had disappeared into the trees, then he reined his horse aside and leaned down to wrench the arrow from the ground. An ice-like calm wrapped around him, trapping the fear and fury deep within his soul. Now was not the time to purge it. He turned Rufus on his hocks and kicked him into a gallop for home.

The ford below the spring. He knew it, not far inside the Intake wood, where there was little cover for armed men to come up unseen. Twenty head of cattle—what, by the One Tree, would they do with that number of beasts? They would never get so many across the border into Wales, either on the hoof or slaughtered and packed on mules. And knew, in gut and bone, what the intended outcome was. Slaughtered beasts and men left lying for the hooded crows, Regan and Dafydd along with them. If they were not already dead.

No. That way led to madness and he needed a clear head for what had to be done. Leofric crouched lower over Rufus' neck and urged him on with voice and heels.

The gateward saw him coming and his very speed was warning enough. The gates were slammed shut as soon as horse and rider were through and armed men stood ready.

"Gather the house-men," Leofric barked. "Swords and spears, but no man leaves the garth save on my word. Wolfsheads," and remembered the lilt of the voice, "Welsh—

have Regan and Dafydd. To ransom, they say." He was vaguely aware of a woman's shriek, knew it was Edwina but could spare no time for her yet. "They both lived when I last saw them," he went on over the rising shouts of outrage from his people.

"I'll send to Swein," Godwine bellowed, "raise the Fyrd, send word to Guthlac-Thane—"

"No," Leofric cut in. "Do you think they won't be watching for that? Until I see their bodies, I will count Regan and Dewi still living—" He found he was at the dais table where someone had already spread the map. Leofric stared at the painted hide as if he had never seen it before, the enormity of what threatened Regan surging against the barriers of his self-control. Be cold, he told himself. Be cunning. None had more guile than Old One-Eye, his father used to say, not even Loki-Trickster. And he'd tap the side of his nose and wink. *Odin, of your wisdom guide me through this maze.*

The ford, the sparse cover of that first swathe of Intake— the wolfsheads had how many men? He had seen only five when his two were taken, though there were more at the burning of Geadas' house. Say they had eight, ten at the most. He could muster twice that from steading and village alone. But there was no way to conceal twenty armed and armoured men. Unless…

Among the countless songs Dafydd had sung for him during his convalescence, the Saga of Odysseus had been a favorite with them both. Odysseus the Cunning, who had conceived the idea of the Wooden Horse that brought down Troy Town, who had won past the Sirens and braved Scylla and Charybdis… The beginnings of an idea began to form, Odysseus and the escape from the blinded Cyclops…

But he needed to get his men in rather than out. He frowned at the map. Slowly he raised his hand and the hubbub in the hall swiftly died. In a clear, emotionless voice he told of the ultimatum, felt as well as heard the shock of it. Twenty head of cattle, near enough a fortune and, moreover, at this time of the year, not so many short of being his complete herd.

"Sifrith," he said, "take four men and muster every plough-ox on my land. Godwine will tell you where they're byred. Make up the tally with heifers first, then the oldest milk-cows. Hold them close to the steading gates and pray to all the gods and saints that we have fog tomorrow."

"You'll not give them what they ask for!" Godwine roared. "Are you wit-lost? May God help them, Lady and lad are both dead by now and those bastards only want you sarkless and unarmed to␣gralloch you as well—"

Leofric looked him in the eyes and smiled and what Godwine saw there stopped the words in his throat.

"Yes," the thane said, voice silky as polished metal. "I will give them all that they ask for." He glanced around the hall, meeting each man's gaze. "See to your weapons and byrnies and get what sleep you can."

He himself got little. Betrayal, the Welshman had said. That made no sense. Regan had betrayed no one and neither had Dafydd, surely, unless it be by guesting in a *Saes* hall— and then his memory gave him the scene he had witnessed the spring evening as his horse crested the rise above Geadas' farm, Dafydd mounted among a group of wolfsheads. Their weapons had been lowered and when Dafydd had spurred free of them, the arrow had come at Leofric, not the nearer target. And Dafydd had shouted something in Welsh. He frowned, hunting after it—*"He's mine!"*

But Dafydd had saved his life, had sworn the most sacred of oaths that transcended all others and Leofric knew that the bard would hold to it no matter what befell them.

Sworn man. It made no difference what race or creed a man was born to, that oath cut all such bonds. Nor did it matter what allegiances Dafydd had held before the ring-giving. The slate had been wiped clean.

* * * * *

Led out into the morning, Regan spent a moment doing nothing but draw in lungfuls of the sweet damp air. Mist was heavy around, thick and chill. The sun might burn it off, but not for a while yet. A group of ponies waited nearby and Maelgwas urged them in their direction, but she paused long enough to glance back at where they had spent the night. If her hands had been free, she would have crossed herself. The long mound of grassed and shrub-covered earth stood some twenty feet high and in the skeining mist had an otherworldly menace about it. *Sleep one night in a fairy mound,* memory whispered, *and wake on a cold hillside with three hundred years gone by and all friends and kindred cold bones under the clay…*

"Up with you, *merch*." Maelgwas hoisted her onto the back of a shaggy black pony, bridled and cinched with rope and as an afterthought threw the blanket over her shoulders to cloak her against the rawness of the air.

Regan was doubly glad of it. Under its cover she was able to work on the slick hide thongs, already slippery with the moisture in the air and stretching as they softened. With a little work, her hands would be free.

She hardly recognized the country they traveled through, partly because she was not paying attention and partly because the mist changed everything with its subtle alchemy. The band hardly spoke, to Dafydd or her or to each other, and the two of them were flanked on either side by Maelgwas and Iorweth. Even with the mist to hide them, she doubted they would get far if they made a break for it. The Sons of Owain might be expecting such an attempt. Best do as Dafydd said and take the chance when it came. If it came.

* * * * *

Dafydd's wrists were raw, but the blood and sweat of his exertions were doing their part to soften the rawhide. He could feel it stretch minutely when he put pressure on it, only a little, but enough. He slipped his hands free just as Iorweth reined in his pony and signaled the band to halt.

They were on the edge of a wide clearing in the woodland that sloped gently down toward the river. The mist lay even thicker there, but he could hear the chuckling rush of water over a shallow stony bed and guessed this must be the ford. The band vanished into the trees, leaving them alone with Maelgwas. There was no way to judge the hour, no sight of sun. The pony under him seemed to have fallen asleep, hipshot and head hanging. Dafydd shivered, feeling as if the damp cold had got into his very bones. Yesterday's sun seemed like a dream. If it was yesterday and not the centuries of the old legends. *Sleep but one night in a howe of the Fair Folk…*

His pony shifted its weight to the other hip. Dafydd glanced across at Maelgwas, but the man was staring straight ahead. Regan's face was pale, her freckles standing out like saffron on dough and she was biting at her lower lip. He gave her what he hoped was a reassuring look. It was hard, waiting. Waiting. The band were so sure that Leofric would come… Not for the first time, Dafydd wondered what it felt like to die.

A sound filtered through the roiling mist, a distant lowing, coming nearer. Maelgwas' pony snorted, tossing its head, and Maelgwas was smiling, fingering the hilt of the long knife in his belt. Other sounds crept in, crackle of undergrowth, hooves on soft ground. Terror and relief mingled oddly in his gut, Dafydd tensed himself for action. Shapes appeared in the mist, dark against lighter gray, firming to the dark red of Leofric's cattle, breath steaming, wide sweeping horns gleaming, grumbling as they were herded through the ford and up the bank and there was a man with them, half-naked and ghost-pale as if it had been he who had ridden from the howe, a king of old days, a warrior out of a dream.

Dafydd threw himself sideways, snatching for Maelgwas' knife as the man was unbalanced and drove it in and up with all his strength. The blade caught in bone and he did not wait to free it, not registering the man's agonized grunt or the hot drenching of blood that gushed over his hand before he released the hilt. He scrabbled to his feet, ducked between the panicked and plunging ponies and caught Regan as she flung herself from her pony's back. "Run!" he instructed breathlessly. "For the ford! And don't stop for anything!" If he could do nothing else, he could buy her safety with his life. He whirled, running like a hare for the river. "Go back!" he yelled at the full pitch of his lungs. "Leofric! Go back!"

Something tugged at his blanket-cloak—and again—and a shaft whistled past his ear. He jinked like a deer, heading for the confusion of milling cattle, but suddenly his footing was gone from under him and he was pitched into the churned muddy shallows.

Somewhere above him a single voice howled the *Saes* war-shout and other voices answered it in a deep baying chant and as Dafydd tried to get his legs under him again, something large knocked him flat again and he rolled to avoid a forest of sharp hooves trampling over him, fighting free of the hampering wet folds of blanket and struggling to his feet. A man lurched toward him, masked in glistening red—as he went down, Dafydd took the blade from his slackened grasp. It came to his hand as sweetly and familiarly as his harp, the *Saes* long-knife, the heavy-spined scraemasax that Leofric had taught him to use. And there was Leofric, at the center of a vicious tangle of hand-to-hand fighting, hard-pressed. Dafydd did not stop to think. He used the blade to hack his way to Leofric's side and fought there for both their lives in a world that had shrunk to a nightmare confusion of shouts and screams and splattering blood.

Chapter Twenty-Eight

Regan stumbled over tussocks and roots, almost falling down the slippery river bank and when hands reached for her, she struck them away in terror before she recognized Sifrith's face. "Across to the other side, Lady," he panted. "You'll be safe there."

Well, so she would, but there were scores to settle first. And if she had not the strength to swing a scraemasax, she still had other fighting skills. "Your bow, man, if you're not needing it."

He stared but did not question, dropping his quiver at her feet as she tucked the trailing skirts of her kirtle through her belt, strung the short yew-wood bow and scrambled up to where the scrub would give her both cover and a good vantage point. Her first arrow overshot her target, but she had the range now and her second struck true, taking a yelling wolfshead in the throat and dropping him in mid-stride. Smiling grimly, she set about choosing her targets with the cool head and straight eye that had been trained into her as a child, and she blessed the father who had not thought such pastimes unladylike.

In the tangle of fighting men it was hard to tell how many of her shafts struck home. It was fortunate that the struggle was brief, for she had her last arrow nocked to the string when someone raised a shout and she realized that the wolfsheads were in retreat. But all she could see was Leofric, standing above a fallen enemy, sword bloody in his hand. His head thrown back, he was baying the Saxon war-shout in challenge and triumph, a paean of victory. She did not hesitate. She ran to him across the clearing and he caught her in his arms, swinging her up off her feet and bruising her mouth with his kiss. "My love, my life! Is it well with you?"

She caught her breath on a sob, wanting very much to cry now that the thing was over. "Very well," she said shakily. "Oh Leofric, you fool, put me down! Where is Dewi?"

* * * * *

Looking back, Dafydd supposed that the battle could not have lasted very long, but at the time it seemed to be an eternity until quite suddenly it was over and there was no one left to fight. He gulped at the moist air, legs unsteady under him, and the knife in his hand was too heavy to hold up. He looked down at it, at the slime of blood and muck that glued it to his hand. He doubled forward and vomited, retching when nothing came up. And straightened, wiping his eyes. "Entirely too well-mannered, is it?" he asked himself softly.

"Are you scathed?" Leofric's voice, with an edge to it that raised the hackles on Dafydd's neck. He blinked up at the man standing before him, Regan held in the crook of his arm. Her hair was streaming loose, the ends snarled and clotted dark — Leofric was bloody from matted blond crest to his boots, the broad chest painted with it, some of it his own by the looks of it, though he seemed to be feeling no pain. The pale blue-gray eyes were brilliant, pupils shrunk and whites showing like a wild stallion's and abruptly Dafydd saw the reality in the old stories of battle madness. Was this how they looked, those baresark warriors of the legends, with the hero-light about them, terrifying to enemy and friend alike? No, this was no baresark, but a leader of men, alight with joy and exultation. "Are you scathed, tiercel?"

"I—don't think so," he croaked, though he was far from certain. The Macsen-fierce face was bright with a laughter that he could not understand and never wanted to see again on anyone's features.

"That's as well." He swung past, his lady on his arm — marshalling his men, counting heads, and Dafydd got his legs to move and staggered down the bank and into the ford, going to his knees there and cupping his hands to drink. Except that the water was running red with mud and blood and a body lay face-up, wedged on the stones. The head was split open, but the river had washed the wound clean, fronding the dark hair like weeds around the great gash that glistened with bone and brain. Still, the dead man was quite recognizable. Coll.

Dafydd knelt and looked at him. He supposed he ought to feel something, be pleased or sorry, pray for the man's unshriven soul. There was nothing but numbness.

"Come up, lad." A hand was urging him to his feet, holding him there. Godwine, bloody as a butcher, concern warring with delight on his face. "God be thanked, you're safe. Is this blood yours or another's? Can you walk? No matter, we'll find you a mount. Was that mist not a godsend? 'Get you in among the beasts,' my lord told us, 'for they'll not be counting legs, only heads,'' and the mist was our blessing and their bane, for we knew they would lie in ambush, while they did not think we would come unseen. By Thor and Odin both, that was a fight! He's his father's son, that cub of ours! I mind, at Rhyddygroes—" The captured ponies stood in an uneasy knot and Godwine guided Dafydd to the nearest. "At Rhyddygroes he fought like a young lion, but that was nothing to today."

Dafydd leaned against the warm hairy shoulder of the pony, too spent for the moment to mount it. But he got a handful of the rough mane and Godwine gave him a leg up and the creature snorted and danced a bit at the smell of blood on the trampled grass. There was nothing worth looting from the dead — they were being let lie where they had fallen, food for wolf and kite until there might be leisure to tip the remains into a common grave. The men of the steading were administering to their wounded, rounding up the scattered cattle, beginning to straggle back home. Dafydd went with them, only vaguely aware of the ride for the aches that were beginning to make themselves felt. Ahead Leofric rode, with Regan in his arms. They had not been apart since the end of the fight.

Poets do not sing of the aftermath of battles. Dafydd knew why now.

* * * * *

Edwina had not slept, though after her first wail of shock when she heard the thane tell of her lover's kidnapping, she had stopped her noise by cramming her fist against her teeth. By making sure she was among the women serving the hastily gathered war-council with food and ale, she had heard much of the thane's ruse with the men hidden among the cattle and the planning of it. She had watched during the night as they talked quietly among themselves and saw to their weapons and byrnies. The women had no place in this, for this was men's business—but she longed fiercely to do something, anything, that would bring her man back safe to her. And the Lady Regan too, of course.

"In the Danelaw, women fight alongside their men," she announced and got a scathing look from her mother.

"Who told you that rubbish, girl? Oh there may be women with an army, but they'll be camp-followers, draggle-tail drabs who'll lift their skirts for anything that can pay. Do not you even think of such things!"

"Lady Regan can fight," Edwina struck back. "She has her father's sword and she can use it too!"

Lucca put down the dish of oatcakes and took her daughter by the shoulders. "You listen to me," she said firmly. "What the Lady Regan—God grant she lives through this day!—does or does not do is for her to decide. While you are under your father's roof, what you do or do not do is for him and me. Take this to my lord and no more nonsense."

She did as she was told, wild thoughts of cutting off her hair and stealing breeks and byrnie still buzzing in her mind as she took Lord Leofric his food. He was sitting chin on fist, deep in thought, but he roused himself to give her a smile of thanks and when he turned to go, reached out to take her hand.

"I'll bring him back, 'Dwina," he said softly. "I swear it."

"Yes, my lord," she murmured, because of course he had to say that—Dafydd was his sworn man and it was his lord's duty to defend or avenge him. But instead of letting her go, he gripped tighter and she saw his eyes, wide and dark as they had been on Beltane night.

"I'll bring him back," he said again. "And my lady with him."

After one frozen moment she nodded, speechless, and he let her hand slip. "Let me come with you!" The words burst from her and he bowed his head.

"I can't. You know that." Godwine was coming toward them, carrying the thane's great sword, and Lord Leofric stood up with a sigh. "'Dwina. Listen. I know it's hard, to wait and know nothing. Women have the hardest part in any battle—we kill our enemies in hot blood, but women must tend their own afterwards and sometimes have them die for all they can do. I swear to you now, on my life, that I will bring Dafydd back to you, God and Jesu and St. Martin witness it, or I will not come back at all. Pray for us both, little sister."

Biting her lip, she backed away and watched the men gather in the gray morning, a thin rain falling out of the mist as if heaven itself were weeping. They had ridden out and she had watched and prayed. She had prayed to almost every saint she could put a name to, with especial devotion to St. Martin, the warrior saint who was the thane's patron, and St. David, who she thought might be Dafydd's, and St. Brigid who was her own. She did not stop praying, going mechanically about her chores until someone shouted from the gate that there were men approaching and a moment after that Lord Leofric rode at their head.

"Now God and His Holy Mother both be thanked!" Lucca breathed and hurried out. Edwina dropped her carding back into the fleece basket and followed after, her heart in her throat.

By the time they got to the gate, it was clear that Lord Leofric indeed led the steading men and that Lady Regan rode with him, held safe across his saddlebow in his arms. But Edwina's eyes were straining past him for another figure. He promised, she told herself desperately, he promised to bring him back—but was it a living man or a corpse with which he had fulfilled his oath?

There—back there, astride a rough-coated pony, a rider slumped forward as if it were too much effort to sit upright, but alive and not too much hurt or they would be bringing him home on a litter. Gathering her skirts, Edwina slipped out of the gate and ran down the track, threading through the returning men until she came to his side and put up her hand to cover his on the pony's neck. She did not speak, but he lifted his head and looked at her and she thought he tried to smile.

She smiled back, though it hurt her heart to see the state of him, all filthy and bloody, with the eyes of him dark and dazed with exhaustion in his face and the shadowing of a two-day beard. "Tch," she heard herself say, lightly scolding, "there is bad company you have been keeping, Dewi."

He shook his head. "They were my father's friends," he said, not making much sense. *He's mazed*, she thought, *he must have taken a blow to the head*. Well, no one but herself should have the tending of him.

"If they were," she said sensibly, "then they should have had more care for his son." But he just shook his head again and said no more until they were inside the garth and boys came to take the ponies. Edwina offered her shoulder, seeing his unsteadiness, but he muttered something about getting her gown dirty and managed a fair enough dismount, though his legs almost failed under him as his feet touched the ground. That was all the excuse Edwina needed. She braced herself for his weight, got his arm around her shoulders and helped him into the hall.

Lucca and Anna were already busy with the worst wounded—Huw, who had a sword slash across the belly, and Aidan, missing a hand at the wrist. Edwina led Dafydd to a bench at the hearth, sat him down and brought a crock of water and cloths to wash the blood from him. He sat and let her do it as if made of stone, even though the herb-steeped water must have stung in his cuts. She found no head wound, which was a blessing, though there were bruises enough there and on his upper body when she eased the ripped and ragged sark from his shoulders. He caught his breath at her gentle touch exploring the dark-mottled patch on one side and she guessed at cracked or broken ribs—but it was when she would have stripped his sleeve that she found the worst of his hurts. Fresh blood welled up as the clotted fabric came away from the deep gash that had opened up his left arm from shoulder to elbow. Edwina flinched as if she felt it in her own body, but he merely stared at it incuriously.

"You said you weren't scathed," someone snapped and Leofric was leaning over Dafydd, scowling.

"I didn't feel it," Dafydd said calmly.

"You will, soon enough," the thane promised. "It's a clean cut, Edwina—stanch it and bind it well and it'll do."

She washed it first, holding the lips of the wound apart as she had seen Anna do, thankful to see no broken edge of bone or severed sinew, and bound on a pad smeared thick with Lucca's green salve. The bite of that on raw flesh made him blanch paler than he was already and she nodded, knowing that the stuff burned like fire.

"Bide still," she whispered. "It'll pass. I'll fetch you something to drink." There was mead poured already, doctored with Anna's best pain-easing potion. She took up a cup of it and saw Regan trying to get Leofric to sit down long enough to be tended. The lady was not having much luck.

"Let be, Regan! I tell you, I'm not hurt!"

"What's this then?" she snapped. "Pig's blood?"

There were rivulets of fresh scarlet among the blackening clots on the naked chest, running down to soak into the waist of his breeches.

"A scratch," Leofric said abruptly. "Godwine, where are you? Gather the rest of the sound men and we'll ride after the two who escaped. The hounds can cut their trail. Padraig? Where is the man? Padraig, I'll need a fresh horse."

Edwina went back to her patient, found him grinning bemusedly at the argument.

"Listen to him bate!" he said wonderingly. "Worse than Macsen. At least the bird can be hooded!"

"I'd like to see anyone try to hood Lord Leofric, though from the looks of her, Lady Regan is like to try," Edwina murmured, smiling. "Here, drink this. Then I'll bind your ribs and you must sleep."

He obeyed, biddable as a child, and she saw him settled before going to help the other women. Sifrith, she found, had a slash across the shoulder-blade that needed careful binding and it was while she helped Morwenna with this that she discovered that prisoners had been taken.

"But Dewi said nothing of it?" she frowned. Sifrith sucked in a breath at the smart of the salve, let it out again in one heartfelt expletive and apologized straight after.

"I doubt he noticed," he said. "Yes, two of the bastards we brought back with us. Padraig has them in charge. My Lord says he'll give them fair trial before he hangs them, which is more than they'd have done for him or your Dewi. Are you done, sweeting?" This to Morwenna, who was tightening the last knot.

Edwina scowled thoughtfully. Dafydd had said they were friends of his father, which she supposed was as likely as anything else, and her curiosity was piqued. She slipped from the hall, making her way across the garth to the forge and Padraig's store, which was the most secure lock-place on the steading. Donal was standing outside the door, billhook, in hand and Edwina breathed a small thanksgiving that it was not Padraig himself. He would have sent her away—kindly enough, but firmly, with a rumbled admonition that some things were not for maids. Donal was a far easier prospect. She sidled forward.

"Sifrith told me," she said. "Are they in there?"

"Hog-tied," he said laconically.

She stretched her eyes admiringly. "I've never seen a wolfshead," she breathed. "Not up close. Are they very fierce?"

"Not anymore." Donal stood up a little straighter under her regard. "Had all the fierce knocked out of 'em, see. M'lord wanted them alive, or they'd be carrion like their pack-mates."

"Sifrith thinks they'll hang," she told him.

"That'd be justice," Donal agreed. "Is he all right, your Dafydd?"

"A slice down from the shoulder and maybe a broken rib or two. And what do you mean, 'my' Dafydd?"

Donal snorted. "Oh come on, Edwina. Everyone knows it."

"Holy Mother, I hope my Da doesn't!" she said prayerfully.

"Then he hasn't asked for you yet?"

"This place breeds rumor as a dunghill breeds flies!" Edwina sighed. "Donal, can I go in and look at them? Just a look?" She wished she had Lady Regan's air of command, but made do with a wheedle instead.

"My Da will have my hide in strips!"

"He won't know unless you tell him."

He looked crafty. "What's in it for me then?"

Edwina was not prepared for this. "I don't know—what would you like?"

"A kiss?" he asked hopefully.

"There is wicked," she scolded, prim. "Oh all right. But after, mind!"

It was dim inside until her eyes adjusted. Holding her skirts tight against her legs to avoid contamination, Edwina stood and stared at the captives. They were very dirty and sullen and more ragged than beggars, but otherwise they were just men. She wondered what else she had thought to find.

"Expected horns, did you, pretty?" one of them said hoarsely. "Cloven hooves and a tail, at the least?"

"Well, we got tails," said the other. "But in front, like. You want to see?"

"Dafydd said you were friends of his father," Edwina said coldly, glad that the dimness hid her blush. "But I do not think that can be right. You would not talk filth in front of a decent girl and his betrothed, else."

"Oh then you must pardon us, mistress, for we did not know." It was a mockery of courtesy. "We should have guessed, mind. The cub-wolf runs with his own kind until he winds the scent of a *Saes* bitch in heat—"

He didn't get further than that. Edwina took a pace forward and swung at him, the flat of her palm cracking across his face and turned on her heel, flinging out the door with their laughter in her ears. She quite caught Donal by surprise.

"Seen enough, have you? Hey, what about my kiss?"

He was dumbfounded when she told him in no uncertain terms what he could do about it.

Chapter Twenty-Nine

Dafydd woke in a sweat, shuddering, fought free of the dream and forced his eyes open. He lay on his own pallet but in the thane's room. It was dim-lit by a couple of rush-dips and his arm ached as if a wolf's jaws were locked there, grinding down to the bone. But there was a deeper pain in him, not attributable to battle wounds.

He could not recall much of his father. The proud brave *Cymru* warrior he had imagined, fierce to claim and defend what had been stolen from his people, had acquired a darker side. If Gryfydd had been all that Iorweth and Maelgwas claimed, then he was—had been—a reiver, betrayer of trust, murderer. On one hand, he, Dafydd, was the traitor, betrayer of all that his father had stood for and believed and died for, choking out his life on the end of a *Saes* rope. Those who had died at the ford had died because Gryfydd's son had come into a *Saes* hold and stayed there and grown to love where he should not. Gryfydd's true son would have opened the gates to his father's friends and let in the wolves to ravage and destroy. His stomach twisted with nausea.

He lay and stared up at the shadowed ceiling and thought of the oath he had sworn, of the reasons he had for swearing it. It made him traitor, yes, to his father, his slain family, his race. But he could not make himself feel regret. When it came down to it, here in this place he had found more love and companionship and simple caring than ever before in his life and that from the *Saes* who should have been his enemies. What had he had from his own people? He could not remember his mother. His father had all but ignored him. Owen his teacher had cared, yes. But Owen had never demanded anything of him save that he be true to the art they both loved. What makes a man *Cymru* or *Saes*, other than an accident of birth? What was he? Oh *Cymru* by birth, without doubt. But in his heart?

Convulsively, hissing at the flare of pain, Dafydd sat up, swinging his feet to the floor. He cradled his arm across his chest, rocking until the white-hot gnawing had eased to a throb that pulsed with his heartbeat. This was too hard and bitter a thing for him to think through now, while the hurt was on him. How long had he slept? It was impossible to tell night from day, here in the shuttered room. Outside, beyond the door, there were voices, sounds of movement on the dais. It had probably been going on for a while, he realized, though he hadn't noticed it. They would be talking over the fight at the ford. He wasn't sure he wanted to be drawn into that discussion. But his arm ached and his belly was empty and there would be remedy for both in Lucca's kitchen.

It wasn't easy to get into his shirt—any movement hurt. But he managed it and the tunic and sat for a moment after, getting his breath, hands spread on his thighs. He looked down at them, at the long fingers calloused on the tips from the strings of his harp, at the glinting gold of the ring Leofric had given him in token of their oath, each to each. He had meant that oath, every word of it, with every fiber of his being. Let that be his touchstone then, regardless of blood or race or what others might consider his duty.

What passed in the hall, he discovered when he eased open the stair door, was no discussion over ale-cups. It was a trial, a court of justice. Two men stood before the dais, hedged about by drawn blades, their hands bound behind them. But it was Iorweth who drew Dafydd's gaze and all but stopped the breath in his throat, Iorweth with his head held high, grim face arrogant under the shock of white hair, so that he was scarcely aware of the other prisoner.

He had not known that any of the wolfsheads had been taken alive. Now, knowing it, he wondered why, for surely there could be no mercy for them, nor did they deserve it. They had killed Aeditha and Wyn and Geadas—they would have killed Leofric and himself and raped Regan before she too was killed. The knowledge did not help. He stood where he was, able to see both the prisoners and the thane and felt pity move in him.

"This is our land!" Iorweth was shouting. "You'll have no joy of it, even while you keep it, which will not be long!"

"Will it not?" Leofric said coldly. "You are mistaken. These hides are my land and I do not let go that which is mine. It has been Saxon land for generations and before that the men of Rome held it. If it was ever Welsh-owned," he said, hard, "then it was long and long ago, and for all your snarling and yelping like jealous curs, it will never be so again." And Dafydd saw that he smiled. "But since you covet it so much, I will give you, at least, a part of it. Enough to lie under."

"*Saes* justice!" Iorweth spat on the scuffed rushes underfoot.

"Yes, *Saes* justice!" Leofric snapped. "Your lives for the lives you ended. Take them out and hang them."

The prisoners were hustled out of the hall and Dafydd pushed through to Leofric's side as the thane stared from the dais. "My lord," he began, grabbing at a sleeve, and Leofric paused, turning to face him. Anything he might have said and Dafydd did not know what it would have been, died in his throat. The pale Saxon features were implacable. Even if he sued for mercy, there could be none.

But had Aeditha and Wyn been shown mercy?

"A priest?" he said instead. "Should they not be shrived?"

"Why?" Leofric said coolly. "Their souls are no concern of mine." And he turned away. There was nothing more Dafydd could find to say, so he walked at his lord's shoulder out into the bright afternoon. The eldritch mist was no more. It was again the lovely May and a cuckoo was calling somewhere near. Godwine had slung two coils of rope over his shoulder and was leading the procession out of the steading and up the track towards Old Top and the forest that ringed it. Trees aplenty for hanging wolfsheads, Dafydd thought and found himself wondering how he and Leofric would have fared if Iorweth had won at the ford. Somehow he knew that the rope-death would be more merciful.

The prisoners were not going meekly to their doom and their struggles slowed the pace, which was just as well, for the following throng included some of those wounded from the ambush. Dafydd couldn't have managed a faster speed himself. His head felt strange and light and a great distance from his feet, he supposed the blood he had lost might have something to do with that, or his empty belly.

About halfway up the hill, a little short of the hawthorn thicket where Dafydd had waited for Edwina on Beltane night, Godwine halted under a great beech. One massive branch extended out over the track some ten feet above it and he tossed the ropes up and over. There was no ceremony. The nooses were fitted around the wolfshead's necks and willing hands hauled them up into the air. They kicked and jerked for a while, choking, before the end came and they hung slack on the ropes, circling slowly. Dafydd was glad he had not eaten. For sure his belly would have rejected it. He shot a quick glance at Leofric's profile. No softening there, no hint of nausea. So looks the executioner, witnessing the death decreed. Gryfydd had died on the end of a rope too and for the same crimes. Rapine, theft and murder. And he was Gryfydd's son.

He turned on his heel and left the crowd, making for the steading wearily. He knew where his heart lay and he was Leofric's man, body and soul, his shoulder-to-shoulder man — but how would Leofric see him when he knew the truth? The man who had just hung his father's friends? And Edwina? Would she turn from him? Dafydd ap Gryfydd, son of a reiver and a wolfshead. He lurched aside from the track and crouched to retch like a cat, spitting out bile, and afterwards could only manage a few more steps before he had to sit down in the grass, head resting on drawn-up knees.

"Dewi?" Sifrith's voice and Sifrith's arm about his shoulders. "Dewi, man, you shouldn't have walked so far! Lucca will have your guts." There was friendliness in the words and Dafydd flinched from it. If Sifrith knew — if Lucca knew — ah Jesu, Edwina would never come near him again and the others would drive him out of the steading. Or hang him. *Reiver. Wolfshead.* "Dewi? Come up, lad, let me help you. Your first time, eh? And you with a green wound on you — no wonder you're feeling faint."

"I'm his sworn man," Dafydd said urgently, desperately.

"Of course you are," Sifrith agreed, puzzled. "On your feet, man, and let's get you back before you take a fever. I can't be carrying you, not with this shoulder."

He would rather have stayed where he was, found a hole to crawl into and laired up like a sick animal, but Sifrith was talking at him, coaxing as he did with his oxen and it took too much effort to argue.

"Didn't I say you should not have gone?" There was clear satisfaction in Lucca's voice as she regarded the two of them, drooping with exertion as they trailed back into the hall. "And Dafydd — I thought you had more sense. Morwenna, metheglyn for your daft swain and Dewi here!"

It was sweet with added honey and herbs, but it cloyed on his tongue and he set it by after the first taste. Morwenna, perhaps better aware what ailed him, brought bread and curds and this went down easier.

"Does your arm pain you?" she asked gently. He shook his head.

"It aches. Nothing more." Her hand touched his brow, a gesture like a mother's.

"There's no fever — that's good. I'll put willow bark in some milk for you, then best if you were back in your bed."

She smiled at him. "Things will seem less weighty come the new day."

He did not know why she had chosen those words, but they were a comfort of sorts. Besides, it was good advice. He was weaker than he cared to admit and lying down would be a relief. Although he did not expect to, he even slept awhile and woke feeling clearer in mind and stronger in body. This was as well. There were things that had to be said to the thane, to the man who claimed to be his friend. Dafydd owed him the truth about Gryfydd—and his son.

Around him, the hall was silent but for the breathing of men and the occasional whimper from a dreaming hound, darkness lit only by the glow of the banked hearth. There was light enough for him to find the latch on the stair door and he knew the stairs well enough now to need no glim to guide his feet. There was a chink of brightness shining through the latch-hole of the thane's door. Dafydd tapped, pushed it open. "My lord," he said from the threshold, "may I speak with you?"

Leofric was not alone. Dafydd realized he should have known that. But he was set on his course now. The Lady Regan, wrapped in a great wolf-fur mantle, was seated with her lord. But both looked up with welcoming smiles.

"Of course," Leofric said. "Come you in." And he gestured to a chair. "Are you too wound-sore to sleep as well?"

Dafydd came into the room but did not sit. "My lord— Lady Regan, there is a thing you should know."

"Then sit to tell us, tiercel." A wariness had been born in his gaze, Dafydd saw, as if he had been warned by the stilted formality. Or knew what had to be said. "Dewi, for God's love, sit down before you fall down, or Lucca will gralloch us both."

He could not, nor could he speak, for words had deserted him, but he dropped to his knees before them instead. He took a deep breath and tried again. "My lord, I am your sworn man and it is an oath I will never break. But—"

"I know that, tiercel." Leofric gave Regan a glance and leaned forward a little. "What buts can there be? Oh in God's name, get up!"

"My father, Gryfydd ap Rhys." Dafydd stayed as he was, head bowed. "He rode with Iorweth until *Saes* hung him, ten years back." Once started, the words were impossible to stop. "He called it war, my father…to drive out the invaders, the land thieves. He would claim hospitality and in the night open the gates to let in the reivers."

"I know," Leofric cut in. "This is not news. Iorweth told me in hall."

Dafydd blinked at him, glad not to be standing. In hall. Then they all knew. But how much did they know? Enough to hang him too? Or merely to drive him out?

"I didn't know before. No, I did, but I didn't let myself think of it. All high deeds it was and a noble cause. Not red death and cold blood and unreasoning hatred. I didn't realize. Not until Aeditha and Wyn…" He hesitated, aware that he wasn't exactly making sense. "It doesn't matter. I shall leave, in the morning, if you will allow me."

"In God's name, why?" Leofric moved lightning swift and had him by the wrist. "Dafydd, are you crazed? Why leave? Do you hold your oath so light?"

"No!" That was close to blasphemy. If only he was not so wound-weary, perhaps he could make the man understand. "My lord, before I came here, I was one of them, the Sons of Owain. Oh I never killed, myself, never shed *Saes* blood, but still I am as guilty as the men you hung this day. Perhaps more so, for I betrayed guest-right. It is your right to do the same with me. You have both the high and low justice. Or if you will be merciful, then I will live as your thrall, or however you wish it—"

"Dafydd, stop this!" Regan cried out, coming to kneel beside him, her hands on his shoulders. "What are you saying?"

"That I was never worthy of your regard, lady." He could not look at her. "Though I would die before I caused you any hurt."

"That I know well." Her arm was around his shoulders now and he was glad of the support. "Leofric—"

"Let him be, Regan." Iron, the voice now. Adamant, as it had been in Hall.

"Leofric, I am your hand-fast wife."

"So you are and I thank God for it, but don't meddle!"

"Meddle? I but remind you, husband, that I have not claimed my morning gift of you."

"Regan, this is neither the time nor the place!"

"I claim it now then. I ask you for this man's life and freedom."

Bemused, aching, Dafydd looked at her then, at the clean profile and the unbound hair that fell over her shoulders, at the proud tilt of her head as she begged—no, demanded—his life. Leofric looked as bemused as he felt.

"Damn you, woman!" But there was no anger there. "Do you think I'd have harmed him? Dewi, listen to me. You will not leave, for I do not release you from your given word to me and the ring I gave you stays on your hand for the rest of your life—aye and beyond. As for your father—what do you want me to say to you? That he was a brave man and a patriot? By his lights, I suppose he was. But he chose his path and paid the price, as do we all in the end. *You are not your father, Dafydd. We know that, my people and I.*"

"That night they held us prisoner," Regan said softly. "Dewi, you told me then that you would die before you would let them touch me. You saved me from death and worse, at the cost of your own honor, when you could have let them do as they pleased and be called hero for it. If we needed proof of where your loyalty lies, my dear, we have had it. Come, sit."

"My lord—"

"Call me so one more time and I'll not be answerable! You are my friend, my lady's savior! Do you think I would visit the sins of the father upon the son whom I love? Neither will your friends out there! Dewi, you are a wittol! Do you think they will forget how you fought at my back and took a wound for it? How you saved me before that, at risk of your own life? Above all, how you saved Regan? You are trusted here, trusted and well-loved. And you cannot leave."

There was a plea under the command, but Dafydd did not hear it, too caught up in the words that had been spoken before—friend, well-loved—his own feelings put into speech and hurting like barbs, though why love should hurt he could not think.

"Sit, damn you!" And Leofric pulled him into a chair. "Has wound-fever addled your mind? Or is there some other reason you would be gone from here regardless of your oath or Edwina—" He halted himself sharply. "Are you so determined to take on your father's guilt? Is that it? Tell me, Dafydd, which is stronger? Blood or oath?"

The blood he bore because he was born with it. The oath he had taken because he chose to do so. "Leofric, what am I? *Cymru* or *Saes*?"

"Tiercel," Leofric said wearily, "if we talk of Welsh and Saxon, we will end by tearing at each other's hearts. You are Dafydd, my lady's bard, my sworn man and our dear friend, whatever blood you bear. And wherever you go, from here to the world's end, that is what you will always be." He straightened in his chair, wincing as the movement pulled at his wound. "I was wrong to deny you leave to go. You are not my thrall, to live or die by my order. Every fledgling leaves the nest eventually, so if you wish to try your wings, my tiercel, then go with our blessing. But know that Edwina will not be the only one counting the days until you return." He looked down at his hands then, studying them thoughtfully. "I suppose I can think of something to say to the Earl to explain why I must go to the Welsh King alone."

Dafydd had forgotten that—Godwin's Great Design. Quite suddenly, the urge rose in him to laugh, but he kept his face straight. "I'm sure you could. Save that you will not need to. *Duw*, let you walk into the Dragon's lair without me? I would be shamed!"

And Leofric was looking at him, the Leofric he knew best, not the Horned One of the Beltane Fires, or the blood-mad baresark, or the stern judge, though he was all of these. This was a tired young man, as wound-sore and confused as he was himself, who had called him *friend*. He felt the smile come, a little shakily at first, but settling and growing into a grin. And Leofric was smiling too and Regan's eyes were bright with unshed tears. But they were tears of happiness.

Leofric held out a hand and Dafydd took it. "Now listen to me. As my sworn man, you should hold land. Don't argue," he went on quickly, "this is a thing I should have thought of before. Geadas held some of the best land around from me and did not get the best from it. I think it would be a good holding for you. The old house place has been cleared completely and we can build anew. If you'll accept it?"

Dafydd opened his mouth, closed it, swallowed hard and tried again. "I don't know anything about farming."

"Neither did I. You don't need to—you'll have Godwine to advise you, as I did. And men to work the land for you."

"Leofric!" Regan reached for his hand and since Dafydd seemed speechless, spoke for him. "Give him a chance to get his breath. He came up here all set to offer you the blood-price and now you're giving him land. Dafydd, think. If you hold land, you can offer for Edwina!"

"I thought he was decided on that already." Leofric was somewhat puzzled.

"Yes, but Cuthbert Coelrigson holds half a hide over by Pyon."

"So he does. What of it? Dafydd'll hold three-quarters." They grinned at each other. "Let's not spring this on Godwine too soon," Leofric suggested. "He gets shockingly complacent. A surprise will be good for him."

Chapter Thirty

Edwina sat on her bed in the corner of her parent's room, fingering the smoothness of the blue beads at her throat. She counted the days on them, from moon-dark to moon-dark—counted again. No mistake. Before, there had been times when her bleeding came late—not often, but it had happened—but never this late. It was too soon to be certain, she knew that, but some deep female knowledge assured her that it was so. She was carrying a child for her man.

She wrapped her arms across herself, sheltering the new life growing within her. She would go and speak to Anna in the morning and then she would seek out Dafydd and tell him—or no, that should wait until she was sure—then again, how could she keep it from him, when he was sure to mark the change in her? It would have to be soon, so that she could be hand-fast to him before her belly swelled and she could no longer get into her best gown. She bit her lip at the vanity of the thought. But was it wrong to want to be pretty for him, to have his eyes take on that look of wonder and love when he saw her? Well, if it was, she would do penance for it—she could not help it.

"Come, my fine lady—this won't do!"

Startled, Edwina stared up into her mother's face. Lucca stood arms akimbo in front of her, face rosy from the heat of the bake oven.

"Oh...Mam...I was day-dreaming..."

Lucca's face softened. "Very prone to it, girls of your age. I suppose I was the same. But the chickens can't go hungry, or the geese, so about it if you please."

"Yes, Mam." Meekly, Edwina straightened herself, fingers lingering on the beads. "Mam…"

"Yes, chuck?"

"Has Cuthbert Coelrigson spoken to Da again?"

"Last I knew of that, they were haggling over your worth," Lucca said shortly. "That fond your Da is, he'll beggar the poor man who takes you to his hearth. But Coelrigson is very keen."

Edwina flushed. "I can't wed him, Mam."

"Can't? What's this can't? He's young and has all his teeth and he's doing well for himself! What do you want, a prince out of story?"

Yes, Edwina breathed to herself, *a harper-prince*. "Mam, I can't wed Cuthbert. I—I'm promised, see."

"Without your Da's word, you are not, so!" Then Lucca's gaze sharpened. "Mary Mother! Edwina, tell me straight. Have you missed?" Speechless, Edwina nodded. "How many? If no more than two, then there's remedy yet—"

"Mam! No!"

"Oh if that's the way of it… Do you know whose it is then?"

Edwina's cheeks felt like fire and her eyes filled. "Oh Mam…"

"Tch, girl, enough. I saw you at the Beltane Fire, even if your Da didn't. Dear me—all the lads around to choose from and you pick on a Welshman." She put her arms around her daughter, patted her back. "There, you could certainly do worse, for he's a comely lad for true and sweet-natured. Will he offer for you?"

Edwina dried her eyes on her mother's headrail. "He says he will. He said he would speak to my lord first and then ask—"

"Did he so." Lucca put her daughter from her, hands on her shoulders. "Then I shall have to act quickly. Leave it to me, child. I'll tell your Da and sweeten him for the shock!"

* * * * *

Regan frowned into the early light of morning, not for the first time feeling a decided queasiness under her ribs and unwilling to move in case it got worse. Her bed-mate snored softly beside her, one arm across her belly and then, half-waking, nuzzled at her neck.

"Little she-fox…" he mumbled amorously. Regan considered. Normally she welcomed his love-making at any time, but now — now would not be a good idea. However, after some three weeks of it, she had a good idea as to what was causing the sickness. Nor could it be hidden for much longer.

"I'm sorry, dearling," she whispered, sliding from his embrace before he roused completely. He sighed, burying his face in the pillow, and slept again. She wrapped herself in her bed-gown of fur-lined lamb's wool, pushed her feet into kidskin slippers and padded down the stairs.

Lucca, of course, was already up and about, breakfast for the household well in hand. "You're up early, my lady! Sit you and I'll fetch fresh porridge, or will you have a slice of bacon?"

"Thank you, Lucca, but a little dry bannock and perhaps a brew of lemon balm tea—?" Regan sank onto a stool. Lucca regarded her sharply and Regan gave her a small smile. "Yes. I think so. But Anna must confirm it before I tell my lord."

"Aye, the less that one has to worry about, the better. I'll bring you a bite and sup, my dear, and if himself notices anything tell him that we fear the bacon last night was too greenly cured. As soon as he's about his business, you go back to your bed and I'll send word to Anna."

"I can go to her, Lucca. I'm not crippled."

"She'd not hear of it," Lucca said firmly and she was right. As soon as Leofric, blissfully ignorant, went out to see to the late lambing, Anna came to Regan, with Lucca in attendance.

"Well, my lady," she said finally, after her experienced hands had made their examination, "this is no Beltane babe you're carrying, or I miss my guess. When did you bleed last?"

"Just before Eastertide." Regan had already made the reckoning. "It'll be born at Candlemass, Anna."

"What? No, dearie, it'll be not long after Twelfth Night." Anna was quick to correct her.

"Candlemass," she repeated firmly. "Anna, my lord is to keep this Yule in Wales, remember. He cannot be there and here at the one time. Where will he choose to be, Godwin's business or no?"

It was Lucca who nodded, a slow smile beginning. "Oh bless you, yes. I should have thought. First babes are often late."

Anna chuckled. "Aye, I'm getting old! Candlemass, of *course*."

The three women understood each other perfectly.

"My girl has missed her courses this last week," Lucca confided. "That one is a Beltane babe, for sure."

Regan's eyes sparkled. "Dafydd's got Edwina with child?"

"Surprised it took so long," Anna snorted.

Lucca gave a grunt. "She's no fool, my lass. Waited until he was sure to stay then claimed him."

"He'll offer for her then?"

"If he doesn't, my man'll have his hide for a saddle-rug. Mind, Godwine doesn't know yet."

"Oh this hall is full of secrets!" Regan laughed. "Lucca, I think I might fancy a slice of the green bacon after all!"

* * * * *

Carry on as normal, Anna had said, just take a little extra care for a while—and stay away from the lambing pens, for it was well known that it was risky for pregnant women to be at such places. Which meant that Regan could not tell Leofric as soon as she would have wished. So she took the track that curved well away from the pens and rode up to the first ridge, knowing he would see her there and join her when he could.

Regan did not have long to wait. The group of men leaning on the hurdles ended their discussion, straightened and broke up. One swung onto his horse's back and headed towards her at a canter, blond hair bright in the sun.

"I'm for Dewi's place," he called. "Race you."

"Wait—" but he was spurring past her, laughing. "Dolt," Regan grumbled affectionately and followed at a more sedate pace.

As she topped the rise she could see Leofric already by the foundations of the new house. He stood at Rufus' head, Dafydd and Edwina hand in hand before him with Arianrhod tethered nearby. Regan began to smile.

"So we would ask a boon of you, my lord," Dafydd was saying as she joined them. He stood proud as a prince and Edwina seemed aglow with blushes, her downcast eyes belied by a smile that was suspiciously close to being smug. "Will you bear witness to our hand-fasting? And give your consent for Edwina to wed me?"

"It's her Da you should be asking for that," Leofric grinned. Edwina's smile faded. "But for my part consent is given, with all my good wishes. When is the wedding to be?"

"As soon as may be," Dafydd said fondly, with an arm around Edwina's waist. "'Dwina wants to wear her Easter gown and—"

"It won't be fitting me if we wait too long," Edwina finished as he faltered. "I am carrying my Dewi's child, my lord."

"Well!" Leofric's grin widened and he pulled her from Dafydd's grasp and swung her off her feet before setting her down and kissing her on both cheeks. "I'll stand godfather! Dewi, you young dog, you've kept this quiet! Or did you fear Godwine would have your guts for cross-garters?"

"She's only told me this morning," Dafydd protested. "As for the other—maybe three-quarters of a hide of land will stand against my being black Welsh!"

Regan dismounted and came to kiss both Edwina and Dafydd. "Hides and Welsh?" she smiled. "They'll not count for much when he knows he's to be a grandsire."

"A—" Leofric's eyes gleamed with a wicked light she knew only too well. "Yes! Let me tell him! A grandsire, by the Rood!"

"No!" Regan laughed. "Lucca will be more tactful. Of course Leofric will be witness for you. We both shall." Regan remounted and reined her horse about. "My lord?"

"In a while. Dewi and I need to plan out the byres—"

"Leofric," she interrupted. "Dewi has other things to plan. The byres can wait. Ride with me?"

He gave a rueful chuckle and obeyed and the two horses moved off side by side at a steady amble. Leofric leaned across from his saddle to kiss her mouth. "You are a scold-wife," he whispered. "And I a poor witless fool to let you command me so."

"Yes," she smiled, her hand caressing through his hair. "Witless certainly, and sometimes a fool. But I love you well for it."

"That's all right then," and kissed her again.

"Besides," Regan went on, when she had caught her breath, "I have something to say to you—not here, these two need their time together. We'll go on to the old willow and talk there. I've a fancy to paddle my toes in the river again. Do you remember us falling out of that tree?" Which distracted him from the present so successfully they were laughing helplessly at childhood follies by the time they reached the bank.

It had been cut about by the winters' floods and the willow slanted over the water at a more rakish angle, but there was still a place where Regan could sit with her skirts about her knees and dangle bare feet into the cool water.

"This is one of my favorite places," she sighed, gazing up at the green-clad branches above her.

"And mine," Leofric murmured. He lay with his head in her lap and she knew he was not talking about rivers and willow trees. "What did you want to say to me? If it's suggesting we should send word to my mother, I'll have none of it. Not yet."

"That can wait on Lammas," she agreed. Her fingertips found the scar that made a natural part in his hair. A battle scar, gained from a Welsh blade. Soon he would ride into Wales on a mission that might mean peace on the border. Or more likely his death— She pushed the ill-omened thought away. "No," she said lightly, "it's a much more pleasant thing than your mother. 'Dwina isn't the only one who's with child."

He gave a snort of laughter. "After Beltane? Half the steading women will be breeding."

"Yes," she agreed. "Including me."

"Oh. *What?*" He sat bolt upright. "Regan?" She found herself praying that Hawiss would keep her cursed presence out of this moment. But after the shock came a dawning joy that told her she was winning him from the past and she was folded into his embrace with a tender care that ridiculously brought tears to her eyes. Thus far his reaction was untainted by fear, though Regan knew that would come sooner or later.

"Anna says Candlemass," she went on before he could think of the Godwin's design and his enforced absence and start to worry at it like a wounded hound with a scab. "The same as 'Dwina. You'll both be back from Wales in plenty of time for the lying-in." *Mary Mother, forgive the small lie.*

"Yes," he said distractedly, his arms tightening about her. "Are you well? Is there anything you've a fancy for?"

Taken a little by surprise, Regan considered that. Pickled walnuts and honey sprang immediately to mind, and cream. And burned bread-crusts, the blacker the better—"Yes," she said contentedly, nestling her face into the strong curve of his neck, "now you come to mention it…"

* * * * *

That night, when the family slept, Lucca turned to Godwine lying beside her in the bed, his head already half buried in the feather-stuffed pillows, and gave him an elbow in the ribs to rouse him. "You were over to Pyon today, man?"

"Uurgh," Godwine confirmed. "God's love, woman, I've done three men's work today, haven't I earned my sleep?"

"In a minute. Listen, you, our 'Dwina's ripe for marriage."

"Aye and I was over to Pyon today arranging it, wasn't I?"

"You'll have to unarrange it then." Lucca settled herself comfortably on her pillows as Godwine's head came round and one eye glared at her. "She doesn't want Cuthbert Coelrigson."

"What do you mean, she doesn't want him?" Godwine demanded in an outraged whisper. "What does she want then? She's a steward's daughter, not an Earl's, to pick and choose!"

"Dear me, not so loud! You'll wake the girls." Lucca decided she was quite enjoying this. "She's had her heart set on one lad for months. I thought you'd surely seen it. Got good taste, my girl has. The lad's got prospects."

"What lad?"

"Better than half a hide of land, certainly, with my lord doting on him and the Godwin."

"God and Jesu save us, it's not—!"

"Blind as a mole," Lucca chuckled happily.

"The Welsh bastard!?!"

"Now hush you!" she scolded. "No name-calling, if you please!" She snuggled closer to him, feeling him rigid with shock and anger. "Didn't I say the lad's got prospects that Cuthbert Coelrigson couldn't even dream about? Our girl could be at court, man! And who knows how high a harper may rise? You think on it. For myself," she murmured, dropping a kiss on his cheek, "I think 'Dwina's made a good match. And we'll have her at home while her lad's off with my lord."

"Not quite," Godwine muttered. "M'lord has had Geadas' land cleared for a new house. Wouldn't tell me who he planned to put in it, the young fox!"

"Geadas' land? You think so? That's—"

"Three-quarters of a hide. Some of the best land hereabouts too," Godwine said mournfully.

"Then she won't starve, will she?" Lucca told him. "And she'll be closer to home than at Pyon." She let him think on it for a moment. Then, "And that'll be nice, for when the babe comes."

Coda

The old road from Shrewsbury ran straight as a bowshot on its high bank and the tired horses were able to make good time despite the weather. Rain-soaked and muddied, Leofric and Dafydd did not need to discuss rest-stops. They were of one mind. The pauses were for the benefit of the two horses, not the men.

The race had begun in Gryfydd's Royal Court on the northern coast of Wales, where the first tenuous cords had been tied between the Welsh king and the Earl of Wessex. Thane and bard had done all that had been expected of them and more, but as February approached, both were eager to be away. At Shrewsbury, they stayed only long enough to report to Godwin and to rest the horses, then they had struck out in the teeth of a storm to reach Staneleigh before Candlemass.

There were, inevitably, delays. Not five miles out of the town, Arianrhod cast a shoe and a smith had to be found. Then a flooded ford and a river too fast and treacherous for swimming meant an argument with a reluctant ferryman and all the time Leofric's features grew more pale and strained.

Dafydd knew well enough what was eating at the man, shared it himself to a certain extent. Childbirth was ever a danger to mother and infant and Edwina too carried a Beltane-child. But he did not have the memory of Hawiss' death to haunt him waking and sleeping.

Candlemass at the earliest, Anna had said, with Lucca nodding her agreement. First babes are often late, they'd said in chorus. No need to fret, God willing, you'll be long home before the pains begin.

Through the driving sleet, Leofric picked out a familiar landmark. "Five miles," he shouted above the howl of the wind.

"*Diolch Duw*!" Dafydd croaked and they pressed on at a faster pace.

The horses were willing enough, they too knew the road home now and before long the palisade and gates loomed out of the murk.

For a brief instant Dafydd was reminded of his first arrival at Ashford—soaked to the skin and battered by a winter gale much like this one. But this was no strange steading, this was Staneleigh, the one place he called home.

A horn blew as they approached and the gates swung open. Leofric let out a groan of relief and swung out of the saddle as they entered the garth. He was home and Candlemass was still four days away. Not that he could do anything to help Regan when her time came, except be there and pray to every saint and god he could lay name to—an image flashed before his eyes, Regan in his arms, eyes staring and blank, blood flowing from her body—

"Well-come, my lord!" Godwine, flushed face abeam beneath his moustaches, enveloped him in a bruising bear-hug. "Did all go well?"

"Yes—where is my lady? How does she?"

"Blooming as any rose," the steward assured him with a kind of misty-eyed enthusiasm that eased some of the ache in Leofric's heart. "'Dwina too, Dewi-lad. By the Rood, but it's good to see you both back safely. Come you to the fire and—"

"Where is she?" Leofric demanded. Beside him, Dafydd called Edwina's name and pushed past him. She stood at the hearth, round as a swaddled barrel, her face both scowling and alight with pleasure.

"Look at her," Godwine murmured. "Beautiful as—as— But swears after she's dropped this bairn, she'll not let him near her ever again. And pigs might fly."

"Regan!" Leofric shouted, grabbing a handful of his steward's tunic. "Where is she?"

"In the solar, of course. Eh, she'll be that pleased to see you, lad—" But Leofric was already thrusting through the welcoming throng toward the stair door. Behind him, Dafydd was kissing Edwina as best he could with the bulging belly between them.

"Regan!" Leofric took the stairs three at a time. "Regan!" He restrained himself from bursting into the room like a marauding Dane, mindful of the delicate state of a woman far gone in pregnancy. "Regan—"

His great chair was pulled close to the glowing fire-basket and she sat there in state, her head bent tenderly over the small bundle she cradled at her bared breast. She looked up as he entered and her face was so bright with love and joy that he was stopped in his tracks by the wonder of it. Then the picture registered in his mind, Regan with a suckling babe— "What—?" he said uncertainly. Then, like an idiot, "Where did that come from?"

"Oh Leofric. You wittol," she laughed. "Us, dolt. Come and greet your son."

"Son?" he echoed, coming closer. Born early to the world. Too early by a month? Dear God, such frail lives rarely endured long— Regan took the child from her breast and got a squall of protest from the scrap.

"See?" she cooed to it, "here's your Dada come." The scarlet-faced thing did not seem impressed. It opened its mouth and howled louder until Regan silenced it with her nipple. "Such a greedy one," she purred and slanted green eyes at Leofric. "Just like your Da."

Speechless, Leofric kneeled at her side and gazed at them both. "Ours?" he said stupidly.

"Who else's?"

"So early? Is he strong? I mean—"

"Not early. Right to the day, he was. And didn't give me a moment's trouble, did you, my petkin? Less than a day he was in coming and popped out as easy as a greased piglet, the dear mite." She beamed at the quietened child. "Look, he has your hair. Though Lucca says it'll fall out soon…"

"But—you said—everybody said it would be Candlemass at the earliest." He reached gingerly toward the flailing fists that beat aimlessly at the air and one tiny starfish paw locked viselike around his finger. "By the White Christ, what a grip for a sword! Regan, you told me Candlemass!"

"Of course I did," Regan chuckled. "With you off into Wales and like to tear your heart out with fretting because we were apart." She gave him the radiant smile of a Madonna. He suddenly knew what his married life was going to be like and rejoiced in the knowledge.

"I lied."

Also by Chris Power & Terri Beckett

Tribute Trail *with Terri Beckett*
War Trail *with Terri Beckett*

Also by Chris Power

Argent Dreaming

About the Authors

೭౧

Terri: Back living in North Wales after four years on Grand Cayman (proof positive that no good deed goes unpunished), I am married to the love of my life, with one son, two cats who deign to live with me, and one very new grandson. I've been working in libraries for much of my life, just to be near books.

I have been writing as long as I could hold a pen, but first teamed up with my writing partner Chris Power in the mid-70s, writing fan fiction. After some time and several awards, we branched out into writing fantasy and historical fiction.

I am published in these and other genres, separately and together with Chris. Writing is a passion—even an addiction. I fall in love frequently with the characters who live in my head, and sharing them with other people is the most fun I've had with my clothes on...

Chris: I live in the southwest of England, in the heart of what once was the ancient kingdom of Wessex, and close to Stonehenge. My home is cheerfully chaotic, since I share it with my son, daughter-in-law, two grandsons and three large dogs.

I've been writing stories for as long as I can remember, so much that my parents gave me my first typewriter when I was 9 years old. In the 70s I started writing with Terri Beckett, sharing plots and characters with happy abandon. At first we wrote fan fiction, but our mutual love of history and fantasy inspired us to spread out to wider fields.

I have been published in other genres and co-writer with Terri, and have several solo writing projects on the go as well as some tandem ones. Writing is something I have to do. It's a necessity, it's fulfilling and just plain fun. Sharing it is an incredible bonus.

Terri and Chris welcome comments from readers. You can find their websites and email addresses on their author bio pages at www.cerridwenpress.com.

Tell Us What You Think

We appreciate hearing reader opinions about our books. You can email us at Comments@EllorasCave.com.

Why an electronic book?

We live in the Information Age—an exciting time in the history of human civilization, in which technology rules supreme and continues to progress in leaps and bounds every minute of every day. For a multitude of reasons, more and more avid literary fans are opting to purchase e-books instead of paper books. The question from those not yet initiated into the world of electronic reading is simply: *Why?*

1. ***Price.*** An electronic title at Ellora's Cave Publishing and Cerridwen Press runs anywhere from 40% to 75% less than the cover price of the exact same title in paperback format. Why? Basic mathematics and cost. It is less expensive to publish an e-book (no paper and printing, no warehousing and shipping) than it is to publish a paperback, so the savings are passed along to the consumer.

2. ***Space.*** Running out of room in your house for your books? That is one worry you will never have with electronic books. For a low one-time cost, you can purchase a handheld device specifically designed for e-reading. Many e-readers have large, convenient screens for viewing. Better yet, hundreds of titles can be stored within your new library—on a single microchip. There are a variety of e-readers from different manufacturers. You can also read e-books on your PC or laptop computer. (Please note that

Ellora's Cave does not endorse any specific brands. You can check our websites at www.ellorascave.com or www.cerridwenpress.com for information we make available to new consumers.)

3. *Mobility.* Because your new e-library consists of only a microchip within a small, easily transportable e-reader, your entire cache of books can be taken with you wherever you go.

4. *Personal Viewing Preferences.* Are the words you are currently reading too small? Too large? Too… ANNOYING? Paperback books cannot be modified according to personal preferences, but e-books can.

5. *Instant Gratification.* Is it the middle of the night and all the bookstores near you are closed? Are you tired of waiting days, sometimes weeks, for bookstores to ship the novels you bought? Ellora's Cave Publishing sells instantaneous downloads twenty-four hours a day, seven days a week, every day of the year. Our webstore is never closed. Our e-book delivery system is 100% automated, meaning your order is filled as soon as you pay for it.

Those are a few of the top reasons why electronic books are replacing paperbacks for many avid readers.

As always, Ellora's Cave and Cerridwen Press welcome your questions and comments. We invite you to email us at Comments@ellorascave.com or write to us directly at Ellora's Cave Publishing Inc., 1056 Home Avenue, Akron, OH 44310-3502.

Cerridwen Press

Cerridwen, the Celtic goddess of wisdom, was the muse who brought inspiration to storytellers and those in the creative arts.

Cerridwen Press encompasses the best and most innovative stories in all genres of today's fiction.

Visit our website and discover the newest titles by talented authors who still get inspired—much like the ancient storytellers did...

once upon a time.

www.cerridwenpress.com